CRUSADE OF THE SOUL

ALLAN JEFFRIES

ISBN: 978-0-9903352-9-0

LCCN: 2022931681

To all writers…never give up, write your heart out, ignore the naysayers, have strength and conviction. One small spark of inspiration may bear fruit, even it it seems as though it takes forever to see it come to fruition.

CONTENTS

Preface   7

PART I
BOOK THE FIRST - THE SEEKING   9

1. Chapter the First   11
2. Chapter the Second   29
3. Chapter the Third   43
4. Chapter the Fourth   63
5. Chapter the Fifth   80
6. Chapter the Sixth   109
7. Chapter the Seventh   121
8. Chapter the Eighth   155

PART II
BOOK THE SECOND - THE FIND   169

9. Chapter the Ninth   171
10. Chapter the Tenth   202
11. Chapter the Eleventh   223
12. Chapter the Twelfth   256
13. Chapter the Thirteenth   283
14. Chapter the Fourteenth   317
15. Chapter the Fifteenth   346
16. Chapter the Sixteenth   364
17. Chapter the Seventeenth   381
Epilogue   408

PREFACE

Not far from the lazy blue waters of the Mediterranean Sea lies a very special grave in a unique city in what was once the land of the Turkish Byzantines. Not far from the city of Tarsus, there has fallen unto the decayed hands of time a mound of small stones that marked the grave of a gentle woman named Claire Jean Beaumont. The resting place sits high on a natural mound long called the Hill of Stones for reasons lost in antiquity, but the people of the valley around it can tell you the story of the one whose flesh slept there centuries ago. And although you might not believe in God, or honor, or even love in this troubled world, you cannot deny that even on the dreariest day the sun has a curious habit of splitting the clouds just above her grave, or that with every storm there is a rainbow over the solitary hill, just as there was so long ago. Of all the gifts God has given to man, the only one greater than love is honor, and this is the story of both.

PART I

BOOK THE FIRST - THE SEEKING

1

CHAPTER THE FIRST

Dreams are many things to many people. Wise is the man who can skillfully interpret his; foolish is the man who ignores their meanings. But there is one dream so utterly horrible as to defy interpretation, although its purpose is never in doubt. One cannot say where dreams come from, whether God or devil, but this dream must come from the mouth of hell for its torment, its hellhound ability to pursue the unwary in a never-ending chase through the gates of slumber until it has him worn and panting, uneven the contest, monstrous the result. Never was truth more awesome or incomprehensible, never was the ability to see such a dreadful burden.

The dream was special; it was of impending death. It was always the same.

Replayed repeatedly until his nerves screamed and dryness stuck in the cracked corners of his mouth, the dream chased him. Eyes closed in terror, he groped in his sleep for some sign of normalcy. But where his hands touched icy wall, he felt only hot wind and where his face met the softness of the duck-down pillow, he felt only the harshness of the blowing dust.

He sat in the high, leather saddle of a great warhorse all clad in his armor with one gauntleted hand clutching rein against pommel in desperation and the other clumsily trying to draw his longsword. Horse and rider sat at the crest of a sharp-peaked hill, gazing with terrified interest into the valley below. The earth was yellow and hot, the grass brown and dry. Overhead, the sun burned a hole in the ebony sky with its white-hot heat, cowing animal and human with its projected power. A voice from nowhere bade him flee that hill, but he sat stubbornly awaiting the challenger he knew would come

The heat was not bearable, yet he bore it. With terrified wonder, he realized that he could see through his leather gauntlets and he watched as the heat withered the skin of his hands, breaking the flesh so that blood ran forth in tiny rivulets that grew and grew.

The voice that urged flight was a soft, musical, female voice, but it became harsh with repeated warning. The blood on his hands dried and caked. It, too, split apart to show the white of his knuckle bones upon the saddle pommel. He hurt past the point of pain.

But still he waited.

Then, when the wind was absolutely at rest and the sun most intense, the challenger came riding up the slope from that valley, his black armor silhouetted against the yellow dirt like a giant beetle.

The woman's voice was gone from his ear; what the young knight heard now was a bitter, off-key laugh that chilled him even in the hellish heat so that his spine turned to water and his baked flesh to quivering jelly. He had never been more afraid as he saw the black knight whirl his sword effortlessly above his head; no mortal man could do that for a sustained time with a heavy broadsword.

The figure lifted his helmet's visor to challenge the young knight and Geoffrey's heart nearly leapt from his chest. Inside the dark helmet, he saw only flames licking forth from the armor. No face, no eyes. But where the fire should have burned silently at that distance, the knight heard the laughter rise and fall with its licking. And as the demon approached, the flame grew brighter and stronger, and the laughter rose until it was deafening, for Geoffrey could not free his sword from the spell that the thing had cast upon him. Hypnotized, he watched the demon of his own death bear down upon him. His gaze turned to his holstered sword helplessly.

He was a warrior; there was no shame in dying afraid, but he could not bear dying without a blow struck on his own behalf. Eyes wide with terror, he saw the attacker's sword raise up and begin the downward arc that would slaughter him like a sheep. The echoing laugh was deafening.

He awoke, mercifully.

Geoffrey turned his aching, sleep-laden eyes to the rough stone wall where he had yesterday made his most recent scratch with the small diamond of his ring, one of three given him by his father upon attainment of his gilded spurs of knighthood. Supposedly, the three rings symbolized the Holy Christian trinity of Father, Son and Holy Ghost yet more than one knight flaunted such gifts to demonstrate his wealthy influence rather than his deep convictions in the church.

It was the last in the seventh line of the eighth square of such marks; it celebrated his seven hundredth-seventy day in Castle Ayrin. In the evening, he would make another scratch for another day of his life lost to captivity, always in the evening, for he held it luckier to do so. If he resigned himself to another day of captivity ere it actually passed, was that not meekly accepting his fate without a struggle? And when did God aid the coward? Never!

And it was strangely curious that Geoffrey might think such a thought on this very morning, for although he could not know it, this would indeed be his last day served as prisoner. He would not make that new scratch in the coarse wall of his chamber.

The first amber beams of daylight made the scratched wall glisten dreamily with the morning dew and the same dampness in the fresh air, inherent in such cold, formidable structures as the High Tower of Ayrin, made the waking man shiver. Yet Geoffrey was all too familiar with his environment to take much notice of this discomfort for it was the same as laced every morning together. Dull indeed is the chain of days that does more to bind the spirit of a man than the chains upon his legs, each day unceasingly as the one proceeding it, until the captive mind becomes sodden and stuperous with the narcotic boredom.

Yet, there was, paradoxically, one phase of his repetitious life that he never tired of and never burdened him with the heart-weary homesickness he felt when the inanity of his situation caused his reeling mind to take him again and again to Westwall and home.

In these first rays of the sun that signaled morning, both home and captivity were relegated to the darker recesses of his mind by the fantasy of what drew Geoffrey unerringly to the solitary, narrow window of his chamber, little more than a widened arrow slot.

With the newness of each sun, she was there, walking the wood's edge with gentle hands outstretched to pet the small creatures that came to her for food and affection. Her flowing blonde hair, a gift of her Saxon parentage, caught and held the sun as she moved and with it, Geoffrey's gaze. Here were his dreams sent walking, taunted by some jesting god or demon, for while she walked free, he but needed to trace the narrowness of his cell's window to realize the true hopelessness of his plight.

Yet, she alone kept a spark of hope alive in his chest, a flickering ember that would not relinquish its life to fatality of thought. For surely, as God gave life and breath to such miracles as she, there was yet promise in the future for a poor wretched sinner such as himself. Yet, it was not her beauty that caused Geoffrey to grip the single-window bar as if it were Phillip de Ayrin's throat. It was her soul.

Each day as she passed in her walk beneath the thick, deep-green yews and towering beech trees of the forest, she would pause to allow her gaze to climb the high conical walls of the tower until they met his, framed by that smallish port of mortared block. Then, she would pause an instant, nay, longer than an instant, in what seemed to be a silent prayer or mayhap a simple meditation. With equal quietude, she would hold up a lovely, fragile hand and make the sign of the cross to his. She had repeated this for so long that the young knight had emblazoned the ritual on his heart and despaired of ever being without it. Yet, it was ever there, with her matchless mercy for the wicked, her eternal hope for the despairing, her benediction for the criminal, thought Geoffrey ruefully. At least, so he stood in old Phillip's eyes.

In his youthful heart was a depth of emotion for her, nearly great beyond human measure. It was an adoration so faultlessly pure that it lacked even the meanest traces of lust or want, those thoughts that men so often mistake for love in their greedy guzzling of the wine of life.

Does a man lust after an angel? The Lord only knew how many were the times Geoffrey had murmured the magic of the word *love* to some strapping village wench or castle serving maid as they coupled in forest clearing or his own bed. But never could it be so with her. He remembered how he had unashamedly hung his head and wept that first time he had seen her small hand make that cross, for most certainly, she had heard the tales of him and his crime. But she still seemed to mourn for his imprisonment, sparing her time to give comfort to his lonely soul. What words were there for one such as her? For how would one translate into rude speech the most ineffable essence of good? Perhaps the poet could come closest with his comely verses, yet never could the poet match her perfection. And in Geoffrey's mind, she was perfect.

Most agonizingly he knew all about her, his graceful benefactor, from his gaoler, although it had cost him two of his rings for the information. And though she passed close enough for him to see her clearly, held between wood and sky like some sprite of the air, he could not hear her speak or she understand him. Because of this, both dwelt in a fantasy of utter silence, perched painfully upon the border of two different lifestyles linked only by the common bond of the perceived connection (love?) between them, although it was in reality, two uncommon types of emotion.

Claire was her name, Geoffrey knew. Small, lovely, with delicate aquiline features and bright, laughing eyes. Infinitely graceful. Fragile, yet sturdy, both in a combination of her Saxon hardiness along with her utter femininity. Aye, a sprite of the forest air, indeed, a nymph of the sunlit morning, an angel strayed from the heavenly flock and landed upon this poor, unwelcoming sphere by mistake. Nay, these still were but words and she was so much more.

She was so completely the opposite to Geoffrey's hard-headed, steel-muscled masculinity that it was nigh impossible to describe her. Her kind hand was never made to wield a sword or lance, hers was a hand meant for stroking the sick and the tired and she alone could still the raging torments of an ailing soul.

She was light, deliciously delicate. Not really full-bodied but made with a superb petite-ness that put to scorn all the earthly standards that attempt to measure the voluptuousness of a woman. She was a Grecian statue come to life, an Aphrodite strolling the wild woods of Cornwall.

He watched, lost totally in the depths of his emotions which were all he possessed in this hostile world.

She was dressed as ever in her spotless dress of fustian homespun, demonstrating that she was not one of wealth yet at the same instant putting to lie, if not shame, such coarse standards of worth by her very bearing. The green frock drifted with the spring breeze as she stooped to stroke some slight, four-footed thing that scampered across her feet and she sprinkled something into the underbrush where tiny heads peeped out with blinking eyes and twitching noses. So very free she was, as free as the creatures she seemed to love so much. How ironic it was that the creature that loved her most was forever imprisoned, denied the freedom that she radiated.

As always, when she attained that one bend in the path where she stood away from the pressing yew boughs that sheltered her, where her hair danced to the light of day and wind of morning, unshadowed and unbound, she paused. No longer in the dimness of the thick wood, stepping free of low plants and bushes that tangled the hem of her garment, she stood in the warmth and beauty of the new-risen sun with her soft skin a golden color against the lush background greenery. And she raised that concern-etched, matchlessly-beautiful face to gaze upon his high window, to study again the coldness of the tower, misplaced in the loveliness of God's world like an accusing finger pointing to the heavens in an unspoken rebuke against some unspoken offense of the Creator himself.

She raised that face to him.

Geoffrey's rough, calloused, steel-thickened hand crushed the iron window bar against his chest as though willing himself through that lone obstacle by the power of his mind alone. She watched in silence that somber, handsome face, beardless beneath the long, slightly curly tangle of auburn hair. Claire could feel his blue eyes boring into hers even at this distance and although she could only imagine their power and depth, she nevertheless felt their solemn intensity.

What was there in that prisoner's face that drew her? What was it that first attracted her to him, that had made her pause to examine the lines of his features? It was more than the traces of grief or self-reproach she saw in that young knight's face. It was a kind of misplaced nobility that one finds often in…she pursed her lips in thought. Well, one did not find it often, at all, in any man. And most certainly never in the face of a scoundrel. There was too much openness in that gaze of his, too little hidden in the caverns of the mind. Then, just who was Lord deAyrin's *guest* in the High Tower?

Claire had heard the tales of the tragedy. She knew that the knight held in the High Tower had slain Phillips's only son and that Phillip deAyrin had sworn to hold him in his son's place for all eternity. The aged lord had even sworn this oath over the body of his son and promised by the love he bore him, an awful oath indeed. And Phillip, who was sometimes called Black Phillip for his temper and vengeance, was just the man to carry forth such an oath.

Still, there was a strangeness about all of this that belabored her innocent mind with doubts. She had seen enough of life to know that all human events were not nearly as simple as rumored. Then why? Why would Black Phillip send more than thirty men these many miles to Westwall and have them lie in waiting for nearly a month for that single night that they might seize Geoffrey St. Denis as he rode home to his family's manor?

That the prisoner's father would not free him was easy enough to understand when one looked upon Phillip's mustered guard. He had fully ten men for every one of Brian St. Denis and boasted a score of lesser knights pledged in loyalty to him. Westwall was but a manor hewed out of the hostile Saxon countryside in the years after Hastings; Castle deAyrin was a fortress built upon land given Phillip by the Iron Duke himself for his service in the field of Hastings. It was even said by some that deAyrin had commanded the archers who had chopped Harold's bodyguard to bits in those final mad hours before the sun set on the field and that William himself had drunk a toast to the man when he set up his dinner table amidst the Saxon dead.

Aye, a man not to be taken lightly.

And Phillip would accept not the largest offering of ransom for Sir Geoffrey's life. All of this lovely Claire knew from the talk of the guards whom she bribed with mead and honey cakes. Yet all of this was none of her doing nor any of her concern. Why should she dwell so upon it? Perhaps, solely because of the haunted look that crossed Sir Geoffrey's face as his eyes came across her. Perhaps because of the way he had wept at her first impulsive sign of kindness. Perhaps...

Perhaps because those few in Cornwall who would seek her hand in wedlock, the hand of a poor craftsman's daughter, were stinking country louts who wanted only someone to stir their kettles and spread her thighs upon command and that they might rut out their lust. So, unknowingly in her own mind, she found it easy to fasten her hopes on something she knew was unobtainable, to fashion a world of "if only" around that poor, handsome wretch confined to the High Tower forever. None had ever escaped the High Tower though some had died trying.

But in the eyes of this caged eagle, she found solace; she could comfort herself that she was needed and appreciated but for herself, a comfort much needed by every human.

Mercifully, tenderly, she raised her lovely hand to the sky and to the tower, to Geoffrey, and made the sign of the cross to him although just as much for herself, if truth be known. Then, unable to watch as he bowed his shaggy head either in shame or grief, Claire walked for home and her day's work.

With her leaving, was an uncanny stillness to nature as if something had been torn free from it, some integral part of the sunlit morning that caused the wind to stir and the insects to give utterance, or so it seemed to Geoffrey as he stared sadly at the empty spot where she had stood. But he hung his head in neither shame nor grief. He prayed.

But not as always did he pray, thanking the Lord God for the promise of another day's light to see her by. This time he prayed an awful, terrible prayer of rage, of a hatred and lust for vengeance that had festered deep within his tortured soul for well over two years. Until it was nigh ready to burst inside him.

It was a slow poison that had accumulated within his system during his captivity, fed by every sign of freedom he took in, from the flight of the redbird outside his window to the laugh of his gaoler outside his door. It danced within his veins as a peculiar witch-fire that was all desire and no action, for he had been given small chance outside of his first attempt. Yet, that was long ago and he felt no longer even the grim satisfaction of at least having tried.

There were only the long hours of frustration. Phillip was a wily fox indeed. He teased and taunted the captive, yet a solid chance to bid for freedom was mere illusion. And for some unknowable reason, all of this overwhelmed the prisoner this bright morning.

So, the prayer he silently mouthed was not to the ear of a gentle loving God as Jesus the Christ had preached; the God he raged before was an elder God—the avenging God of Israel, the one who had wiped cities from the face of the Earth with his wrath and cast the entire world into the sea.

Geoffrey lifted his eyes to a warrior's God and demanded, not begged nor pleaded nor cajoled, for a chance, even though it might be one in which he would die trying. He prayed for God to tear down the mighty stones of the Castle Ayrin and cast the High Tower into the dust from which it had risen. And if the utter anger of the helpless knight could have been shaped into one of God's thunderbolts, it alone would have been sufficient to grant his wish.

But the clear blue heaven was ominously silent before him with its slow drifting of lazy white fleece and unhampered sun. Geoffrey sighed weakly. It was not, simply not, the day one might expect biblical revenge to be delivered. Everything seemed much too harmonious in nature; there were no storm clouds, no gray thunderheads, no streaks of flickering quicksilver across a blackened sky. Was he that alone in his imprisonment?

Aye! He laughed ruefully and spat from the portal, watching as the little cloud of moisture fell those many yards to the ground below. He was indeed that alone. Abandoned out of necessity by his family, out of what...disgust, anger? By God himself from the day he broke that wretched commandment?

Abruptly he snorted at his own misery. Robert One-Eye said self-pity was a damnable offense.

Thoughtfully, he stretched and tensed his youthful muscles, feeling the warmth of the sun and yearning for more action than the hour he spent each day practicing with sword and axe, lance and morning star and all the other knightly tools of rapine and slaughter. Geoffrey was a product of harsh times. In his idealism, these brutal blades and clubs were but tools of his trade.

Phillip was excruciatingly subtle in his torture. For one hour each day, Geoffrey was allowed to practice his art in the courtyard of the High Tower so that he might more fully come to appreciate his captivity, enjoy more readily the long, dull hours with no end. But the punishment was a two-edged sword to Geoffrey for while his antics provided amusement for the castle, his exercise also gave him health and strength and enough devastating skill to become a master at his trade. Common to all human nature, when a man has but little to pride himself in, that little often becomes all. For Geoffrey, this martial study was all he thirsted for after his mornings, for it alone could save him, he knew. He developed into a true champion for all his few years.

For one hour each day, regardless of what torment the seasons provided, despite thirst in summer and the cold in winter, he moved with learned masculine grace from weapon to weapon, from target to target, never stopping to catch his breath. He changed. Where there had once been firm muscle, there was now sinews of thick-coiled rope and slabs of moving steel. His speed and agility increased and doubled until his sword thrust was a whispering blur and his axe-swing a glittering rainbow of double-edged death. He had tempered his exercise with intelligence, unlike many of his peers. He had studied what made a man a fighter and why some perished in battle where others triumphed. He dredged from his memory the uncouth gems of wisdom of Robert One-Eye. He knew that there must be strength behind the arm, quick-flowing, continuous strength for the sword arm that falters in battle belongs to a dead man. There needed to be a rhythm between the man and his metal, a harmony so that the swinging of his longsword was as effortlessly done as the swinging of his naked arm, so that the weight of his armor and weapons was as only the bodyweight of the warrior.

He had attached leaden weights to the heaviest, most cumbersome weapons that the armory maintained and swung these without stopping until he reeled drunkenly and the massive two-foot-thick practice posts were but handfuls of splinters in the dirt of the yard, and the muscles of his legs, arms, and back stood out like sculpted marble. At first, the guards jested with each other over him for of what use was such practice to the condemned?

Phillip smiled sardonically at both the stupidity of his men-at-arms and the foolishness of his captive, hoping against hope. The old man dearly loved a contest between minds. He let this mewling puppy build himself up in the arts of combat and so build his faith as well. It would be all the more gratifying to dash these hopes in the end, dash them like a jug cast upon stone, dash them like he had dashed Phillip's hopes for a feudal dynasty carried on by his son.

But the guards learned not to laugh at the madman in the tower. There was a day nigh a year past when some damnable imbecile had left the portcullis of the High Tower raised after the guard changed. Coincidentally, Geoffrey was honing his skill with his heavy Danish axe at that moment and the men of the tall tower realized all too late that the captive had other targets for his terrible weapon than the crumbling, scarred posts of the court. In the swift passage of a few minutes, he had slain five of the watch and sent the rest howling for pikestaffs and crossbows to keep the wild boar at bay. In truth, had not the very outer gate of Castle Ayrin been bolted heavily, it was probable that Geoffrey St. Denis would have hacked and bashed his way through the entire garrison of four-hundred men-at-arms and perhaps even Black Phillip as well in the bargain.

Geoffrey had drawn up cursing, chest heaving like a hunted stag, sweat running in rivulets down his back and arms, and had eyed the gate warily. He knew then that his rush for freedom had failed, yet still he was loathe to relinquish that fleeting feeling of power that he had experienced. "I am a free man!" he cried out in anguish.

Then there was silence in the courtyard, save for his panting and the crunch of boots on gravel as the guard moved in cautiously to surround him. None would approach closer than the distance of ten paces.

"Where is your mockery now, dogs?" he had roared at the still crowd, but no one replied. They cast side glances at each other and prayed silently that the madman would not choose their position to break through. Geoffrey faced over a score of men in a standoff while the dead were led off on muleback to the mortuary, trailing blood like butchered sheep.

In the end, it had been Black Phillip who had halted the contest when he confronted the knight with several crossbows that could not miss at so short a range. Mindless of his own safety, Phillip had smiled benignly and held out his hand for the axe. Geoffrey could have slain him easily then and there. But instead, he grinned openly at the old man's courage. Whatever the old villain might be, he was certainly not a coward. With a contemptuous sniff, he cast the weapon at deAyrin's booted feet and walked unconcernedly past the double line of sweaty, hard-faced guards back to his chamber.

But all of this was past, long past. The guards feared him now; they followed his every mood with hard eyes and apprehension, all save the lout Henrik. The fat gaoler felt he had a bond with Geoffrey and should the knight ever stare at him with even the slightest trace of antipathy, Henrik had only to change the subject to the girl with the golden hair. But even he wondered how long it would be before the knight exploded in another crimson rage. No one, not even Black Phillip, underestimated Geoffrey again.

Still, time has a curious habit of running in circles. Perhaps there is something to the notion of destiny as the sages maintain, for there was soon to be another bloodletting in the castle. God was silent to Geoffrey's vengeful prayer that morning, but there was the chance that other, darker ears heard the plea and understood the red-rage within the young man's soul, ears that were grossly tapered and companion to cloven hooves. If Satan heard Geoffrey's quiet cry, he felt no pity nor compassion. But it's also been said that even the devil dearly loves a good jest.

And although Satan hurls no thunderbolts in the same manner as the true God, still the weapons of his wrath or mirth glare awful indeed. And one of these now approached the doomed castle.

In the scattered underbrush that littered the huge, dry ditch of caked, cracked earth around Castle Ayrin, a furrow two-men deep that had been in wetter weather a sort of moat, scurried in a half-crawl, one who was to have a profound effect upon Geoffrey's future. The moat was now awash with garbage and less likely offerings of human habitation, but this did not in the least deter the ragged, grubby figure that skittered from scrub bush to dung pile.

In this dry sewer, scurried a most unlikely warrior, and even less likely a saviour for the Norman knight, in a sort of round-about dash for the castle. As the figure ran through the garbage, it could be seen to pause here and there to examine tidbits that, in his estimation, should never have been cast away.

His name was Eadric Siwardsson, a Saxon, and he was a stinking, scraggle-bearded, louse-ridden bandit as burly in build as a bear. His flaming red hair was a true sign of his temperament and the leather patch he displayed over his left eye was a reminder of too many dark adventures. He wore a tunic of patched furs bound by a broad belt of silver ovals, and high boots of wolf hide. In his hand, he carried a large-headed, double-bladed axe and in the other, a coil of heavy rope on the end of which was affixed a grappling hook made from his ship's anchor. Eadric Siwardsson was an outlaw. A notorious outlaw, it might be added.

He was a fugitive from his native England, having left at the Norman Conquest in 1066 for the countries that had spawned the Vikings. His entire family had fled after Harold fell bloody and beaten at Hastings, choosing exile to Norman rule. He, too, was a warrior but not a knight of lineage as was Geoffrey St. Denis. Instead, he was a reaver, a plunderer, begotten upon a drunken serving wench by his father late one night who, equally drunk, had found her charms more appealing than those of any of his wives. From the beginning, he had practiced thievery and village-raiding with his sire and progressed until the grimy clan was raiding the coast of their own country and giving the blame to the Northmen. Eventually, Eadric rose to command his own ship and at his father's death, assumed control of the clan of brigands. The motley group had continued to grow after their flight from Britain until it was now a sizeable group of cutthroats. Wild was the army of Eadric Siwardsson.

Eventually, even the fierce Vikings gave the Siwardsson a wide berth. Quarrels with the Northmen started with the father who just couldn't accept the fact that the Vikings were the undisputed kings of the North. Siwardsson had traveled to their lands to negotiate a treaty, chose to mix politics with honey mead and settled the matter by splitting open the head of some minor jarl. Unfortunately, this minor jarl turned out to be the son-in-law of Ragnar Irongrip, called by some the Jarl of Jarls. From this point, the clan's relations with the Northmen had progressed steadily downhill with the result that when Eadric Siwardsson fled Britain, he had no ally in the North to run to. Undaunted, even unconcerned, Eadric carved out a niche for himself in that cold land reasoning that the loss of one country justified invading another. Siwardsson the Saxon was no weakling himself when it came to dealing out axe strokes and he was eventually accepted by the Viking neighbor, no mean accomplishment in that hostile land.

Peace can be a fickle instrument of pleasure, however. The blue-green fiords, high, grassy hills, and snow-capped peaks that had once welcomed the Siwardsson's small army soon became tiresome. Eadric Siwardsson was not weak by any stretch of the imagination, nor could he ever be accused of small thinking. At the onset of his latest madness, he was content to harry the British coast and the Norman conquerors. But then, slowly the worm twisted within his brain until he decided that he would liberate all of Britain and make himself the first Saxon king since Harold.

This theory sent chills up the spine of many a stout man of Eadric's for his willpower was irresistible and none could gainsay him. He would always come up with the argument that, "Even should we fail, you gutless snivelers, the worst thing we can expect is death! And I say death is better than this boredom!"

Quite naturally, the cheers for the speech were rather weak, but Eadric had his will anyway. So far, they had not failed and his men discovered, to their immense joy, that political liberation also meant rape, rapine and plunder. That was all they needed to know.

Again and again, they stormed over the English coast and many was the cry, "Vikings!" which went up unjustly at the sight of Eadric Siwardsson's blood-red flag. Worse was the luck of the British when it was found that the warrior, wild-eyed and irresistible, belonged to them. One could more readily reason with a Viking, especially when the more talkative of the English tended to be the cursed Normans who spoke with their ill-

concealed French accent reminiscent of Hastings and Harold. Quite naturally, those who could boast proper Saxon lineage were not likely to
suffer, though this was for the most part, irrelevant since they made up
the poorer classes anyway and had little worth taking. Ah, but the
foreigners from damp Normandy got a warm welcome at the hands of
Eadric, Wild Eadric as he was most often called, in a mixture of both awe
and respect.

So, on this spring morning, bug-crawling, ale-breathed, soul-stinking
Wild Eadric crawled and scurried as a mad ant might amid the garbage
and dung piles of the great castle Ayrin, axe in hand, dagger in mouth,
rope in hand. Murder in heart? He was alone now, but better than a
hundred displaced Saxons, like himself, and accompanying Norsemen
awaited him in the deep woods.

His first objective stealthily reached was a large, squalid dung pile
that lay built up far beneath an out-thrust castle turret. The small conical
turret, an aperture of wood plank and stone sat out over the moat,
meeting at the corner of the south and west walls. It was supported by
angled beams connecting bottom to walls, with a brief distance between
beams so as not to obstruct what might fall through the bottom of the
turret.

Aside from being a watchtower and arrow port, it was also an
outhouse, or toilet in the most modern sense of the word.

Planks formed a crude seat at its base with a medium-sized hole
centered there. The waste dropped into the moat below and followed the
moat channel, ideally, to the river in wetter weather. Poor engineering
and dry weather caused the moat to be a stagnant sewer more often than
not when earth-slides blocked the flow into the river. And now, in this
unseasonably dry weather, the river had shriveled within itself until the
moat was nothing more than a dry, cracked ditch full of beached squalor.
It stank like the wind in hell!

But the nearly overpowering stench of the dung heap, crawling with
flies, was all the same as a fresh summer breeze to Wild Eadric, for his
large, misshapen nostrils had only room enough for his own putrid odor;
a rich fragrance enhanced by the fact that he had not bathed since the
season before. And the stink of the mud was nothing too much, either, for

he had crawled through worse and remained unconcerned. By now, he was beneath the vulnerable turret, upright on his feet and swinging the grappling hook he had made. He drew back and thrust out, a wheeze trembling the thick layers of fat around his middle, aiming for the supporting beams.

His one eye was expert enough. It caught on the first cast and the huge villain chuckled delightedly to himself. In an instant, it was solid enough to bear even his great weight and Eadric scampered like a demented monkey up the rough stone wall, hidden from inquisitive eyes by the overhang of the turret. However, he did mark his trail up the wall in footprints inked upon the rock in some wretched slime that attracted greedy flies. Fortunately, or perhaps unfortunately, it was still so early that the watch took no notice of him, so sleep-drunk were they still.

And none heard the soft thud as Eadric's dagger slipped from his teeth and fell to the tall mound below him, along with a hideous muttered curse that rolled through the Saxon's clenched teeth. But now, all was ready. They awaited him below. Destiny was at hand; he felt it. He was more right than he knew.

It was already becoming warm in the unshaded sunlight. Eadric blinked his single eye against the sky and surveyed the forest. All was ready. He licked his thick lips, still glistening with fat from his morning meal, and waved at a certain tree at the edge of the wood.

Hanging from the twin beams of the turret, Eadric watched as a second wild man appeared, scurrying low and carrying an axe similar to Eadric's in both hands. He also raced up the rope with practiced grip and lodged himself in the beam work. Both men grinned at each other. Then the two spat into heavy hands, gripped their stout axe handles and drew back.

But suddenly there was clatter and commotion. A female voice sounded from within the turret and both Saxons froze in mid-swing lest they be discovered and the castle alerted. They pressed themselves flat against the wall and scarcely dared to breathe as a plump pair of buttocks adorned the round hole. With a short pause, nature took over. Unfortunately for Eadric the Wild, the hole was a bit closer to his position than his cohort's. His fellow bandit turned away lest he laugh and give up the game, or Eadric Siwardsson forget himself and dash his comrade to the muck below with a swing of his great axe.

"A right fair arse," hissed Eadric, unmindful of the danger. Dark eye smoldering, his hands clenched and unclenched upon his axe handle.

"Aye," snickered his comrade, a brigand named Pigfeet for some obscure reason. "Dare you give her a smack with your…" he indicated the handle of Eadric's axe. The Siwardsson gave a satanic leer.

Then, unrestrained as ever, he gave a ferocious guffaw and kicked at the grinning Pigfeet. Naturally, this sound did not go unnoticed by the person and the bottom was abruptly replaced by a fair face framed by long black hair. The girl's eyes opened wide in utter astonishment as she perceived the source of the laughter and her mouth gaped, although no sound came forth, so horrified was she. Eadric screwed up his already unpleasant countenance in a demonic mask that undoubtedly scared the girl to no end. With no hesitation, the face was gone.

"A fair arse, a fair face!" roared Eadric with unholy glee. "By Odin, I shall have that little pigeon before night sets."

Both strong Saxons put their shoulders to the axes and leaned to the stroke. Boards from the turret seat flew up in great clouds of splinters as the entire bottom of the structure disappeared. Feet pounded along the walls toward the turret, but Eadric was already within the castle with Pigfeet directly behind him.

Lady Alice deAyrin, daughter of Phillip, turned in the doorway where she was desperately trying to make one of her maidservants understand what was happening. She wheeled in time to see a terrifying, ruddy, face swathed all around with dripping red hair and with one gleaming eye emerge from the opening where she had just recently sat down. As a rabbit transfixed by a snake's stare, Alice watched as the wood flew to pieces, and shoulders, wide and powerful came through, followed by an arm, naked from wrist to shoulder except for a wrist cuff of red leather and holding aloft a wicked-looking axe.

She found her voice and screamed. "Vikings! she shrieked, shrilly. Her maid collapsed in a faint upon the chamber floor.

"Vikings?" Eadric roared, quizzically, "Vikings?"

ALLAN JEFFRIES

"Vikings…" she cried again but his hand was then across her soft lips halting further warning. With a fierce grunt, he spun her to face him.

"Saxons, wench! By Thor and Odin, Saxons!!" he howled and his mad laughter filled the room. Then he was past her in a rush for the parapet and drawbridge, pausing only long enough to pull her quivering form into his arms and taste her fear-sweetened lips. As Pigfeet ran by, he was a trifle more thorough in his exploration of the girl's charms, then he too was for the drawbridge, lustily swinging his war-axe.

"Make yourself ready for the victors, my lamb!" was his final encouragement to the sick Alice deAyrin as he thundered past.

Lady Alice licked her ravaged lips and shuddered. Then, she too swooned.

Pigfeet caught up with his thane in time to see the big man embroiled with seven or eight of deAyrin's watch. He had struck one so hard that his axe had passed through the victim and lodged him in a thick-planked door where the axe could not be freed for all his strength. Undaunted, Eadric the Wild was howling like a dog and busily engaged in hurling those of the defenders he could lay paws upon, the twenty-odd feet to the courtyard below.

Pigfeet was cheekily singing an old Saxon song of harvest as he jumped into the struggle, "We grow the grains we cut it down, we cover the face of the mother ground."

"Thwack!" went his axe as it crashed through the shield of another Norman soldier, hurling him from the walkway to the ground. And still the old song continued.

2
_____

CHAPTER THE SECOND

G eoffrey started as he heard the frantic pounding of feet in the corridor outside his cell and the echoed cry that brought a lump of fear to his throat. "Vikings, in the castle, Vikings!" Then drawn out silence accompanied by the faint smell of woodsmoke.

He had no way of knowing that destiny for him truly was at hand or as at hand as the mocking fates allowed. The drawbridge was down; the chains to raise it severed and a milling crowd of smelly, hairy Saxons clad in furs and swinging axes from behind huge round shields were hacking at anything that moved. Even though they lacked the close combat discipline of the Norman invaders, they made up for lack of skill with grim enthusiasm.

The smell of smoke in the air grew stronger; Geoffrey sensed its acrid taste curling beneath the door to his chamber. So! They had fired the castle already.

Eadric was cunning to attack at break of day for only a fool or a madman would attack the lofty walls of the Castle Ayrin in broad daylight or a wild man with no concern at all for death. The guard was about to be changed, those on duty bored and sleepy, those who had already replaced them at some posts still half-asleep and stuffed lazily with breakfast. The morning was peaceful and clear, the weather mild, the breeze warm. Why should they fear? Attacks on this coast came more often in the gloom of night or at sunset when shadows masked the lurking outlaws. In daylight, they would be too much exposed to hope for much success.

Or would they? Now, it seemed that they had underestimated those such as the wild Siwardsson for there were cries of anger and anguish all throughout the great fortress.

And the castle's men were killed as they ran, surprised, into a crimson swirl of Saxon men with fierce weapons. Women screamed and ran every which way. Pigs and cattle ran abandoned within the walls and fearful peasants leapt into earthen cellars and beneath stationary carts as the hard-bitten men-at-arms stubbornly struggled to delay what both sides sensed was now inevitable.

The attack had been perfectly executed; Castle Ayrin would soon be only the merest shadow of a memory. And the shadows of here and now in the fortress were mostly flickering for long tongues of flame shot skyward from keep and towers, sending a pall of blackness rising for the sun.

The smoke was as a demon messenger fleeing from a dying world for here, death was everywhere. There was no romance in such adventure as the bards oft sang; those who sing bravely of death have seldom experienced it. Both sides knew the weak would die.

Then there came the moment Geoffrey had hoped for and feared both. There was the sound of a key being placed inside the lock of his door.

But who?

Black Phillip come to finish him off? Vikings come to either slay him or make him a slave in the cold North? Henrik trying to free him for personal gain? There was more fear than hope.

Geoffrey turned, heart racing and sweat beading his naked chest, as the door was roughly thrown open and he peered straight into the single bloodshot eye of no less a person than Wild Eadric himself. His heart sank; this was not a man come to free him.

The Saxon's axe dripped blood over the flagstones of the floor.

The young Norman tossed his square-cut hair and moved into the best defensive position possible, though he knew with sickening certainty that he no chance for survival. He had learned from his own practice what such a weapon as the Saxon wielded could do, and how futile was a defense, barehanded, against it. But he had little choice; he tensed his muscles and moved into a crouch, warily watching the blade.

Eadric threw back his massive head and laughed, nearly gagging Geoffrey with his foul breath. And he raised his axe high. "Saxon?" he asked none too gently, his solitary eye gleaming.

Geoffrey, seeing death full upon himself, snarled and spat full into Wild Eadric's ugly face. "Norman! You great stinking coward! And I am proud that it would not be mine own axe that would slay a defenseless knight!"

Eadric's roar seemed to shake the entire tower but, incredibly, it was a noise of sheer, unadulterated mirth, not rage.

"By Thor, you show me how even a cub of a Norman can meet death with both eyes open and honor! Now tell me, child, before you die, why did your countrymen hole you up in this chamber? What was your crime?"

"Well, I'll tell you, even though it is none of your concern you maggot-brained drunkard," grinned Geoffrey, growing bolder. He sensed instinctively that this was a man who appreciated and respected both bluster and pride, and it would not be the first time Geoffrey had saved his hide with the force of sheer audacity alone.

"I'm here for killing Black Phillip's only son!"

"He whose manor this was, d'ye mean?" pondered Eadric.

"Aye, ale-breath. Now, either slay me or give me a weapon that I might slay you, for your stench sickens me to the bone!" Geoffrey thundered.

Again, the Saxon howled with glee. "Ha! There is yet time, little cub. But tell me, why was the son against you?" he asked, casually testing the axe edge with a calloused thumb.

Geoffrey shrugged, curiously numb at the mention of the duel.

"Gold?" suggested Eadric.

"Worse! Over a woman!" Geoffrey spat at his feet.

Eadric winked, "Was she worth it?"

The young knight shrugged again, philosophically. "Is any woman?"

Eadric roared with merriment to Geoffrey's chagrin, until tears of joy ran down his face into his beard and he pounded his fists upon his knees in elation.

"So be it, cub!" he bellowed, for he never spoke in less than normal voice. "The lecher slays the lord's son and is himself thrown into a tower to rot forever! Har, har! Here is a wayward villain after mine own wicked heart!"

Geoffrey nearly vomited as Wild Eadric threw down his axe, hugged him hard enough to squeeze him dry of breath, and then cast him to the floor. The Saxon retrieved his axe and laughed. "Such a man, Saxon or Norman, is a criminal of mine own blood!" And with that, he stormed out of the room, leaving the door wide open and inviting, singing a Saxon drinking song at the top of his lungs. He pounded down the stairway to join his men in the looting, his exploration of the tower complete.

Geoffrey choked a minute on his good luck before he ran for the armory. It was hard to accept that he had escaped death so easily by the recklessness of his action, but he was not one to second guess the fates. If he hurried, he might catch Phillip deAyrin before the raiders did. Geoffrey had a good idea who his "saviour" was, for the madman's fame had spread as far inland as Westwall, although fortunately, his military prowess did not.

At the foot of the staircase Geoffrey found Henrik, sword still sheathed and several wounds in his back. Someone had already finished the coward. But the young knight could shed no tears on that account. Too bad they had also taken Geoffrey's two rings from the fat gaoler's fingers.

Smoke was much thicker now. Before long the entire fortress would be engulfed. It occurred to Geoffrey that every man he ran into here would be thirsting for his blood, the Saxon because he was Norman, the Normans because of Black Phillip. So be it! He stretched his powerful back muscles with the imagined heft of an axe or longsword. Let no man stop him now for what coursed through his veins magnified his power by its force. It was the will to survive, to live…and with it…vengeance!

Utter chaos greeted the knight as he fled the High Tower. The odor of charred and burning flesh assailed his nostrils from the smoke-filled windows and doorways. Instinctively, he knew that there was no time to be wasted to seek out DeAyrin, that he could do it later if the aged bastard were still alive. For now, a sword and a horse was all he asked, a chance to complete his escape. Vengeance had given way to sense. The young knight was learning.

The sword he found easily enough, sticking upright in the body of a chain-mailed Norman serjeant; the horse he pulled from a flaming stable. Twice, he was rudely challenged, once by a blood-stained Norman and a second time by a foam-mouthed Saxon.

Mercilessly, he cut them both down. He would not allow himself to jeopardize his liberty for misplaced feelings of brotherhood. Robert One-Eye had taught him this cruel law of war. More than one noble fool had been cut down from behind by the enemy he had just spared. Knightly contests were one thing with their pageantry and chivalrous process; pitched battle between armies was entirely different. So, let these fools beware his sword strokes; he asked no quarter and he offered none. He wanted too badly to live now.

Spattered with men's blood, naked to the waist with his long hair tangled and wind tossed, sweat-drenched, he hurled himself into the saddle and raced for the gate.

Let them all make way for him!

He felt the white-hot heat of better than two years of damnable darkness breathing down his neck as he thundered over the drawbridge, his horse's hooves striking sparks on the metal bands of the lowered platform as he stormed past reeling guards and blood-drunk Saxon raiders.

Now, all was burning. The castle was dying terribly amid creaking timbers, twisting and moving with the heat, making portions of the walls shudder like the hide of some huge animal in its death throes.

Freedom! He was past the gate; they could no longer stop him! He wheeled the charger and looked past the trees of forest edge, back at Castle Ayrin. Gray-black smoke hung like a shroud over the mighty fortress and was even starting to fill the wood. Much of the castle was burning fiercely, the High Tower blazing like a tall tree. There were fewer screams and shouts and Geoffrey reckoned rightly that the slaughter was almost over. By now, the Saxons would be sorting through their plunder, sifting gold from jewels and pretty girls from wrinkled or fat, and guiding their captives toward the ship where it lay beached. Within the space of another hour, all this would be but a gory, pain-filled memory.

But it was over for Geoffrey. Thank a foresworn God, he had lived through.

The territory surrounding the castle was totally foreign to Geoffrey. He had seen it but once on that night so long ago. Starlight had been little enough to make out landmarks by. Wisely, he picked his way with caution down the strange roadways, trusting himself alone and asking directions from no one. The odor of burning hung heavy in the air even here in the deep of the forest and Geoffrey saw why as he came upon a crossroads with a small village. Every house, every shop, blazed methodically. The torching had been meticulous despite the Saxon lack of discipline.

The few people he saw were those that lay sprawled dead in the street, mostly men. Undoubtedly, the raiders would save the women and children for either mating or slavery. He tightened the grip on his sword-hilt.

Even the most isolated huts of the wood dwellers were ablaze and Geoffrey wondered if all of Cornwall must surely be afire. It was then that the soul-chilling, gut-wrenching fear that had been building in the back of his mind took proper form and sent his other calculations scattering. If the country was ablaze and being slaughtered, then what of...

"Claire!" he cried hoarsely, turning his mount so tightly about that the poor animal's neck was nearly wrenched out of joint. She dwelt within walking distance of the castle.

He put his heels to the horse's ribs and thundered down the main road back to the castle with both curse and prayer upon his tight lips. It was risky taking the main road but he had no time to spar. Only once did he meet up with any of the Saxon men.

He raced down upon several of them walking close together, axes slung carelessly over their shoulders, blood-soaked and laughing. Over each shoulder, two of the men carried sacks of the spoils, a third walked relaxed, but both hands were clear to swing the axe. There was no time for second thought.

Time had run out for them all, and he knew it. Frustration and desperation mingled in his ageless war cry.

"Ha! Rou!" he shouted, exactly as had his father before him against the Saxons in 1066. It was William of Normandy's cry. "For God and Westwall!" he cried, though Westwall was leagues away and the land he now fought for, by proxy, was enemy territory.

Then he was in among them, sword held high to crash down on the first surprised face turned toward him. He barely caught a ruddy, sweat-beaded face, seamed across one eye with an old scar, before his sword glimmered brightly, creating a red line between the eyes. The man never had a chance to cry out.

The two raiders with sacks full of plunder were sheep before a lion. The third fared better, but not much. Warned by the deaths of the other two, he leapt at random with ready axe and Geoffrey turned his mount barely enough to let the whistling axe slash past him so that the fellow overreached himself. The knight's sword slipped easily into the outlaw's chest and, with a gasp, the fellow sank to his knees. "Die slowly!" Geoffrey snarled. Then, he was past the fighting parties and stragglers, heading for the coast and the raider's ship.

He cursed as he took one wrong path after another, his inexperience with the land slowing him to a walk almost. *Damn! Damn!* The seconds ticked off in his mind like grains of sand passing through the neck of the hourglass and with each grain he saw the girl's fate slip a bit more. Geoffrey never considered that he might find and join her only to die himself in the meeting with the raiders.

But what else was there? He had more than his youthful arrogance in his skill as a warrior; he had confidence in his ability, and more importantly, confidence in his purpose.

Optimistic well beyond reason, he was certain he could save her if he could but arrive in time. But then, many great battles have been won by ungrounded optimism, Geoffrey was not alone in this.

He noticed not the forest, not the meadows where forest ended, nor the beach where sea began. Geoffrey's mind was filled with only one thought as he urged the horse down the beach, doubling back to where the raiders must have landed and left their longship.

Before him stretched only empty beach, a ribbon of neutral-colored pebbles and rocks winding along the coasts. Here and there a tree grew at water's edge nearly obscuring his view, but for the most part the coast lay open and deserted.

Gulls frightened by his voice as he demanded more from his horse, rose squealing from the rocks. By now, he was as winded as his horse. He must find them soon or give up the chase.

~

EADRIC SIWARDSSON MOTIONED ABRUPTLY FOR THE FEW REMAINING prisoners, mostly women, to be brought onboard his longship. The water-craft was modeled wisely after the habits of the Norse longships, except that it was built on a larger scale which provided space for a raised cabin between oar banks, to the rear. This cabin could be used either for the storage of cargo or for sleeping quarters, although the crew rarely used it as such, for they felt it weak to seek shelter from the weather of the sea and ungrateful.

The sea was their mistress as it was to the Vikings and perhaps all who sailed since the start of time. She fed them, helped them travel, hid them from pursuers and most importantly, gave them adventure. Their love for her waged with their love for the rough life they led.

Atop the cabin and its stuffiness, little alleviated by a few portholes the size of a double fist, was a fair-sized open deck, railed on all four sides and with shield-hanging posts for better defense. Wild Eadric was clever in his design, despite what angry Britons wished to think in their ballads of the man. This special deck sat higher than the oar banks of conventional ships and thus, could fire down into attacking ships.

He had won more than a few sea battles because of this. From this vantage point, he mentally checked off the store and booty being loaded. But as the last of the prisoners were brought to the ship, he, with a fero-cious oath of rage, burst down the stairway to the nearest guard and without further ceremony, struck him to the deck with a mighty blow of his huge-knuckled fist.

"Fool! Scum from a thousand aged whores!" he roared. "I told you to steal none of our own people!" Wild Eadric bellowed so that every mouth became still, awaiting the outcome of this display.

The stunned man held his un-helmeted head, his helmet lay nearby with a colossal dent in the back of it, and groaned, turning a bloodshot gaze to the woman the Siwardsson had referred to in his own distinctive way. The maid stared back at both of them, eyes full of fear but much too proud to let her gaze drop. And although she trembled violently at the gross robber's swaggering approach, she did not try to flee.

The Saxon outlaw pulled on his beak of a nose as he stared, first at her and then past her lovely fierce eyes, over her small shoulders to the sea. Now, it was calm and clear as glass, greenly mirroring the sun and clouds. It was an odd illusion of peace, he thought philosophically. How different from the butchery he had just commanded. Was it not said, however, that peace came only as a gift of Odin? And was not all of the sun and sea contained in the realm of this high king of the gods?

And warfare was man's realm. Ah, well, he thought, tis to no end anyway. He turned his attention back to the girl for too much philosophy gave him a headache directly behind his eye sockets.

"Any dog can see that you are of Saxon lineage by your straw-colored hair and fair coloring!" He turned to the fallen guard, now barely able to stand. "I'll have your lust-filled balls for this, Besfric," he spoke sharply.

"But, my thane," protested the fellow, cowering slightly from his master's wrath. He was near the Siwardsson's size and weight, yet, within Eadric's dark, stormy eye there burned the soul of the berserker…and this made all the difference in the world.

"I asked the bitch her name and it was as French as Duke William himself, may he burn slowly in hell!" He tried to dodge, unsuccessfully, as Eadric responded in his natural way to the mention of William the Conqueror.

"My knife!" he howled, fumbling with his sheath and foot-long dirk. The man, Besfric, tried to escape but Eadric caught him by his long brown-blond hair with one massive hand tangled in it and the other holding the dagger up to his throat. The man was nearly choking out of fear and Claire watched his Adam's apple bob dizzily as Eadric turned the captive to face her. She saw the pain in his eyes and it repulsed her.

"Tell me he lies, girl, and I will free you to cut his throat. I can see well enough that you've stout Saxon blood in your veins; just tell me you 've got a name to match it and you can kill this bastard!" Gentlemanly, he offered the knife to her.

She was silent, her eyes unreadable but her mouth twisted with scorn.

Puzzled by this reaction, Eadric hawked noisily over the gunwale and blinked expectantly. What was wrong with her? He certainly knew what he would do if someone hinted he was a member of William's putrid empire. Possibly, she was slow-witted, didn't she understand?

She smiled a little, as if to herself, "My name is Claire Beaumont. My father was Norman-French, my mother a Saxon," she said in a sotto soft voice, scarcely audible at all. It was no more than a whisper on the wind but it stung Eadric like salt in a wound.

"What!" he exploded, hurling the prisoner Besfric from him as he advanced upon the girl. "Your whore of a mother chose to sully the noble stuff flowing in her veins because of her she-dog rutting? Could she not find a Saxon with a horn to suit her so that she must dirty her line instead?"

The slap that Claire stepped forward and dealt the red-bearded ox resonated sharply over the stillness of the ship. Even Wild Eadric ceased his ranting, so amazed was he by her action. Then his normally ruddy complexion grew slowly redder and redder until scarlet turned to purple. His fists clenched and unclenched and he half raised one heavy hand in case he should decide to dash her to the planking.

"You dare!" he blustered, "Why, I'll have you..." but he halted his threats when he looked into her eyes. There were tears there but also something past hate, past rage, past fear. What he saw froze his voice in his bull's throat.

"My mother was a good woman and my father a good man. They joined out of love and I forbid you to say, or think, otherwise."

"You...forbid?" pondered Eadric, unsure what to add.

Claire continued, "They loved each other and when she died of the fever, he mourned her the rest of his life. Neither of them have harmed you, so you do no justice in trampling their memory. I pray you, mighty thane, you are strong enough that you can afford to be merciful." Then she put her pretty head down, defiance defeated by sheer exhaustion.

Eadric eyed her appraisingly in silence. Then he glared around at the others who still stood there with slack jaws and mouths gaping like fools at a fair. Instantly, they were busy again, not daring to goad their thane. His patience had been sorely tried by this impudent girl and anger hovered over his head like storm clouds just waiting for a victim that he might feel safe in punishing. It was odd that he had not cuffed her teethless and then cast her overboard. It was not common for a person, man or woman, to strike the wild Saxon and live, much less stand before him and lecture on charity.

If he were not such an old thane some would swear...and they would be right, for the mind remembers when the body does not, but they would be right in a way they had not thought of.

"Stow her with the rest and see that they are comfortable!" he thundered, eager to display his old authority. Then he turned to his second in command, the man Pigfeet, who had stormed the castle with him earlier.

"Are all back?" he asked.

"All who are coming, I think Lars has stayed watch. Here! I see him by that big rock!" Pigfeet laughed and pointed to a figure swimming mightily for the ship. A heavy rope was thrown over the gunwale and a half-naked figure climbed aboard, axe in hand.

"Cast off!" the tall, tanned Saxon cried. "I saw a scout upon the beach riding for us, no doubt the lead man for a party of Normans!"

All eyes were on the man but an instant, then there was work to be done and quickly.

"How many, you limp-pricked whoreson? That's what I need to know!" bellowed Eadric as Pigfeet called for oars.

Lars leaned against the rail, gasping for air.

"Cast off!" the cry echoed across the water.

"I heard one and didn't wait for the rest! What would you have me do? That I politely stop the fellow and ask him how many serjeants might be behind him or that I...," Lars began, excitedly.

"Arsehole!" Eadric dismissed him. "Well, you women, have ye not put distance between us and the riders? Put your weak backs to the stroke, think about your share of the loot and women later, but now, ROW!" he bawled at the laboring crew. The red sail went up and the ship gathered speed.

In the distance, the smoke rose and shaded the sun.

The Siwardsson scratched the seat of his britches, uncouthly, as he stood lost in thought. Oddly, his thoughts were on that brash young braggart he'd freed in the fortress. As he watched the ragged coast of Cornwall fade with every sweep of the oars, he remembered what the young man had said and found himself regretting that the young knight had been unable to claim Saxon parentage. A shame, really. The knight was a fighter, not an overfed, overbred noble fop fit only to mince at the king's court and kiss the king's royal arse! The Saxon grinned crookedly as he remembered the wicked blue balefire in the knight's eyes as he watched the axe and had prepared to die fighting. And the way he had arrogantly spit into the Siwardsson' s face! Ah, now that was a gesture worthy of Wild Eadric Siwardsson himself.

Ho! Ho! The lad was young and overbold, but he was a warrior, no doubt, and he must have escaped the flames and murdering. For an instant, Eadric felt a tinge of guilt that he had not done more to facilitate the knight's escape, but he suppressed it. No man needs to be led by the hand to safety, and he had little worry that the knight had not made it. It was just that there was something in the Norman that reminded Eadric of himself somehow and he felt a whisper of paternal interest.

He shook off this alien feeling. Sympathy for a Norman, pah! Then he turned about, to stare at the blond Norman-Saxon girl he'd taken, although now he was wishing that he had left her in peace. That type of girl was bound to be a thorn in his side, sooner or later. She had a will of her own and there was no reasoning with her and worse, she was not a fighter so Eadric had not even the satisfaction of beating her! Oh, he well knew her spirit. She would never defy him openly, meeting each command with grim resignation. But she would never yield her spirit to him, and she would remind him every day of his life that he had wronged her. She could bear him children and love and raise them as a mother, but she would never be more than ice to the man who took her.

Eadric had taken one like her years and years ago, the mother of his only son. She had never refused his favor or withheld from him, she had never disobeyed him and had raised him a son as best she could, though the son had been a viper at her bosom since birth. She was always gentle and well-liked by his band even though she was just a slave. And because of all this, Eadric had spent twenty years trying to earn her love, though he would never admit it, nor would he admit, even to her, how much she meant to him.

She died cursing him for what he had done to her. And, oddly for him, he had actually treated her very well.

No! Give him a woman who would fight him, who would try to stick a dagger in his ribs when mad and with whom every night would be a challenge. Let the woman show her hate for him openly that he might teach her submission! These soft ones hurt too badly. They were too fierce inside, too unrelenting. An eagle that fierce deserves no cage. She had a quieter, more deadly sort of courage, blood-strong nevertheless. He knew that if she had been less feminine, she too would have spit into his face. Huh! This knight and girl, both. He, too, had been that proud when he was their age. But, still, these British-Normans were strange folk.

Claire was also sunk deep into consideration of her own fate as she watched the familiar landmarks of Cornwall take on an unfamiliar cast as the ship gathered distance. She was losing the only life she had ever known. A breeze had sprung from nowhere, smelling of salt and open air. It tossed her hair and dampened it with sea spray, but it could not blow away her feeling of utter hopelessness. But what life was she really leaving, in truth? What or who would she really miss from Cornwall? She no longer had family there. And no love, or even lover. There were only her dreams and no one can exist upon dreams, no matter how sweet and tender, forever. She had tried for so long.

But why must it be THIS way? Why must she be spirited off by some blood-drunk barbarian raider to a miserable slave's life in the cold-covered mountains of the North? She was better off dead, she thought with a bitterness foreign to her character. She laughed inside at the irony of the situation, how she had spurned village louts only to fall prey to far, far worse. With tears glistening in her eyes, she looked up from the stern section of the slave deck and bade England farewell forever.

But as she did so, she thought she saw something bright glitter in the afternoon sunshine amid the few dark trees that grew by the water's edge. Then, it glittered again on that bleak beach and Claire saw that the brightness was the metal fastenings of a horse bridle.

In the shade of those silent sentinels by the water, there sat the shadowy figure of a man on horseback, watching, only watching, As if in slow motion, the figure rode out into the water where the sun struck him directly. Eadric turned, caught by her attitude of attention. He also saw the figure.

He laughed, "He'll never catch us now, methinks!" The figure was powerless to interfere now, even if riders were behind him. Hmmm. Curiously enough, the shape of the fellow's shoulders, the way he held his head jauntily, even in silhouette, suggested something to the one-eyed bandit.

"Why, he looks like that young rascal I freed from that wretched High Tower!" he growled to the oafish Saxon beside him. But the dull churl barely heard, let alone understood.

The lovely girl who knelt upon the deck behind him heard the growl well enough, however, and her head lifted higher as her eyes tried hard to focus. Her concentration was intense as she willed her eyes to see further towards the shore, to span the distance more clearly. She sat upon her heels, hands folded gracefully in her lap, pretty lips pursed in thought and examined the rocky beach minutely.

Why would it be him, unless…?

Eadric noticed her movements, although he did not remark upon them. Nor did he comment on the soft smile that flickered briefly over her features before she again lowered her head.

Nor did he appear to notice the silent tears that cascaded from red eyes and washed through the sooty grime on her beautiful face.

Goodbye, England, goodbye my love, goodbye my life!

Then there was nothing but sea about them.

3

CHAPTER THE THIRD

E vening's salty, sea-wet breeze lifted the surf at his feet and still the young knight stood on that miserable, desolate beach, thoughts lost on the horizon. It was still warm, although clouds now swirled in front of the sun with promised rain, insuring that the darkness would fast close in. Wither had they taken her? To the North he thought, but where?

He had not arrived soon enough as he had feared. The rustling whisper of the waves over sand and pebbles seemed to taunt him. T-o-o-o-o late! T-o-o-o-o late! Losing this race was a pain that ripped into Geoffrey's heart and stomach.

A gull flew past, headed for the far horizon. About him, the warmth of the weather beat upon the canopy of leaves that shaded him and horse and nature seemed silent. The stillness at the forest edge made his dark thoughts thunder loud in his temples. Two more gulls flew squealing for the sea, their cries mocking the flightless human.

Agony was an iron yoke across his shoulders. He could not cry, nor curse, nor moan, however, for its weight was the heaviness of an infinity. For him, an era had ended. Geoffrey felt misery on the verge of cowardice. Youth's view of love and a knight's view of duty allowed no excuses. Grief bent his spine and slowed the breath within his lungs until his shoulders felt leaden and he hunched forward as a cripple might. The emotion was overpowering; he dropped to his knees and vomited.

In his disgust, he cursed himself with the vilest of names, knowing as he did so that none of them rang true. But self-pity was the only luxury left to the knight now.

He needed to establish blame and it was easy to blame himself for having failed her. Now, some heathen churl had her...her softness, her beauty and gentleness...all mated to some smelly animal. He hung his head to laugh black oaths at God's will, at its vile irony. Surely his God laughed humorously at fickle mankind. Geoffrey had said over and over to himself that if he could only be free of that damnable tower, he would never want for happiness again.

And now? Now he had lost sight of hope and happiness entirely. The smoke-red eyes he turned to the heavens were clouded and stormy and it was no prayer he uttered. But then, it was probably not the first time puny humanity had cursed God by his own name.

Then, he turned his horse for Castle Ayrin, for he would need clothes and armor and another horse for what he intended. The armory of the fortress was of solid stone; it would be intact yet. He shivered at the thought of returning to the place of his misery, but there was no alternative for him. And it suited his humor well enough. What he would take from the store of Black Phillip would be small enough payment for those 770 days and nights. Logically, all those in the wood would be dead or fled, but should any remain, then let them choose other than to stop him!

But yet, for all the hardness of his intent and the fervor of his desire for the girl with the golden hair as he thought of her, he could not know then that it would be nearly two years before he would see her again.

THE CASTLE AYRIN WAS INDEED DESERTED IN THE BLEAK QUIET OF THE afternoon. Here and there a fire still raged in one of the windblown outer cottages, but most of the flames in the larger structures of the fortress had burned themselves into exhaustion. The High Tower was left a gutted cylinder of stone, hollow as a chimney, with all the interior woodwork of floors and roof burned from their stone supports.

Like a stark sign from heaven, the sky had grayed over harshly into a clouded bowl and a damp-smelling wind rolled in from the coast. It was good, Geoffrey thought wryly. Let the tears of the Creator wash back into the sucking earth the final offerings of his children's folly. Let the thirsty earth quench its appetite with man's blood. Let God's majesty sweep away the crumbs of man's foolishness, the markers of his civilization.

He threw back his head and yelled into the rising wind. The first gusts spattered raindrops at his feet and he felt the wonderful coolness that was coming.

Then he turned to his work, slightly sickened at the sight of the corpses. It was one thing to slay a foe in the hot press of battle when the will raged coldly, *kill or be killed*, yet quite another to gaze upon the still, twisted forms of the dead. It was not so much the gore that sickened him, as the folly.

Vultures were here at the fortress, also, their instincts sensing the terrible carnage as a free feast. They flew low to prise loose some morsel from the defenseless. It was so pitiful, but at least the courtyards and grounds were deserted.

Geoffrey had little trouble seizing another destrier, for they wandered throughout the compound, unsure of what to do or where to go. They readily flocked to Geoffrey's human touch and eagerly followed him. For his warhorse, he took a massive, reddish-brown stallion, similar in color to the mount he rode now, yet larger and heavier, more suited for battle.

"I shall call you Chestnut, old fellow," he decided, rubbing the horse's neck affectionately and the animal nuzzled him, feeling more secure now with this new master than when running free. The horse was too disciplined to ever be happy with freedom; it was trained for battle, to be a partner with its master. And it sensed Geoffrey's strength and respected it. "Chestnut, new friend, would you away with me?" he murmured silkily as he stroked the creature's muzzle. As if to deliver an answer, the noble beast snorted and pulled at the reins. Geoffrey laughed at the animal's spirit, as heavy as his poor heart was.

The gate to the armory hung open, creaking on dry hinges in the stiff breeze. Inside was a reddish twilight of furnaces left to die, the fire now un-stoked by their human masters. The light of the coals played weakly over the immense array of new and used weapons hung on the stone walls, and sadly, over the silent forms of the two smiths draped awkwardly across their anvils. Geoffrey fought back tears of pure rage for these two had been friends to him in his captivity, stout colleagues in that they shared his opinions of weaponry and aided him gladly in his wild ideas of weighted swords. They had helped make him the warrior that he was, yet oddly enough, both brawny giants were men of peace themselves. Their love was in the beauty of a fine weapon and its clean lines, not in what to wear to the court of William Rufus itself. Upon his pack horse was the suit of armor, finely wrought yet unadorned with any symbol that it might soon bear upon it the twin trees of St. Denis. With it, he stowed weapons that might accomplish much in meeting human flesh.

Geoffrey thought to bury both men, but he realized with some degree of trepidation that deAyrin's vassals would soon arrive as the news spread and he had best be gone by then. There was no reason to die for an old score.

Kindly, he laid each smith out on the floor and closed their eyes. He draped a cloth over the wounds of each so that they might retain some dignity in death. He would want the same for himself. Then he stood before the wall and selected his tools.

In the middle of a disaster, one of the most burning wishes of every young knight was fulfilled, the wish of every warrior. He now possessed weapons, fine weapons, and excellent armor equal to that which any vassal might have, those awesome weapons of warfare that he had become so formidable with: battle-axe, mace, lance and longsword with a two-handed hilt, just the thing for turning a mounted enemy from his saddle. He clad himself in simple chainmail and cast off his soiled rags for a surcoat of blue linen, the color most near that of his own crest. Around his trim waist, he belted a double-edged broadsword in scabbard and its companion dagger. The kite-shaped shield he selected was ample protection, if plain, but to Geoffrey it completed the image. When he had been held by Black Phillip's serjeants that night long ago, he had been but a raw boy-man, early in his gilded spurs of knighthood and otherwise poor in everything except spirit. Now, he would return to Westwall a stronger man, young still perhaps, but a full knight seasoned with the weapons of his duty and confident in manner.

And relieved from his poverty by the very man who had sought to ruin him. Geoffrey grinned cynically at this thought. It was fitting that Black Phillip had brought this about, and Geoffrey suddenly realized that he had beaten the aged warlord at his game of minds; he had turned his skill to his own advantage and won his freedom with it. And with the help of Eadric Siwardsson, Eadric the Wild.

God rot him! The man who had slaughtered his friends with his foes, who had stolen *his* Claire with the women of his enemy. But for a reason he did not understand, he could not bring himself to hate this bear of a Saxon.

Geoffrey understood the Saxon raiders. The Norman-French were still considered invaders of Britain, even if Hastings had been fought some thirty years past. Duke William had proclaimed himself king; the natives had had no say in it. Some said William was the legal heir to the throne. But whatever the legality of it...Geoffrey's people were still strangers in a strange land of wild-tongued Saxon names and even wilder people, descendent of ancient races and eldritch times before even the Caesars put the stamp of their rule upon Britain. It was a land where even the overbearing and over-striving dominance of Old Rome had come to nothing but the ghost-shadowed ruins one found built into castle walls or standing off alone in deserted fens. No, to Geoffrey St. Denis, his enemies were still of his own misplaced nation.

He turned to cross the drawbridge, now useless with its lowering chains hacked through so that it was but a platform across the moat, stationary and immobile, and cantered past the great hall. It was then that a hoarse shout broke the river of his thoughts and caused him to reach for his longsword. Black Phillip, the Lord deAyrin, stood within the vaulted recess of the huge archway leading into the great hall.

"Sacred name of God!" Geoffrey swore softly, his sword leaping from its scabbard. Here was the chance to put right his suffering, to cleanse his anger! The dark gods of vengeance laughed.

But the old warrior reeled blindly as a man besotted with drink; his movements were uncoordinated and only the wall stopped him from falling down the wide stone stairs. Blood ran down his tunic in several places and he left a trail of it in bloody hand and footprints as he lurched along the wall. A man of strength even upon the eve of his death, Geoffrey thought.

Geoffrey hesitated, sheathed his sword, and then dismounted to walk up the stairsteps.

Black Phillip hung to the wall like a mollusk and bloody saliva trickled down his close-cropped gray beard. His now-palsied hands gripped the rough stones in an agony of utter helplessness as he struggled to remain erect. But his voice, though hoarse from shouting and weak from loss of blood, still held all the brittle curtness of the old Phillip deAyrin.

"Ha! It's you!" he spat. A rattle shook his chest. "Of all who died, you alone had the temerity to survive."

Geoffrey seized his mount's reins again and made to leave. He was too disgusted by the pitiful sight of the elder knight to wish him harm, although the man deserved it. Black Phillip was dying on his feet.

"Have you come to finish me then, Sir Geoffrey?" deAyrin asked with heavy sarcasm.

Geoffrey eyed him coldly but said nothing.

"Well?"

"Nay, deAyrin! I have come but to offer thanks for your courtesy and your weaponry," he smiled grimly.

DeAyrin looked him over and nodded approvingly. "You wear the armor well, Sir Knight. You have learned much."

"Praise from the devil?" Geoffrey sneered.

Phillip laughed though a terrible cough wracked his stooped body. "Your arrogance becomes you, puppy! You hate me, but you hate even more the fact that I made you what you are; it was hatred for me that made you into a warrior! Nothing can change that!" He coughed again.

"Burn in hell slowly, you bastard!" the knight spat and made ready to leave.

"Wait, you rogue!" shouted Phillip hoarsely, bubbles of red gurgling hideously at the back of his constricted throat.

Geoffrey turned back to him for reasons he himself disclaimed.

"And where will you go with this plunder, boy?" Phillip asked weakly, but there was the ghost of a smile upon his tight lips. Geoffrey saw a jagged wound running up his neck and curling around to the front where it disappeared into his blood-stained beard.

The knight eyed him coolly. "After them," he answered laconically. What more could he say?

"After them all?" Phillip whispered. He clawed his way forward a pace, only to sink to his knees, his breath and speech coming in quick gasps. "After them all?"

"Aye!" grated Geoffrey, impatient to be on his way.

"Then they took the girl, didn't they?" Phillip muttered.

"You filthy bastard! What do you know of her?" the knight cried.

Phillip shook his head in amusement, "Christ, lad, the whole castle knew about her from the swine Henrik," he coughed.

Geoffrey walked slowly up to the old man and knelt next to him.

"You bloody torturer! Not even Christ would forgive you."

But suddenly, Phillip cried out in anguish, "My son! My son!" and he clung to Geoffrey with desperate strength. Puzzled, the knight helped him up into a sitting position against the wall. Still kneeling, he gazed into his foe's eyes and what he saw there touched him with pity for the man who had lost all while Geoffrey had life and liberty.

Phillip's voice now was almost still; the drama was nearly played out. "I know you slew Michael justly, so I could not slay you. And even having you here, I needed your...youth." His feeble voice died to the barest whisper as he looked deep into Geoffrey's eyes, "I saw Michael in you, my son. Now, go ride them down and do as my son would have done." He coughed from deep within his throat and Geoffrey heard much of the sound come from the gash in his neck.

"Go with God!" he finished in a gulp. His quivering hand reached out blindly, for his sight was gone now, and took the hand of the knight.

He held Geoffrey's hand affectionately, gently. In this gesture of supplication, Black Phillip made restitution for his wrongs to the young St. Denis, and Geoffrey, despite himself, accepted.

He lay the body back and closed its eyes. Impulsively, he made the sign of the cross over it. Then he rose and stared down an instant at his fallen enemy. "Old bastard," he said softly, "you are cruel to the end, for you have stolen any satisfaction this hellish day has brought me. May God have mercy on your wretched soul."

Then, Geoffrey was seized with a terrifying sense of haste, a feeling so strong as to be denied by nothing. The dead were finished, but life awaited! He was clutched in an iron grip of despair that caused him to flee to his mount and race for the gate, tugging the other animal fast behind him.

Why was there this chill wind sweeping through the caverns of his heart? Perhaps it was the aura of death at this doomed fortress, perhaps it was the stench of the bodies lying in the sun. But there was more. He had seen things in Phillip's eyes that caused him to wonder at the secrets of life and more.

No more! No more! There were no premonitions, there were no omens! He had only one cause to worry and the longer he tarried the sooner she was lost! Geoffrey had an idea of the direction he must take from the sun; he set spurs to Chestnut and pounded down the path still vacant of human life. He would be out of the shire before Phillip's allies arrived and well on his way home to Westwall.

Westwall! Home and aid! Ha! He laughed wryly, enraptured with the idea that would have seemed fantasy to a listener. Men to back him as he stalked the wild, shrewd Saxon, a ship to carry him and a detachment to the North, money and supplies delivered by his father! But Geoffrey was sadly mistaken; although he was not to understand it yet, there was no longer a chivalric mood to life that sent well-meaning nobles chasing after peasant girls with their family's blessings. Perhaps there never had been. Perhaps even then, romance lay in song and story but not in life.

Geoffrey was suffering the curse that change brings to all prisoners regardless of where and when they are captive. Imprisonment gives a man nothing so much as time, time to think his own thoughts, time to formulate his own theories and opinions of life, and to develop his character more so than those who wander idly from day to day seeking amusement.

The prisoner, released, retains a directness of thought that can paralyze the unwary; in his years of loneliness he has examined the same ideas again and again, minutely stripping them down to the kernels of wisdom, or falsity, contained within as if building a machine. One idea builds another.

The theory is constantly torn down and rebuilt, examined precisely from each and every angle. He has made use of his long hours in a way that those with freedom can never do, because his wisdom is forced upon him. But at the same time, he has only his thoughts to judge by, for in the years of his captivity he lacks the greatest essential for true knowledge—the experience of others. Thus, while he can, with intelligence, delve deeply into life's accepted theorems, he cannot compare them with the theorems of others. It is not uncommon to assume that those on the other side of the unclimbable wall feel as you do; every human craves acceptance.

But Geoffrey's mind was already clouded with emotion; he failed to see truths he would have otherwise accepted. He would have laughed himself if one of his comrades went chasing after a country wench, would have made coarse jokes about the fellow's mighty lust and not understood at all.

But love alters the mind more than even captivity. The discussion of love's effect is better left to the philosophers, or possibly wise men. But there is one truth universally accepted about love, deep and abiding love; it can be a form of madness, a torment, an obsession to the stricken. So, Geoffrey knew too little of how he would be received for the real world was possessed by an alien madness all its own.

Chestnut's massive muscles bunched and flowed as he set his hooves to a steady, mile-eating pace and Geoffrey, with a grimace for pain already sprouting in his buttocks, settled himself for a long ride. The one practice deAyrin had denied him for the last two years was the practice of horsemanship and Geoffrey now thought his arse to be as soft as an old man's. But he was stoic in pain, as he had always been; it was the one trait he would never outgrow from youth.

The ancient, rune-marked distance stones clipped past him rapidly and neither narrow path nor rushing brook held him up for longer than an instant. For six days and six nights, he rode when he could and rested only as his drawn mounts needed. He ate little himself but foraged constantly for his animals. Strangers were passed without so much as a nod. More than once, he forced some rider off the trail in haste, yet even when he was twice challenged by irate cavaliers from some local manor, he did not draw up to reply.

Undoubtedly, they thought him a coward, and the second encounter even accompanied his thoughts with verbal abuse and strong-worded challenges. But Geoffrey cared not a bit, for despite their insults, he had but one enemy now. Although, the second opponent was hard to ignore when he called Geoffrey the "spawn of a Saxon bandit!" Still, the rest of the ugly spinning world could sink itself into hell for as much as he was concerned, preferably taking that second rider with it. Geoffrey was hard-pressed not to stop, regardless of his anger, and argue manners with his sword.

Had he slowed enough to reply to the fellow, he would have seen that the man was a messenger from the court of none other than William Rufus himself, King of all Britain, And ironically, had he spoken to the messenger, he would have learned that the man was riding from West-wall, having discharged his duty in a message that would change the face of the world.

It was a declaration with more destiny in it for the young St. Denis than he could comprehend, a destiny of dreams and love and death.

Six days and six nights passed him with an ease of time that seemed magical. He rode with single purpose and kept but one sight before his red-rimmed, swollen eyes…the forest scenery or the sun rising in an eastern meadow were all one to the fevered lord for he pounded along entrapped by his own idealism. There were but blurs of greens and blues, a backdrop ever changing for the sight that haunted him internally, wrenched him forward in the saddle at a gallop and hounded him with such longing as he had never known before, even in his sleep. Was she a witch to affect him so?

No, he had only to remember the infinite softness of her gaze and the muscles of his hardened heart would burn. It was an awful mixture of desire and rage that chased him relentlessly until his eyes shone hollow and sunken, and the smile lines of his mouth were pursed and set, lips turned tightly inward to press against clenched teeth. His hands grew cramped from his grip and the muscles of his back and legs grew knotted with the hard ride. He was oblivious to the pain.

In fact, it was the dull sensation of pain that put his tired senses on edge and stayed him from dropping. He knew that with every additional minute he could remain horsed, he was that much closer to help. So, on he raced, through rain and night as lampblack as the underside of hell, until horses reeled drunkenly, trembling now with the exertion of movement and he leaned over to cough up bile upon the ground from his weariness. And still he rode on.

The morning of the seventh day found him at the border of the lands held by Brian St. Denis, Earl of Westwall, since the Conquest three decades past. Geoffrey knelt at the crossroads that marked his father's furthest field and as he wept, gave thanks to God.

But God heard him no more this morning than he had the morning of his escape from Castle Ayrin. No more than He had heard the girl's cries as she was dragged aboard the Saxon ship. God was deaf to all these cries, but he could not know that then. God was tired, even then, of the cries of these little men and women who prayed for peace while they slew each other.

If God were made to listen, it would take a mighty cry to do it. With a final act of boyish impulsiveness, Geoffrey put on the rest of his armor that he might display himself to his father and the others at Westwall. He took up his shield, also from the packhorse, and splendidly arrayed in his chivalric finery, rode for the manor house.

In two years, it had changed mightily. Before, there had been but a manor house of stone with a single high watchtower adjoining it for defense. Now, a wall of possibly eight or nine feet of stone swept around the building in a wide oval with a tall, square platform of stone at either end, the foundations for towers. A ditch, deep and wide, ran around the wall, implanted with sharpened, wooden stakes set at an angle to halt a charge of leaping horses.

Entrance was gained by a wooden bridge set across the ditch, leading to two large iron-bound doors. The bridge was quite practical from the standpoint that it seemed an easy entrance to Westwall proper. But Geoffrey knew what his father had planned; those timbers comprising the structure were soaked in pitch. In the event of an attack, it would take little effort to raise a fire upon the planking, thus burning the entrance off and undoubtedly roasting a detachment of enemy soldiers. Others would be trapped on the narrow space of land between castle and bridge, easy pray for archers or burning oil. Geoffrey noted with pride that his father was a well-seasoned old warhorse. The men of Westwall could sleep securely.

High above the old watchtower flew the pennant of William II, King of England and directly below it, as propriety dictated, drifted the colors so ineffably dear to Geoffrey. He could make out the triangular field of blue so pure as to be almost indistinguishable from the sky behind it, and upon the background, the twin splotches of brilliant green that marked the twin trees of the clan St. Denis with their leafy boughs spread wide and roots dug deep. The herald of St. Denis was the union of the two halves of nature, land and sky. And in this union, there was formed a whole, a completeness that symbolized strength, certainty, and steadfastness. The family of St. Denis upheld these ideals in their ruggedness and their ties with the hostile environment that they had mastered in Britain. They were men of the land…strong, sturdy and honest vassals a king or lord could depend on, even for his very life. Never was Geoffrey prouder of all this. The Conqueror had needed men like Phillip deAyrin to command the slaughter of the enemy, but Geoffrey knew that the real strength of the Norman host lay with men like his father, who, while he would never forge ahead on his own initiative, would never give ground either. Westwall had never looked better to a tired, hungry son.

Slowly, he approached the sentry at the foot of the bridge, trying to determine if he knew the fellow. He did.

Alfred, who still headed the watch, failed to recognize the voice of this curious visitor and Geoffrey's face was masked by the high chain-mail collar and the long, narrow nose guard of his conical helmet. Alfred studied the strange knight closely as he sent one of the watch for Lord Brian St. Denis, bidding him come that a messenger had arrived in obvious haste from the condition of his horse with word of his captive son.

The old serjeant stood silently, arms akimbo in his leather jerkin, sucking at a hollow tooth and trying to understand why this odd knight was somehow vaguely familiar to him. Two men-at-arms eyed him with outright hostility for the very mention of Sir Brian's son was enough to cause tempers to flare in Westwall; messengers had come and gone now for two years without accomplishing anything. And this grim, silent, well-clad knight boded news of some importance.

Geoffrey's death? Had Black Phillip finally committed his greatest outrage? This was far more likely than his release they knew, for the legends of the deAyrin was not rife with stories of Christian charity.

The elder St. Denis raced for the gate, heart pounding. Brusquely, he wiped breakfast from his mouth with a tunic sleeve and took up position in front of Alfred. He gave Geoffrey a look full of warning and the son was glad he was not the messenger they all feared. Brian St. Denis had altered much in two years; his hair was now fully gray and thinning. Geoffrey felt a twinge as he realized it was probably due to his captivity, and all that caused by him over some village strumpet.

"Oh father, I am sorry!" he thought silently as he returned the man's stare. Sir Brian's eyes no longer sparkled with his usual lust for life, but they held a power his son had no trouble in distinguishing. The eyes seemed vacant, fear-filled at first as the old knight had approached, but now they were molten with hatred for this presumed man of deAyrin. He was still a man to be reckoned with, on or off the battlefield.

His mother, Lady Alice St. Denis, ran behind Brian, faster than dignity allowed. She was still as plump and pretty as he ever remembered her and he was glad that she, at least, was spared the physical signs of worry that had plagued his father. As it dawned on him how great their love for him must be, he fought back an impulse to end the surprise too soon. It was hard to stifle a smile as Geoffrey saw her eyes grow hard for the man who had brought word of her son.

But no. Sir Brian would expect him to be proud!

"Sir Knight!" began Sir Brian coldly. His voice trembled slightly with the anticipation of what would come. "By your rich dress I ask you, do you come from King William with answer to my plea for his aid to my son?"

Geoffrey shook his head in silence. The two men-at-arms reached for their swords and edged in closer.

Sir Brian's eyes clouded over at once with a deep measure of malice for this unknown knight who had dared to raise their hopes, albeit unknowingly, only to destroy them. The knight that sat astride the massive chestnut destrier was a mocker of his last hopes.

"Then I ask you, sir, do you come from Phillip deAyrin?" Sir Brian was mercilessly polite, pretending not to see the unsheathed swords in the hands of his men.

Geoffrey nodded and he saw even his mother's gaze go black with hate. Alfred stopped one of the men-at-arms but he himself set a hand on the hilt of his dagger and would not move his eyes from Geoffrey's face. The hatred of this small group generated awesome vibrations, so much so that Geoffrey decided not to carry the jest further lest one of his own soldiers be impulsively spurred to attempt to strike him down.

Brian's voice was full of terrible menace and Geoffrey saw more men move behind him to bar escape.

"Then what say you, villain!?" the old knight roared with as mighty a voice as he had ever owned. Geoffrey saw him pale with fury, the tired eyes aglitter with promised death. And he doubted not that had he been in truth Phillip's messenger sent with such ill tidings, he would have been at once cut to bits for the faces before him were those of a family pushed to their limit. There was no quarter left within them to give; their next step was vengeance, despite Phillip's measure of strength.

Thank God he could be the one to stop this, to prevent a feud instead of birthing one. "Why simply, my lord, that your son has survived!" And he threw off helmet and threw back coif to show himself, and blindly found his way into their arms.

∼

CLAIRE STOOD ALONE AND FRIGHTENED IN THE GREAT HALL OF THE thane Eadric Siwardsson, or jarl, as the Norsemen were accustomed to calling him. The only other presence was that of the jarl himself, although guards barred the two exits from the other side of the doors.

The hall was not lofty as she had expected and was smoke-filled from inadequate ventilation. It was shaped almost as an inverted boat set upon walls, built entirely of rough-hewn wood. The earthen floor was dug out about a foot to allow for more headroom and in this depression two firepits sent a constant cloud of smoke skyward with a quantity of it not leaving as it should.

The floor was covered with furs and rugs stolen on raids, and judging by the thickness of the carpeting, the adventures had been many. Rough-hewn benches and tables were carelessly scattered everywhere, over-turned from last night's feasting. Loot from the castle lay carelessly spilled throughout the hall and Claire was shocked to see actual piles of gold pieces in the least likely places. The hall smelled foul like its owner, of ale and vomit and even women's blood upon the furs where virgins were deflowered in a night long of drunken insanity. Now, the Saxon sat before her, obviously no worse for a night without sleep, behind a table of massive oak. He regarded her slim beauty as he ate, his strong teeth snapping and crunching the fowl bones as he sucked the meat off them. With a grunt, he wiped his hands in his beard and looked at her. A long rolling belch escaped him and he looked as surprised by its depth and intensity as she was.

"Are you a virgin?" he asked casually.

She gasped at his insolence but did not answer, so outraged was she.

"Answer me or I'll find out for myself, girl! I'm not one to be taken lightly!" he snapped.

She glared at him. "If you could see my hatred, you would learn that I do not take you lightly!"

"Your hatred is unimportant; you are a slave. Now, answer!" he said sharply.

"Yes!"

"You are a liar," Eadric said casually, Claire gasped again and clenched her fists.

"If I were a man, I would kill you, you brigand," she hissed, her light complexion clouding over redly.

"If you were a man, you would already be dead," he replied casually. "Be glad you have that soft pelt between your legs, woman!"

"You are a pig, Eadric Siwardsson!" she fumed.

He delicately picked his nose as he regarded her.

"I have been called that," he said mildly. There seemed to be something amusing in her anger, she thought. She had the idea he was laughing at her. "You are much like my wife was!" he said with an odd merriment.

"Oh, my God!" cried Claire, certain of what was coming next. She felt sure she was either going to faint right there, dead away, or vomit. Or both! Surely, he didn't mean that..."Then she must have died hating you because I know that I will!" she shouted at him as he sat musing.

The Siwardsson looked up suddenly, startled. Claire was puzzled as she saw a flood of emotions across his grimy face, anger, sadness, hopelessness, and finally, understanding.

"Time runs in circles as the sages say," he muttered, "Perhaps I've outlived mine." Then he straightened his demeanor and regarded her once again as a jarl.

"Do you know why you were brought here, dressed as you are, golden hair?" Eadric pointed a drumstick at the clean linen dress she had been allowed to put on.

She shook her head dumbly, not taking her eyes for a moment off the fierce Saxon bear. She was sure that he intended to hurl her to the furs and rape her at any second and she was deciding how best to get hold of his dagger.

Eadric grunted again, noncommittally. "The other women we took are slaves now. Do you know why you are not?"

"You said I *am* a slave," she answered.

"Pah!" he scoffed at her, tossing a bone to the rug. "You have no idea what it is to be a slave and probably never will, at least not a slave like the other women. Their own desires make them slaves."

She shook her head, bewildered.

Eadric nodded in some quaint show of secret satisfaction. He could see her as she could not see herself, as those most worthy who do not understand what it is that they have, what makes them desirable. "You are a brave little girl and I think it a great waste to make a butter maid or pig tender out of you. From such loins as yours, stout warriors are brought forth." He paused to refill his gaping mouth for it seemed that it must be constantly filled for him to speak properly. She studied him intently, shock written tragically across her lovely face. She had lived to hear her nightmare pronounced. Never had she felt so alone before.

At a call from the jarl, a tall man entered the room, as tall even as the Saxon robber himself, with a cruelly handsome face and a short-cropped beard instead of the wild tangle that distinguished Eadric's face. His hair was blonder than even Claire's. He eyed her with a condescending appraisal that stripped her naked in his mind and slowly ran his tongue across his lips in a gesture calculated to make her feel even more helpless.

"But I thought...," she began in even more fear than before.

Eadric smiled, almost kindly, "I am too old for such sport, little one. Although regretfully so, looking at you."

She blushed, feeling a confused kindness towards this man who had stolen her.

Slowly, the second Saxon nodded his approval to the first. "Eadric Siwardsson, you have done right by me this time! I accept this gift freely given!"

Eadric laughed loudly, a trifle drunkenly as he swilled ale. "Wulfhere Eadricsson, spawn from my loins, take her and bear for me many warriors!" Then, he turned to peer again into Claire's pale face. "But treat her with mildness for I look upon her with favor, as she is a different lass."

Wulfhere nodded, but his lips sneered. He could not wait to get at her.

"His mother was Norman also. Perhaps together you can both find your true Saxon blood and let it flow wholesome through the veins of your children and the children after!" The old jarl's face was impassive as Claire registered her shock at what was happening, and when Eadric's son took her by the arm, she lashed out at him in desperation as she had done to his father.

"No!" she cried. " You cannot! You..."

Only this Saxon struck back and a large open hand sent the floor rushing up behind her. She arose trembling, his vise-like grip upon her arm once more and, horrorstricken, allowed him to lead her out the door.

Eadric laughed sadly, it seemed. "I should have told you, lass, patience is a virtue of mine, but not necessarily that of Wulfhere the Reaver. And he is a bit more prone to express his dislike with open hand or fist. But you have the spirit he needs in a wife, for he needs to make himself the master, not have it given to him!" Something clicked in Claire's mind as he said this and she saw the evil in Wulfhere's face, evil for evil's sake. Here was a man who would take what he wanted, including Eadric's command. She saw this at that instant with a certainty that seemed almost clairvoyant and wondered why the father did not see this in the son. But Eadric was blathering on still.

"And see that you bear him sons!" he called as Wulfhere half-dragged her down the hallway. With that singularly repulsive benediction, the burly Saxon returned to his feast. That evening, there would be another feast in the celebration of Wulfhere taking a woman, but if he knew anything about his son at all, he knew that Wulfhere would already be starting his own celebration within the confines of his own chambers.

Poor girl! Eadric thought obliquely, but it was all he could do for either one of them.

Poor girl! Then he heard her first cry, and his hand went abruptly for the ale horn.

Claire sat without speaking on the edge of a low couch made of logs and covered with a pallet of rushes and furs. Her slim legs shone golden in the torchlight where her gown could not conceal them and her lovely face was turned to the wall, not looking at the big, bare-chested warrior standing before her.

He drank from an enormous horn, letting the frothy brew flow down the corners of his mouth and over his naked torso. "Drink!" he said, shoving the horn to her.

Disgusted, she pushed the ale horn away, but Wulfhere was too quick and too brutal for her. His left hand entangled her hair and snapped her head back; the right forced the horn against her lips, cutting them until she opened to drink. The ale splashed down her dress and Wulfhere tightened his grip when he saw she was faking.

She swallowed the bitter brew, coughing and gagging.

Wulfhere smiled the smile of a fox to a hen and kissed her savagely, his eye agleam with lust.

She felt warm, feverish from the large quantity of ale that she had eventually been forced to swallow, yet it was still not enough to dull the dark trepidation she felt at what was to occur. She had had men make advances to her before, but never like this, never in such a barbaric showdown or such utter terror. There was no place to run to, no place to hide.

She was abandoned in this chamber with a stranger who had merely taken her as he might an object or an animal. She had tried to think of herself as other than slave, yet this man treated her with a callousness bordering on contempt or even dislike. He gave no care at all to her. What manner of man was he?

Wulfhere the Reaver was more animal than man. He cast the ale horn away and with a semi-drunken sweep of his arms tried to enfold her. He had stripped himself naked now and Claire drew back in the presence of his arousal. She had never feared a man's loving until now, for Wulfhere Eadricsson cavorted around the room heavily like a bull seeking a cow. A rough, calloused hand cupped her chin and forced her eyes to meet his. She was determined not to show any fear for she knew that such a display could only encourage him further in his brutality.

She tightened her lips against the kiss that must inevitably come. But it was not a tender kiss, or even a lusty one that met her pale lips, but the back of his hand slamming her down to the couch. Her entire form convulsed with fear and she could conceal it no longer.

"Please! Do not hurt me," she wept. He had crushed her, not so much with the physical blow but by the look upon his face that promised so much more.

She did not resist further as Wulfhere took her dress from her to reveal her deliciousness, nor as one uncaring hand methodically fondled her small breasts. He examined her as a man might a horse or steer, stroking and seeking knowledge with his fingers. But it was a detached form of fondling that offered no excitement to either partner, Wulfhere was merely exploring the property he now owned. And it made her feel totally degraded, not even being touched as a human being.

"Please..." she began.

"Please," he mimicked her, his eyes unfathomable.

The pressure on her breasts tightened until she winced.

"Please!" he mimicked again.

Then he bit her, as if testing experimentally how much pain she could withstand before crying out. At first, she ground her teeth in silence, but soon the pressure of his jaws increased and she could not stop a low cry from escaping. Wulfhere laughed softly and massaged the bruised areas, apparently satisfied with her reaction. She knew now what she might expect from him in the future.

Claire's senses danced crazily as the alcohol finally reached her head and she relaxed somewhat to his fondling. It was softer now. Almost gently carried out.

He was easier on her now that his dominance was established. She loathed him still; she did not need him nor want him. But her mind became duller and duller with drink. Claire felt the fight ebb out of her and she allowed him to lay her back upon the couch.

Wulfhere laughed.

And in spite of the misery and horror of this man in her mind, an image that would never change for as long as she would know him, and because of her treasured fantasies being left on another shore, so far away, she had no choice but to yield to him. Her mind had drifted to sleep as she surrendered.

The torch sputtered smokily, annoyingly. Wulfhere reached up a hand and extinguished the light, plunging the chamber into darkness, but not into sleep.

Eadric Siwardsson walked away from their door, satisfied.

4

CHAPTER THE FOURTH

"In God's sweet name!" roared Geoffrey with a fury that his elders at Westwall had never seen exhibited before. His chainmail and leather gauntlet smashed the crockery upon the dining table before his seated father and the oaken table itself rocked and groaned precariously.

"Is there nothing you will do? This is how you welcome me home, is it, my father? By forbidding me my heart's dearest desire?"

The other nobles quietly left the hall, unsure of exactly how Geoffrey would continue. Sir Brian rose, his face bleak and tired.

"At your age, my son, every desire is your heart's dearest."

"Don't patronize me, Father! I'm no longer a child!" Geoffrey sneered.

"Then cease acting as one!" said the elder St. Denis sternly. Enraged, Geoffrey cut his father to the quick with an observation he knew he would never mean. "You are a coward. You let me rot in deAyrin's tower and now you will not help me in punishing these raiders and freeing one I hold dear!"

Sir Brian's look was stony, but he did not reply. For two days, the father had postponed an answer to the astounding request Geoffrey had made his very first day home, saying that he needed time to consider the matter. Which was a lie, but a well-intentioned one. During these days, his incredibly strong son practiced as he had in Castle Ayrin with sword and axe and lance until even his stupefying vitality was exhausted. He was up at first light, clad all in his heaviest armor and would continue until evening stopped him by its waning light.

His purpose was relentless. All of the knights and men-at-arms at Westwall were sore from being coerced into battling this young champion, and in the end, only agreed to combat Geoffrey in twos or threes. None could even hope to match his skills, or his ferocity, for none had been trained in the school that he had been—the school of desperation. It was the fever in his mind that made him truly fearsome, for as each man raised sword against him, the familiar face vanished to be replaced by the scraggle-bearded one of Eadric Siwardsson. Two of his friends he had injured, although he had not meant to.

Now, this was how he returned to his elders this evening, late for supper, storming into the hall with blue eyes smoldering—the eyes of a fellow knight and noble. Not those of a son.

"Father, I will have your answer!" he demanded, regarding his sire with eyes of flint. Spurs and broadsword clanked on the flagstones; he threw his coif back to show a haggard face.

Sir Brian slowly pushed away his trencher of bread, folded his hands upon his lap, and regarded his son with cautious eyes.

The silence was electric. By now, Geoffrey knew what the answer would be. Somewhere, a dog chewed noisily upon a bone; two sentries outside the windows exchanged crude jests, but between the father and son, there were no words for the longest time.

Sir Brian repressed his anger at the intended rebuke at his son's attitude, after all, it was deAyrin's fault, wasn't it?

"I cannot help you, Geoffrey!" he said quietly. For another instant, there was deathly silence in the hall as those terrible words sank into his son's consciousness, that phrase he had dreaded so much, yet knew what it would be.

Sir Brian steeled himself for the protest that must come; old Robert One-Eye had advised not provoking the lad, for he knew Geoffrey's temper. Robert One-Eye usually knew best in these matters; he knew

Geoffrey as well as his father might. But even so, Sir Brian paled before the fury of the verbal assault.

Geoffrey's eyes narrowed wickedly and his lips twisted into a half-sneer. A great vein stood out, pulsing, in his throat where the metal links were opened and his entire face seemed gray and drawn. It was as if Sir Brian addressed the ghost of his son.

Without taking his eyes from his father's face, Geoffrey stripped off his gauntlets and, for one second of gut-wrenching fear, Sir Brian feared that his son would hurl the heavy gloves into his face in the universal sign of a challenge.

Geoffrey cast burning eyes about the hall and saw that he and his father were, unsurprisingly, alone. Even the servants had left as they heard the elder St. Denis refuse the request. They all knew what the young knight was like now that he had returned home; they had witnessed his frenzy these past days. And now, his father had the agony of refusing to acknowledge the weight of what tormented his son. Poor father, his son was quite mad. But none dared say so to either St. Denis.

Poor family, having lost their only son and heir to the land in this way, to be maddened by the curse of a woman was the worst way to go, the old sots said. Who had heard of a noble raising such a fuss over a peasant girl; why if he couldn't have one, there were plenty of others who would accept his love.

They were all authorities, of course. Ancient lovers revealing the sacred secrets of the mystery as they sat around tables of spilled brew and drunken companions. No one speaks of madness to the mad, however.

They had all seen him joust and do contest with war's implements, by now. Geoffrey was an imposing figure in his own shire and those who had traveled said that he might meet the best in England and not be shamed. His sword was respected, his good will honored.

And, too, sure of himself with his newfound importance, he felt he would soon ride with legions at his back and be permitted to set his own course for the North. But his certainty waned a little as time passed and there was still no answer given; certainty waned and rage set in.

And again, his hopes were shattered.

He raged as a wounded lion rages, ferociously and unreasoningly. He called his father a knave and the men of Westwall cowards and shirkers. With a backhand stroke of his sword, one of the benches was kindling for the cooking fires.

But now he was met with equal fervor by his father. Sir Brian had seen that this sort of anger could not be met with patience, for it was as all-consuming as a forest fire; only a rainstorm could smother it, not a shower.

Now it was the older man's turn to pound the table. "Cease, you young ass! I'll not tolerate this boorishness in mine own manor. If you cannot control yourself, then get you back to the field and lose yourself of your vigor!" he snapped.

With a grunt, Geoffrey cast his sword down upon the table in an unstated agreement to watch his manners more closely. He was not, after all, oblivious to his father's authority.

"You talk of God's name! Nay, not yet, but it will come! For now, in the name of William the King of England, do we assemble." said Sir Brian. There was a secret held here, there was something Geoffrey had not been told, something of tremendous importance. Geoffrey was so taken aback by this extraordinary statement that he stood speechless.

Sir Brian continued, encouraged by the awed silence he received. "You have put the question to me right bluntly, more bluntly than you have any right to. But I will answer it for you, nevertheless, and equally blunt! You are self-centered in your pursuit of lust."

"Love!" Geoffrey interrupted hotly.

"Whatever," agreed Sir Brian equably. "But consider this, for thirty years, England has been a nation of warring factions. Regardless of what accomplishments we Normans have made, we are still invaders and still resented by these Saxon churls!"

"I do not fear their resentment!" Geoffrey muttered. He spat into the fire in disgust.

"You should," Brian said simply.

"They are a conquered people..." Geoffrey began.

"Aye. But they own this land no matter what force of arms takes it from them. They are a people divided from us and England can never be strong as long as there is rivalry and warfare between nations of its own peoples. You were born here; you are not of Normandy even as I am no longer. But to the Saxon people, we will always be the invaders from Normandy, even if the hundredth generation of them is birthed on English soil. At present, England grows weak, despite our government. We are easy pray for other countries as we still harry Saxon outlaws in the hills and fens. If this continues, the day will come when another people will drive us under, and we will be the Saxons then."

"Nonsense!" scoffed Geoffrey.

"Who will help us if we war with another country? The Saxons? You forget, there are still far more of them than there are us!"

Geoffrey was silenced by this thought. "But where is the truth, Father?" he asked finally. "Is it not that we Normans jumped the channel and smashed a people and civilization we should have let live? That we, the outcasts, have wrongly made them outcasts in their own land?" The young St. Denis spoke with little regard for who might be listening, and his words were calculated like blows of a sword to sting the father of an immensely proud line and heritage, and proud of what he and his family had carved out of this alien, hostile land.

"Truth?" the father queried. "Truth is determined by the history writers. We are more concerned with pragmatism."

"But it's only the victors who write the history. Truth is the point of a sword, not a writing quill."

"I will give you truth, you idealistic puppy. The truth is that Duke William was promised the crown by Edward the Confessor in 1051, and the Duke reinforced his bid for England when Harold himself, then merely the Earl of Essex, was shipwrecked along the coast of Normandy."

Geoffrey gave a bitter laugh. "Who writes your history for you, Father? Did you hear all of this from the Iron Duke himself? Or were you actually there when he and Harold settled the affairs of this land?"

Sir Brian ran a tired hand through his gray hair in a sign of impatience. "There are stories…" he said, darkly.

"Stories, aye!" mocked Geoffrey. "If it's stories you like, then I'll tell you one heard from Robert One-Eye. The Iron Duke reinforced the bid, you say. I'll tell you how he reinforced it; he threw Harold into his darkest dungeon until the Saxon Earl promised to king him should the occasion ever arise. What could be fairer than that, eh?"

Geoffrey's words had an ominous ring of truth to them. What he said, Duke William was more than capable of doing. "Was Harold really expected to hold to that contract, to honor such blatant nonsense? Tis no great wonder he fought so fiercely at Hastings, undoubtedly, he still tasted the stale bread and wine and smelled the rat droppings from beneath his bed. It seems to me that he was trying to save his country from an unscrupulous bastard!" he went on. Geoffrey idly played with his dagger as he thought out loud, eyes downcast to the table.

"Unscrupulous? All men of power are unscrupulous; that's how they become men of power. They have a fine way of thinking that they are always right; if they are strong enough then I suppose that they always are," Sir Brian parried.

"Cynicism well becomes you, sir!" replied Geoffrey.

"As idealism does not become my son. In your time of captivity, you have forgotten what the world is really like." Sir Brian stroked his beard as he studied his beloved son's hard face.

"And forgotten how to tell right from wrong, also, I don't doubt."

"Nay, not at all," said Brian in all seriousness. "But you attach all too much import to the act of being right. This world is not full of rights and wrongs, only choices, each choice with its own penalty or reward. People are either weak or strong; the strong win and become kings. The weak become the serf. Better to choose out of strength than be right and be weak also."

"I disagree!" Geoffrey grated.

"That is your right," allowed Sir Brian with a condescending shrug. "But what you feel does not alter the rules of the game."

"Then why bother with knighthood, Father? On my oath of fealty, I swore to uphold the right. Is it all that false?"

"Again, nay. I, too, try to do the correct thing each time I make a decision. But I never confuse ideals with saving the skin on my arse!" Brian laughed.

"And William, a bastard, no doubt."

"Bastard, yes. Tis well known. But you talk of scruples. Am I to believe that when King Edward lay upon his deathbed and Harold sent all the other attendants away, that the dying King suddenly changed his will and gave the kingdom to Harold? Tis odd, methinks, that he called for no other witnesses to attest to this. We had only Harold's word that he had been named the rightful king, and when is the word of some Saxon to be weighed with a kingdom in balance?"

Geoffrey shrugged ineloquently at the sound of these words.

Sir Brian continued, sensing that he was winning. Geoffrey was arguing with him now, but the mad roaring was gone. "And at any rate, Harold was merely some jumped-up Earl; King William was the choice of Edward. But Harold got greedy and seized the throne upon Edward's death in 1066. What would you have done, my son? Be made a shame-faced fool and lose a kingdom in the bargain?"

"Or march for the coast?" Geoffrey asked.

"You never knew him, son," Brian went on almost gently. His eyes dimmed at the thoughts of memories long past, decades past, when he was Geoffrey's age, or not much older. Memories of a commander he had revered. "The Iron Duke was a man's man with fire in his veins and ice in his soul...even as you and I are! He, himself, led the force that landed in September that same year at Pevensey, an army sadly lacking in numbers for the contest to come, if truth be known. The landed nobles across the coast had no desire to squander their men under the command of some hot-headed bastard, born of Robert of Normandy. But on a flat-topped hill six miles this side of the town Hastings, they locked horns, he and Harold the usurper."

"King," Geoffrey corrected.

Sir Brian ignored him; he was in another world where he had won the glory of his life. "The rest you know. There's no gainsaying that Harold was a brave man, or that all his men were equally brave. Afoot, they withstood the brunt of the Norman cavalry for an entire day, until they thought the day won and broke ranks to chase our fleeing ranks. But William turned his men, regrouped them according to his plan, and they mauled the broken-ranked Saxon bears. Harold's men ran back to the hilltop and regrouped, but by then it was too late to turn the tide; William's archers cut them to pieces as the cavalry backed off."

"Black Phillip's archers," Geoffrey interjected.

"Aye, that scum, so they say."

Geoffrey spat at the thought of the old, dead devil. *Those who live by the sword, so shall they perish by the sword* echoed in Geoffrey's mind. He wondered if Black Phillip and the Iron Duke were together again in hell.

His father continued, "But what has happened since then is more to my point. Look you how wretched the land was, how it has changed in thirty years! William revived learning in the church and extended power to ecclesiastical courts! He took the rude methods these Saxons called justice and tempered them with trial by jury. He has vastly expanded trade and altered the very appearance of the landscape with architecture. William Rufus has followed in his father's footsteps."

"Grand for us!" laughed Geoffrey mockingly. "I cannot imagine why the Conqueror has not been canonized."

"No saint ever led a nation."

"No king ever became a saint," Geoffrey replied.

"Tis all the same. We say the same thing, son. The hand that holds the rein of a plunging horse must be strong, even harsh, else the horse will break both their necks."

"But what does the horse say? Does it not plunge for a reason?" retorted Geoffrey.

"Perhaps it is mad," stated Brian.

"But here, the horse says only that William was a royal bastard, the son of the Duke of Normandy who readily earned his name *The Devil* and that the man followed after his father!"

"Do you listen to horses? Then you are the mad one!" Sir Brian smiled.

"And the English Saxons are charmed by your Norman arrogance."

"That's irrelevant. They are the horse; we are the rider," the elder St. Denis said coldly.

Geoffrey held up a weary hand as he settled himself on a bench and called for dinner to be served him. His anger was all but abated in his interest of the talk. When a boy, Geoffrey had often talked with his father like this, now it was somewhat soothing, despite the subject; it brought back the security of childhood.

"This I realize, Father. But what has this to do with me and with the house of St. Denis?" His anger was turning into despair, and with its exit he realized that, for all his faults, his father had never judged him harshly without good reason.

Brian smiled grimly. "There was a messenger here but a day or so before you arrived. There is in the wind a happening so great that it will cement together the house of William II and this land; it will change the very course of history–to unite Norman and Saxon alike under God's banner and melt the peoples of this still-warring nation into one piece of iron for eternity! I speak in the name of his majesty William II, King of all England, when I say to you that the entire house of St. Denis is pledged to this cause as are all true Normans, and with the will of God, every Christian knight, Saxons included!"

Geoffrey smiled wryly and tapped his dagger blade against a goblet of wine sitting before him. His blue eyes studied the ripples in the deep red liquid as he pondered his father's words. Odd, he thought, how life was like the ripples in the cup, how a series of events sprang from but one action and continued to spread until they reached their limits and then faded. In the goblet of life, some ripples would not fade, however, they were too strong. Perhaps they might disappear from the surface of life's sea, yet they were always there. What his father was doing was setting a limit for his feelings. Had Geoffrey been the goblet, the ripple that started with Claire's capture would supposedly be fading by this time, to be overwhelmed, *negated*, by this new feeling of honor that his father had initiated.

But it was not so easy with people as with objects.

Sir Brian continued, "I cannot spare you a single man, my son, no matter how great you think you love this girl. I do not agree with you pursuing her but I have always allowed you to make your own grief, which you have done handily enough, I might add. But now we will all soon be in mortal combat ourselves with perhaps the very fate of England in the balance. If we succeed, the world can never deny what we have done, for we will do what no other civilization in the world has ever done."

"Unite two warring peoples?" asked Geoffrey, puzzled.

Brian laughed, a guffaw full of pride and excitement. He was young again in his anticipation; his fatigue was gone. His eyes gleamed as he stood and reached for his sword and sheath, lying across the table. Slowly, he unsheathed the longsword and held it up to the torchlight. "In God's name, we will free Jerusalem!" he cried, sword flashing.

Geoffrey leaped to his feet, horrified. His strong features went ashen with the disbelief and anger he felt.

"You jest wrongly, Father!" he cried. But the silence told him more than words that it was no jest.

He cast his dagger into the table, rude again without thinking. The madness came over him again at the import of his father's statement. The dagger vibrated in the planks of the table so that its hilt rang out metallically against the goblet, sending ripples churning through the wine so strongly that the red splashed over the edge and onto the table. The sound of dagger and goblet was that of a funeral bell to Geoffrey.

He stood splay-legged, arms akimbo, his blue eyes cold and forbidding; the corners of his mouth twisted slightly in the semblance of a snarl. Fists clenching and opening repeatedly, he slowly, and with visible effort, hung on to the last of his restraint. Words came slowly now, forced from a rage-thickened tongue and numbed mind. The intent, however, was crystal clear. His disgust was of such measure that he could not have hidden it from the king himself.

"You are mad!" he thundered. "What can England do against the might of Islam that we have heard so much about from the traveling minstrels? A power so great as to hold numberless nations within its grasp! Has their might been so greatly overrated? Are their men cowards that we might sweep them into the sea? How can you think such a thing?"

"No, they are not overrated," Sir Brian said calmly, trying by his attitude to instill some degree of composure back into his son. "It will be a great struggle, but it will be won in God's name! "

"How pious you suddenly are, Father! Did you take vows while I was gone? Explain to me, please, how we will conquer the infidel? Mostly, I am curious as to what makes you think we can conquer the heathen world when we are still thirty years into the conquest of this land. England is still but half-tamed and the fens are still full of reckless, raging Saxons. Do you count these bandits in God's army?"

Brian stood to face his boy turned man, his lean features dark and the barest hint of resentment in his eyes. Yet his voice was cool and full of chilling reason. "Those Saxons with honor will fight for the Holy Land, if not under the banner of England, then under their own. The rest of your speech belies your maturity! But I shall enlighten you…

"In a few months, Pope Urban II will make a plea to enlist the martial and financial aid of our brothers across the channel. At present, he is negotiating in private with William for our aid. And I assure you with all confidence, that the king will stand in the forefront as leader. What can these wild Britons say when it is their king that frees the Holy City?"

"That he is not their king," Geoffrey replied, ironically, with a shrug.

Sir Brian laughed and sipped at his wine. "You misjudge the common mind, boy! These peasants and down-at-heel nobles need success that they can claim; God knows we have left them little enough else. If William succeeds, they will acknowledge him as their king."

"And if he does not?"

"He will. He would not attempt it if he thought he could lose. William understands the precariousness of the situation; he is no fool."

"I still do not see what will make the Saxons ally with us. Should we conquer, what then? Will they not return to continue worshipping the sun and seasons as they have since time began? A city of another religion will not hold them in awe. Now, say rather that it is William who captures the King of the Otherworld, or something equally practical to them, those that are ignorant—now that would be a real cause for support. But a city that is holy because of some man they nailed to a cross of wood? Why no *civilized*, self-respecting Saxon peasant would believe that."

"Do not blaspheme so!" Brian admonished.

"Do not chide so!" Geoffrey countered, sitting with a grunt. "I only say what the savages will think and do."

Brian gave a wry smile. "Tis known even to you, my son, that the magic days of the druids and wood painters are far past. Christian culture is Saxon as well as Norman."

"Go to the hills in the fens, Father. Look at the stones carved into altar and statues; watch the gatherings at twilight. Tell me they are Christian."

"They are few."

Geoffrey laughed loudly, without humor. "Still, it seems outrageous to think that events in another land will so change the situation here. There is nothing but time that will melt the English, all of the English, into one culture. Even the greatest sword cannot do this, nor the greatest quest. You are a fine one to call me dreamer, Father!" The young knight's voice was tired and hoarse. He sensed the wisdom in Brian's argument; William was many things, but the least of these was a fool.

"Tis but William's dream, my son. My heart, like yours, is here."

Geoffrey looked up, blue eyes glowing. "Nay, Father. My heart is across the sea somewhere, in the North where they have stolen her!"

Sir Brian gave him a look of sharp distaste. "Then I tell you that as my duty to God and king comes before mine own heart, then so does yours, sir!"

Geoffrey eyed him scornfully. "And these legions of others that will flock to William's banner, are they also moved so much by duty to God and king?"

No," said the father thoughtfully. He leaned back and scratched his beard with a splinter of wood from the table. "They will come for the gold."

"Gold? Does William pay mercenaries?" Geoffrey asked blankly.

"No, my innocent, he does not need to. The lands of Islam are rich with gold and women; there is no matter if while we are restoring the true religious order of the world, if we help ourselves to some of the goods these heathens have stolen from others. Even the Saxons will believe this."

"Oh, my God!" gasped Geoffrey, suddenly understanding. "You and your hollow piety, and William's! All you want is to fill your coffers with gold! How long have you all planned this, Father? Even Black Phillip would have joined you in so gallant an undertaking for he was the Christian the rest of you are!"

"Silence, fool!" roared Sir Brian. "I did not tell you that it was my dream of wealth; I am a soldier loyal to mine king. If he tells me to fight, then I fight, for him or God or gold, whichever is irrelevant. We are the vassals to the son of William the Conqueror and we do as he says. I am simply telling you what logic he will use to recruit the more practical who owe him no allegiance. The truth is that there will be much gold, but foolish is the minor lord who thinks he can snatch up a lion's share before the kings. For many in these armies there will be more death than gold. If I am rewarded for my contribution, so much for the better; but the standard of St. Denis will fly for the good of England and for no other reason. If God chooses to align himself with me, he is welcome."

"You make an idol out of William."

"I make an idol out of my love for my home."

"And the Pope?" Geoffrey asked sarcastically.

"He has his own ideas, I'm sure."

"Are they of God or gold?" struck Geoffrey again.

Surprisingly, his father smiled. "I cannot answer that. You should ask him."

"I shall, if I receive an audience," muttered Geoffrey.

"By God! I believe you would!" Sir Brian laughed. "I believe you would!"

"My love for her is real," the young knight said suddenly, abruptly. "I won't squander it on hypocrites."

Sir Brian's humor faded as suddenly as it had sprung. His face was white with anger as he studied his son. "You are my son and my vassal. You will abandon this nonsense and prepare to leave with us. There needs be no more said on this matter!" His father gazed down at the table as he finished, unable to face the pain that he knew was clawing its way out of his son's eyes.

But Geoffrey was cool as he drew himself up to his full height and looked down at his father.

"On this, at least, we agree!" grated Geoffrey. And with no further words he turned and left the hall, his dinner untouched. Sir Brian smiled to himself at his son's iron. When the last trumpet sounded, the young knight would be by his side, he was sure of this. But as he mulled all of this over in his mind, he became morose with some barely sensed premonitions and he also pushed the rest of his food away, uneaten. When the servants went to bed, he was still sitting there, staring into the huge fireplace. He was wondering what the flames of hell were like.

His son did not sleep either. Geoffrey paced the confines of his living chambers in frustration. Candlelight gave the small room a cheery glow but could not dispel the knight's gloom, nor could the thought of what his father expected him to do on the morrow. He had had these chambers as a boy growing up, yet these rooms contained no warmth for him now; no residual lingering of a child's familial love as should have been. Instead, they held for him all of the cramped oppressiveness of his tower room at Castle Ayrin, perhaps more, for it was his mind that was now oppressed. Each night, he had awakened in the dark and lonely room and wondered which was a dream—his sleeping memories of the High Tower or his being home. All rooms are much alike in the dark and though Geoffrey had been a prisoner, then he had at least had her.

Now he had to content himself with hope, a meagre fare indeed. He stood free but more helpless than when he was captive. And now, too, there were even those who would deny him his hope. Perhaps his heart should lie with Westwall, but here she was only a dream to him, bittersweet and distant.

What then of his honor? Was it not also a dream? A dream of hypocrites of a united England, of golden dreams of a free Holy Land? But whose dream was it? It belonged to William II and the elder nobles, those with their grasping plans and grasping hands—to shape England's future.

But was it not, through his oaths, his dream also? Did he not owe more to his family's honor than to run after a captive girl he had never spoken to? Geoffrey laughed mockingly as the irony of the situation became clear...worlds, or countries at least, hung in the balance and he thought only of Claire.

On one side, his honor, for it was really inseparable from his father's, the future of England, the fate of the Holy Land, his knightly vows

before God, his trust in his golden spurs, his entire way of life to date…
and on the other…Claire, only Claire.

But the "only" was misleading, for it is a term often used to imply a
small degree of worth, to demean, to condescend. Here, it denoted the
singular, but this degree of "oneness" overpowered kings and countries,
and if He was as the priests and pious nobles said, then Geoffrey idolized
her above Him to his soul's lasting damnation.

Beautiful "golden hair" with her matchless compassion for human
wickedness, her unhuman gentleness. What choice was his, really? He
had sworn a life of allegiance to God and king when he received his
spurs, to abandon them now for something as selfish as his own desires
made him more than just a false knight—it made him a traitor in his own
eyes. How could he live with that?

As with much of youth, there was no room for the ground in
between, no gray border where truth and falsehood overlapped. Either
something was true or it was false, either he loved her or he did not,
either he would become a traitor to all that he loved, or he would not.
But he was uncomfortable because the monks who had tried to educate
him had insisted truth is a straight line through life, as is what is false;
one must simply follow the line to one's own destiny they had told
him–truth led to truth. But here the truth that he loved her led to the
truth that he would be a traitor. He was confused by the logic; it
contradicted his heart. It never entered their logic to allow for feelings
and the needs of a man as a good man and one entirely human as God
had ordained it. He was neither machine nor perfect knight—he was
but a man. But he found it hard to consider this in the situation; his
manhood was lost to his chivalry. The ideals that made him an excellent warrior also fettered him with a weight greater than the chains of
Castle Ayrin.

Then, in his aching heart, he learned the first of his great lessons of
life, a lesson that had brought tears to stronger men than he. He had
learned that a man's feelings for another, be they justified or unjustified,
be they worthy or not, good or bad, may supersede all else, come ruin or
riches. If it was merely lust or jealousy, his honest heart would have won
out and he would have followed the dictates of his iron conscience. But

all he could see when he closed his eyes was her still form, kneeling on the bow of that awful ship.

And it was not that he discounted his honor, not even for all his love of her, nor that he held his vows any the lesser for seeing their value next to hers. Rather, he counted himself fallen, lost from the position he had wanted more than anything his entire life...until he saw her. In his swollen heart, he knew his shield would never bear the twin trees of St. Denis against that blue sky. Indeed, how could he ever face his father or his father's men, again. He could not.

Could he abandon them in their need of every man, allow them to risk death while he took a ship for the North? False knight! False knight! False knight! The words pounded through his tired mind like hammer blows upon an anvil. His veins throbbed; his heart raced as he reached for his traveling cloak and spun it around his broad, steel-wrapped shoulders. He would not pause to even eat or change; let him be gone before he repented his sin and conscience forced the mind straight. Let him flee like the coward he was before he was discovered and rebuked into staying.

Geoffrey kicked awake one of the stable pages and bade him saddle Chestnut. He took only his sword, shield and mace with him that he might travel light, along with the dirk that he kept on his person at all times and the heavy pouch of silver and gold coins that had been a welcoming gift at his first dinner home. Now it was one of farewell.

The young page gazed at Geoffrey through sleep-crusted eyes. His blond hair was uncombed and he seemed habitually embarrassed to be standing so before the lord's son, a great warrior.

How long ago had it been him standing there, Geoffrey wondered. The boy was puzzled by his master's haste, yet he knew better than to ask awkward questions about his night's work. Mayhap, it was some lass excited to feel the master's lust. The page chuckled to himself as he worked. Geoffrey continued to fret, lest he be discovered.

"She must be well worth it, master!" the boy laughed as he cinched the saddle tight.

Geoffrey started from his melancholy and stared intently at the lad, his eyes clouding at last with some unfathomable emotion. "Aye, fellow.

She is worth my soul!" he muttered, pulling tight his riding gauntlets. The blond boy smiled, flattered by this confidence.

Geoffrey turned and surveyed the dimly lit stable for what he knew was the final time. He knew he would not see it again, ever. And he was right.

His eyes moistened briefly as he glanced up to the loft where he and the other pages had hidden from searching squires and trainers more than a decade ago. The smell of straw was rich and fragrant, the aroma of horses warm and reassuring. And then, with a suddenness that startled the sleepy page, Geoffrey hurled himself into the saddle and thundered across the cobbles of the courtyard. Two familiar faces saluted him at the main gate, happy to have him home again.

Then he was through the gateway and free from his second imprisonment in three years, this time one of honesty and honor. The wind was soft and warm like her breath must be, the night slightly damp with the fleeting hint of rain. Dark trees were still around Geoffrey as he cantered along in the silver moonlight, bound again for Cornwall and the coast.

And then? He did not care to think about it. But as surely as the sun would rise tomorrow, he knew that he would one day find her, if it took ten days or ten years. And if he could not free her, he would die for her. But that part was unthinkable, God would not permit that.

In this beautiful foolishness of thought, this utter impracticality of dedication, Geoffrey had encompassed the most ancient secret of man. He had learned, harshly perhaps, the eternal truth and lie, about manhood and men and their women. He had discovered in his heart what it meant to be sufferingly and totally human despite the artificial discipline of years of training, to care, despite the protests of the ego, for another. He had seen revealed the most painful secret and the most devastating, defeating purpose of manhood with all its bittersweet reward. He had learned so very well. There is no power stronger in a man's soul, than the love of a woman. Geoffrey had entered his third captivity now; it being the most terrible.

5

CHAPTER THE FIFTH

E xactly three months to the day after Geoffrey's decision, destiny
had caught up with the men of Eadric Siwardsson.

Wulfhere Eadricsson spurred into the Saxon camp, cloak flying with
his steed in a slick lather of foamy sweat. He was a man in a hurry. His
once fair skin was now burned almost black by a hotter sun than the
Saxon camp on the high fjord had ever witnessed. He looked around at
the crowd come to meet him, satisfied. He had always counted himself
the real leader of the group, despite his father's decisions. There were
many who listened to him, many who would follow should he leave for
good.

The settlement was exactly how he had left it, beautiful and
unchanged. It was perched precariously upon a grassy cliff that jutted out
over the narrow strip of water that housed Eadric's Nykr, the ship named
for a water sprite with partly human form. Eadric's longhouse smoked
peacefully amid thirty or forty odd dwellings and tents in a placid scene;
one could almost see shepherds walking flocks in the hills. But the peace
was now over; Wulfhere had brought news of war, war that would see
them all rich. He surveyed the camp in some sort of hidden appraisal of
strength as he jerked his horse to a halt before the longhouse. He nodded

once more, satisfied. He could match the many swords he had boasted of in his correspondence.

Although he was cloaked in furs against the mountainous cold, he no longer dressed with the rude barbarousness of his clan. Hide leggings were replaced with soft leather boots and he wore a tunic of soft, yellowish fabric that was quite unlike anything the civilization of the North had turned out. His beard was gone, leaving only the moustache which he now wore longer, so that it arched past the tight corners of his mouth. His blond hair was no longer of unruly length but had been trimmed masterfully. In appearance, he was now civilized in the manner of the eastern lands; his entire mode of dress altered even to the wicked, curved blade he sported instead of his sturdy longsword.

And there was an air of contempt about him as he looked at the dirty slaves, and their equally dirty masters, going about their duties. Wulfhere Eadricsson had always been sure of himself, perhaps as having been raised a jarl's son. But there was something undeniably sinister about the brigand, something that lurked just out of sight in his eyes, hidden back in the shadows of the eye sockets. Eadric had sensed this periodically when Wulfhere gave vent to fits of temper. When he was a boy, Eadric would give him a slap up the side of the head to calm him down, and he would run to his mother in tears. As he grew older, he was harder and harder to control because his authority inside the tribe had increased with maturity and all had to admit, including Eadric, that his son was clever… devilishly clever.

Wulfhere was a natural leader and the men knew it. But where they loved Eadric, they feared Wulfhere. He was too much lost in himself, too quick to inflict punishment or rebuke to define his power. He had not the security of his father, but he was listened to and followed. Above all, Wulfhere the Reaver had a stout sword arm and courage to back it. In the frozen North, only the strong are worthy of being followed. But still, there was this strangeness about him.

Even familiar faces did not acknowledge his return for Wulfhere Eadricsson was not a man to be taken lightly or addressed with any degree of familiarity by his inferiors. He was burdened with an exaggerated sense of his own importance, yet, thus far he had found the ability within himself to check his ego.

He was both feared and respected, and his place as Wild Eadric's equally wild seed acknowledged, yet there was no affection for him in this camp as there was for the great jarl himself. Those who are overly ambitious are never fully trusted and a scheming mind is often a two-edged sword, eventually slashing the wielder as well as the foe.

Claire looked up from her loom where she sat spinning with the other women. For an instant, she opened her mouth to greet him, but thought the better of it and did not speak. He passed her without so much as a look. That was his way. The other women looked at each other but said nothing; it was not their place to notice such things.

The way of Wulfhere Eadricsson was harsh; he lived by his own warrior's code. He could never bring himself to show tenderness to anyone, not even her. Nor could he exhibit the basest elements of love, excepting, perhaps, when he really wanted her. And this fleeting taste of gentleness was gone as he climaxed within her. His expert caresses were poor substitutes for words of endearment, words she needed as does any woman. Perhaps she needed them more from him, to make up for the way he took her. Some thought there was bit of affection between them.

But love is ill-defined on the tongue of gossip and appearances deceiving. Women are peculiar in that if they are saddled with a man, they often try to make the best of it, even to hiding or attempting to justify his actions. They will mask their despair and concentrate on the man's accomplishments, not wanting to acknowledge even to themselves, just how very much they been wronged. They would rather bear their cross in silence than hear the world moan for them. The good ones, that is. Men are just the opposite; they look for excuses to find comfort between another woman's thighs. Human logic is frail.

But love or affection between the two of them? She could not say, for herself. True, he was never wantonly brutal to her after the first few times when he established his dominance. Now each time he struck out at her, he had a valid reason to. At least in his own mind.

Knowing this, she found it in herself to try to ignore his excesses. It was all she could do for her own sanity. What use to hate? There was no escape from the grassy cliffs overlooking the fjord. Where could she run to? There was nowhere.

Thus, it was easier to ignore. If she could right his wrongs within her own mind, even at the expense of her own respect, then she could establish a security within herself; she could negate the anxiety she would otherwise feel. No one can live without this feeling of security, even if it is wrongly established. Claire was no exception. And it was easier for her to create this in her own mind now for she was with child. But the pregnancy had affected Wulfhere differently; while Claire accepted his clumsy lust for many reasons, he now viewed her in an odd way. They were more strangers than they had been before.

She showed but little, though she and the oldwives in the camp knew for certain, but he rejected her as if there were resentment for his own child. He had first accused her of taking another man, but this sounded ludicrous even from his own lips. For reasons she could not fathom, he now denied her his touch. Her thoughts were confused on this; was this a good thing or did it mean she would no longer be under his protection?

For now, he would not even touch her. He had tired of her with the sowing of his seed and now he would look to others.

Eadric disapproved, but thought it wiser to remain aloof, in the end. Wulfhere would only take out his pain on the girl.

There were more than willing maids in the camp; this she knew. More than once she had seen Wulfhere cast lust-filled eyes upon the voluptuous figure of Margaret deAyrin. who served as Eadric's slave, and some said, bed warmer. It pleased Wild Eadric tremendously to enjoy the rites of submission with the daughter of a vanquished foe, though in truth he treated her not unkindly for all his uncouthness. She was often seen doing chores with the butter maids in the fields, a disgrace to her lineage. But curiously, she sang as she worked, and wore her hair loose like the Saxon maids. With some, the rites of submission can be made agreeable.

Wulfhere, doubtless, would have liked to administer these rites to the Lady deAyrin, her submission being all the sweeter for the knowledge that she belonged to his father. This was known to all, even Eadric. But none thought Wulfhere fool enough to try; he had too much to lose. With him, it was always the bid for power. No matter how inconsequential.

Claire turned her moist eyes to the hills, to the cool greens and grays so unlike the English forests she had grown up in. Here, the east wind was always cool and carried the scent of the sea. The land of the Norse was a vast, barren place, it seemed, and cold. Wulfhere understood how it affected her, how she feared the wildness of the land, but still he made a show of confining her to camp.

She was denied even the solace of limited freedom and trust, responsibility that even other slaves had been granted. Wulfhere demanded that her slavery be absolute and in this, he was a fool. But then, he was a fool in so many things about her. How could she flee now, even should she feel the need to? Did she not have two lives to care for instead of one? There was no salvation in leaving for she knew not in which direction to travel and she could not jeopardize the tiny soul locked inside her. There were times when she walked the cliff just at camp's edges when the wind rose with coming storm clouds and the sea churned below about the Nykr…when the tall grass bent to the breeze and it felt like the wind was forcing her to the edge of the jagged cliff…when she felt a fear unlike any she had ever experienced. There was an aloneness to the land that could drive you mad and she wondered what it must feel like to fall to the sea and rocks below. Claire feared this dizziness and feared the land for giving it to her. It was better to stay with Wulfhere and his vices. But all of this was lost on Wulfhere. He could not think of others past his lust or past using them for some end. Men were such fools.

She would wait for a dream, again, as she had waited all her life. She would resign herself to her fate and raise their daughter or son as best she could, alone, within the same longhouse as the child's father. But still, she knew that she must have a girl child. She prayed each night that it be so. She must! With a woman's instinct, she knew it had to be, or was it hope to find surcease from her apprehension, apprehension at what a man-child would become in this camp? She could not bear to have a boy sprung from the loins of Wulfhere Eadricsson, for they would corrupt him with their warfare as they had Wulfhere. The boy would be coarsened by these brutes until he could spit at his own mother and be another instrument of pillage and murder. Better such a child be born stone.

Perhaps if such a birth took place, if she birthed a boy despite her prayer, then she might flee. Death on the lonely cliffs could not be worse than seeing her child taken from her, day by day.

~

WULFHERE CAST ASIDE HIS CLOAK OF WOLF FUR, TOSSING IT CARELESSLY to the grass for a slave to pick up, and swaggered into the lodgehall where his father sat drinking with some of the captains. All of the scraggle-beards turned to him expectantly, ale horns held motionless halfway up to slavering mouths and oaths dying on the tongue that birthed them. Centered within them was Eadric, measuring with his single dark eye the stride of his son. Wulfhere was a strong right arm, but oft-times, Eadric wondered, if not the arm might one day grow too strong for the body and turn the clan to harm. More than one jarl had had to clench his teeth and cut loose such a limb when it became diseased.

Eadric studied him closely. The eastern lands were full of diseases, those that preyed upon the mind of an ambitious man. And Eadric knew that Wulfhere was greedy beyond mere ambition.

His eyes, however, betrayed nothing; Eadric was lulled for the moment. Now there was a future to be bought and paid for and with heavy Byzantine gold at that. Wulfhere was his link to riches; he had sent him chasing after the wildest of rumors, yet rumors that promised wealth beyond measure perhaps, if true.

Beware, Eadric! Some diseases are contagious without being noticed.

Eadric stood as did his captains following his lead. Lifting his ale horn high with one meaty arm, he roared out a drunken greeting that echoed out the long hall and over the fjord.

Wulfhere studied his mentor now, trying to discern his degree of inebriation. This was an old game, a battle of wits. Often Eadric would feign drunkenness to worm answers from Wulfhere. While drunk, he could say what he wanted and often goaded Wulfhere into revealing more than he had intended, for Wulfhere's pride was arrogant. But not this day. Wulfhere played for too large a prize.

"By Thor and Odin!" Eadric bellowed, "Who is this perfumed foreigner that comes before us as if he owned our allegiance? Phew! I can smell the drift of sandalwood from here and look you, my captains, the creature sports not the beard of honest Saxons!" Comically, Eadric thrust out his hairy chin, tangled with burrs and the remnants of the morning's repast. "By Loki's mischief, is this a woman who dares enter the hall unbidden, or worse? Have the Byzantines turned him into a boy lover? Note how he walks spread-legged. Has some dirty Turk injured his arse?" Politely, the lesser jarls shook with laughter, not a hard feat in the least as they had been drinking for several hours now.

Wulfhere smiled condescendingly and held up his hand for silence. He would not reveal his secrets today but Eadric had goaded him to anger. "Indeed, you might not be the one to judge, my jarl!" Wulfhere sneered. "For a group of ale-sodden ancients as yourselves must be fit for nothing better than wenching. It seems, that is, if you still prefer wenches. See if you can still find the prick that sired me amidst all that ale gut hanging over your belt!" he laughed. "Or does it take a young warrior to make the flesh tall now, my father? Tell me, is it true that Lady Margaret is still a virgin?" Wulfhere ducked as a heavy pot of brew sailed over his head to explode with a pop against the door behind him.

"My sword!" roared Eadric. "Where is my sword?" It was Eadric's turn for anger.

"Save your anger, old fool!" shouted Wulfhere, gloating. This time it was the father who lost the exchange. "I bring you greetings from the Emperor Alexis himself!"

"That boy-lover!" Eadric snorted. But he looked up from beneath the table where he was blindly groping for his sword amid gnawed bones and sleeping dogs. He blinked expectantly, allowing his eye to clear. "Ugh," he grunted. "What say you?" He rose to display the knees of his breeks sodden with ale from the puddles upon the floors and less likely offerings to the god of drink.

Wulfhere shook his head contemptuously. "I say gold, old man! The stories we heard were true!" shouted Wulfhere.

Eadric pushed his way through the men and grasped his son by the shoulder, looking deep into his eyes as he spoke. Now he must be sober, he thought. No, he must regain his perspective for the men would demand a decision of him and Eadric knew well enough that the story he would hear would be only Wulfhere's part of it. He had learned long ago that to be a jarl meant to be able to see through the words of men, to understand the truth beneath their words and actions. No man is completely honest, Eadric knew, not even to himself, and a man is more likely to lie when he has something to gain, the degree of gain often determining the degree of the lie. Ambitious men were the worst, and Wulfhere was ambitious to the point of treachery, Eadric had often thought. But he could never pin down Wulfhere's indiscretions; his son had learned too much, too well.

They were not talking about another coastal raid this time, however. The stakes of their game was infinitely greater, both in loss or gain. If they won this time, they would have looted an entire treasury—the treasury of an emperor.

"Say you so in truth?" Eadric asked quietly. Something flashed through Wulfhere's eyes under Eadric's powerful scrutiny. Fear? What? And then it was gone as the son composed himself with the knowledge that Eadric could not possibly know what he was thinking.

Eadric cursed himself inwardly for the sign was there and he had missed it. There had been a secret unlocked briefly in his son's eyes and he was too slow to interpret it. But he hid his disappointment well.

Wulfhere's smile took on the faintest tinge of cruelty as he looked at his father standing more than half-drunk before him, his red beard dripping the brew he drank and his leather eyepatch carelessly rubbed to the side by one big hand.

"Aye! And I bring communication from Alexis to you. We are to depart as soon as possible for Byzantium!" Wulfhere held his head a bit too proudly for Eadric's taste, yet better to have an excess of pride than none at all. The son held out a sealed scroll to the jarl and smiled to himself as he saw that the old man was hesitant to take it. Eadric Siwardsson could neither read nor write, for all his wit.

This was not uncommon, for in those times, only the scribes or noble youth who merited tutoring had these abilities. By and large, the populace was usually ignorant, but the nobles would eventually learn that it was to their advantage to understand the curious runes the monks called "letters." Even the interpreters could be bribed by a wealthy adversary.

The correct meaning of a scroll was the difference between peace and war, ruin or riches.

Wulfhere's mother had been a learned woman; she taught him these skills against Eadric's will so that someday he might surpass his father. Was the day here? Eadric doubted not that Wulfhere presented the scroll publicly only to embarrass him with their contrast in learning.

Wulfhere smiled again, the very picture of politeness. "Tis in French, my father. I had Alexis's scribe put it in the language that your woman, my mother, taught me so that I might do you the service of interpreting it myself."

Eadric studiously picked at his beard. He looked at the parchment and then back to Wulfhere. The others sat in silence, several of them half-smiling. They understood what was happening.

"Read!" Eadric commanded. The hall was silent.

Oddly, as Wulfhere read, Eadric seemed to find interest in a myriad of other things so that he did not concentrate upon the scroll. Twice, Wulfhere stopped in exasperation as Eadric noisily tried to catch a fly or gargled great mouthfuls of ale. The captains scratched their heads in puzzlement.

Wulfhere finished and stood silent before his father. Nothing. No reaction, as Eadric merely sat there nodding pleasantly. It occurred to Wulfhere that the jarl was more inebriated than he had at first suspected.

"What...?" the son demanded, growing impatient.

Eadric smiled and let loose a rolling belch. "Fetch me my son's woman. She is Norman enough to read this; I have heard she has learning." Then he turned away, pretending not to see the hot rush of scarlet beneath Wulfhere's tanned skin. The insult was less than subtle as was the jarl's explanation.

"I am afraid at my age, my mind wonders," he apologized as the others gaped at the scene. "I have not heard what was upon the scroll and rather than have Wulfhere the Reaver humor an old man and read the message again, I shall have little Claire read it. Reading is woman's work anyway," he said with a shrug.

Wulfhere glared at Eadric, then at each captain in turn.

Suspicion. Distrust. Jealousy. And between kindred.

Why do you bother with her, my jarl?" inquired Wulfhere with a cold, piercing formality. His left hand toyed with the leather-wrapped hilt of his scimitar as his right smoothed his long moustache, but his eyes never left his father's broad back. "I would gladly read it again to you, in truth. I would enjoy practicing my skill."

"I wish to see how worthy your woman is of you, Wulfhere," muttered Eadric, turning back slowly and staring Wulfhere down. His smile was ice.

There was a lie here, and both knew it. In fact, the entire hall knew of it and the mood became electric as they watched to see who would break first, the father or the son. Eadric was testing the word of his son, and each man understood this. That he did not trust his word was plain enough to all, but to insult him with his own woman? No man would bear such an insult. Not for any price. Except Wulfhere. And he alone knew the full price.

But should the jarl catch him in a lie now, with so much at stake… Wulfhere nodded, a sneer upon thin lips. His eyes blazed. *So, it was this way already,* he thought. *You dare to question my word before the council of captains, do you, old fool? Very well, then. You have fallen into my trap unwittingly; you will be proven wrong and I will make much of it, so much that you will not dare to question my word again lest your men lose faith in you. And I will wait until the time is ripe for deceit; did you think me so crude that I would try treachery in reading a letter to you? You old fool! You fat old goat! Did you really think me idiot enough to try a trick so simple, you who taught me to love cunning?*

He laughed to himself. Eadric had thought to surprise him but he had traded with the gullible jarl. Ha! And it had once been his father to tell him what cunning a jarl must have. He who, in the end, knew nothing!

The young wolf smiled thinly and crossed his arms as he stood before the captains, as if to say to each, "Look what dishonor my father holds for me; see how he is suspicious of his right arm; see how he would question you!" He was confident that this would end in increased stature for him. The captains would judge Eadric old.

And Eadric was, he thought. His wits were failing him if he hoped to catch Wulfhere so easily. And age meant weakness after wisdom faded.

The world of the Saxon raiders was not one for the weak. Only the strong survived the fighting; only the strongest led the clan. Eadric Siwardsson was no stranger to the laws of Odin, yet he sometimes felt, in what might be self-pity in another man, that surely the years of leadership beneath his belt should count for more than some puppy's cunning and youth. Could he not gracefully hand over his command in the years to come, in a time when he would be through with war and pillaging? Must he have to fight the flesh of his flesh for leadership before this time had a chance to come? He knew the answer to be yes, for while the raiders loved their war chief dearly, they could not afford to be sloppy when it came to their tactics. Whether Eadric Siwardsson realized it or not, his son was backing him into a corner and those captains, still intensely loyal to Eadric, the older ones mostly, wondered if he understood the game.

The path of a leader is often harsh. Eadric studied Wulfhere's face as the guard escorted Claire before her husband and her jarl. He watched how his son stared at her with hostility but with no alarm at all. There was no need to have her read before the captains. Eadric's years of observing men's faces, and the masks that hid them, had well served him this day.

Claire entered the smoky hall barefoot, clad only in her short gown which dropped barely to her knees. Her lovely legs were emphasized. She kept her eyes before her as she walked, oblivious to the men that gazed upon her, appreciating her fragile beauty. The eyes of the captains moved from her face to Wulfhere's and back, waiting. He never removed his gaze from her, but what they saw in his eyes was unfathomable. It was certainly not love, far from that.

Wulfhere had suddenly realized that beneath Eadric's thumb, here might be an instrument to shame him with. His father would use his own woman against him and if he tried her once, he would try her again. Silently, Wulfhere resolved that if this day went awry, he would slay her. He gazed at her as he might an adversary.

"Woman!" he said sternly, "I did not send for you!" His voice was metal on flint. He would provoke the confrontation; he would play it for Eadric's benefit. Claire stopped and turned slowly to face Wulfhere.

She quietly knelt down before him in the manner she was accustomed to.

"My lord Wulfhere, I was sent for in your name by the jarl's messenger."

"You lie," he said simply. He struck her only once, a stinging slap across the mouth that did not hurt so much as it forced tears from her eyes by its force. Wulfhere looked up at his father, triumph flashing across his swarthy face. There were many accusations he could fling; Eadric had tried to use Claire to shame him by summoning her instead of bidding Wulfhere do it. He would try to entrap Wulfhere with her reading of the scroll. Ha! So much the better! Let the old bear get himself into the deed thickly, then would he spring the jaws of the trap!

"My lord, it was in your name I came," she protested in a low, hurt voice.

"You have not learned!" Wulfhere grated, drawing back again.

"Save your blows, Wulfhere Eadricsson. She tells it true! Knowing what your sire intended, I summoned her in your name, as he undoubtedly meant." It was Pigfeet's huge bass, booming out over the hall.

He and Eadric interlocked glances, and the jarl's aide smiled ever so slightly. He had smelled the trap before Eadric and nullified the jarl's mistake; now Eadric had an opening to completely disarm the situation while the rest of the hall sat puzzled, Wulfhere more so than the rest. His accusations died on his tongue.

"Of course!" laughed Eadric, gruffly. "Didst thou think I would insult my own son? Wulfhere Eadricsson, you are obtuse as a bull! Can you not see I called her in here to welcome you back, as befits you? And see her belly now; the old wives tell me it will be a son! Come, come, twas but a jest at the girl's expense. All of you, drink up to my son's health, and that of his son and his woman!" Furiously, he fired a hornful down his gullet, all the time praying to Odin that the mood caught.

It did. The captains were drunk enough to see it as a jest and before Wulfhere could spit out his claims, the hall was alive again with drink and song.

"And the reading of the letter?!" Wulfhere shouted to the jarl. He was like a dog worrying at a stubborn bone.

ALLAN JEFFRIES

Eadric's ugly face was almost innocent. "Why, son, you read it to me. What of it? Do you wish to read it again?"

He banged his horn on the tablet. "Hear, hear! My son enjoys the arts of scribes and women so much he would read the letter again!" The hall shook with cheerful guffaws and well-meant derision. Wulfhere snarled his rage and Eadric ducked gracefully for all his bulk as a bench arced past where his head had been. There was another storm of laughter. Wulfhere drew himself up to his full height and shot a glance at Eadric that promised trouble, although his lips smiled.

"Ah, Eadric Siwardsson, I had forgotten how much I missed your witty jests when I was in the land of the Byzantines; they have a somewhat more subtle sense of humor."

"They are subtle in everything, I understand. From humor to poisons to their love of young boys. What else have you learned from them besides a new taste for jesting?"

Wulfhere smiled thinly. "Tell me, my jarl. Do you think the day will ever come when one of my jests might surpass your own excellence?" His eyes were mocking. He turned to Claire who was still kneeling, and idly stroked her injured mouth. "You are mine as my captive, dove. Do not ever forget it!"

He missed Eadric's reply to the question in his attention to the girl. "Praise Odin, you shall die first!" the old jarl had muttered. He was sorry for Claire, for he knew she would pay the price of his victory, and he knew that Wulfhere also understood this. The price would be high this night. Wulfhere studied Eadric as he brushed her cheek lightly, reveling in the soft, sweet skin.

The jarl fought down his temper, realizing that to lose control would be to play his son's game and ruin all that he had established this day with the captains. He could not win this way. But if one could not win by the rules existing, then should not the rules be changed?

Now it was Eadric's turn to press the attack. "While we are on the subject, girl, is it true that you can read? Or is it all talk? Such a slave would be very valuable to her master!"

Claire nodded as she knelt there, hands clasped before her and eyes lowered in pain.

92

"Yes, my lord; I was taught as a child by my father."

"She has a nice voice," commented Pigfeet from one side.

"Agreed!" laughed Eadric. "Her voice is soothing. Let us hear more, girl!"

"Aye. The girl!" the others chorused drunkenly, unable to figure out who the girl in question was now.

"Speak for me, my darling!" Eadric cooed. Wulfhere stood sullenly, knowing that he was being led like a tame sheep but unable to figure out how to stop the situation.

"What shall I say, my lord?" Claire asked. "I do not know what you would hear."

"Well, speak to me in that funny gibberish the Normans speak. No, well, I would not understand that! Hmmm!" He made a great show of giving some thought to the subject as he sat with lips pursed and brows knit. "Oh well, let us see; here, just read this to us. Wulfhere already told us what the words say but it will sound pleasing if you do the same! Shall the girl read to us?"

"Aye! The girl!" echoed drunkenly throughout the hall.

Eadric thrust the letter into her trembling hands. Wulfhere shook with rage and made odd choking sounds that the drunken revelers missed, all except Pigfeet who played with his dagger. Before Wulfhere could reach his father, the dirk would be buried to the hilt in his broad back.

Claire's eyes went from Wulfhere to the letter and back. Instinctively, she sensed she was the pawn in a brutal chess game and was stricken with indecision. She peered around the room, her throat numb, thinking desperately. Somehow if she read, her master would be the fool; but if she chose to disobey the request of a jarl she could be mutilated or put to death.

"Well?" fumed Eadric. "Have the breaths of ale in the air so addled your senses that you cannot collect your wits enough to speak? Answer, girl!" he shouted only for effect; he understood the crisis within her.

Claire, more terrified by the roar than by thoughts of future violence from Wulfhere, hastily snatched up the roll of parchment and read it, at first to herself than aloud for Eadric.

"Aye, lord, I will read it," she sighed. Her pretty eyes went uncertainly to Wulfhere's and the hardness she saw there told her she had chosen wrongly. But there was nothing for her to do now but to read it, she thought.

Eadric smiled benevolently to her. He was truly fond of her, especially so, since she would bear his first grandchild. And now this affection was sweetened by the fact that she could help him against Wulfhere, simply by using her talents openly. What was done was better done openly for deceit often left a film of scum behind it to mark its passing and remained in subtle traces to poison the minds of those involved. No, if he exposed Wulfhere's plans to sunlight, they would shrivel and die. Let the kings and courts play with the Pandora's box of treachery, thought Eadric. He knew from experience that the way of open force was better.

Claire was speaking now, disturbing his reverie. Wulfhere had fled from the hall, unable to contain himself.

"It is from the emperor of the Byzantines, my lord," she repeated. "He says that he wishes you to know he desires your services as agreed upon by your son."

Eadric's hand, held upright, silenced her as he turned the words over in his mind and in his mouth as well.

"By my son," he murmured, thick lips pursed in thought and brows drawn upward until they formed a single patch of red fur over eye and eye patch. "My son...I see. Well, go on, little one."

So! Eadric may have been wrong, but not altogether. When Wulfhere had read the letter, he read it accurately save that he omitted the phrase concerning himself, an easy mistake to make and to justify should he be caught. But a significant one in thought. Eadric rose and spoke to Pigfeet, "Clear the hall of these sots. Then tell Wulfhere Eadricsson that I would talk to him about his journey. Here. Now." Pigfeet heaved himself to his feet, belched indelicately, and threw a captain across each shoulder to begin clearing the lodgehall. This was done briefly for all were by now semi-comatose, and Wulfhere again entered the hall. He had changed his riding outfit for another, also cut in the splendor of the East. Eadric hawked loudly at the sight of his curled-toed slippers and silk cape but refrained from commenting.

Claire was still trying to spell her way through the formal French of the letter, but clearly Eadric was inattentive. He had fixed his eye upon his son and the younger man seemed a trifle ill-at-ease at his stark scrutiny. Eadric held up his hand again for her silence.

"What means this in the letter, this part that services were agreed upon by us, wolfling?" Eadric asked harshly. "I gave you no leave to bargain yourself into this!"

Wulfhere shrugged, seeming all the more foreign by the minute. Something had happened in the land of the Byzantines to give his soul a final shaping. He seemed to have made the choice there, one that he had trained for all his life and Eadric suddenly regretted that he had not raised him differently, for the sages said that snakes are not raised by ewes. But it was done. Wulfhere had decided what his fortune would be and he had chosen wrongly in his avarice, if this letter meant what he suspected. The old jarl hoped he was in error. If Wulfhere had told the emperor that he could make the decisions for the clan, then he had succumbed to the heritage of treachery that was the empire of Alexis. Poor Wulfhere! The Byzantines were at home in intrigue as a fish in water and the knowledge and the lifestyle they imparted to the unwary, helpful or not, was oft times nothing less than the bite of a poisoned apple. Had Wulfhere set himself up as jarl? Had Alexis the Emperor convinced him to? Had Wulfhere sold out his own father and jarl?

Eadric stared at the ale and wine stains on his big belly, studying how the colors blended richly with the dirt on his tunic. Idly, he reached down and popped a couple of lice, wiping his fingers free of their guts on his breeches. Ergo, if Wulfhere was not a complete traitor, then he had been swayed.

As was agreed upon by your son. Only words, but what treachery they might conceal! He had never given Wulfhere the power to bargain for him. And now, he must trust his son's word, or lose forever this chance at real fortune. He could send another messenger to Alexis but that would take time and the emperor would wonder at two emissaries from the same jarl.

Alexis was suspicious enough without Eadric furthering any doubts Wulfhere had given him. Damn! If only the offer was not so inviting. But

Alexis's generosity to his faithful was legendary, and Eadric had enjoyed the part of the letter where the emperor had promised him his weight in gold for coming.

That was generous, but obviously Wulfhere had not described Eadric's bulk to the Byzantine king—a bulk which would increase during the ship's voyage, he was certain. Eadric wondered if Alexis knew the trick of hiding a lead rod up the rectum to add weight, or of swilling ale until you could not walk. He was sure the emperor was no fool, but on the other hand, it would not do for Alexis to appear ungracious to a new detachment of his personal guards, especially with war brewing.

Eadric impatiently motioned the girl to leave the two of them and she sighed in relief. But as she strode past Wulfhere, he caught her roughly by the arm and turned her so that he might gaze into her eyes. A sinister smile played over thin lips as he ever so gently stroked her bruised mouth, cupping again her proud chin and letting his fingers drift through the curl of her hair.

In his hard eyes, she saw the warning, and tried to look aside. One hand was under his robe fingering his dagger and Claire paled at the measure of his rage.

But Eadric also noticed the placement of his hand.

Wulfhere held her pretty face firm, and with easy strength he guided her lips to his. It almost appeared a gentle kiss, but Eadric surmised that Wulfhere the Reaver was never gentle. And he was not now. The force of the kiss increased until Claire again tasted her own blood from her injured mouth.

"My dove, my delicious dove!" he breathed into her face. She blanched at the sight of her blood upon his hard lips. He passed a metal hand over her trembling flanks as he guided her to the doorway. "Await my pleasure in our chamber," Wulfhere murmured with a charming smile that fooled neither Claire nor Eadric. Looking back slyly, he saw a look of concern rush across his father's face, only to vanish just as quickly and completely as Eadric again assumed the mask of the jarl.

When the girl had left, Wulfhere approached Eadric warily. "What do you wish to say to me, Eadric Siwardsson?" he said formally.

Eadric leaned forward, raised one ham-like fist and brought it down upon a bench. The bench splintered into pieces under the blow; Eadric had once killed a bull with a single blow to the head. He had a power Wulfhere could never hope to match.

"Never forget what I have the power to do, boy!"

Wulfhere said nothing.

"I fancy your girl, son! Perhaps she should have been mine."

"Even as jarl, you have no right to interfere with what I do with her!" Wulfhere protested.

"Do not make me slay you over a woman, Wulfhere Eadricsson! She will be mine if you do not take care of her properly," roared the jarl and Wulfhere went white but knew better than to say anything. Eadric felt a tad bit guilty for using Claire and this was his way of protecting her.

Casually, Eadric picked up a heavy double-bladed axe and passed a calloused thumb across its edge. For several seconds, he was silent though still breathing hard from the force of his fury as he watched a narrow rivulet of crimson course down his thumb toward his palm. Eadric studied the blood as thoroughly as any seer and Wulfhere wondered if the old man might think he could see his future in the slow trickle. Which was ironic, for it was often said that the future of every great jarl is in blood. And it was seldom a figurative meaning.

Then Eadric the Wild looked up, his face matching his name an instant, and Wulfhere wondered at what he must be thinking. But the look faded to be replaced by an expression of deep study and he peered into Wulfhere's eyes. The old man's eye was both proud and fierce as Wulfhere remembered from his youth, though the jarl had had both eyes then, eyes like a falcon's, he had thought in his boy's mind. There was something in his gaze even now that belied his slackening gut and unquenchable thirst for ale.

He was a great jarl, and for an instant, Wulfhere regretted his treachery, but only for an instant, for his want was too strong. Eadric had had his day. Soon, it would be the time of Wulfhere the Reaver.

But caution, Wulfhere! The jarl was seeking within your eyes, and even you could not know what it was he searched for. And Wulfhere would die not knowing; he could not understand what he had never possessed.

"By what right did you bargain with Alexis the Byzantine?" Eadric asked softly in a voice that was not quite a question, more nearly approaching a condemnation in tone. Indeed, his words carried such tension that Wulfhere momentarily forgot himself and blanched at the menace held within them. Yet, he was stung by the thrust and would not hang his head before such a man as his father.

But now, his only defense was a brazen accusation. "I did what I had to, what needed to be done for all of us," he growled, subtly making a show of his dagger hilt between twitching fingers. The dagger, like the scimitar he sported, was long and wickedly curved with an edge of the finest Damascus steel. Several rubies winked from the hilt pommel and Eadric wondered where Wulfhere had gotten the money for such a bauble. The jarl studied him impassively.

Wulfhere returned the gaze, unflinchingly, although his skin slowly burned red beneath its deep tan.

Impassiveness became open distaste as Eadric stroked his bushy red beard. He spat into the palm of one hand and rubbed the growth vigorously in a feeble attempt to restore some order. It was readily apparent that the red thicket had never conformed to any known plan before now. "For us, or for yourself?" asked Eadric, quietly.

Wulfhere's flush deepened. "For us, naturally," he said calmly, causing Eadric to mark his self-control. Evidently, the warrior had learned much in the East; he could still be goaded into an outburst, but he recovered very quickly. Perhaps the poison apple of their wisdom agreed with his rotten soul.

"My interests lie with the clan, Father," Wulfhere finished, although the title he finished with he so seldom used, that it sounded ironic, if not a trifle sardonic.

"And they run with mine, then?" asked Eadric, owlishly, arching the eyebrow over his grimy leather patch in a comic display of curiosity.

"For the most part, aye."

"And where do they part company from mine?" wondered Eadric aloud.

Wulfhere's voice was the hiss of a snake for all its bass, "When you become too weak to enforce them!" he sneered. And without asking leave, he turned and swaggered from the lodgehall. Eadric watched him in bitter silence as he swirled ale about his drinking horn's rim, pushing various plans and ideas about his head as he reached for the ale pitcher. Both men ended the argument unsure if Wulfhere had given himself away at last.

∾

CLAIRE CRIED OUT AS WULFHERE ROUGHLY PUSHED HER OVER THE COUCH of pelts tearing her frock from her body as he did so. She looked at him in consternation, not knowing what to do, or if even to cry out, as he pulled free his leather belt.

"Ambitious little bitch!" he laughed wolfishly, relishing her fear. "So, you would use Eadric Ale-breath to gain revenge, eh? You would let him use you so innocently, eh? I should slay you here…slowly!"

"Please, my lord!" she wept in fright. "I did not understand what was wanted of me!" she protested.

Wulfhere laughed a cruel, mocking rasp. Lust for pain was glazing over his eyes as he watched her legs and arms tremble. Lust stirred his loins as well. His hand knotted one end of the thick leather around his fist so that it might not slip from the grasp of a sweaty palm. Already, he was perspiring profusely and he moved close to her, his free hand gently slipping off her undergarments from her until she was naked before him. His mouth was dry; his hands shook as hers.

"All so sweetly innocent," he stated. "Were it not for the fact that the Siwardsson would have me killed, I would beat you until you drop that brat you carry, and which, by custom, keeps me from you. But I shall make certain that you remember whose woman you are the next time the jarl sends for you!" And the heavy lash caressed her white back with an obscene smack.

"Please, please, master!" Claire cried out but Wulfhere pushed her face to the pelts that she might not be heard.

Again, the stroke fell, and this time, it was Claire who forced her face into the pelts to hide her tears from the brutish Saxon. Her soft form quivered like a poleaxed calf as Wulfhere welted her back. He surveyed her shaking form and listened to her deep-throated sobs.

"My sweet slave!" he murmured huskily, turning her over and gazing into her tearful face. She closed her eyes for what was to come yet this time he kissed her as tenderly as was possible for him and began tracing the curve of her throat with his lips, while his arms shifted her more comfortably to the couch. Wulfhere's breath was hot, wet in her ear as he verbally claimed her. But deep inside, her violated soul shrieked and shrieked in awful, silent fear-dominated silence.

"Mine!" sighed Wulfhere as he buried his face in her sweet-smelling hair. "You are mine alone."

BUT WHILE THE GREAT JARL SAT IN SOMBER STUDY AND HIS TREACHEROUS son punished a slave, events were turning the world topsy-turvy in a change that would alter the course of mankind irrevocably. Little did the Siwardsson know when he read the letter from Emperor Alexis that his action of taking allegiance for money from the man would embroil them all in what was to become the greatest holy war of all time—that which would later come to be called The First Crusade. They understood only that they would form the nucleus of the emperor's hand-picked body-guards of ferocious Vikings, Saxons and Danes, yet only Alexis knew what this would entail, he and Pope Urban II who was the then-undisputed leader of all Christianity. This was only the beginning.

Eadric was oblivious to the rest of the world; his camp was isolated and he was self-centered to the point of monomania in his ideas. But the same fervor that had taken hold of him and summoned him from the cold North to the sweltering East, had swept all of Europe with the same promises of gold for most, and salvation for many. All of the feudal lands were stirring with the dreams of wealth and glory, women and power, conquest and prowess against their centuries-old enemies, long ignored, while current enemies became "friends" under an uneasy flag of holy truce. The people, from prince to pauper, yearned for the East and its mystic wealth. What better way to become rich than beneath the proud banner of God? Or as Urban the Pope played his role beneath the banner of a proud God, a silly but meaningful distinction.

Aye, brothers! Seek out all the gold you can. This appealed to every man, but there was no gold for the taking in Britain or France or Spain. Only one land had this wealth, a land where the towers of their onion-topped churches were plated with solid gold!

And for the peasants who had no horses to carry the gold, there was land to farm, to carve out virtual dukedoms for each dirt farmer from the plains of the infidel excesses. This was the land of Canaan, the land of milk and honey they had been foretold. Life was sweeter than on the foggy, rock-strewn coast of Normandy or Cornwall. What was there to lose? Your life, perhaps.

But fie! Had not the Pope promised true salvation for anyone willing to take up the sword for our sweet saviour? Why, there was to be no losing…either you won the kingdom of man or the kingdom of heaven, but either way, there was no sinning to be punished. God himself would relish the infidel blood you spilled; every monk would tell you that.

It was so simple, actually. Too simple, almost, for the poor fools believed that the God who had warned them not to take life would sanctify carnage, that He who had warned them not to covet what their neighbor had, would sanctify rape and pillage. Each churchman was a magician, with a wave of his hand he wiped away the sin in a violated commandment and granted you the right to take another man's wealth. Some of the more warrior monks even dared to say that the commandments were created by the heathen Jews anyway, so what was the harm in putting them aside for a bit.

God would love you for it, brother! If he hadn't wanted us to slay infidels, he wouldn't have given us the Pope! And there was still a score to be settled with the damned infidels! Had they not nearly overrun Europe in their brazenness once before? They were dangerous, these slender, swarthy men who dressed in silks and satins, yet who fought with such cunning and vigor as to seem half-animal. And they were as numberless as the stars in the heavens and growing more each day in body. They were a perpetual threat to Europe and their civilization was growing stronger instead of succumbing to the disease of the ancients, succored by their deep faith in Allah. Could one afford to wait until their strength grew enough that they could attack a second time with impunity? Would there arise another Charles Martel when the hoards came again? And there was so much gold in their possession.

Now then, salvation was a thing, an event, a happening to be desired by every man with any sense, for who with his brains intact would choose to push hot rocks in hell with the devil for the rest of time? And if you asked any true Christian knight he would choose to be saved at once, but a purse full of gold on the belt certainly made the times easier awaiting that salvation.

What then of the City of Our Lord, Jerusalem the Holy? What of the true cross being held in infidel hands, that miraculous cross that had been sold as literally hundreds of thousands of splinters to the pilgrims seeking a souvenir, yet still remained intact in its shrine. What of the fate of the Christian women held in the wretched slavery of Moslem harems? Do we turn the other cheek? And what then? Nay! God loves the bold!

And service to God has always paid well; there was so much gold in those lands, brother, so much you must see it to understand. Let us rise as one, they cried, and march for Jerusalem! Let us lay beneath our feet the Moslem jackals and take for our rightful own what is now theirs. Arise, brothers, arise! Onward, ye Christian soldiers!

And there is land enough for all of ye to be barons. And they rose up, these vigilant Christians across Europe. From king to lowliest brigand, they caught the challenge and made their armies. Their fervor was indescribable as they rode, secure in their own hypocrisy. Goodbye, my love! We march now for God! And later for gold...

So, it was not merely Eadric Siwardsson and his sturdy clan of outlaws and cutpurses, rogues, pirates and assorted brigands that answered the call to fame and glory. Indeed, Wild Eadric knew nothing then of either the god the Moslems worshipped or the one of the Christians with his three magic parts. He worshipped only one deity outside his curses to Odin, one universally worshipped since the beginning of time. But then, that alone put him in common with the rest of the Crusades, at least the more human ones.

And thus, it happened that while Urban II was still preparing his speech that would voice his formal plea for aid in late November of that year at Clermont in Southern France, Wild Eadric's band was already on the quest. They had made their longships ready.

The cliffs of the Northland had never become familiar to Claire; she had never allowed them to. She fought with a secret fear that when she looked upon the cold crags as her home, they would be so and she would be trapped forever so far from her England. But for her, forever was relative; each day she spent with Wulfhere the Reaver was an eternity. She had been trapped long ago and not realized it. Perhaps the fjords of the North never had become home, but she was an eagle without a nest.

Now, their beauty haunted her as the cliffs faded into the distance as had once the cliffs of Britain. Columns of smoke rose from Eadric's camp that he had fired himself, symbolically destroying their lifestyle so that none might look back. The clan must look forward now, go to their future in the East under Alexis the Greek, to their struggle for him in some vague little holy war, or Jihad as the Moslems called it. It was Eadric's understanding that Alexis was caught up in a messy little war, a war of only minor consequence with a few of the more rabid Moslem tribes. Although as emperor, Alexis could undoubtedly handle the affair; he and Eadric apparently agreed that a band such as Eadric's would considerably hasten the defeat of the infidels. Alexis had mentioned obliquely that the King of England was sending a few soldiers to reinforce, but the Siwardsson did not expect them to help much; after all, if they could not even protect their own coastlines, how could they police an entire nation? No, he and his several hundred stout Danish axes were what was needed. Eadric rubbed his hands together with glee when he thought of slender, dark little men waving their fancy curved swords at him. Ha! They would soon learn to fear the name of Eadric Siwardsson, Eadric the Wild!

A chill sea wind had sprung up now and Claire wrapped herself deeper in a woolen shawl. She must not chance sickness now; she must choose for her child instead of herself. The salty wind brought traces of tears to her eyes as she sat in the open beneath a canopy of cured and decorated leather. Around her, the men rested at the gunwales as the longship bobbed in unison with the rest of its small fleet The fresh strength of the wind had made more rowing unnecessary. There was a curiously peaceful feeling to be had here amidst the tossing of the sea, a feeling of being but a grain of sand floating through eternity with the tide of unvaried human existence. It was a lost feeling, a stark sensation of being swallowed whole by the universe with jaws cast out of the sea and the sky, of drifting eternally, carried as a seed pregnant with new life upon a storm breeze. And it was comfortable, for it drove from her fears and trepidations about the future; it lulled her into a delicious semi-boredom that was balm for her worries, those open wounds upon the organ of the mind.

Again, she was but an infant in the womb, with an infant still within her own womb as if they were a succession of Chinese boxes leading to the final mystery of life. But the womb Claire rested in now was the sleepy cradle of nature, a shelter rocking with the raw vitality of existence upon the floor of that open sea. The clouds were the canopy for her soul and the breeze was her guardian. For the first time in a great while she smiled, a gentle, lovely, dreamy smile as she forgot who and where she was, heeding only the impulses of creation as they washed over her.

Till Eadric's gruff voice broke the dreaminess of her spell. "How fare you and the little one?" he asked, not unkindly. She rode in the jarl's own Nykr with him and his family because of both her station and her pregnancy. Wulfhere rode out far into the horizon with one of the sleeker scouting raiders.

"Well, master," she smiled, "quite well." She drew her woolen up higher about her throat and turned from him to the sea.

Eadric studied her elegant profile as she stared off into the horizon. "It was with just such a look that you bade farewell to your first homeland," the jarl said, quietly.

"My only homeland, my lord," she murmured, without thinking. Her face showed a momentary flicker of her former defiance and Eadric frowned, but the mood passed for she was too enchanted with the sea to harbor bitter thoughts.

"And hero..." added Eadric laconically, but Claire understood who it was that the jarl referred to. He watched her closely. Her eyes sparkled with salt spray or were those tears he saw there?

"Only dreams did I leave behind, master. Reality is here and now," she whispered, watching the waves.

"Spoken like a Saxon!" Eadric laughed. "But I have watched you sit upon the highest cliff in camp and scan the sea for hours, watching for a sail. I understand what it is that you feel, and I believe that he would have fought for you if I let him. But we covered our trail too well, my dove. Now, only the will of the gods could cast him into our laps or the fickle whim of fate. I place not much reliance in either so I advise you to forget what you can never have. I had hoped Wulfhere could win your affection."

She gave him a look of infinite sadness and pity for him. By now, she understood better what motivated the old warrior in affairs of the heart, how he hoped over and over to prove that he had not been mistaken about the woman he had loved so deeply and abused so much. "I bear you his child. Is that not enough, my lord?" she asked.

Eadric's face softened. "I suppose it must be for now. Perhaps in time, things will change between the two of you. He is still young and untamed; you need to grow together."

"No woman can grow to the oak that is Wulfhere, my lord. You do not understand how I have tried for the sake of our child. But in the forest of men, Wulfhere Eadricsson is a tree that stands alone, brooding."

"And I?" asked Eadric good-humoredly.

"You are the great oak, the grandfather of trees that towers over the forest and shelters the rest with your branches. You are the strength of the group and as long as you stand, they will stand. But..."

"But what, little seer?" he smiled, stroking his beard.

"But beware, master. Even the stoutest oak falls prey to the axe of the smallest woodsman."

"True. But this tree swings its own axe, Claire. And it is strong."

"Strength fades with time. Axe blades rust into nothing, master."

For a moment, Eadric was shaken by what seemed to him a prophecy. "You deal in dreams, little slave," he muttered.

"Only the dreams I left behind me, master," she replied.

Wild Eadric laugh huskily. "Is not all of life but a dream? Love, hate, compassion? Are these not but things given reality only when we will that it is so? I know who it was by the signs in your eyes, that Sir Norman who came to the beach that day. I freed him; I gave him his life. Yet I know if we had been but a minute slower in casting off, I would have had to slay him."

"You could not have slain him! He is a great warrior!" she snapped, stung.

Eadric nodded equably, "Perhaps, but that is not the point. Where is he now? You talk of the reality of feeling, but it is so weak that a length of water has ended it."

"No!" she cried.

"Claire, I do not judge your heart, nor do I condemn the lad for not coming for you. I am only saying that it is foolish to hope that the barest dream can become reality. Feelings are the reality of the soul, but there dreams and reality end their intertwining; hope is a poor cart to carry your dreams in. What you wish for is better left unspoken, especially to yourself. It is kinder that way."

Claire glared at him, angry at having her memories soiled in such a crass manner. "You say feelings? We have never spoken to each other; I doubt that he even knew my name. Mayhap, he was simply seeking you on the beach that day to repay you for saving him!"

Wild Eadric laughed uproariously. "I saw what type of man he was, my sweet! More like he sought to repay me for taking you from him and with a cleft skull at that! But let us suppose it so anyway, for if it was not true, would it not hurt that much more? Which is worse, little one? To know your lover was stopped from taking you, or to know in truth that he was not your lover?"

She turned hot, spite-filled eyes upon the old Saxon.

"And you, my master? Have you never loved a woman so much?" she asked deliberately, knowing full well the story of his misery. "Not even when the love lay unspoken deep within the chambers of your heart, in some misty recess so carefully hidden that you yourself scarce knew it was there?"

"Never!" fumed Eadric. "Love's only following is that of fools. Only folly is the child of love!"

"You must have loved her very much, Eadric Siwardsson, to feel so," she said gently.

Furious at having been found out he turned to her, his eye burning with anger and drew back his huge paw to strike her. But the blow was halted when he looked at her eyes, those eyes that said, "That is how you struck her."

"You know so little of life, golden hair!" he snorted. But she held him with her beautiful eyes as he tried to look away.

"And what of Wulfhere? Tis been said you tolerate him only for the love you bore his mother."

Eadric's face went white with rage and shame. His vast bulk shook as with the ague and he could not speak in reply. Some secrets are common knowledge, but still they are never meant to be spoken. To know they exist is enough to bring forth humbleness, to speak them aloud is to destroy an illusion—an unforgiveable offense of human nature. To speak them aloud is to call the secret's object a fool for trying to hide behind a mask.

Claire looked at him with immense sorrow, only then understanding what she had done. "I am sorry, master," she said quietly. "I meant no harm." She gave him a truly beautiful smile and her eyes glistened with warmth for the old Saxon brigand. "It seems that neither of our dreams can stand the sunlight of reality."

"She hated me until the day she died," Eadric muttered hoarsely, as if speaking to himself. "Wulfhere was the only thing I ever gave her that she found she could love." He closed his eye in pain at the memory and tried to act as if he were but casually leaning on the rail.

"And you would change this through me. You would make me love your son in her place of loving you?" she asked, her face compassion-filled.

"You bear his child!" Eadric growled sternly.

"Yes," she said.

"You bear his child, girl!" he rasped again as if that explained everything.

Claire smiled disarmingly. "As she bore yours, master?" she asked. "Was yours then out of love?"

Eadric ignored her and strode on up the deckway apace. Clearly, she had bested him in the heavy exchange, for it usually took more than mere words to halt the Saxon's wild mouth, more than the words of a mere woman, anyway.

It was so odd, she thought, how she could detest him and pity him at the same time. The matter of Wulfhere was far simpler; he was worthy of only detesting. But the Siwardsson was more complicated than that. It must be terrible to love so and see it unrequited, to see each day that all the nobleness of the human heart matters not a whit to another.

She thought upon this last for quite a while, until the waves lulled her senses and she slept, curled into her woolen shawl as the tiny babe lay curled within her.

6

CHAPTER THE SIXTH

The sun hung cold and friendless in a barren sky; the landscape was a field of icy crystal and menace that promised injury or death to the unwary rider. Snow upon ice was a bad combination back in England's harsh winters, but here it seemed that there was nothing else but rocky shelves and mountain sides all covered with powdery, granular snow that could send a horse from its path without warning. The climate was bitter and the land empty, for the most part, of human life. Geoffrey wondered if all of the North was like this, and if so, how could even the Vikings survive? Here there was nothing to eat, no shelter worth seeking, and the wine froze within its flask. Never again would he curse the bleak moods of English wintertime.

The young St. Denis pulled his cape closer about him as protection from the snow-laden wind that pushed down through the pass, echoing a shrill, mournful note against the high mountain walls. Damn this country anyway, he thought ruefully. It was cold and inhospitable and it seemed as if he was doomed to cross one wretched mountain after another. Here, even the Spring sunshine was frozen, not to mention the seat of his breeches.

Damn Eadric Siwardsson to hell! he thought. No, that was a mistake.

Hell was warm and he wanted the Saxon to have the cheeks of his arse frozen, too.

Chestnut moved slowly, instinctively, at a slow walk against the driving wind and Geoffrey chewed one of his strips of dried, salted pork against hunger, washing it down with a mouthful of water he kept in a skin next to his body for the heat to keep it thawed. His journey was beginning to seem but one great hare hunt after all these three months of traveling from mountains to coast and back again. By now, half of Scandinavia had heard his uncouth cursing as he learned to live in their often-harsh environs.

Apparently, everyone in the Northland had heard of Eadric the Wild but no two people agreed upon where his camp might lie. The coast seemed logical, yet there were those who insisted he moved inland between raids to some mysterious mountain fortress as protection against the Viking jarls who wished him ill for usurping their lands. This, too, seemed logical. But was Eadric Siwardsson a creature of logic?

Geoffrey paused for an instant in the sleet to ponder exactly what type of animal the old bear was. He had thought on this many times as he lay camped alone with only Chestnut for company, but he could still reach no conclusion. Certainly, the jarl had had his share of success in combat, and this was usually acknowledged as a good sign of a logical brain. But the Siwardsson had this odd way of making success seem almost accidental for he constantly took gambles to win that no military mind would accept, at least as casually as Eadric seemed to, yet he constantly won against the greatest of odds and enemies. Beloved of the gods? Or just plain lucky? Or a strategic genius. Geoffrey frowned at the thought of that one. But still, some evidence was irrefutable. And some as elusive as the Saxon's carefully hidden camp. Well, he thought, if nothing else...

Suddenly, his meditation was interrupted by a short cry of pain somewhere ahead of him. The wind had stopped and with it the fine sleet and Geoffrey was quite sure he had heard a plea for help.

Here in this desolate pass? A traveler perhaps? But it was hard to say where exactly; the mountainside played tricks with sounds.

As Chestnut rounded the bend in the path, Geoffrey found himself face to face with six or seven shaggy, blond-and-red bearded giants clad in heavy furs wearing conical helmets adorned with horns or steel wings and sporting terrible, heavy broadswords and huge round shields of iron and wood.

Viking warriors! And this far into the mountains. The group of men blocked his path, warily watching his every move in silence with panther-ish eyes. They were ready to kill, these men, and Geoffrey felt his heart sink at the odds. Perhaps he could pass them in peace; he had no quarrel with them provided they had none with him. Behind the gathering, Geoffrey saw a dark-haired, slender man hanging nearly naked, by his wrists, from a narrow tree branch stuck in the rocks. Clearly, he had interrupted some sort of justice.

"What do you here, stranger?" snarled the largest of the giants, brandishing his sword hotly. His apparent lack of sanity was so damnably disconcerting that Geoffrey was at first tempted to reach for his own sword and get the battle over with. Yet, he had no quarrel with these fellows and it was the act of a fool to risk his own neck for an imagined grievance. He would try for a peaceful approach.

"I wish to pass as a tired traveler, only but enough of your land to clear these mountains and that only long enough to do so. I have no claim against any one of you; I am but a traveler seeking…"

"Ho, ho! Orme will have to do better than that! Tis no good, I say," cried the hanging man suddenly to Geoffrey. The leader of the Vikings was almost as amazed as Geoffrey was and the knight drew evil looks from the group.

"They can spot a warrior like you a spear toss away, my friend! Best draw and chance a fight while you can!" the hanging man shouted again.

"What?" gaped Geoffrey, looking at the prisoner's cunning face. The man had dark hair and eyes with a moustache curled down and neatly trimmed atop a narrow chin-beard. Clearly, he was not a Viking, but what was he playing at?

"Ho!" roared several of the warriors in one voice, and they moved a step closer to Chestnut. Their glittering swords struck beams of reflected sunlight through the gently swirling snow, and their colorful painted and studded round shields moved up into a defensive wall.

"Hang him with his friend!" someone bellowed.

"Hold!" cried Geoffrey, fear rushing so suddenly through his lungs that it became hard to breathe; adrenaline began pulsing through his veins and he felt the madness coming on. These ones would try to keep him from his Claire. "I know not this treacherous rogue, and by the trickery of his words, I see why you condemn him! But by our sweet savior, I swear he is naught to me, fellow!"

"We swear by Odin here!" growled one.

Again, the prisoner cried out. "Orme, you coward! Would you abandon me to these beasts? They want to remove my maiden's delight!"

"Knave! Bastard!" roared Geoffrey anger foaming in his mouth. "I will give you in an instant what these dogs wish if you do not cease your prattle."

"Orme!" the man wept. "Do not betray me now!"

"Coward!" sneered the nearest Viking to Geoffrey. An older warrior with a crisscross of scars across his bearded face and three fingers missing from his shield hand reached abruptly for Geoffrey's stirrups.

"I give you warning, dog vomit!" Geoffrey shouted, edging closer to madness. He reared Chestnut away from the man's grasp and the fellow reached for his longsword.

"Hold him!" cried the leader.

"You will hold a handful of your own guts if you try, you jackals!" Geoffrey stormed and tossed his cape from his sword arm. "I warn you all now, I will slay every one of you if you press me!"

Several laughed, not seeing what was in the young knight's eyes. They were the berserkers of legendary ferocity, but what pounded through the Norman's heart made them wild dogs before a wolf. And they could not see it. It would mean their death, for Geoffrey no longer knew who he was or where he fought. He only wanted to release his anger against his circumstances.

With a low growl, Geoffrey flung his cape from his shoulder into the nearest man's face, blinding the varlet with the voluminous folds long enough to pull his sword free. The cape glistened red in the snow as Geoffrey buried his blade in the man's skull, striking with such force that the fellow's helmet was split into halves to fall from beneath the cloak.

The act was met with animal noises and curses as the other six swarmed in about him, eager for bloody revenge.

Chestnut reared, as he had been trained by the men of Black Phillip to do, crashing down heavily on the shield of the leader. The brawny warrior was sent sprawling with a broken arm, for strong though he was, he could not take the weight of a plunging, full-grown destrier.

Geoffrey laid about lustily with his razor-edged broadsword, but it was the horse that won the day, for his speed, coupled with his agile, muscular mass as pitted against that of each opponent made him unstoppable despite their dangerous weapons. Geoffrey was expert enough in the saddle to keep his mount away from the swift sword thrusts and the horse was swift enough in return to be a readily usable weapon, one of awesome magnitude to these men who were more at home fighting from the decks of ships than battling cavalry.

All Geoffrey need to do was turn aside each thrust with his own weapon and keep the animal moving. Twice more lethal hooves lashed out and twice more did men fall.

Panting, the remaining Norsemen drew back and surveyed their foe in frosty silence. The snow had ceased completely and the sun had finally cleared the sky, reflecting brilliantly off Geoffrey's chainmail armor and dripping sword. He was an imposing figure, astride the magnificent brown horse with his blue eyes icy with contempt for his enemies.

"I warned you!" he snarled, pointing his own heavy sword at the leader. "I asked you for peace but you would not listen! God's witness that I gave only what you demanded.

They looked at each other with pain-filled faces but said nothing.

"Well?" Geoffrey asked, silkily.

The leader of the Vikings spat a mouthful of blood into the snow. Wistfully, he tugged at his long beard and sized Geoffrey up. "I for one, am inclined to believe that you are telling the truth, my friend." He grinned in wry humor as he held one hand beneath an armpit, trying to staunch a steady flow of blood.

Geoffrey glared about at the rest of the fair-haired warriors. All of them desperately wanted to kill him, if for no other reason than to avenge their honor. But all of them kept a safe distance from Chestnut, enough of their number lay silent upon that chill carpet.

"Aye!" muttered the rest and backed off that he might pass.

"Hold!" ordered Geoffrey, by now thoroughly irritated at their stupidity. He had no objection to killing a man if he had to, or defending his honor if he needed to, but this carnage had been senseless. He wanted the man who had caused it.

He turned hot eyes on the prisoner with the mouth of silk and the Vikings turned their heads with him. It seemed all were thinking the same thought.

"I wish to know what this rogue has done to warrant such punishment!" Geoffrey said firmly.

The others exchanged glances.

"By Loki!" muttered the Viking leader, his eyes narrowing. "Stranger, you push too hard, methinks!"

"Save me, Orme!" whined the hanging man.

"Best save your wind, varlet!" Geoffrey snarled. "Your mischief has already cost me enough discomfort and them their friends! And you, you dog!" added Geoffrey ruthlessly. Addressing the Viking leader, "I did not ask for the fight. If you wish, take up again your sword and let us put an end to this nonsense!"

But the burly Norseman knew he looked death in the face as he peered into Geoffrey's hard eyes. "No," the man said slowly, never taking his eyes from Geoffrey's, "I am not the fool you think me. The bastard's name is Guvi Leofricsson, a half-Finn who is a plagued-ly good thief. He has tormented us for a year now with his adroitness, but this time we have him. He shall entertain us with his screams as we remove a few of his body decorations."

"Lies! Lies, all of it!" cried the Finn. One of the men turned and caught him in the groin with his sword hilt so that, save for a low moaning, he became still once more.

Geoffrey laughed, suddenly amused by the fellow's boldness. Truly, a skilled rogue indeed with fleet feet and satin tongue. Useful perhaps, if he could be trusted, which of course he could not.

"Castration?" Geoffrey snorted, "I had thought you men of the North were made of sterner stuff than that. Why, in England the penalty for such a brigand is..."

"Friends!" interrupted Guvi. "Why, we are all friends here, good gentlemen who can surely reason out our differences with logic rather than by resorting to the crude barbarianism of our forgotten ancestors! Come, enough of a joke this has been, though funny, mind you, and every man enjoys a good jest now and again even if it is set upon himself. But enough of this humor, good friends, come cut me loose so that I can dress and we might all drink together and then..."

Silence followed the sword hilt again.

"Whew!" Geoffrey shook his head. "How that rascal can talk!"

"He speaks pretty enough," agreed the chieftain. "But it is all snake oil poured out to still the violent waters of his crimes. He means not a word he says!"

"Impudence!" murmured another.

"Cut his balls from him and end the talk!" grated a third.

"Friends!" pleaded Guvi.

Geoffrey threw back his head and laughed loudly. "Tell me, oh prince of liars, do you know this land?"

Guvi groaned in what Geoffrey took for assent. One of the warriors had struck him again and he was having trouble speaking. The knight looked at the chieftain for agreement.

The stout warrior shrugged casually, sucking at the torn flesh of his hand. "He should. He has been run from one village to the next. Ours will be his last."

"What has he done besides thievery that you hate him so?" queried Geoffrey

"He raped my oldest daughter and Jaggar's as well!" thundered the chieftain.

Geoffrey whistled appreciatively.

"Twas not rape!" sneered Guvi proudly.

"So say you, pillager of households!" roared the Viking leader.

"Ask your woman if I raped her, then!" mocked Guvi and all of the Vikings closed in on him with fire in their eyes.

"Hold!" shouted Geoffrey. "What is past is past, I do not doubt that your quarrel with this fellow is legitimate, but I have need of him to guide me!" He edged Chestnut in between the warriors and their prey, his sword casually laid across his lap. Again, there was an air of menace about him; he would let nothing come between him and his purpose.

"No!" roared a chorus of voices, the Vikings picking up their weapons again.

"By my life, no!" shouted the leader. "He owes too much!"

"How much?" asked Geoffrey laconically, idly studying his sword, an act not lost on his opponents.

"Over thirty silver pieces counting the worth of a necklace, and not counting the worth of my daughter's virginity!"

"Add one lead penny," shouted Guvi, his arrogance returning at the thought of salvation. "I took not what was not there, Sir Knight!"

"What?" bellowed the furious chieftain, reaching for his dagger and edging around Chestnut.

"Phah!" snorted Guvi. "Why his wife was less used than..."

Geoffrey turned in the saddle and kicked the Finn in the chest, hard. The air left his lungs with a whoosh and he fell silent, gasping. With a flicker of sunlight, Geoffrey's sword point was touching the Viking leader's throat with a pressure that promised death.

"My honor!" snarled the Viking. "Surely, you understand!"

"You ask a man without honor, sire. It has lost its luster for me so you see where it must leave you. You will have to settle for money instead, but perhaps enough of it can buy mead to drown your lost honor and bury your frozen dead. I sympathize with you, my friend, I really do. But what I seek is more than honor, it is life to me. You must try to understand."

"You must seek a rare prize, my young lord. What is it? Gold? Treasure?"

Geoffrey shrugged. "My jarl, you would not understand. But it is worth whatever existed of my honor."

"Oh ho," laughed the Viking, "Then it is a woman who has maddened you, I understand now."

Geoffrey stared at him, uncomprehending.

"I, too, was your age once, my young knight. But now I am older and wiser; how much money do you offer for his life?"

Geoffrey sighed and hefted his pouch in his hand before tossing it over to the chieftain.

"Tis more than he owes," murmured the man, appraising Geoffrey anew.

Geoffrey pulled back his coif and shook his auburn hair free, relishing the feel of the cold air on his hot, sweat-soaked neck.

"Tis for your men slain, though rightfully done. I have no wish to travel your land with your men stalking me for a blood debt. Now fetch friend Guvi and see if he can walk after the buffet your man gave to his horn."

The leader nodded at Geoffrey's wisdom as he pocketed the purse into his broad belt. "You are wise in the ways of the North. But you have the word of Bengt Sigurdsson, who is the man of Jarl Olaf, son of Goll the Merciless, that you may pass in peace." He laughed. "By right of steel, you have won this man but it is often said that silver is a metal stronger than steel in the long run. Today, you have bought peace and the friendship of the jarl in whose name we were to have punished this man."

Guvi was led to Geoffrey, clothed now in his own furs and leathers of much worth. Geoffrey eyed him appraisingly, judging just how skilled a thief he must be.

He walked with a pronounced limp from the blow he'd been given and rubbed his hands, raw from the rope. Geoffrey leaned down to peer into the Finn's face. "Will you follow me and lead me through the North?" he asked, anticipating pledges of loyalty until death.

Instead, Guvi eyed him with crafty glances, looking around at the trail and the remaining Vikings. He gave a crooked smile. "For what price?" he asked silkily.

Then he jumped forward against Geoffrey's destrier with the speed and force of a crossbow bolt, pricked deeply in the arse by Bengt's dagger.

"Master!" he cried, "Where do we go?!"

Geoffrey grinned wryly. "Your gratitude is touching, varlet. How do I know you will stay with me, not stealing off at first chance?"

"He is known, Sir Knight. I will speak to Jarl Olaf. If he is found without the Norman by his side, he will die," Bengt smiled benignly. Guvi blanched.

"What if something happens to my master?" Guvi asked.

"Pray it does not," suggested Bengt the Viking.

"Do any of you know a man called Eadric Siwardsson? A Saxon?" Geoffrey asked them.

"The Saxon!" Bengt roared, answered in anger by the others. "What business do you have with him that you seek him at the cost of my men's lives?" The air was suddenly electric with danger when Geoffrey saw the look of utter hatred that passed over the Viking's face and his men's as well.

"His death!" grated Geoffrey, brandishing his sword high for them all to see. "Let no man hinder me. He has robbed me of what was once my dearest possession and I seek him for the debt!" There was dark defiance in the Norman's eyes, challenging the Vikings to try to stop him. Again, he was maddened.

But Bengt merely barred his teeth ferociously and nodded. "So be it. So, too, did our Jarl lose his dearest possession to the Saxony in battle and by a deft sword stroke unmanfully done!"

"We speak of different possessions, friend Bengt," sighed Geoffrey. Even here, in the frozen beauty of this chill wasteland, her face came easily to haunt him.

"Perhaps!" agreed Bengt with a short laugh. "But one is of little use without the other, eh?!"

And Geoffrey then realized how great a pain the Jarl Olaf must have in his heart for Eadric the Wild, perhaps as great as Geoffrey's.

"Clumsy!" shouted Bengt as Guvi slipped on feet still numb from hanging in the icy wind and fell against him. "Usually you are better skilled at moving than that! Has your reprieve so upset your feet that they will no longer work for you? Ho, ho! The dog will have to take up an honest trade now." All of the Northlanders laughed at the crude jest and Guvi with them, in rare good humor.

"I am no match for you, Bengt Leofricsson! I shall do better in the future," smiled Guvi ingratiatingly. Bengt nodded in acceptance of the compliment.

"You are learning, Finn. You are learning," he said.

"The sages say every man has much to learn, but that he never does," Guvi added.

Geoffrey shrugged. "Spare us your philosophy, friend Guvi. Let us hasten for shelter before the daylight leaves us. You have cost me much time here with your foolery." The knight waved farewell as he started off down the pass, but Bengt stopped him. The Viking presented him with a gleaming ornate dagger with a handle of wrought silver and gold and adorned with Nordic runes, intricately worked.

"It is a token of Jarl Olaf, son of Goll the Merciless. He wishes it to be buried in the throat of the Saxon. If you meet him ere we do, see that this blade bites deep into his filthy hide!"

"Aye!" grinned Geoffrey. "Your jarl need not fear on that account; his present will not go thirsty. I will carry it as a sign of our friendship!"

"I had thought it so," laughed Bengt and waved him on, giving Guvi a final kick in the arse as he passed.

"Behave yourself, brigand!" admonished Bengt. And Guvi smiled humbly and nodded.

The man has no pride, Geoffrey thought to himself.

As the knight on his huge destrier and his walking companion left the men of the North behind, the Finn turned to Geoffrey and asked, "How long am to stay with you, Sir Norman?"

"And how do you know that I am Norman-French, though of England?" asked Geoffrey easily, lulled into good humor at the thought of a competent guide to help him seek out his enemy.

"It shows in this Northland, in your every way," replied Guvi, caustically.

"You will stay until you have earned the worth of your debt to me," said Geoffrey, halting Chestnut to regard the slippery Finn. There was little doubt that he was up to something.

"Which is?" enquired Guvi casually.

Geoffrey spat contemptuously.

"A heavy pouch of silver, my friend. Now let us go." Geoffrey turned Chestnut for the path again.

"But wait, Sir Norman!" called Guvi, not moving. "If I give that to you, then I am free?" Geoffrey looked back at the obtuse fellow, irritated.

"I have said so, varlet. You owe me more than a pouch of gold for your greasy hide, yet I will settle for that. At present, that price is as far from you as the sun and the moon."

"Perhaps they are closer than you dream, sir. I hope this 'sun and moon' you seem obsessed with is as close to us as my payment of the debt is." The young knight was thoroughly nonplussed by the Finn's words.

"What are you nattering about, Finn?"

"And after the debt is paid, if I stay to guide you?" Guvi persisted.

Geoffrey was amused at his recurring nonsense. "Then you will be paid your worth!" he replied. "Now hasten before it grows too late!"

Casually, Guvi thrust a hand beneath his thick furs and withdrew a heavy leather object. Geoffrey stared at it but his thoughts were interrupted by an echoing cry floating down the pass from where he had left the Vikings. "Thieves! Thieves, bastards, traitors!" It was Bengt Sigurdsson's voice and it raged on and on in furious oaths.

Guvi tossed the hidden object to the knight and walked off down the trail in no small degree of haste.

"Come, Sir Norman!" he called back over his shoulder. "It grows late and soon wolves may find our trail. Snow comes; it will hide us till we find shelter. And my price is a silver a fortnight!"

Geoffrey watched the fellow in stark amazement before he again looked at the object held in cupped hands. It was the pouch he had given Bengt Sigurdsson.

7

CHAPTER THE SEVENTH

E adric the Wild cleaned his large nose on the back of his hand, wiped it off across his breeches and held out a calloused paw in greeting to the magistrate. As usual, he stank of ale and now in the heat of Byzantium in his leathers and furs, almost overpoweringly of sweat as well. Patches of bright red heat rash dotted the cheeks of his face where not covered by grimy beard and the veins in his nose stood out blue and swollen from days of excess drink. His eye patch was off slightly, giving the really curious a close-up view of a part of human anatomy most never see, and great sweat stains decorated the chest and underarms of his tunic darkly. He was an imposing sight for both his height and girth in this land of slim warriors, and a standout for both his unorthodox dress, and more so, for his rich aroma in this land of clean silks and spices.

The sun glared harsh and friendless, as friendless as the emperor's magistrate. The thin, darker-skinned man muttered something in Greek about feces and Eadric mistook this for a greeting. Uncouthly, he parroted the phrase back at the little dignitary, grossly offending the man. He refused to accept Eadric's hand.

The Saxon shrugged. Byzantium was a strange place so he was not offended by the fellow's rudeness. However, he was quick to learn and memorized the "greeting" the blunt magistrate had given him, using it liberally on the curious folk who approached his band at the wharf.

Eadric waved to them all in a friendly fashion and roared out mirthfully in a close approximation of their tongue. "Allah forgive me, you stink like shit!"

The crowd drew back in awe before this immense bulk of a man, talking darkly about his lack of manners, yet his apparent friendliness. They had seen many strange sights before in this vast city where the East met and blended with the customs of the West, but now they had seen everything. The emperor was hiring madmen to fight for him!

These people were too jaded to take real offense at this barbarian's use of Allah's name for, after all, it was his own soul that would not travel to paradise. But still, they wisely left when Eadric, in his enthusiasm, transposed some of the words and blurted out roughly, "You forgive me, Allah stinks like shit!"

They dispersed, mumbling Allah's name in prayer that they might not be judged in company with the strange barbarians.

Eadric lowered his arms and stopped waving, puzzled by the crowd's behavior. Didn't they realize he was finally here, ready to save them from the devils of the eastern desert?

"Who' s this 'Allah' they keep going on about?" growled Eadric out of one side of his mouth as he watched them all depart hurriedly.

Pigfeet shrugged. "Who knows, my jarl? Perhaps tis their local jarl of some sort to have his name in the greetings around here. Have you heard anyone talk of Alexis the Emperor?"

"Nay," rasped Eadric, his throat growing hot in the sun. "Whoever this Allah is, perhaps he owns the local alehouse and we can quit this thirsty dock. Odin knows my throat is tight and dry!"

Wulfhere shook his head in exasperation. How could he begin to explain to the two of them what this land was? How could he show them that here in these teeming streets and mixtures of all peoples and religions, that here was all the treasure and beauty of the world for the taking.

Byzantium was a truly remarkable place, even Wild Eadric had to grant that to these greasy barbarians with their thick intrigue and even thicker wines that a clean Saxon palate would choke on. Twas not really the antiquity of the city that impressed him, for in truth his mind could not comprehend the concept of seventeen centuries. Rather, it was the size.

The white city sprawled majestically the length of a peninsula that thrust itself out into the Sea of Marmara, surrounded in length and breadth by high stone walls. Intricate layers of buildings rose from the sea itself to the walls in a virtual honeycomb of Byzantine civilization. Never had Eadric seen such a culture, all the people packed thick as the fleas in Pigfeet's beard as Eadric explained it to the traveling companions. All laughed at this comparison, including Pigfeet who had twice bested Eadric in flea and lice hunts through their beards.

The inside of the yellow-white walls gave Eadric even less cause for reassurance as a captain in the Imperial Guard led him through the streets. The man was a hulking, blond, giant of a Viking, or so he appeared. In reality, he was a Varangian, a descendent of the Norse who had migrated to this land generations ago and who spoke only Greek, to Eadric's immense chagrin. He greeted them in broken Norse and bade them to follow him, but that was as far as the captain's limited linguistic ability took him.

Eadric could not be restrained at the fellow's rudeness. The Saxon swore profusely at the obstinate countryman who refused to answer his questions and was on the verge of dealing the fellow a blow to the side of the head "to calm him down."

Fortunately, Wulfhere, suave and polished in his new environment, informed his father with some mirth, on the curious course of events in this strange land.

"Thor's hammer!" cursed Eadric roundly. "What manner of odd-matched villains have we thrown ourselves in with?"

After a tour, they ended up back at the docks where that rabbit-livered magistrate had met them and had the nerve to tell him, Eadric Siwardsson, that the Emperor Alexis was much too busy to welcome the new arrivals to his Imperial Guard in person. Huh! For all their civilization, these fancy-dressed Easterners knew little enough about common hospitality. Eadric asked the man three times if Alexis did not know who he was, for surely Alexis Comnenus would come in person to see the man who had traveled here to save his civilization for him.

Oddly, the darker, slight man of authority seemed unimpressed. Rather, he was studying Eadric's motley crew unloading the ships, with a somewhat disconcerted look upon his pudgy, beady-eyed face.

Then there was the matter of Eadric's supposed command of the Imperial Guard. The magistrate informed him that the position was already filled, but that hardly deterred the Saxon brigand who nodded in understanding and eyed-up the commander who had accompanied the dignitary. The Commander's name was Constas and he spoke fluent Saxon so Eadric was able to begin provoking him full throttle. Constas held out a large hand in reserved greeting.

Eadric spit on the hand and loudly trumpeted, "Your mother was a scabby whore and your father the emperor's entire arm!" He grinned expectantly.

Constas went white, withdrew his hand, and reached for his sword.

Wulfhere and the magistrate stepped between the two and co-announced that it was beneath a commander's position to be subjected to this. Constas was dismissed but Eadric further endeared himself to the gaping throng when he dealt a ragged beggar a huge clout up the side of the head, downing him instantly. Unfortunately, no one had explained to Eadric that the beggar was a holy man in this Eastern culture and that such men were humored, if not revered by the populace.

"What?!" the Saxon roared. "They worship beggars here? Tell the dirty little bastard to find himself some honest employment and to quit sponging off people with my good nature!"

"Can you not control yourself?!" hissed Wulfhere into his ear, feeling the foolish shame his father could not.

"By Odin! I cannot!" roared Eadric again in a gruff bellow that caused all of the passersby to stare. "This is the most arse upside down land I have ever landed in. Satan, take this plagued anthill of a city. Let us end the dainty formalities and begin killing these infidels I hear so much about. Here, it is still light enough, let us start the slaughter today!"

"Eadric Siwardsson!" snapped Wulfhere in disgust.

"That is why we came, is it not?"

"We are here to protect and serve the emperor, you great wild boar!" lashed Wulfhere, as he smiled ingratiatingly to the officials who strolled by the group giving the Saxons black stares.

One of the city police guards stopped and gazed at Eadric with open contempt and the Saxon jarl spit on the man's boots in defiance. Wulfhere hurriedly grabbed his father's arm and turned them both away.

"Tis all the same!" grunted Eadric. "Where are the infidels?"

"It's more than infidels we must fight, as you will see when the Norman host arrives!" smirked the Reaver.

"What?!" thundered Eadric. "By Thor and Odin, how many men does that idiot think we can slay by ourselves?"

"You misunderstand," smiled Wulfhere, disarmingly. "We are to fight *with* the Normans against the desert tribes of infidels."

Eadric looked at Pigfeet who spat into the dirty street. "What?" Eadric shouted again. "Fight *with* them? By Odin's prick, you conniving son of a bitch, what is this you say? Bad enough we come all this way to kill Normans; we could have done that to better purpose in England. But I am easy enough to please; you tell me we are here to kill Normans and I say, well, all right with my blessings. The only thing that matters is that they be slain. But now the sun has broiled your meager wits until you think the usurpers of our nation are brothers and that I will risk the seat of my breeches to fight with them! Balls, say I!"

They were standing before the formal gardens to the palace now, having toured the city as they talked. One of the emperor's Turcopole guards eyed Eadric reproachfully as the Saxon cleared his throat loudly to show his disgust and spat upon one of the stone lions guarding the entry steps, spattering the guard.

Wisely, the guard said nothing, His gaze was unfathomable as he watched the uncouth Saxons, but it was hard to tell what the renegade Turk was thinking. Like Eadric, he had abandoned his land and leader to serve Alexis as a mercenary, but the Turk's position was not enviable, for the people he fought against now were his old Moslem kinsmen and they reserved special treatment for traitors to Allah. He was a Christian Turk now, a bitter enemy of the infidel Seljuk Turks that fought under the banners of Mohammed. Eadric questioned Wulfhere about the swarthy man regarding them and Wulfhere wearily restrained his father from drawing his sword when he found out the fellow was a Turk, just like those he had been sent to kill.

Wild Eadric was furious now, cursing like a madman. "By Odin, what sort of madhouse have you driven me to, Wulfhere Eadricsson? You tell me I'm to kill Turks, yet you stop me; then you tell me I'm to protect Alexis from the Normans yet you won't let me fight them either. When does the killing begin? By Odin, I did not travel all of this way to walk guard before the palace like those greasy Turks..."

Wulfhere shook his head. "First, you came here not for any of those reasons. You remember what we discussed on the ship? But if you want the facts behind this country, they are these: Alexis fears the Saracen so he talks to the Franks, as they call the Normans here, into fighting for him. But we know as well as Alexis, that the Normans are ruthless and greedy, so he fears these ally-Franks will turn against him when the dust clears. We are to escort them into the lands known to the mapmakers as Asia when they arrive and see to it that they push directly for the infidel cities, to keep them out of mischief here. We will guide them and keep them in cheek; it is our task to report on them to the emperor."

Eadric snorted and fiddled with the new helmet he had been given, a high conical one with steel wings. "This thing smells rotten to me, boy," he said at length. "But what I want to know is when do we pull guard duty on the emperor's gold, like we discussed before? As soon as we get into that..."

"Silence!" hissed Wulfhere. "The very walls have ears in this land. Never mention again why we are really here; leave the planning to me. Trust me!"

Pigfeet pulled at his nose and eyed Wulfhere suspiciously.

Eadric calmed. "Of course, I do, we are Saxons!" he whispered.

But not one of the three believed him; gold has no nationality.

Wulfhere sneered. "I have not said that this was not a rotten land, have I? But even a rotten tree can bear delicious fruit!"

The jarl looked about suspiciously before he continued, "Alexis thinks to use all the Frankish kings and princes to fight his battles and clear the Seljuk hordes from his lands, expanding his sphere of influence.

He is crafty, that one. I have not personally spoken with the last emperor but it is said that Nicephorus was forced from power by the faction of Alexis, mutilated to terrify him, and banished forever to the care of some secret religious order that Alexis might wear the purple robe."

"He is not a man to trade jests with, nor underestimate," responded Wulfhere.

Nor are you, son from my loins, thought Eadric. But he said nothing. He belched delicately, still full of the syrupy, dark-red, spiced wine they had forced upon him when he had landed. Ugh! Was this stuff actually supposed to quench a thirst? He looked around idly at the street full of dignitaries before the palace petitioning for an audience.

"Are there any tarts around here?" Eadric asked. "I've heard they are something special in this city." He squeezed the buttocks of a passing female dressed in poor quality silks and she turned to regard him coolly. She supposed he was of the emperor's guard so merely smiled politely and hurried off. Eadric grinned and filed this away for future reference. Then he thought of business and the myriad things that could go wrong with their hastily planned skullduggery, for they had much on their minds besides service to his highness.

Nervously, he picked his nose while he asked, "And how do we fit in? All I had thought was that we were supposed to join the palace guard at a heavy rate of gold. Now, you hint that we are caught between Normans and Turks and the empire to boot. All this without stealing the gold we had decided on. I have known you for twenty-nine winters, Wulfhere Eadricsson, and I understand you. You, as well as I, know that we do not fit in here nor would we pass as real Varangians. You have altered the plan we first discussed when you perceived the complications of the situation. Where does the profit lie?"

Wulfhere nodded and glancing about, then pulled Eadric and Pigfeet into the mouth of an alley where they might talk. But before their plan was made, they were interrupted by a squad of horsemen thundering past the gate to the outer courtyards, palace guards, more Turcopoles. The swarthy men raced past, clad only in light armor with conical helmets wrapped in swaths of red silk as their uniform standard. They sported small, round shields with center spikes little bigger than a serving platter and Eadric chuckled at the thought of such a shield meeting his axe swing. The only weapons they carried were short scimitars and long lances, slender and supple as they wobbled in the rush. They looked ridiculous to Eadric in their high saddles with the short stirrups set upon horses vastly different from anything he'd ever seen before. These were not the heavy war destriers of the conquering Norman knights, but much smaller, high-stepping, high-strung racehorses, infinitely maneuverable and very capable of outrunning the fleetest Norman warhorse. To Eadric, their very lightness was a drawback, however, for as he expressed it, "Ugh! Look at them racing about like mites in a summer storm! Give me but one stout axe and I'll separate that torrent of horseflesh like a rock set against the waves!"

"Big enough waves cover the rocks, Father," smiled Wulfhere, being more of a sage than he realized in his sarcasm.

Eadric would soon learn that there was more to the warfare of the Seljuks than lances and fast horses alone. They were also masters at the short-curved bow they kept so often at their saddle horn with its flat quiver of arrows with red feathers to match their helmets. And just as a horde of mites could sting when massed, so too could the Seljuk lancers, circling always beyond axe or sword stroke, sending arrow after arrow into a compacted foe. And while the pounding charge of Frankish destriers was awesome beyond telling and powerful beyond description, the swiftness of the Arabian ponies allowed them to judge the rush of their relatives and gracefully dodge and outflank them where needed. The Franks would suffer much before they learned. They would lose many because they thought their weight and power were all.

But let them all rot in the sand, thought Eadric. He was a sailor and a raider and hated them all. But fate sometimes had odd notions; Eadric would soon find himself receiving direct experience from these little men that he had such contempt for.

Two mornings later with the sun newly sprung and the wind fresh and clean, Eadric stood outside the gates of Zeytinburnu with his Saxon clan, watching as several hundred Turcopoles led their sleek ponies up the ramps of waiting ships. The Siwardsson commanded his own flotilla of ships and they were to act as escort, accompanying the emperor's men, seeing as how Eadric's men were rovers and sea fighters whereas the dark Turks were cavalry only.

Eadric the Wild's joy was boundless. Apparently, the emperor was no fool when it came to planning but he was excused for having never met a man with Eadric's audacity before. He ruffled his tangled red mane and eyed the large chests that were being loaded carefully upon a final, larger vessel, and with them, a multitude of Greek bowmen.

"Gold!" he breathed, licking his thick lips greedily.

Wulfhere and Eadric had been routinely briefed by the paymaster according to plan. The sea-going caravan was to travel the coast, distributing payroll to the garrisons, heading generally for the gathering Christian hosts at the vicinity of the Bithynian city of Nicaea, in a roundabout of cities along the Marmaran coast. Eadric had just received word from his son who was acting emissary to the emperor, that an army of the Franks had pulled up from Nicaea and were moving along the coast in a more direct route for the Holy City.

Greeks, Turks, Franks. Eadric had this foreboding feeling that he would have to fight his way through the entire lot of them before his thievery was over. Alexis had made only one small error in his planning —he had stocked the guard companies on board the ships with Greeks and Turcopoles who came from inland towns and, as such, were absolutely terrified of water in general and the sea in particular. They were counting on Eadric to fend off any pirates or Saracen raiders but had neglected to satisfy themselves that they had no wolf in their own midst.

Lambs, thought Eadric. Little boys playing at war. Well, he would teach them what kingdoms and politics were about; that he would. And he would teach Alexis Comnenus to snub such a personage as Eadric the Wild, son of England and all points North. Before the day ended, he would be rich beyond his dreams, providing he did not meet up with these sea-Franks. That might be a different matter altogether; they had marines with them and ships that could match Eadric's, no doubt. But then, nothing ventured, nothing gained, they always said. He tested the heft of his axe and heaved a sigh into the rising wind.

Apparently, this Bohemond of Otranto was not the puppet Alexis thought, chuckled Eadric to himself. The wily Greek leader had obviously expected the Franks to charge hell-for-leather across the breath of the Seljuk lands, beginning on the other side of Byzantium where massed Saracens were waiting to massacre them. In their rush for Jerusalem, they would wear down their armies as they went, until by the time they liberated their goal, they would not only have freed the empire for Alexis's rule, but would have also decimated themselves in the effort and thus removed the Christian host from being any future threat. Alexis was not oblivious as to why the Franks swarmed around his banner. And it was certainly not due to the ignorant prattling of Pope Urban II. At least, not in concern to the Frankish kings and princes. They were men of ambition. One did not lightly match wits with the Emperor Alexis; he had been fathered by intrigue and suckled on greed.

With the Empire pushing in one direction and the Frankish leaders a maze of entirely different and entirely selfish directions, the crusade, never-the-less, progressed along the coast by ship, horse, and for the poor men-at-arms...by foot.

And trailing at a safe distance were the ships of the emperor carrying supplies and gold for the troops carefully guarded by a Saxon clan, not so much out of duty, but out of a strange feeling that the gold belonged to them. And it did really, all they had to do was get past the Greek bowmen and the Turkish horse soldiers.

Ah, the poor little witless Iambs, doomed to die for their emperor if they could not be otherwise persuaded. When Eadric was through with them, there would not be a dry eye in the court, especially on Alexis's part; he hated to be made a fool of. But such was the fare of war. Some were born to fail; some had the stuff needed to succeed. The Saxon chieftain preened slightly at the rail as he considered himself well within that second category. A delicate rolling belch escaped him as he considered both the gold and also the salted carp he had had for breakfast.

It mattered not a whit to him that at Khios and Patmos they dispensed with nearly two of the large chests, though Pigfeet wept openly at the sight of their leaving. There was still much gold left, so much that had Eadric tried his best, it still would have taken him years of wanton spending to shed it all. After all the garrisons were paid, there was still to be much left over as a goodwill present for Bohemond of Otranto and the other Frankish leaders. In other words, a bribe.

Eadric licked his lips again. So be it, lucre from the hands of one great scoundrel into another. Surely, it was no large crime to also dip his hand into the till. And even if it was, his conscience was not unstained with the life he led. Long ago, he had come to terms with his revolting conscience and the two lived under an uneasy truce. Gold was the best balm for any wound, he reasoned, and guilt went better with enough gold to buy forgetfulness. Gold was only useless for a wound of the heart; but even as he thought this, he wondered that he should come up with such a poetic theory; it was alien to his lusty nature.

He hummed happily with his lips as he scanned the deck crew and saw them making ready their weapons. It would not be long now! He tested the wind uncertainly. There was a squall following the convoy, but he was unable to say when it would hit. This Eastern sea weather was as strange as the land. But this thieving the emperor's gold, he was comfortable in this. It was his forte.

The others felt the same, he knew. They were ready. Eadric had not failed to notice the expression on Wulfhere's face when he caught sight of the gold chests in port. Naturally, he had known the stakes of the game from the very beginning, yet even he had no way of knowing how much wealth they were to help transport. The enormity of it staggered even his aplomb.

Eadric had to tread quickly and quietly now, for he made his way through a pit of snakes. He needed only to wait and watch.

Surely the fates loved a wicked rogue, for the expected opening for his dark desires came fifty miles off the coast of Cyprus two days later. His last port of call was Aydincik at the bottom of the thumb of land that was Turkey and the squall that had stalked them for two days was blowing in. It was too perfect to pass up; the wind and rain of Odin would do the work for the Saxons and they need not betray their desires by force of arms, which would be both mutiny and piracy.

For nearly two hours, they had sailed on beneath a coal-black covering of clouds on a sea that was dangerously still. The inexperienced captain of the ship carrying over half of the emperor's horse soldiers called to Eadric that they should put into land for a storm was coming by the looks of things, but Eadric called back the Seljuk equivalent of "sissy" and sailed on, hesitantly followed by the two ships full of horse guards—the one carrying the Greek infantry and the gold—and his other longships. Eadric was a bit nervous about the storm for the rearmost ships carried their women and children, contrary to accepted policy. However, these charges had been boarded in secret so that once the gold was in Saxon hands, they might fly in force from the Empire. Eadric had told them all at the boarding that he would neither stop nor return for any man, woman, or child, for after their treachery, to return would certainly mean a slow, hideous death. Well, the women and children were Saxons, too, or at least members of the clan. They must take their chances with the men. Wulfhere had begun a debate of Eadric's decision but ceased when he caught the crafty glint in the old pirate's eye and the smirk etched across his ruddy face.

"We can weather any squall!" laughed Eadric. Wulfhere smiled greedily for he knew their crews were excellent sailors; but what of the emperor's ships? They also had their sailors, yet Alexis, in his security precautions for the gold, had stripped the crews bare to clear the weight allowance for the Turcopoles and infantry. But the soldiers were not seamen by any imagining.

Eadric the Wild chuckled as the wind rose; he laughed aloud when the first lightning split the lampblack sky. He pounded his knees in mirth as the Empire ships finally guessed what was happening and turned for the deserted coast, far from any of their garrisons. The Saxons moved after them but they knew there would be no battle; the storm was moving too swiftly for them to escape its jaws.

The wind was so strong that it drove the rain horizontally, ripped their large sail and sent mast and boom crashing down onto the panic-stricken crews. Already, the Saxons had cut sail for the storm and made ready. Eadric stood at the prow laughing as his red mane became soaked and his beard finally lay down flat and wet. He spat contemptuously into the raging sea and hurled curses at the thunderbolts as if Thor could hear him. Then the storm began with a vengeance, sea and a mad whirl of foaming whitecaps caused even the larger of the longships to keel dangerously. Eadric still stood at the prow, clutching the dragon figure-head for life itself, but laughing again now and shaking his hairy fist to the heavens where the clouds' bellies had been ripped inside out and torrents of water gushed from them in a blinding, smashing union of sky and sea.

"O-d-d-i-i-i-n-n-n!" he called to the wind, "Send us death in the wind and the rain! Swamp the heathen ships and drown the little men like rats!" he demanded.

"But spare the gold ship!" he added as an afterthought. *Whew!* he thought. *That was close!* It would be foolish to lose the treasure for the vehemence of his curse, he decided. And one could never know when Father Odin might decide to take a man literally.

Wulfhere eyed him with ill-concealed derision but he took on a more thoughtful expression when the first troop-ship of Turcopoles slowly took on water beneath its decks, drowning horses and riders quartered below, and keeled over onto its side, sinking gradually into the deep water. There was a horrible cacophony of burbling screams as over a hundred men and their mounts went beneath the sea, and the few that escaped the tragedy were soon lost in the storm.

"Pull about!" roared Eadric, rushing to the steering oar where Pigfeet fought the squall determinedly. The other two Turkish ships were running sloppily for the coast but the ferocious, devouring sea overtook them both. They died cursing Eadric and his band. But now, there was trouble brewing, for as the longships drove in to snatch the treasure from the waves, the first of them slid into coastal rocks and burst like an eggshell spilling Vikings and Saxons into the brutal sea. *Damn!* thought Eadric. And worse, the treasure ship, while fortunately remaining afloat, also still had a complement of those damn bowmen who were loosing arrow shafts into the teeth of the storm at the Saxon longships. Another ship lost control in the wind and sea and smashed against the reef that held the other Empire ship.

Eadric threw his helmet to the deck and jumped up and down, bellowing loud curses as he saw what was happening. But his own Nykr scull overtook the beached ship despite the opposite-pulling wind. But the sea was rougher than he expected and it suddenly pulled them for the reef. A cloud of Greek shafts, grey-feathered and invisible in the storm until they hit, swept his deck with incomprehensible death and even Eadric winced as a shaft pinned his left hand to the deck rail.

But then the worst happened and Eadric saw too late a second row of huge rocks, invisible also in the dark sea, jutting up out of the coastal waters ahead, craggy knobs of water-honed rock, polished and worn to piercing traps for the unwary sailor.

He had only time enough to snap the arrow shaft from his hand, wrapping the wound with a piece of dirty linen, and cursing the unsympathetic and mocking fates that had done this to him. "Shit!" he bellowed as the harsh waves lifted his ship over the worst of the rocks only to smash it down savagely on the second ring of reef and directly into the stern of the Empire treasure ship, pitching the fuming jarl headfirst into the swirling waters where he barely avoided smashing his thick skull against even harder out-croppings. As he went under a second time, he heard the wrenching of heavy timbers as the Nykr ground out its beautiful guts upon the jagged stone teeth of the Turkish coasts.

A burble of hair-raising curses rose from the spot where the jarl sank. But Wulfhere was commanding admirably in the confusion. As the Turcopoles and Greeks swarmed on deck they were met with whizzing arrows in return for theirs and the renegade crew half-swam and half-climbed over the rocks to engage them in hand to hand combat. Behind the ruined Empire troop-ship, Pigfeet was assaulting the ruined treasure ship in the shallow waters, trying to do minimal additional damage so that they might salvage it for further use. But it was to no avail, for the treacherous, roiling waters sawed the galley back and forth on the toothy reef, grinding the hull into splinters. As the last of the men of the Empire abandoned ship and tried to row in several smaller boats for the coast, Wulfhere and Pigfeet sank three of them; then the remaining two fled into the storm and left those to guess whether they had survived.

ATTACK AND SQUALL ENDED AT ROUGHLY THE SAME TIME. AS THE SKY ceased its fury and began to clear, Wulfhere stood upon the slanting deck of the treasure ship and took stock of the disaster. Perhaps twenty of the Saxons had been slain in the combat on this single ship; how many more were lost to the storm he had no way of knowing yet. Nowhere did he see a live soldier of Alexis. Several had attempted to surrender when they saw how hopeless the situation was but Wulfhere was taking no chances. "Cut their bedamned throats and cast them back to the sea!" he ordered callously. "A few more dead Turks won't matter to us or the emperor!"

Wulfhere glanced briefly at the near coast where the men were carrying the stores salvaged from the ships and the gold. A party of them were also erecting crude shelters for the women and children, still scared witless by the viciousness of the past hour. He shrugged, unhappy to have them clinging to him and the rest. *Better they had gone under and the warriors had lived,* he thought. Women could easily be replaced and children were but pests. Ah well, he decided, there were those in the clan that felt differently and he could not afford to alienate any swordsmen. A glance at the reef showed Eadric puffing and snorting like a beached whale as he hauled his waterlogged bulk from the water, his red hair matted darkly against his craggy skull.

Another unfortunate toss of the dice, thought Wulfhere. Better for all had the old man drowned and relinquished his command in death. Now, for certain, that there was gold handy and the clan weakened, Wulfhere had no intention of giving the jarl back his authority.

But, thought Wulfhere, if he could not praise the old man's ingenuity, then he could not condemn it either. True, they had fatally lost all but one of their ships and they had not enough room for all of the clan, let alone people and gold together, but they did have a good portion of the wealth of the Emperor Alexis, and they had salvaged a good number of floundering horses to transport stores and treasure. And true it was, that by Wulfhere's reckoning that they were within a day's march of a number of coastal villages loyal to the Empire after having been reclaimed by the Frankish hoard. It could have been worse.

They were safe enough as long as no survivors had escaped to take word to these villages, forwardable to either the Franks or the Byzantines. But where then did this actually leave them, he pondered. On foot, they had but two choices—either cast in with the Franks or cast in with the infidels. Ugh! One was as likely to take all of their gold for a little assistance as the other, but should the Franks, loyal to Alexis in their own fashion, find out that the clan was full of traitors to the Empire, then they would have a handy excuse for a full day of throat-slitting. There would be hell to pay if they opted for that choice. No, the only logical alternative was to press on to the infidel strongholds, claim themselves enemies of the Empire and try to deceive the Seljuks into helping them for a share of the gold.

At present, the Franks were encamped in the vicinity of Erdemli and Tomuk, awaiting reinforcements. Hopefully, the Saxons could win favor and be away quickly, refitted out of gratitude from the Turks, before the Lion of Otranto stood pounding at the gates of Tarsus. How much he could dupe the Seljuk emirs, Wulfhere was not exactly sure, but it was now impossible to flee for the North again as they had originally planned. The one ship left would carry perhaps seventy men and provisions which Wulfhere would need to survive.

But no gold. So, they must trust their luck to the land routes. Ugh! But a meagre chance was better than no chance at all.

Hmm. But would not a very small band travel faster? Say, one half the size as now existed. Or less? And would not that mean twice the take of gold for each man, each man except Wulfhere? He would have ten times as much!

He gazed at the semi-comic figure of his father, wildly gesturing his orders to his men and smiled a smile of pure malice and greed.

Unfortunately for Wulfhere Eadricsson, as well as his father, the days following the squall were placid and, ironically enough, if the storm had been a gift from Odin Stormbringer, then the calm sea and blue sky was his curse for the mild horizon swarmed daily with Frankish troop-ships and escort squadrons from the Empire's fleet.

Undoubtedly, a search for the missing gold-ship and its complement of soldiers was being held . Even not knowing the true story of the wreck, Alexis would be scouring the coast for clues. He was neither a stranger to the effects of greed on men and bad luck, nor a fool. Time was slipping away for the band.

Twice, in fact, galleys landed companies of Turcopole horse soldiers

136

along the length of the coast to search for reasons the convoy disappeared. Eadric had not been lax in his security, however; at the instant the squall had left, he had men upon the reef dismantling what was left of the wrecked ship. The longship that had survived carried as much of the ruined planking and rigging as possible out to sea and down the coast. If Alexis wanted to believe that the storm had scattered and sunk the convoy elsewhere, he was more than welcome to his thoughts. At present, the Saxon camp was doubly protected; they were two miles inland leaving only a scouting party, horse mounted, at the beach as a watch. The reef stretched menacingly across the sand, flanking their camp. A direct ship-borne frontal assault on them would see all of the invading ships caught upon the reef; Eadric's only real worry was that a flanking movement of horse soldiers would land further down the coast and come in from behind, catching them unaware. Plainly, the emperor was not a man to write off so much gold.

Eadric had sent off scouts the first day after the storm, seeking a path to safety. To date, none had returned and the men were growing restless.

Fortunately, they had found a town some ten miles inland called Vechut, a watering hole for caravans along the coast. But it was enough, for it had both shelter and food, and, most gratifying for Eadric, the headmen of Vechut were more loyal to the yellow metal he flaunted than they were to their emir or emperor. Thus, when the Turcopoles of Alexis came to Vechut, they were told that no, no Varangian details had been seen in the area and that yes, the men of Vechut knew the coast intimately for miles. Even when they suspected the village mayor of complicity and made him watch as they tortured villagers, he could not break the spell of Saxon gold. Eadric merely gave him five times the amount of gold as promised.

The deal left a bad taste in Eadric's mouth but he was fighting for his life now and that of his men, fighting with chests full of the only weapon that really worked. Life was cheap and easy in those hills, gold was not. So, the Turcopoles passed by Vechut without ever understanding that the tents of the outlaw Saxons were pitched right under their noses in one of the innumerable valleys that ran through the low hills.

Two more days passed and still no riders returned. The Siwardsson had an inkling of what was happening yet held onto hope of the men being delayed rather than being waylaid somewhere and having their throats cut by Turkish brigands. Eadric and his ferocious bunch were safe enough in Vechut, but they could not stay there forever and while they sat eating, drinking and dreaming of their gold-bought palaces, hostile bands of warriors swarmed over the routes surrounding the village, bands in such numbers that for once even the men of Wild Eadric were outclassed. There were still Turcopoles of the emperor maintaining the Empire's peace, straggling groups of Christians and pilgrims traveling the coast in an effort to either flee from, or catch up to, the main Frankish armies who had passed not long ago, and behind them all detachments of Moslem horse-soldiers sent to harass the Crusaders' flanks. Equally as bad were the huge bands of paltry bandits roaming the hills and preying on Christians and infidels with no distinction between them. Indeed, these were perhaps the worst for they took only loot, no prisoners. The best a person could expect from them was a quick death by sword-thrust but quite often, it was otherwise. Death was only granted painlessly to their fellow Moslems. Christians were summarily tortured to death for the amusement of the brigands, women and children included.

Not a good group to fall in with, Eadric thought, pulling his nose. Even more bothersome was the fact that these bandits had some idea of the guests of Vechut, though they surely did not realize the treasure that the fair-haired warriors guarded. Routinely, one of the bandit captains had entered Vechut in disguise to spy upon the townsmen and he had, by merest chance, come upon Eadric, Pigfeet and Wulfhere embroiled in a discussion with six of the headmen. The clumsy outlaw had the audacity to actually confront the Saxons and demand a share of whatever it was that they were hiding in return for his blessing of silence, even proceeding so far as to leer devilishly at Eadric and make a slow cutting motion across his dirty throat with a hand that rivaled Eadric's for uncleanliness. Eadric looked at his companions, decidedly unimpressed.

The headman interpreted for the bandit, "Eadric, he say that you be dead by sunset if you do not count him in on what you are guarding!"

Eadric spat onto the fellow's boots and said to the headman, "Tell him that what he says may be good and true, but he won't be here to see it happen!"

"He say, Eadric, that he spit on your mother's grave."

Eadric laughed and looked at the others an instant before he rose slowly and grabbed the bandit by his long dirty hair, pitching him out the door. Pigfeet smiled grimly as Eadric hitched up his breeches and cracked his knuckles as he followed the man outside.

Then, there was a long, drawn out gurgling scream that made Wulfhere's hair stand on end until it ended in abrupt silence. Trust Eadric to do the job indelicately. The six headmen looked at each other in trepidation. Eadric the Wild was unpredictable. Hurriedly, they excused themselves, wishing to be gone before the jarl returned and started interrogating them.

But now the others in the bandit horde were making less-than-discreet inquiries into the man's curious disappearance. The trail is full of snakes and poisonous lizards, the headmen would say, shaking their heads sadly. Allah is wise. Allah gives and Allah takes. And the outlaws were lulled. But only for a while longer.

By now, the Saxons had been in Vechut nearly three months and the tempers of the men were soon running as short as their luck. They were tired of the thirsty, dry days under a naked brazen sun; they were tired of the chilly nights that drank the last vestiges of the day's heat from the ground, for by now they were used to the warmth of the land. They were tired of blowing sand and winds that could knock a rider from his steed; they were tired of the dry taste of the land, dull and lacking the salty freshness of the sea. But most of all, they were tired of being the richest outlaws of the entire East, and still with nowhere to spend the money. The girls of Vechut were accommodating enough but soon grew bothersome. The men thirsted for the excitement of a city, either to loot or to run rampant in with their pay, as all soldiers do. But the problems were more severe with this band for they were stranded out of their element and as such, it often breeds insecurity.

Men whispered curses upon Eadric Siwardsson for this. Why had he not taken them out of the desert before this?

Wulfhere drummed up more support for his unspoken claim to the clan. Something had to give soon for the climate was so depressing to these giants of the North, that lately two stout Saxons had been slain in paltry quarrels. It was not out of enmity for their fellows that they had perished, but more out of their lust for action that ran soul-deep among these huge warriors. These were men born to battle, hardy and fearless. Even Eadric could not expect them to let their swords rust in this forsaken half-dry oasis.

They were more used to boarding enemy vessels under the pelting of both arrows and icy squalls or in high-gated harbors. In a pinch, they could raid a coastal fortress or loot a manor; yet here they sat with their feeble brains baking beneath a strange, hostile sun with little to do except continually sharpen and re-sharpen their broad axes and longswords against the day when they might leave their hospitable prison. The craggy giants sat inert and useless beneath the clear, hot sky that topped their hill-strewn furnace while flies the size of half a thumb crawled over their darkening, severely-bitten skins with neither fear nor mercy. At night, mosquitos and various other noisome insects invaded their tents and their beds, and these stout, lusty warriors that had slept naked next to their women in the frozen North, now had to cover their vulnerable nudity against the pests of the desert, the relentless heat, and the eternally blowing dust.

Ugh! Let the dim-witted infidels keep this underworld of a land; Odin had addled the wits of the Franks to make them think that they wanted it, also. Give these Saxons only the cool sweet wind of the North and an endless sea to sail the length and breadth of. But first and foremost, Great Lord Odin, grant them escape from Vechut.

But Eadric knew that there was no escape, short of a miracle, for so large a group of men, and the noose grew tighter daily for more and more Franks were making use of the coast. The renegade Saxons were very likely to soon be in the midst of the swarming Christian host if they watched irresponsibly, and consequently face to face and sword to sword with a detachment of the Empire's best troops.

As soon as word reached that damned Greek, there would be hell to pay, but if all this was true, what now?

What indeed, thought Eadric, staring out to sea from the guard post.

Desperation gave rise to the most fantastic plans, plans that were eagerly discussed around the campfires and councils but which Eadric always vetoed before their fruition, for they were the brainstorms of half-crazy vagabonds wanting too badly to go home.

Pigfeet wanted the men to sweep down the coast to the nearest village during the night and steal their fishing vessels. But fishing ships were not made for war and the Saxons were not made for night travel in the desert. In either event, they could be surprised by any number of enemies and annihilated.

Gundar Besfricsson wanted to post naked slave girls on the beach with simulated wreckage and hopefully trap the Franks when they came in to rescue the tender prizes. But Eadric knew that the waters were awash with ships from Frankistan and beyond, and there was never any more "just one" single ship. Eadric knew the Norman mind well enough by now; a group of naked girls would have the entire Frankish navy beached before they could escape.

And there were other plans proposed, even more improbable, but readily received by yearning ears. But they were only plans, idle talk that continued night and day and meanwhile, the merchants of Vechut grew fat and prosperous on the gold of the Empire, and even the littlest street urchins had pockets full of gold coins with Alexis's profile stamped upon them.

Sooner or later, the word would fly and they had stayed in the village for so long that the *later* they had talked about was now the *sooner*. Time was running out for them all.

Curiously enough, Wulfhere had no plans to suggest on his own, he whose head was always full of strange thoughts. Eadric followed him to the guard post one afternoon, determined to see if he could milk anything out of his son's twisting mind. What was needed now was animal cunning and Wulfhere was nothing if not full of snake oil.

He stood with Eadric and two other captains atop one of the higher grassless hills and pointed a dagger blade to a large force of men moving along the coastal highway in the distance. The flat road was thick with them so that they looked like warrior ants on the march, only these ants wore armor that struck a man sunblind and waved pennants of rainbow colors. There was little doubt that this was a formidable force; the men that were arriving now were different from the ambitious princely fops and wild-eyed warrior priests that had first massed to the call. Now, the word had spread far over Europe and armies of the best, long in the making perhaps, were now arriving. Eadric hated them all equally, but he saw now the cloud on the horizon of the Saracens. Mayhap these men were not the warriors he and his bunch were, but their armor was thick, their horses heavy and weapons sharp. And Eadric had the distinct feeling that the Seljuks were in for the largest of surprises.

"More Franks!" he spat in disgust. "Surely the bowels of Europe have turned themselves inside out to cast forth all this fine chivalry. Daily grow their numbers and I fear it is but a matter of days until their horde waxes great enough to dominate this entire area of land!"

"We must move now, Eadric Siwardsson, if we are to move at all," said the Reaver slowly. "I think the Franks are not ones to welcome us with open arms since we are scarcely Christian to them and have the gold to boot."

"Loki, take all Christians!" snarled Eadric. "Why can't they stay home and tend to their own affairs?!"

"As we do?" smirked Wulfhere, sardonically. "You are selfish, my jarl. You would deny them this land of opportunity that we have found, this land of wealth and women, milk and honey, this land of..."

Eadric rounded on his son, furious. "Spawn of a dog! If you have nothing better to spout from your twisted mouth then take your tears to the desert and out of my sight! Why, I should..."

"Patience, old jackass!" laughed Wulfhere, holding up a hand for silence. "You asked for advice, now you shall listen and learn."

"I suppose anything is possible in this land," said Eadric dryly, idly shaking out some sand mites from his boots. He placed his large rump on an emptied wine barrel and took to the task of examining his toes. Wulfhere noted the mold growing inside his boots and the tinge of darkness across his feet. The stench was gagging.

"Well, go on, snake that I have spawned! Your mind twists and turns where mine does not. I would fain see your miraculous plan of salvation.

Do we ride a wind from Odin or do we simply swim the sea with gold chests strapped to our backsides?"

The Reaver laughed mockingly. "If it were as easy as that, then you could carry every man's share on that galley stern you call an arse. But listen, Eadric Siwardsson..."

Wulfhere paused and smiled mysteriously, yet Eadric was much too intent upon his feet to notice. Jagi, one of the two captains noticed, but he was Wulfhere's man.

"The Franks are slowly moving to surround the city of Tarsus, my jarl. This we know from the talk in the village. From there, their net will expand to cover the surrounding countryside, creating a huge barrier too widespread to skirt with women, children and gold." His voice trembled slightly as he pronounced the final word but Eadric was busily working a stick between his gnarled toes, scraping loose a year's dirt. Wulfhere continued, "For now, there is time to pass around in front of them for an army moves slowly. We can enter Tarsus before they seal its gates with siege, exchange gold and slaves for better horses and run the length of the coast before the advancing Franks, until we can reach a port where we might take a ship for home. It will cost us richly in what we stole, but we will have enough to sate the avarice of most of us!"

But not yours, Eadric thought obliquely. Still, Eadric nodded his lion's head in agreement. "But what if the Franks have already encircled Tarsus from the far side and we hurl ourselves blindly into their host advancing from another direction? Had I the armies and kingdoms, tis how I would play the match."

Eadric was polishing his toenails with a greasy rag now and Wulfhere considered emptying his stomach. He had adopted the Eastern custom of bathing daily, for all of the old jarl's remarks about him growing breasts by doing so.

Wulfhere cursed him wickedly. "Gold, fool! Can you not glean from the constant parade that the highway displays that the Franks are nowhere near fighting strength? Are you afraid?"

Eadric shrugged philosophically and spat casually at Wulfhere's feet, a subtle reproach for his son's disrespect. "Who can say how many Franks, Wulfhere Eadricsson? Can you, in truth? Huh, braggart! Your words dance like a fart in a whirlwind! There is an endless river of men and supplies flowing from Christian Europe and these native Christians here in the East as well, endless because all their Pope has to do is whisper 'pax vobiscum' and at his cry another generation of ripe manhood marches off to save this barren land. But you are right in one thought, young wolf, even the mightiest of rivers can dam itself up at an obstacle and fill an entire valley with its churning backwash. I suppose now it is a question whether or not this river of ants, with their crosses and swords, has hit the obstacle of Tarsus yet and started..."

"The columns move easily, my jarl, and with haste as when a river rushes to find an open space!"

Eadric nodded easily. Perhaps this was their only hope. "What you say is true. If the walls of Tarsus are ringed with Franks, then that damned Greek will surely be with them now that he has an entire army to stand before him and the emir. But we may be both ways damned if we wait much longer, for we will be caught in the end and torn like a hare between two hounds. If we run for the emir of the Seljuks, we may only be fleeing to our deaths; but who can say? Perhaps a few riders at a time would gain ground unnoticed by night and secure ships that we might escape as Pigfeet wants."

"Phagh!" snarled Wulfhere. "Well you know that every ship around is busily engaged in hauling Frankish supplies and soldiers. There is small chance of finding several sitting with empty bellies and slack crew. And if you think to put to sea amidst the convoys with fishing boats then..."

"Perhaps we might find one ship empty," mused Eadric.

"Oh? And who would leave with the gold, my jarl?" asked Wulfhere, craftily, his own ideas beginning to show.

Eadric gazed at him a moment without speaking as he again put on his boot.

At length, Wulfhere changed his tone of voice and began to speak in a coaxing tone. "Be reasonable, Eadric Siwardsson. We can outrun the heavy Frankish horses easily. It is but four or five days to Tarsus where the legions of the Saracen emir are gathering for battle; what is the worst that might happen? Would we be so very trapped within the walls of such a fortress? I have seen the walls of the citadel; they can withstand any siege!"

Eadric's head jerked up at this. "When did you see the walls of an infidel city, Wulfhere Eadricsson? Do not lie to me!" He rose and wiped his dirty hands on his breeches.

The Reaver smiled modestly. "Why, what think you it took me so long in my visit to Alexis? I also visited the emir of the Seljuks and he was most receptive to my suggestions."

"A snake's mouth!" snarled Eadric, reaching for his broadsword. "Or is it three?"

Wulfhere backed off ten paces while his father ominously swung his heavy longsword. "Would you have done less?" he asked.

And Eadric's rage wilted because he knew that he would have tested both sides before joining either. Wulfhere was sometimes his father's son. "But you still talk of unknown things," Eadric admonished him. "Have you ever experienced a Frankish siege, boy?" growled Eadric with dry humor as he watched more riders pass in the distance, their plumes and pennants fluttering in the carefree breeze of the sea. All felt the old jarl's mind working in the silence and there was no sound, save the rustle of the hot wind. At length, the red-beard wiped again both greasy palms on his pants, hitched up his sword-belt and turned to go.

"You have decided, my jarl?" asked Wulfhere, almost contemptuously.

"I have," grated the old warrior. "Tonight, a rider follows the coast as far as Erdemli before returning. If he finds nothing in the way of ships, then we will ride for Tarsus as a last resort. Who will ride? Not you, Wulfhere," Eadric added.

Without so much as a glance towards his friend, the dark-featured Jagi spoke up, "I will, my jarl. Let our fate rest in my hands!"

Wulfhere turned away as Eadric looked searchingly first at Jagi with his scarred countenance and then to Wulfhere.

"Where lies your loyalty, Jagi? Swear to it, by Odin."

Jagi bristled. "Do you insult me without reason, my jarl?"

"Do I?" retorted Eadric. "Tell me."

"Only as much as you insult your son!" The captain tossed his dark brown hair and the scar that ran the length of his left cheek flamed red.

"Swear!" thundered Eadric, clenching his fist about his sword hilt.

"By Odin! I am your man!" bellowed a furious Jagi, staring unflinchingly into the bloodshot eye of his jarl.

Eadric beamed benevolently and clapped a rough hand upon the warrior's leather-covered shoulder. "Good. Good!" laughed Eadric. No one, surely, would break an oath of that nature. All was well.

Jagi returned the smile a bit awkwardly but laughing still to himself. Eadric and the other captain turned to camp. But as Jagi and Wulfhere followed behind the other two, the dark captain caught the Reaver's eye and held it.

Later, the last rays of the arid sun found Jagi and Wulfhere crouching in their capes in a wadi behind the Reaver's shelter. Both laughed softly. "Brother, you have cursed your spirit by a false oath to father Odin," mocked Wulfhere with a sarcastic chuckle.

"Brother," returned Jagi, "for such gold as we strive for, for such as will be mine, I can buy a new spirit or buy the good will of Odin himself! Huh! An old man and his old gods! Did he actually think me to be bound by such an oath? But what shall I tell the old fool? Surely, you do not actually want me to run after ships, for there are none."

Wulfhere pursed his lips in thought.

"Eadric knows this as well as you or I. The bastard is up to something; you can depend upon it. He is buying time and I would bet my share of the gold that he no more trusts you now than he did before the oath. His display of ill trust was patterned only for the audience of the camp, for the word will travel and with it, his renewed trust in you. But I cannot tell why. I think he will use my plan, or try to, for it is his last chance whether he trusts me or not. Who can say what the great ox thinks? Perhaps he only wants credit for making the decision to leave."

Jagi chuckled. "Unfortunately, he will miss the journey."

Wulfhere paused, looked about for spies, and then leaned closer to Jagi conspiratorially. "Let him think that you have found ships enough to remove us. Whatever it is that he plans, he will have to leave it for you will spread the news throughout the camp. The entire clan will make ready to leave!"

"Only not all will make it!" laughed the captain softly.

"No. We will take the slaves and our women and children. Other than that, we will take but twenty trusted men, each one picked by me personally, along with the gold, water, and horses. We do not need any revenge-seeking fools following us!" Wulfhere grinned wickedly.

"What of the people of Vechut?"

"I have tended to that, friend Jagi. Without his gold to buy favor, the people will never supply Eadric Siwardsson with so much as water. To insure his doom, I have paid one of the headmen of the village to ride to the Franks tomorrow eve and tell them that the Empire's brigands have been found. As a final gesture to him who spawned me, I will give him warning that I do this so that he might flee to the desert and die rather than be hanged by the Franks or be boiled in his own grease by Alexis."

"You are more generous than I would be, my jarl," said Jagi.

Wulfhere shrugged in all humility. "After all, he is my father."

Jagi nodded, understanding. "How will you separate our chosen from the rest? They are still many."

Wulfhere's smile broadened as he held up a small leather pouch. "This is an addition for the celebration wine, brother; it will choose!"

Jagi laughed with him as he drew his cape closer about his broad shoulders, against the cold of the barren desert. "But why do you not simply poison them all?" Jagi queried, ever practical.

Wulfhere looked at him in mock reproach. "What? Do you fancy me a slayer of my own kin? And my loyal comrades? How little you understand, friend Jagi!" And again, laughter rose on the chill desert wind with the naked face of the moon watching. Thus, was the plan for treachery.

When darkness was solid about the camp, Wulfhere crawled out of his hiding place and skulked to his tent of hides. He paused a moment to listen as the hoofbeats of his co-conspirator grew faint in the open air and then threw aside the door flap, entering to find his slave-mate suckling their infant daughter, seated before the small fire of wood shavings and horse dung. For a brief instant, he lusted at the sight of Claire's petite, pale breasts for she was almost naked to the waist. But the look of unguarded anger in her beautiful eyes stopped him, not with fear, but rather curiosity.

"Why look you so, my Frankish princess? You stare cuttingly as a moor with your eyes catching the fire. What do you hold against me now, the fact that I take others to bed as much as I take you? Or have not taken you as much as you wish?" Even in jest, his words were cruel. But she was far too furious to pay heed to his banter.

"You would betray your own father for gold! You have no honor!" Had she not been holding their baby girl, Wulfhere would have beaten her senseless.

"Put the babe down," he ordered.

But Claire only clutched their child closer with both arms.

Wulfhere walked forward slowly, an evil smile spreading across his face. He was Satan personified, she thought. He took Claire's lovely face between his two large hands and pressed the soft flesh of her cheeks until she winced in pain. But he did not let up even then; his arm muscles knotted with tension as he kept up the intensity.

The big Saxon bent down and peered into her eyes, almost sadly. Then, he kissed her softly about the lips and mouth, tasting and relishing her tears.

"So," he smiled gently, "you have listened to our plans, have you, my treasure. A pity. A genuine pity. I cannot trust you, you know. But come little sparrow, I will have you one final time before you pay the price of your stupidity. Put the babe down, I will not harm her."

Claire paled as she saw the hardness in his eyes. She had underestimated his wretchedness and now she wondered how she could have ever done so. His eyes glowed bright with two kinds of lust as he stared down at her, one with desire and one for death. In the weak light of the tent fire, his dark face was even darker and more shadowed, gaunt from life in the desert and hollow as if it revealed his shriveled soul. All she saw was his eyes and in her mind the hands that now knotted her hair were becoming talons. His gaze was removed from any semblance of humanity; its heat was a perfection of evil and she felt the fear of terrible death churn hideously in her belly. "If I..." she begged, "if I were planning to tell him, I would have done so already, would I have not?" Tears poured from her horrified eyes and trickled over her pale cheeks as his grasping fingers wormed deeper and deeper into her tresses.

"Tis not love that has held your tongue, bitch!" he grated, kissing her again, slowly, lingeringly. He loved the taste of her tears, the sensations of her misery. He was aroused by her vulnerability and his power.

She stared into his eyes, unspeaking.

"You fear me that much, do you?" he asked quietly, slackening his grip on her somewhat.

She nodded, trying to avert her eyes. But he forced her head back that he might look into her features. All of her anger had vanished, to be totally replaced by her tearful submission.

At the sight of her weakness, something primitive stirred again within him. Slowly, he kissed her again, this time with no malice. Only one lust remained, that for her sweet, warm flesh.

"Put the babe to bed," he said huskily.

"She will cry! She has not finished feeding, Wulfhere," she protested, looking anxiously at their daughter.

By the terrific pressure of his hands, he forced her to her feet and shook his head slowly before he kissed her trembling mouth. Yielding, Claire placed little Helgi in her cradle. Surprisingly, the child cried not at all but lay looking up at her mother, intelligent eyes wide open, brilliant for all their tiny-ness. In the shadowed light, those eyes seemed questioning and lively and Claire knew why she had not run to Eadric with the news of Wulfhere's dark treachery. Then, Claire felt her master's hands upon her waist and reluctantly, turned to face him.

"The child," she murmured as Wulfhere began kissing her throat, giving her gooseflesh with his unshaven beard bristles. Twas useless to protest, she knew. If she submitted, there was the chance that he would be merciful in his use of her; if she resisted, he would beat her until she either gave in or was unconscious. She felt her robe snatched from her hips, leaving her naked, and she knew herself mastered. It was a woman's ill fate, she thought. It was wrong, but men were always stronger. And eager to use that strength. She wondered momentarily at the unfathomable wisdom of God to create life such as this that existed. She wondered at the feeling of helplessness that made her shiver. And she wondered as she always did when he took her, why she did not let him kill her instead?

With a sigh, she let the fight go out of her as his searching lips found hers, she tasting the wine upon his breath sourly but feeling the moist heat of his desire as well.

"If you inform upon me, I will flay the skin from your back with a whip before I kill you!" was the last thing he whispered in her delicate ear before he took her. Then, smiling down at her, he lifted her trembling body in his arms and carried her to their bed.

A DAY LATER WHEN THE SUN WAS HIGH AND MERCILESS IN AN UNCLOUDED sky, a dust-covered rider pounded into camp and threw himself down from the saddle, stumbling and laughing before Eadric the Wild himself. It was Jagi, of course. And he played his role well. "My jarl! You were right! We are saved! I have secured four trade ships that have just disembarked Frankish soldiery and were about to return home! They will carry us wherever we wish; all they require is half fare before we leave! They come this eve!" He turned to the thronging camp and waved his hands in the air. "We are saved! We are rescued! The jarl has saved us!" he shouted.

The cheers went up. Warriors brandished their weapons and hot, dry mouths croaked out Odin's blessings upon their jarl and upon the courageous Jagi for his part in the mission.

Only Eadric Siwardsson did not smile, there in the unshaded sunlight. His eyes were piercing as he studied the captain, now drinking deeply from a wine pouch. There was something wrong, something very wrong here.

There was a general acclamation of congratulations from a sea of eager, sweaty faces surrounding him, warrior's faces now beaming with a childlike pleasure; their many prayers had been answered. All shouted for Odin, Eadric, and Jagi! But the Siwardsson continued to gaze at his dark-faced captain with thinly disguised skepticism, though he dared not dampen the spirit of the ecstatic crowd.

He knew well enough as their leader that there were times when even false hope was better than none, for now, at least. They all needed something to celebrate, something to take their minds from the torture of their arid prison. After all, his clan had been through and participated in, they needed a change of mind, some refreshment to their frame of reference. And it was possible that Jagi really had found such ships, perhaps ones recently emptied of their cargoes. And perhaps the Franks were looking for easy wages on their return trip.

Possible, but not very probable, he realized. He made a conscious effort to dispel the hope he felt choking his own throat with emotions. It was all too neat; Odin never worked miracles like this, at least not for Eadric Siwardsson.

He had sent Jagi out for the reason Wulfhere had guessed—to buy time. He, himself, believed that there were no ships, but it was hard to judge. Even at his age, it was easy to fall prey to wishful thinking, and was not Wulfhere embracing Jagi the Dark with the happiness of a brother, wild with happiness as the rest were? Or was Wulfhere too happy with the turn of events? Eadric cursed his own indecision. Now more than ever, he needed his ability to differentiate fact from suppositions. Was there a trap somewhere? But how could such a trap come about? They would all board the ships together and Eadric would make certain that he had Pigfeet ride the ship with the gold or should it be spread among all the ships? Along with trusted axe men? Where then could his plan go awry? Unless there were no ships…

But why such a charade? Damn! Damn! The change in fortune was all too sudden. But in all his suspicions, it never entered Eadric's mind that Wulfhere would seek the death of his own sire. Gold was worthy of any treachery he had learned, but murder in his tight-knit clan of warriors? No, that could never happen.

Still, there was something that nagged at him. All his life, Eadric had lived from day to day, outwitting both the gods and fate. Never had he prospered so by a gift from the powers that be, for he was convinced that if Odin felt the emotions of man, then he must be jealous of Eadric's success in war and his noble bearing. Well…he could do naught but watch and wait.

The next four hours were spent in feverish preparation. All of the tents, including Eadric's of royal-colored silk, were abandoned along with the still-flying standard of the emperor that Eadric sported out of sheer perversity. In a fit of wry humor, he had placed it in the center of the camp for all to spit upon, him foremost. Now, it hung stiff in the wind, molded crudely by the Wild's expectorations. Then, came all the miscellaneous hardships and goodbyes that the leaving entailed; he had to summon several of his men from the village where they had been adopted by the families of several marriage-minded maidens, maidens no more. He had to pay off the families of several more whose girls were now carrying sturdy Saxon bastards and one odd fellow he even acceded to leave behind by the man's own request. Left with the man was his share of the gold which undoubtedly made him the richest man in Vechut. If he was not caught by the emperor, Eadric shrugged. Or bandits. Or Franks. But to deny another man his pleasures… He was the last one regardless of how impractical the situation might be.

Then, there was the preparation for the feast to mark their leaving, for these stout warriors passed no grand occasion without a feast. Wulfhere understood all of this and had known all along how Eadric could be undone. This celebration was Wulfhere's idea, met with general agreement, though. Eadric, for once, would have just as well been on his way for the coast. But the clan was joyous this eve, tomorrow would see salvation and comfort; tomorrow would see them on their way home. As Wulfhere said, they would never tread this bitter, yellow-brown soil again; let them give thanks. And they did. Mightily.

In truth, it was never overly hard to persuade Eadric the Wild to drink and no one was any happier to be leaving the Holy Land than the wild one, for all his guarded optimism. So, what remaining goats they had were slaughtered and the last of the wine ration turned out. A makeshift table of gold chests with a throne of the same for Eadric, of course, was erected in the center of camp and ornately decorated with the trappings of royal service that had been salvaged from the shipwreck: cloths and scarves of purple, red and blue, richly embroidered flags of the Empire (now used as tablecloths and napkins), and golden serving vessels honorably filched from the Emperor Alexis's own kitchen before sailing.

Torches and fires were lit. Songs were bellowed into the coming darkness. They were free! Free!

Despite the heat of the last of the sun, the clan sat and drank about the tables, ate and drank, talked and drank, sang and drank, and on and on. Naturally, the topic of conversation was unanimous, how to spend gold. No one took note that a certain twenty of the men and all of their women and children were served from a special wine cask, nor did even these selected persons understand. Jagi and Wulfhere had chosen them at the setting of the smoldering sun and would tell them they were selected to go when the rest of the camp was unconscious. If they refused the treachery to remain loyal to Eadric, there would be enough out of the group to slay them for their share of the gold. But Wulfhere had chosen his men carefully; he thought there would be no fools among them.

Wulfhere was fabulously sociable with his sire, so much so, that the great red-beard should have surely suspected. But Eadric was drunk, so drunk that by now he did not even recognize his son when Wulfhere personally poured him four flagons of wine, cursing the old man silently for not falling over with each one. Odin! How the old bastard could drink! Why the mild poison should have rendered him unconscious hours ago, but such was the strength of his system that still he sat upright, laughing and drinking with the rest.

Exasperated, Wulfhere suggested they go to his tent, ostensibly to take a look at the gold pieces and vessels that Eadric was keeping for himself. Eadric mumbled something darkly as he shrugged his way through the oddly heavy tent flaps, into the sweaty dusk of his own unlit pavilion. He appeared somewhat bored as Wulfhere, seemingly in slow motion, unpacked gold bracelets and crowns of gem-encrusted silver from mighty chests. Eadric found the rippling motions of his toes inside his boots to be vastly more interesting as he moved them; the notion sent ripples coursing through his body heavily and up to his drunken mind. Eadric the Wild let out a short giggle.

And Wulfhere knew his sire was past the point of discovering the plot. Still, ever cautious, Wulfhere allowed Eadric to turn for a lamp beside his couch, and as he did so the Reaver deposited the remains of his powder into Eadric's goblet.

Eadric smiled as the Reaver proposed another toast. And downed his drink. But a frown furrowed its way across the red-beard's face as Wulfhere threw back his head and laughed a laugh of purest evil. Eadric's piggy eyes fought the glaze that covered them and dry lips worked noiselessly as he stared at the dregs of his wine.

Then he knew. Even through the drunken haze of wine, Eadric, ashen-faced, struggled for his sword. But meaty hands were leaden and uncooperative and he could not free the tool.

Wulfhere sneered as he watched his leader fall, spittle bubbling from the corners of his mouth. And again, he laughed.

8

CHAPTER THE EIGHTH

Time and fate move in odd directions, never failing to complement each other. A man may outlast his time but it has never been said that a man can truly avoid his fate. He may reap the obvious rewards or escape the punishments of his actions from time to time, but in the end, it is all the same. Each of us, in reality, plods on through time's days unmindful of what the end result will be. But it is always there, always just over the hill in the next sunrise or around the next corner in the coming dusk, until the man runs out of hills to climb or corners to turn and he usually sees where time has taken him, always to his regret. The face of destiny is, at best, a terrible thing.

During these months of intrigue, deception and chicanery that were daily occurrences for Eadric Siwardsson, he searched first for a way to deprive the Emperor Alexis of his gold, and then searched equally diligently for a way to escape with enough of his hide intact to spend the great wealth. Meanwhile, there was another search half-a-world away, a search no less desperate for all the fact that it was for a single person rather than staggering wealth. But that is wrong, for it too, was a search for riches but only as those few who think with their hearts could understand.

As the Saxons moved about the splendid cities of the East, a half-frozen duo traced the chilled villages and fortresses of the North, never halting for more than a night, always asking the villagers about a band of legendary outlaws...and a woman. The people of the North were friendly and each night the pair were welcomed to sit at a new fire where there was feasting and laughter. But always the laughter stilled a little when they saw the hard set to the one stranger's jaw and the unthawed hatred in his eyes as he spoke of his seeking. There was a hint of bitter madness there, a tale of a wrong long left unpunished and a love long left unconsummated. Such a man was dangerous for he could not be reasoned with. His companion with trim features, curled his lips in contemptuous amusement and never failed to drink himself into a stupor.

These two were markedly out of place, if not out of time. What business could a rogue English knight have in the frozen whiteness of the North? A woman? A woman, by Odin?! Phaw! More likely some intrigue to do with the Viking raiders and the kings of the English coast. And what of this knight's companion, this man of thin smile and dark eyes who rarely opened his mouth, save to drink or threaten?

No, there was more to it then was being said and the shriveled old hags of the camps, the ancient wives thick in both wisdom and superstition, prided themselves that they were being instrumental in opening up the entire coast of England for Viking conquest. What jarls this knight had left behind him he did not say, but his importance was easy to tell from the dagger he bore, the one embossed with the runes of Olaf, son of Goll, a mighty jarl whose name was not spoken lightly even in these cliffs. The dagger was a magic key for Geoffrey in every town or village, for it marked him as one of trust. But oddly enough, it was not until Geoffrey loaned the dagger to Guvi, who had lost his own, that he achieved the results he had longed for these frustrating months.

Geoffrey pounded down the narrow, winding path onto the plateau that had shimmered grassy-green in the frigid sunlight and was dotted with buff circles of bare earth where tents and rickety cabins had been. A few of the more solid buildings still stood, made of roughhewn logs with roofs of tanned and tarred hides. The plateau itself nestled secretively between several mountains and terminated at its open side, in a high cliff overlooking a fjord hundreds of feet below them. The height dizzied

Geoffrey as he stared down into the waters and he laced his fur jerkin tighter against the unbroken wind. *It had been a well-planned camp, imminently defensible and secure from attack, the fortress of a skilled warrior and his soldiers,* Geoffrey thought. *Hundreds of soldiers from the size of it. It was the camp of the Siwardsson, God rot his bones.* This he was sure of.

Guvi was not so certain, but then it was of no real consequence to him. All things considered, he would prefer to avoid the outlaws. For months, he had tracked down and analyzed the stories of the wild Saxon for this knight who had saved him from certain disaster, and with each story his apprehension of Eadric Siwardsson grew until the bandit was an ogre to be reckoned with. Once Guvi had grown irritated at Geoffrey's unswerving obstinacy and stopped their ride to ask, "Here now, friend knight. We ride and ride and for what end? What will you do when we find this Siwardsson and he is surrounded by his minions?"

Geoffrey's gaze then would have melted steel. "Kill him!" the knight said. There was no plan, no caution, this mad knight simply intended to run this Saxon, the greatest of all bandits, into the open as he would a hare and kill him in front of an army of enemies.

Guvi's lips formed out a small, "Ohhh..." and they rode on in silence. All Englishmen were insane, no? Of this, he was convinced. And to think it was still because of him that they had found the outlaw's trail! Sometimes, this knight's earnestness could affect a fellow's reason.

It was Guvi who, with Olaf's dagger, had persuaded an old woodcutter to dispense his information, facts which he had originally tried to sell to the honest knight.

Geoffrey had offered the old bastard the remains of his silver, causing Guvi to stare aghast at him at the unjust-ness of the situation. What? Spend the silver on some silly old fool when it was just es easy to clobber him one on the noggin? The idea of it! But Geoffrey was adamant until the little shriveled churl set his thrice wrinkled jaw, ancient eyes flinty, and held out for more. He could sense how badly Geoffrey needed to hear his story.

Exasperated, Geoffrey offered him their food and drink, causing an audible gasp to escape Guvi's tightly pinched lips. Then he offered him his horse. Guvi muttered and fingered Olaf's blade.

But the churl held out for more silver. One couldn't spend food and they needed few horses here in the North, he advised.

Guvi had had more than enough and as Geoffrey argued with the man, he thrust the dagger into the campfire and heated it until the runes on the blade glowed gold against a fiery red. Approaching stealthily, he jammed the sizzling blade against the man's buttocks and looped an arm about the man's frail throat at the same time.

"You refuse our food, friend, but I tell you truly that if words are not spoken quickly now, I will make you a present of your own roasted arse. Though, I'm sure the meat is tough and stringy, you robbing shit!" Guvi cooed softly into the peasant's white-fringed ear. The heat of the blade coming through his smoldering pants said the rest.

Good fellowship seized the old woodcutter and he told Geoffrey in graphic detail all that he knew of a camp high in the mountains, and when he was through, he refused to accept any silver as his reward, though Geoffrey would have willingly given it. Guvi offered to escort the man through the darkness to the trail, for the mountain could be treacherous at night. The woodsman vigorously protested this especial kindness but Guvi would not hear his protestations and with an arm about the fellow's shoulder walked him from the light of the campfire toward the sloping mountain trail. There was an instant of silence before Geoffrey distinctly heard the sound of a boot striking something firm but yielding, a short cry, and the sound of something rolling over and over down the gravel of the trail.

Guvi returned, whistling cheerily and winked at Geoffrey. "What better way to pay a man than in his own currency?" Guvi asked, sagely, and sat down for another drink. Geoffrey watched through half-closed eyes as the Finn idly massaged the toes of his right foot as he drank. By now, the dagger was Guvi's prized possession with its deep blood track and runic message, and Geoffrey stood in Eadric's camp, finally. A fair trade. Perhaps even a bargain.

But now the information was academic for the camp was deserted, long such, by the looks of the place. There were not even ashes remaining in the fire pits, for the wind and the rain had long separated them from the earth. Time's bony fingers had sifted through the remains of the mountain fortress and had cast much back to the sea and soil.

Geoffrey could not determine how long ago they had left, save that it was over a month and that they obviously had no intention of returning.

He tied Chestnut to one of the buildings, now sagging crazily in disrepair, and wandered slowly through the windswept area. Here and there, broken or discarded cooking pots and utensils or broken weapons cluttered the grass, only passing reminders of the presence of man here.

Geoffrey felt as if he were choking inside. *How long would you torment me, God? How long would you continue to mock me?*

Guvi said nothing, touched by his comrade's anger.

The Norman kicked in a planked door to the main house, dislodging a flock of frightened birds nesting inside and warily entered the darkened structure. Stale odors crawled out of every corner to assail him and he coughed at the stench. The only light came through the great rents in the hide ceiling, but it was enough to see by. Overturned log benches lay everywhere, some closely around sturdy heavy tables with the largest of each drawn to one end of the long, low-ceilinged room, the table of the Siwardsson himself, no doubt. Small scurrying, squeaking things ran through the shadows at his feet.

Slowly, Geoffrey walked over to the table of the bandit chieftain and gazed solemnly at its ale-and-wine-stained surface that had once held food for the leader and his family. Would Claire have eaten here? Had the Saxon taken her for his own? What of this son he had heard of, the son of Eadric who the Vikings called the Reaver? Had he been the one…?

Damn! Damn all creation! This was not how it was supposed to have ended! He was supposed to find them sitting around here drinking and laughing and he was to appeal to their courage and honor and fight the Siwardsson in a duel and free her.

Odin, but what was the price of death now? This was so much worse that he felt he could not stand beneath its weight. This was not how it was supposed to have ended. But then, a man always loses when he tries to outguess his own fate, even for the most noble of reasons.

He brought his sword crashing down upon the table and snarled as it flew to splinters. He roared blindly as he kicked the pieces from his path and then was suddenly still, weary, overcome now with the accumulated fatigue of months of frustration and searching. He kicked aside a final bench and entered the private quarters of the Siwardsson and his family, a small series of cluttered, stinking rooms centered about a long hall, one man wide. He found what he took to be the leader's chamber for it had the largest floor area and the best, most heavily built sleeping platform covered with an incredibly-stained cloth mattress of gull feathers and furs. But there was little else remaining to mark the habits of the occupant.

Then, he sighted a slightly smaller, though ample-sized chamber at the far end of the hall. Geoffrey found another bedroom with a similar bed, also lavishly furnished, though not as much so as the first, in keeping with custom and rank in the family. And upon the bed he found something that made his heart pound even harder with a sick, furious foreboding. There was a pile of discarded furs and rough clothes, obviously no longer desirable to the one who dwelled here, and among them was a soiled dress of green homespun that Geoffrey recognized at once. He turned it gently in his hands; the back was ripped as if by a whip, into a pattern of slits. Several of the slits had bloodstains upon them. There was no longer rage, nor hope, nor even passion. He was dead inside.

So here she had dwelt, had she? Here were her sufferings. And God was either an evil schemer or a doddering incompetent. For long minutes, he gazed at the dusty, perspiration-stained bedding and wondered who had claimed her beauty. Apparently, it was one of Eadric's family from the chamber. His son? The man called the Reaver, said to be a great warrior, and monstrously merciless?

Yes, the benevolent sire brings home a present for his son and the future jarl of the clan, a toy to while away the cold nights, a woman ripped from some other man's life.

It was too much to hope for, to expect to find this Reaver. Geoffrey held the dress in tight hands, turning it over and over although his eyes did not see it; they were full of visions of the woman who had once worn it and cared for him. He held the dress to his chest, torn and bloodied.

While he was pondering this, the door banged open and his

companion strode in noisily, rupturing the bubble of Geoffrey's daydreams. "Anything worth taking?" he asked callously, or at least it sounded so to Geoffrey.

Without turning, the knight shook his head sadly. "Nay, naught save perhaps this, friend Guvi."

"That rag?" the Finn asked in amazement. "Huh?"

Geoffrey gave an immensely sad, but at the same time, beatific smile as though he held the shroud of Christ in his hands. He tore off a strip of the rough material and wound it about the cross-guard of his blade carefully entwining the cloth so that the last wrap displayed the marks of her blood in a brown strip about the grip and blade.

Guvi smiled sarcastically at the hard knight's sentimentality. "Will it aid your stroke in battle, friend Norman? If magic it be, then I must have a strip of the cloth for my own weapon!"

Geoffrey stared at the cloth, not speaking.

Guvi shrugged and nosed about the chamber, grinning broadly as he found a small coin beneath a rug, overlooked in the departure.

Geoffrey's voice came as if from far away. "Nay, Guvi. The magic works only for me."

Together, they exited the lodgehall, the Finn pacing behind as Geoffrey strode toward cliff's edge. His heart and mind laden with more emotions than he could speak. He stood silent, looking over the peaceful waters of the fjord.

"Don't jump," Guvi suggested.

"What!" Geoffrey thundered, turning livid with rage that was not all Guvi's doing.

"Well…" stammered the Finn, "isn't that what all you lost lovers do? I mean, I just don't want to be left here…"

"You dog's arse, you simpering bastard!"

Guvi shrugged, "I just meant we are friends."

"I know," said Geoffrey lowly, "I know, friend."

How long had it been since Eadric the Wild's ship had lodged there?

The wind was chilly but the sky clear and blue, making the mountains so beautiful. The horizon was lined with a drifting array of wraith-like fleece and Geoffrey saw mountainsides that seemed miles away from his vantage point. It was a wondrously tranquil setting, the sea, the open sky. It was a scene to send a man's soul flying free with the swooping gulls, yet Geoffrey retained a stark leadenness within himself. Memories he could not escape fettered him to the ground. Where was she now?

Guvi seemed to have read his whirling mind. "The old man mentioned that the camp had packed up and gone seaward, though I took it as an excuse in case his information proved false and he still wished to have his life.

"Where to?" whispered Geoffrey, a hard lump in his throat. "It took us so long to find this place."

The Finn spread his hands wide in apology. "He did not know. There are many stories, but one never knows who to listen to. Perhaps your friend felt this area was too well known for him anymore. Perhaps he smelled richer rewards elsewhere. Who can say?"

Geoffrey was silent again. The wind whistled mournfully through a crevice in the rocky ledge; a gull chased another past the two.

At last Guvi spoke, "Where will you seek her now?"

Geoffrey half-sighed, half-cursed. "Where shall I seek her? Why, it would be just as easy to seek her in the clouds and wind. Nay, I think this is an omen of my fate, for there is no path to follow from here. I think my quest is finally ended. She is gone and taken with her my heart and my honor as well; but these gifts to her I willingly and knowingly give. And do you know, Guvi, for her, I would have given more and never thought the less of it. But she has vanished in this land of frozen earth, gone from me what must be forever unless the fates will differently. But I have done all that I can think of to do and cannot say where I will go now. I cannot return to Westwall for my family thinks me a traitor, a shame-filled wretch who has lost his last vestige of honor in a chase after dreams, mere smoke-filled illusions in the air as castles built out of clouds. Strange, how real they seemed to me."

"What illusions!" Guvi spat into the wind. "So, you loved a woman a little too much and wanted the man who had taken her. This camp shows that we might just as well have found them all, and, in this moment, you could have fulfilled your dream and been lying here dying with her weeping for you." Guvi smiled sardonically. "But dreams? This was no dream; your reasons are odd, I must say, but the logic of your chase was fair.

"And honor?" continued the Finn, "who knows what honor really is? You speak to me of not having it, yet in my eyes, you behave so honorably as with that fool woodcutter, that you embarrass and disgust me! But still, though I pity you for your cramping code, as your friend, I would advise you that where such is lost, if it is, then it is possible to be found again if you but look for it."

Geoffrey smiled sadly. "You speak as if it were but a ring."

"No, it is less to me than a ring. I turned the phrase wrongly."

"Stillness of the tongue is not your problem, knave. But I see now; I think you are right. Perhaps I can be true to my country and king after all."

"Not to mention your father," muttered Guvi.

"How say you?"

"Nothing, friend knight," smiled Guvi. "I was but wondering where you thought to find this gold for the soul."

"Ere I left, the storm clouds of war were gathering in the Holy Lands. Father said it all to me, the speech for king and for country. But there will be fighting and gold and honor for some."

"And death for many," added the Finn thoughtfully. "But tell me of this gold to be had!" He was oblivious to all but one thought. Guvi stroked his narrow beard in thoughtful anticipation.

"Aye, for some fortunate ones. Perhaps such as we two."

"Ah, gold. Lovely, bright, delicious, shining precious metal," sighed the knight's companion. "If I knew there was enough gold there, I could stick my thumbs up my arse and run there on my elbows!"

"I think there is an easier way to travel, if I am not mistaken," said Geoffrey dryly.

"But there is gold, mountains of gold?" asked Guvi anxiously.

"They say so."

"Then there is certainly enough to go around that we might be included! Are we agreed, my dearest friend, my protector, to set our course for the East? You, for your wretched honor, and I for my lovely gold?" Guvi inquired, laughing.

Geoffrey stood silent, watching a line of clouds drift past the sun, first masking, then revealing in a small pageant of nature. This seemed to him to be his fate, his personal fate if not that of all men, that it was far easier to find war and bloodshed, while love remained distant and ever elusive. And honor? His only path to regain honor was again through war, it appeared. What he had taken for granted with the acceptance of his gilded spurs, he now saw the full price of.

The trumpets always moved him, and the heraldry, the pageantry, and the martial music, as they did all men of his time. But he had to force himself to kill, deep down. It all seemed so senseless to the philosopher side of Geoffrey. Intelligence and introspection often brought guilt.

He put the feelings aside. He was a warrior in an era of warriors. And he was fearsome in battle. Why not travel to the war's reward in the Holy Land? There was land and property to be taken, gold and power to be gained. Could he not find solace enough in these material things, as the greedy Finn did? Bah! Money could buy any amount of women, he knew. He could have his choice; he could satiate his lust instead of his love.

But it was his second choice, he knew. Phaw! It was the only choice he had left himself. He was fed up with dreams. The seeking was ended; let God keep her safe now, he could not.

There was no way left to turn, no more running and aggravating his conscience. Let them ride to the East and salvation of his soul, of his conscience of high honor. He would find his father's Englanders and join them for the march.

Cynical though he felt at this point, it was for none of these imminently logical reasons that he nodded his head to Guvi's question. Rather, it was some instinctive feeling within his bones, deep set and certain, that made him opt for this course. Did he sense destiny drawing near? Or was it merely the remnants of his murdered faith, heaving about in their final death throws?

No matter what it was, exactly, that stirred him into decision and action; it was done. He nodded and turned with a feeble smile to his friend. "But here your pay ends, you conniving rogue. You are no longer my guide. We travel as equal companions and comrades, for my purse is as empty as your hard, cold heart!"

Guvi snorted in mirth at the supposed insult. "You call me avid, friend. Yet, are we all not so? Tis only a matter of some small difference in what each of us longs for, is it not? My greed is centered about a small variety of matters, while yours is an uncommon type, that is, it is centered about another person. But I can see by your actions that of us both, it is you who are, by far, the more avaricious.

"But I do not deny this. I will take everything that's coming to me and more if I can get it without getting hanged or hamstrung. But you want past the point of wanting; you are obsessed, bewitched. The feelings that drive you control you; you do not control them. I am merely a thief; if I can take twice my share, I will. But if I fail to, I merely shrug away a silent tear and wait for the morrow. Obsession is frightening. Its denial cracks the very bones with agony and gives a first taste of what death for a sinner will be like."

"Spare me your theology, Guvi!"

"I have seen you pushed to the limits of your body in this hunt and your patience as well. Do you remember how you had the food sickness and finally heaved your blood up with your bile? And still you rode on, not wanting to lapse even a day. You are an iron-willed bastard, that I must say. And I have seen you fight; you are terrifying. But what does this all amount to, my friend knight? You have driven yourself to near disaster, for what? For what?"

"Have you never felt love, then?" the Norman asked quietly.

The Finn tossed his head in a noncommittal gesture. "One man's love is another man's lust," he said.

"Then you think it is lust that drives me as I am driven?"

Guvi gave the suggestion an instant of thought. "Nay, tis not so simple for you to want to feel her stuffed with your manhood. Would that it were. But it is no less a desire for possession than that. Methinks you underestimate the power of lust; look what it has done for the Vikings on the English coast."

Geoffrey shook his head, a slight smile creasing his lips. "You err, friend, I cannot say why it is that I am driven, yet I know it is not such a selfishness."

"There is not all that much wrong with being selfish!" said Guvi, haughtily. "Selfish people tend to outlast generous."

"Indeed?"

"Indeed!" spat Guvi. "But since you broached the subject, I shall explain my view to you on love!"

"Please do!" murmured Geoffrey, making a sarcastic bow.

"For all its facade of nobleness, all love is selfish because, if for no other reason, it is an emotion of man who is, you might have noticed, a selfish animal." Guvi waved his comment away. "You may deceive yourself and you may also deceive others."

"I have noticed," laughed Geoffrey, thinking of his friend.

Guvi continued, "But if you strip away the guise of nobility you will notice that want alone is the solitary motivation. Any unselfishness shown is in spite of love's basic nature, not because of it. People are fools is what it distils down to. They run after dreams and false hopes that they need to mask the bitter taste of real life. But pity them when their dreams are realized for they realize then just how hollow their illusions are and they collapse inside. The more they firmly believe in the dream, the more poisonous the aftertaste of realization!"

"Then my aftertaste would be especially potent if I were to find her and free her for myself, say you?" asked Geoffrey with a crooked smile.

Guvi scowled. "You say it true. The only lucky ones in this life are the ones who die without seeing their dreams turn to ashes before their eyes! She would have grown fat as a cow on you and ended up sleeping with the stable boys when you were off on the hunt."

"And what of your dreams for gold and power, my friend?" smiled Geoffrey, sure he would make his point.

Guvi eyed him suspiciously, stroking his beard again. "You mistake dreams for realistic objectives. Your wants are firmly rooted in reality and ever shall be. You'll not find me heartbroken over a few gold coins or a parcel of land."

"Finding the heart would be the largest quest, determining if it were broken would be easy."

Guvi smiled and nodded sagely. "That is as it should be. Emotion is an inconvenience at best."

The Norman laughed into the North wind. "Then how might the uneducated, as myself, understand the difference betwixt dreams and objectives, my Finnish sage, oh magic lad of the heart and mind, oh holder of untold secrets?" Geoffrey asked snidely.

"'Tis more simple than I can say; objectives are felt and lusted after by the mind. Dreams are felt in the heart."

"Bah!" stormed Geoffrey, striding back to Chestnut. "How can such a putrid fellow, such a thief and godforsaken villain pretend to understand a man's heart as well as his mind? You speak with much assumed wisdom for one who has dedicated his life to dishonesty."

"There is more wisdom in dishonesty than in keeping your God's commandments. It is a wicked world."

"Please," groaned Geoffrey, "spare me your further opinions."

"Perhaps it is because I am so wise that I have shed the moral skin mankind imposes upon himself, at least civilized man. In the end, even the noblest of men is less than the lowest animal. Aye, human nature is corrupt inside; some merely hide it better than others."

Geoffrey turned in the saddle and laughed. "Then come, you pig. You with your selfish objectives and I with my selfish dreams of love and honor! Let us set our course for where all may be won, from salvation to women, and there we will find ever so much to test out your black theories on the pettiness of our existence!"

Guvi grinned broadly and mounted. "Aye, friend Norman! Perhaps I will convince you how much more sensible and pleasurable, as well, objectives may be than dreams!"

"God grant that you can, friend. Dreams hurt too much to do any good," muttered Geoffrey as the two turned their horses for the mountain trail at the plateau's edge. There, it wound down miles and miles of treacherous gravel and rock to the coast where they might find a ship.

PART II

BOOK THE SECOND - THE FIND

9

CHAPTER THE NINTH

Geoffrey leaned against, and sometimes over, the ornately carved rail of the rocking tub of a vessel and appraised the coast as he had been warned to do. It was little help. The damned horizon seemed to dance up and down in his bloodshot gaze and the troll within his stomach started kicking again. Ah! It was always the same! Give him a horse anytime where only the saddle rocked and the ground remained firm beneath his feet, instead of this eternally wretched sea where the very stuff beneath a good knight's feet jumped and fell in the most appalling of motions. But between his libations to the sea gods he had time to wonder at the beauty of this dry climate.

The sun was hot overhead but the wind pleasantly cool from the sea. The sky gleamed a brilliant blue, bluer than he had ever seen it, it seemed, and his entire surroundings seemed crisper, more sharply focused in the clear, clean air. It was not what he had been told to expect, but he assumed that the horrible deserts were inland, carefully hidden behind this alluring coast. The horizon was ever changing toward land and totally enchanting with its hillsides of baked brown and dull green and the small whitewashed villages along the coastal roads. As they passed through the water that their captain called Antalya's Gulf, Geoffrey saw the tall peaks of the Taurus Mountains that were visible all along the coast and noticed how they seemed to move toward the sea where the land butted out into the Mediterranean. His heart thumped loudly in his armored breast as he thought of where he was, sending the nausea fleeing for an instant as adrenalin shook his sword arm. Around that great bulge, he knew, he would find the Christian armies encamped, moving all the while for Tarsus in a steady churning-out of armored columns. This was where he thought to find them.

Along the steep hills, the young Norman saw herds of goats wandering and, here and there, the isolated call of an anxious goatherd floated down to the seacoast. Everything was deceptively peaceful for a land just recently at war but paralyzed with a savage clashing of major armies, nevertheless. There was evidence of the war, however, as they passed a boat full of sponge divers, rowing their flat-bottomed craft close to the shore. Then he saw three others in the near distance, hesitant to put in at the sight of the passenger vessel. Geoffrey noticed that all of the divers were invariably boys just out of childhood, brown from the sun, standing dripping and naked in the slow dories. Their only guardians were several old men who sat, equally naked, in the growing heat of the sun. Geoffrey was tempted to remove his hot chainmail shirt, but he was not that naive. In it, he would drown if he went overboard, but in a battle, it would be, very probably, the difference between life and death.

All of the young men were either with the Red Lion or Islam, their soon-to-be-seen enemies, or serving the other side as Turcopoles of the Emperor Aexis. Impartiality was impossible in this land of fierce loves and even fiercer hatred; a man needed to choose, for to remain neutral meant that he was, in probability, a spy for one side or the other, and neither side was tolerant of such creatures. Better to fight and die beneath a banner, than to perish horribly in a dark chamber full of racks and thumbscrews, where men in black demanded information one probably never had. These were harsh times, breeding harsh men.

Both sides tortured their prisoners for information, though this was never publicized as both hosts had their own tradition of chivalry. While diplomats walked enemy camps and feasted, minor prisoners were buried in unmarked graves. It made Geoffrey's skin crawl.

Guvi approached him, lustily chewing a strip of dried beef and swilling noisily a flagon of heavy Turkish wine. Geoffrey gagged at the sight of nourishment and bent closer to the glimmering surface of the water.

"A right, fair day, friend!" announced the Finn, waving the flagon expansively out over the side, in the direction of land. "Good weather for sailing, eh, and eating? Have you tried the salt beef? Have you eaten at all, friend Norman?"

Geoffrey rubbed puffy eyes and glared at his comrade. "A rank plague upon you and your gluttonous belly both, you Finnish oaf! What devil has goaded you into tormenting me with your ill humor this wretched morning? Have you no decency?"

"None whatsoever!" snickered Guvi, smacking his lips with relish. Guvi laughed deeply, obviously enjoying his friend's predicament.

"Why, Idir the Captain suggested I see how you feel this morning. He seems to believe that you had a rough time of it last night, for some reason. Indeed, you kept me awake for some time with your soft-belly sounds; I cannot understand how one who has eaten so little still has so much in his gut to give up to the waves."

"Kiss my bare arse, swine," growled Geoffrey.

Guvi laughed again and guzzled the wine so that it ran down his chin and shirt. Disgusted, Geoffrey lost patience and moved to cast the Finn overboard but the sight of the running wine made him nauseous again and he raced to the rail, moaning.

"Well," observed his friend, "if the Saracens take us alive, I certainly hope they don't discover your aversion to water. Another voyage and you would've lost everything!"

Geoffrey's reply was lost in the sound of his retching.

"But rejoice, my friend!" Guvi smiled benignly. "You soft Norman lout, you soldier with the little girl's stomach, we will soon put into land again. Once we sight Silifke, Fat Idir swears by the Prophet's Tomb that he will put in no closer to Seljuk nor Christian camp as both opposing forces have ungraciously burned his vessel from under him in the past. It seems that the Fat One cannot convince anyone that he is but a simple businessman intent only upon his earnings and without political signifi-cance. Both sides see him as a traitor—the infidels because he is of their

God and yet ferries Christian soldiers along the coasts and your Christian Franks because he is a Moslem, and they trust no infidels. Odd how religion and goodwill cannot mix sometimes," mused Guvi.

"Odd, my arse!" muttered Geoffrey, wiping his mouth, "Idir is a smuggler and a slaver, not to mention thief. He but fails to conceal his motives from the rest of the world."

"Every man needs a vocation," said Guvi equitably. "Perhaps there is little money in shipping."

"Huh! Undoubtedly less than in smuggling ale and wine to thirsty Saracens, forbidden by their God to drink such."

"Well," began Guvi," If it's morals that..."

But Geoffrey was not listening. With the back of his hand, he finished wiping the foam from the corners of his mouth and pointed to a large port coming up. Vessels of every size clustered about the wharf that jutted forth from a long finger of land. The Norman's laugh was a shout and he snatched away Guvi's drink, draining the mug.

The Finn eyed him reproachfully but was loathe to end his first merriment.

"Silifke!" Geoffrey thundered. "At last! I had begun to think of myself as more a sailor than a horseman!"

"No danger of that!" sneered the Finn, good-humoredly. "Idir told me at last supper that if you lived to rival Methuselah, you would never make a pimple on a seaman's arse!"

Geoffrey swished a mouthful of drink around his mouth to collect the bitter taste there after many days of seasickness, spitting it all out into the sea.

"Hello! Hello!" Geoffrey called out to sailors on the dock in his joy.

"What are you doing?" asked Guvi casually. "That is not Silifke."

"But it is!" protested Geoffrey. "Do you not see the ships? We are off."

"Geoffrey, my friend, Silifke is an inland city on the river Goksu, not a seaport. I must say you are certainly uneducated in this geography."

There was a hoarse cry from Idir on the quarter deck, and then a flow of invectives accompanied by the crash of a jug against the mast behind Geoffrey's head. The Fat One stood, shaking his fist at the pair of them and pointed angrily at the port where they could see all sorts of sailors and dock workers frozen in amazement, staring at the vessel of Idir.

"What did he say?" asked Geoffrey, puzzled.

"He said that you are less than the seed of a castrated camel in addition to several comments about your mother, and he wonders greatly that you do not heed the red pennant with the silver crescent upon its flying over the port, one of the flags of Islam. He says further that you will be the death of him yet, fool that he is for carrying two Franks beneath the nose of..."

"Spare me his tears!" grated Geoffrey, watching as Idir shouted gruffly at the sailors on the dock and pointed expansively at Geoffrey and Guvi.

"He tells them he has two Franks bound for the torture chambers of the Lion of Islam and that he will display our heads only when he passes this way again."

Geoffrey paled slightly. "How much longer am I to endure this purgatory of bobbing land and drunker idiots? When will we be off at Silifke?"

"I told you, not 'off at Silifke,' dolt. But we should soon see it, perhaps tomorrow. It is an interesting place, I hear. Once loyal to the Lion of Islam, also called the Red Lion, but with the sweep of your Franks along the coast, all the garrison there was transferred to the citadel of Tarsus which will certainly soon be besieged."

Geoffrey gazed skeptically at his companion. "And the people?" he asked. "Where lies their loyalty?"

Guvi laconically flipped a gold piece in the air so that, in the sunlight, it shimmered dully. The message was obvious. Like Captain Idir, the people were merchants first and heathen fanatics second.

Geoffrey nodded. "Aye! I will feel safe enough as long as we have full purses. I suppose the loyalty of man to gold is a loyalty not easily shaken, as those to religion."

Guvi nodded quietly. "Every man can be bought. It is a question only of the price and the way the price is presented. The merchants of Silifke, their moral—have a lower price than the others. Some must be bought discreetly so that they are not shamed by the offer and forced to reject it;

therefore, the price must be sufficiently high. I wonder what your price is, friend Geoffrey."

"You have already seen it, Finn." Geoffrey scowled. "But silence now, for you make me uneasy with your talk of deception and treachery. These people invented them both!"

"They were not invented, friend. Man crawled out of the slime with these instincts foremost in his plotting mind."

Then they stood without speaking for a while, watching as the coast passed with monotonous fluid motion.

Silifke was a small river port nestled very securely inland about ten miles or so from the mouth of the Goksu in the Mediterranean. Sullen-eyed villagers, swarthy and stinking in the heat, watched the Franks disembark in sour disapproval. They had had a belly full of Christians by this time, these strange men armored under a scorching sun with their words of repentance and brotherhood and their hearts full of rape and rapine. Men of God? Ha!

Many were the times these same Frankish knights that knelt before their Sunday altars raced down the narrow streets on their mighty destriers, hooves churning the dirt into dust and sweaty horsehide hurling bystanders into walls, overturning market stands and snatching up the prettiest of the girls to spend an afternoon with. How many times had the village's small, harmless mosque been pulled down, only to be rebuilt? Had these Moslems, these peaceful traders as with others, earned the right to hate the sign of the cross?

So, they hid their produce and horses and daughters whenever a sail was sighted, and only with much prodding and a display of gold or silver, could they be persuaded to open up their shops again. Such fear was a loathsome thing, Geoffrey thought. Men being pretty much the same the world over from his experience, he wondered if these particular men were such devils as to justify their punishments.

Did they really eat Christian babies? Did they really rape nuns? Geoffrey mentally compared these stories with what he had seen of the *Christian charity* of his own lands. Perhaps Guvi was right.

But still, he could not condone their fear, their uneasiness. Better to die in battle than to live in fear, as half a man. After all, did not cold death strike everyone equally in the end? Then what price honor, a few more years of living wretchedly? God knew he loved life enough and he was not one to cast it away lightly, but he was also young and full of pride. If he could not meet life head on and accept it as a gift, his own terms were not much better than a coward's. Were these men cowards?

But if the people were cowardly in their hatred of the Franks, they were at least helpful in the arrangement. Silver secured them provisions and water, enough for their mounts as well, for their journey. Idir directed them to a neutral caravan route but a mile south of Silifke. They had but to stay upon that route, the Fat One told them, and they would arrive in the Frank's camp, for by this time, the Christians now almost completely ringed the city of Tarsus. They controlled the roads about the city, yet it was thought possible to still skirt them if one wished to enter the walls. This was limited, however, as more and more Franks arrived daily from all over Europe and soon the net would be closed.

"Tell Idir that we thank him for the information but that when we enter this city, it will be at the head of the Christian host!" Geoffrey laughed.

Guvi smiled dreamily as he thought of the plunder.

Spoke Idir to Guvi in Arabic, "Have your master keep to the trail and in a long day you will pass through Vechut, then Erdemli, Tomuk, Mersin and if robbers have not slain you by this time on the trail, you will see the immense Frankish fleet at Kazanli. Most likely, though, you will meet your brothers long before this as they have moved their camp north of Mersin at Tarsus, last I heard. Be wary on the first part of your journey in particular, for although the caravan route is ostensibly neutral and openly without patrols, both bandits and the Emir's cavalry claim the land, neither group acknowledging the other, nor the Christian knights that thunder the trails in their dusty armor as if they have lived here for centuries! When you reach Vechut, it is best to skirt the village for it is certain the outlaws have spies within the town, reporting on those fit for plunder. You two do not give off the impression of obvious wealth, but around here, it is considered good to slay a Christian for no money at all, and anything that is fit for taking is a bonus. All the bandits are of my true faith and I advise you strongly to avoid the town and keep your fool heads. Anyway, all the girls are ugly there and the water bad," Idir ended with a grin.

Guvi raised an eyebrow at the knowledge Idir had not disclosed in his attempt to have them avoid Vechut. But the advice seemed sound, so there was no reason to pump him further. Idir was honest, for an Arab. Guvi punched him affectionately in the gut as he swung into the saddle.

Geoffrey had already mounted.

"Lust is blind, did you not know?" laughed the Finn.

Idir's eyes went hard. "Death is a blindness for eternity, Frank!" replied the usually good-natured Turk soberly. "Beware the desert people!"

"We shall, oh gigantic one. Worry not!"

Idir nodded and said something to Geoffrey in Arabic which the Norman took as a blessing but which Guvi later told him was a request to never book passage on his vessel again.

This finished, the fat captain was again benevolent to the two. "Now, ride. May Allah keep his hand over you as you ride, for remember that we are friends even though you are infidels and hopeless fools!"

"And may the fires of hell be only warming for you, you wretched Saracen who is also our friend! Farewell, oh Fat One! Live long," Guvi called as they rode into the wind. "Odin keep you."

"Aye," breathed Idir softly as the two rode off, so sure of themselves. "May all of our gods keep us in this time."

The scenery had changed now with the ride and Geoffrey began to perceive the truth behind the grim stories of this Holy Land. The sun seemed hotter and closer and the dust was dry and gritty in his mouth. For the entire day, the two plodded on in impatient slowness over the rutted trail, watching the horizon change, yet somehow remain the same. Geoffrey soon tired of the land, the bone-dry riverbeds and sparse patches of scrub underbrush blooming sporadically in the heat. The heat! It was all encompassing against the cloudless sky. Here and there, he saw the silent backdrops of far-off mountains, but he dearly missed the fresh, clean forests of his England and the soft mossy ground beneath the trees. But far more than this, he missed the delicious streams and running brooks with their reassuring babbling, and the first snows of winter.

It was so damnably hot in this heathen land and first was Geoffrey's observation that the Saracen infidels richly deserved this. Let them learn what hell must be like in the dead of winter, if winter it had.

Geoffrey was constantly thirsty, but he dared not drink as he wished, for in this land even the water was rationed. Drink today and die tomorrow. But he was consoled by the fact that Guvi the Finn seemed to be suffering even more so than he, being used to a colder climate. They both sweated and aged that miserable first day, slumped in the saddles with intense headache from the unaccustomed heat and stark dryness, and both too proud and too tough to mention it.

They smiled sardonically at each other, tongues stuck to the roofs of their mouths and their saliva thick and adhesive.

Night, which seemed long in coming with its brilliant sunset, was a different matter. Both smiled in relief as the sun dropped in the mountains painting the sky purple and red and halting the torturous glare of light reflected from buckle or even rock. The first tinge of coolness on the evening breeze was welcome, but all too suddenly turned chilling, a dangerous contrast to the day. Geoffrey dismounted with his teeth chattering.

They made camp just on the other side of Vechut, intent upon a quiet meal and cozy fire. But the night wind of the open desert was no small sprite in the legions of nature and before long both men were huddled in their fur capes, Guvi postponing Geoffrey's sleep with a never-ceasing array of curses delivered to the countryside and its wretched climate.

"Let it be either hot or cold! I care not which! But Odin save us from a land fickle as a woman's desires that cannot make up its mind and needs do both! Odin damn me if I do not die of the cold this night."

Geoffrey laughed lowly, staring at the fire. "Peace, old woman. Your native land was far colder."

Guvi spat into the fire. "Aye, but there one had his body fat to keep him warm. The day's heat has cost me dearly."

Geoffrey muttered dreamily, hypnotized into complacence by the soothing flames. "Rejoice, my dearest friend. We live. We breathe. We have a future in gold and glory. What more can a soldier ask for, comrade? Your thoughts on what might be otherwise will make you angry, if not mad. Life goes on and we go with it. Let us live for each day only and forget, except in dreams, what might have been."

Guvi sneered. "Sound advice, comrade. Easy to give, hard to take. When you can follow it yourself, then explain it to me. But you know as well as I that heart and mind do not often cooperate and that some needs cannot be so lightly sloughed aside. Let your own heart heal itself before you seek to heal mine!" The words were blunt, but the tone of them was not and Geoffrey smiled to himself at how easily Guvi read him.

Then Guvi discovered his first desert bedbug and concentrated his energy in that direction.

Geoffrey barely heard him. He was drifting rapidly, too exhausted by the environment and the ride, calmed in the solitude of the campfire. Man might try to emulate the efforts of the gods, but even the gods must sleep. Do the gods dream as well?

Suddenly it was hot again, and he was in his armor astride the warhorse. The landscape was that which they had covered the day before, but now he was alone and terrified. Something was wrong. He wanted his sword but it was stuck in its scabbard and he saw why. Thick, jelly-like and dark brown goo oozed from the scabbard and around the blades, making the surfaces sticky and glistening. It would not slide free, this fearsome blade.

Then there was that lilting woman's voice, urging him to flee. But, he could not. He gazed at the ground and saw, awe-stricken, skeletal hands worming their way through the sandy clay to grasp Chestnut's powerful hooves and hold them motionless. Geoffrey heard the hooves of a challenger's horse echo through his dream, though he could not yet see his stark foe. Then the sun exploded into the blackness of a million crows and he awoke screaming.

Guvi was there beside him, broadsword drawn and narrow eyes widening in surprise.

Geoffrey felt himself flush as he realized where he was. "My apology, Finn," he murmured.

Guvi eyed him strangely. "Who was he?"

"I do not know. Death, I think," said Geoffrey mildly, "He came for me...again."

"If I were Christian, I would cross myself to ward off the nightmare."

"How does a pagan do it?" inquired the knight.

"Here! Drink!" smiled the Finn with a wink as he shoved a flask into his friend's hands. Then they were silent for a long time.

WITH THE FIRST RAYS OF DAYBREAK CASTING THE RED SHADOWS OF fever across his swollen eyelids, Eadric the wild awoke, rolled over on his side with a thick gurgling grunt, and vomited painfully upon the terrace floor. Treachery!

"Thieves! Robbers! Whoresons! We've been plundered! Great God! You have cursed me to let me live to see this evil day when my own rotten son of a...Wulfhere! You bastard scum!" Eadric roared, holding his throbbing head. But cursing gave way to moaning as it only made the drum in his head beat louder. He would have bellowed for horse and sword but he was too ill to speak any further.

Thrice cursed by the gods is the fool! What had that conniving son of a doe's womb put into his goblet! Ah! The pig louse had not even had the decency to slay him and get it over with. Instead, he would leave him three-quarters poisoned to meditate his folly! Moaning mightily, he rolled onto his back again and threw one brawny, red-haired arm across his eye against the harsh light. His belly sickness was nothing. But his heart hurt worse than his head. That filthy pile of offal! *I began his life with my seed*, snarled Eadric to himself. *I will end it with my sword.*

Then he laughed. Wulfhere had learned only too well from his father. It was all so damnably clear to the down-at-heel bandit chieftain; for once he had let his drink get the better of him. It would have been so much wiser not to drink, and worst of all, he had known this from the beginning. Odin's arse, but he was a great lout of a fellow! How could he have ever thought that the weight of so much gold could ever be outweighed by mere familial relations? Sometimes, he wondered if he were not his own worst enemy, caught up in some morbid experiment in trying to test other men, Wulfhere in particular. Eadric sensed that it was useless to rise and pursue the thief. His own mind, long accustomed to treachery and double-dealing, found it easy to think through the plan of his traitorous offspring. Either the ships had come for him or they had not. If they had, then Wulfhere and the rest were merrily on their way to the Northland.

Perhaps Wulfhere had left horses that Eadric and his men might survive. Ha! Perhaps Odin himself thought to rescue the Siwardsson! Nay, it was another stupid thought, for these Saxons meant revenge if Eadric had to follow his own into hell for it. Wulfhere knew this.

And water. Now the son must've left them enough water for a few days—not enough to ensure survival, but enough for Eadric and the rest to ponder the magnitude of Wulfhere's deceit. To think how slow of wit they were.

He removed his arm from his eye to stare at the peg on the tent pole where the water bag always had hung. No water. No ships. It seemed clear that there were no ships, he reasoned with himself. Wulfhere and his vultures needed all of the water to run with the purloined gold for Tarsus. May the sands of the desert bleach his bones. But even a fox outsmarts himself sometimes.

Eadric wondered then if his son had not perhaps been too clever for his own safety. What if Eadric were right and Tarsus was being ringed in by the avenging Christians? Then Wulfhere the Reaver would be trapped in his own web! The red-beard smiled broadly at this pleasant thought and wished the nasty Franks good hunting and swift progress, a hunting he would have relished. But with no water and no horseflesh it was not likely that he would live to enjoy vengeance. How many had he left? Were they as crippled as he?

Wearily, Eadric the Wild turned himself over onto his rotund stomach, wincing at the cramps there, vomited, and crawled on hands and knees to the tent flaps.

Outside the dark pavilion, he heard a dull cacophony of moans and retching and the bandit knew that the hot sunlight had revived those of the rest that were fit.

Great God in Stormbringer! How his belly ached! The Siwardsson crawled into the full sunshine.

Ha! Apparently, Wulfhere had learned much more from his brigand father than anyone realized, if one were to judge from the effects of the poison on the rest of the band. And the gold was as long gone as the traitors. Ah, well.

The red-beard blew his nose noisily into shaking fingers, wiping his hand clean on his fur breeks, and, trembling with a temporary palsy, arose like some great red giant. The tent pole danced before him like some brazen hussy bent on teasing and curiously everything leaned sideways, like the rigging on a storm-tossed ship.

And odd it was that what had once been solid beneath his feet was slowly shifting waves, intent on sucking him back to their hot, dry caress. Wulfhere was a wizard to have wrought such change in nature! Thor's hammer! How his head pounded!

With a sigh, he blundered back into his open tent, tripped over his sword and landed upon a couch. Weakly, he sat there and poured himself what was once a bucket of ale, now lukewarm swill. Stranded and dying. he grimaced and gagged, intent on rubbing away the beads of icy sweat from his forehead. Suddenly, the sweat was gone but the ale he swallowed was on the floor. This was more serious than he had first suspected; when had a stout Saxon jarl lost his blessed ability to contain his ale?!

Ahhh! No mounts and no water! Gods! What a wretched fix he had gotten himself into! All he needed now was the wrath of the gods to take hold of him else...

"Saracens!" came a hoarse cry from somewhere outside in the camp. "Take arms! We are attacked!"

"All-I-I-I-lam All-I-I-lahuakbar," roared a voice outside and a swift, light desert pony thundered past his pavilion. A spear slit the fabric and struck, quivering, almost between Eadric's feet. Contemptuously, Eadric wrenched it free and snapped the wooden shaft in his hands like a twig. His massive strength was creeping back into his dead body.

He groaned at the confusion of shouts on the other side of the silk wall and gingerly rubbed his temples. His good eye burned; his skull was exploding with the strength of the pain he felt and he wished nothing so dearly as to be allowed a week's sleep.

The tent flap was torn aside. A wild face in a burnoose peered in at him, swarthy hands holding a torch and a sword menaced him. Almost casually, Eadric stuck two fingers in the fellow's maniacal eyes, pulled the torch from his numb fingers to set the attacker's robes afire and booted him into the sunlight, screaming.

"Arrogant dog!" muttered Eadric, pulling his sword belt tight about his middle. I'll send the bunch of you heathens to your god!"

Eadric turned a rueful eye to the heavens as another figure stormed into the slight shelter of the tent, only it was Pigfeet this time. Most certainly the Christians were right, Eadric had decided. Their god can read minds. This was the last thing he would have wished for!

Pigfeet stood pale and shaking and appeared strangely puny this morning. He panted and sagged as he clutched at a drapery and his tunic was almost as stained as Eadric's own; plainly he was in no condition to fight.

"Saracens!" he rasped. Then, tongue thick in a dry throat, he sat down next to his chieftain. Outside, men were locked in deadly embraces and roars and curses mingled with death rattles and pounding hooves.

"Not so loud!" snapped Eadric, putting both hands to his head.

"You look more dead than deaf, my friend!" Pigfeet replied.

"How many?" Eadric forced out. forced out.

"At least a score. All riders."

"And us?" he questioned.

"Not enough to live. More than enough to die." Pigfeet cursed in a low voice, sweat glistening upon his big arms and forehead.

For a brief minute, he and Eadric sat in silence. Eadric's hands attempted to steady trembling knees and Pigfeet's mind just drifted off into space. Pigfeet missed much this moment. Like Eadric, his home was far away, and he missed the revenge they might have had.

"So be it!" grated Eadric, rising. "So be the will of Odin. Only now let us fight and let us die." He pushed both huge hands into the small of his back to straighten himself as an old man might.

"Come, dog brother!" He kicked at Pigfeet almost playfully. "Let us spit in death's black face a final time."

Pigfeet shrugged. With a bitter laugh, he reached for an axe and arose.

The sun burnt the poison from their veins. As they stepped into the white-hot glare, Eadric's aching eye burned fiercely and he saw the desert landscape through a thick amber haze. But the kiss of the fresh morning wind and the clean smell of the air revived him and suddenly, wondrously, the great axe that he had also picked up was not nearly so ponderous. And as if this were not enough, the scream that sounded behind him flushed the last of the narcotic poison from his system with an electric, pulsating burst of adrenaline.

"Al-l-l-l-ah! Allah A-k-k-k-k-b-b-b-b-a-a-r!" cried a hairy Turkish lancer riding low to split a still-staggering Saxon across the compound. The Saxon fell, undoubtedly uncaring if he was as full of pain as Eadric was, but the Seljuk Turk made the gross mistake of continuing across the camp in a rush to overpower the Saxon bear.

"O-o-o-o-d-d-d-i-i-i-n-n-n!" roared Eadric the Wild, now well and truly wild. His lips snarled with a gigantic surge of berserk fury at the sight of his dead comrade. The change was immediate; the poison was defeated. Again, the Siwardsson was the warrior.

The Turk's beady black eyes widened with what seemed to be fear as he caught sight of the insanity within Eadric's single orb, saw the wicked smile of rotting teeth beckoning, and heard the intensely guttural chant that had lost its roots in dim antiquity. The Saxon's visage was terrible to behold. Froth saturated his beard and he wore no helmet so that his wild mane flew free. His solitary eye was glazed over with anger and blood ran down his arms in rivulets where he had bitten open the backs of his hands in his frenzy. With a bellowing laugh, he shoved Pigfeet head over heels out of the line of combat and waved his massive axe of oak and steel, an axe made for use with both hands because of its weight, in one terrific paw and cried like a banshee.

Time seemed to slow down, to pause a bit. Ever so gradually, the Turk watched the long-handled, double-bladed axe, steel gleaming, sun-glittering, rise until it was first vertical above the Saxon's head then held nearly horizontal behind him. It fell so fast he could not see it, let alone parry the stroke. He saw the taut play of iron muscle beneath all of Eadric's fat as those huge arms tensed on the downswing, and that bull-necked, red-bearded head went back with laughter that held a hell's worth of madness.

The Turk carne so close that he could see the decorations upon this brute's breastplate marking him as the emperor's own; he came close enough to choke over the Saxon's stink. Then he was too close! He could not turn his mount in time to evade or deflect that death-dealing stroke. He jerked abruptly at the reins but the horse half slid sideways in the sandy soil, presenting Eadric the Wild with as broad a target as he might ever hope to get.

"Allah!" cried a frightened voice—the Arabic equivalent for mercy. But the Siwardsson was a right merciless man this day.

There was a soul-chilling whistle of air rushing over the deadly steel head of the weapon and an instant of the fiercest pain that the Seljuk had ever known. Then there was nothing but darkness. And peace.

Eadric spat at the shoulder, arm, and half a head that lay wrapped in bloody cloth at his feet while the infidel's horse raced off, terrorized in the extreme. Blood splashed in great gusts everywhere as the creature crashed into men and tents like an evil omen of doom. Scornfully, the Saxon giant kicked the mangled flesh from his path and searched for another target. By the gods! If all the Seljuks were this easy to polish off then perhaps the day might yet be carried. Unfortunately, they were not.

At least not for a weakened, cadaverous-looking bunch of wasted sea bandits, still all but overcome by the treacherous wine and ale of the night before. Eadric grimaced as he witnessed two more of his own fall beneath the railing hooves of the fierce desert ponies and their blood-thirsty masters, transfixed on long lances through the breastbone and dead before their knees touched the dirt.

"Kill!" cried a Turk near Eadric and the Saxon recognized the foreign word so that it caused his anger to burn even hotter. Something twisted inside his throbbing brain and slithered down his spine toward his stomach. There, this uncanny emotion was transformed into bile to begin its course up the bandit's gullet and into his mouth, and he choked mightily on the dark taste of his own fear and rage.

And how he raged now! He raced forward and hurled himself head-long into the melee, savage and indominable. "Aye! You stinking scraggle-bearded son of a rabid bitch dog! You say 'kill' but I'll show you how to do it!"

And the man could not even turn in his saddle before the stinging blade bit through his spine and sent him spinning off into space, limply thrashing out the remains of his life. His blood-chilling screams took a long time to die out.

The red bear laughed insanely as he ground his booted heel into the dying man's face. There could be no quarter asked in a contest such as this, and none given. They had attacked, bent on Eadric's destruction; let them beware his foul tricks!

~

GEOFFREY WAS AWAKENED BY THE FINN'S CONTINUED CURSING AND opened sleepy eyes to find him engaged in another hunt for tiny predators.

"Are you seeking breakfast, friend Guvi?" the young Norman smiled.

His comrade answered him with a scowl and a curse. "If I am, then tis yours I must be seeking! I do not understand how you can sleep so soundly against the swarms of vermin in this wretched land!"

"Why, little flower! That you will learn quickly enough when you become a man!" snorted the knight sardonically as he arose and stretched, hungry for both breakfast and adventure this morning. The chill of the night had cooled the fever of the day and soothed his headache. He felt whole again. But before he could unpack the provisions to feed, there came a strangling cry from somewhere over the hill at their rear. The cry echoed a long time, unintelligible and metallic in the still morning, before it finally ended.

Then it came again, more urgently. And with it the clamor of combat. Even Guvi felt his interest stir.

Geoffrey raised a mocking eyebrow. "Mayhap there is your gold," he smirked.

Guvi nodded, pulling his shirt on again and hastily the two put on what armor they carried. Here was their first combat in this strange, alien land and both were as over-eager as newly-knighted cavaliers. Geoffrey's mind was thick with dreams of honor regained and dazzling stories to tell while the ever-sly Finn smiled wistfully, hoping to all his gods that it was a wealthy caravan being plundered, where rich rewards might be forthcoming. Hmmm! Or even better, if the caravan were finished just as they got there and with it as well most of the raiders, then there would be easy pickings with little risk. Guvi licked his lips in anticipation.

But distance was deceptive in the open desert, and the noise distorted so that it was difficult to determine exactly where the battle was occurring. Geoffrey danced his mount madly from hill to hill searching. Guvi was a bit slower, not wanting to rush into an ambush and willing to let the raiders do their work on the caravan he saw in his mind's eye. All the unending hills and valleys made it easier to be lost than to be found and it was only with the greatest of effort that they finally discovered the conflict. They paused at the base of one great hill, sure that they had finally arrived at their destination. Over the hill, the sounds of fighting were strong.

"Good hunting, Finn!" Geoffrey shouted, spurring Chestnut up the hot rise.

"Odin keep us!" muttered Guvi, directly behind him.

A despairing cry came from just over the hill, a cry out off with devastating abruptness. It was certainly death, grim and inescapable. Geoffrey felt the blood drain from his face beneath his helmet but was so overwhelmed with adrenalin that he seemed to be floating in the saddle.

At the crest of the hill, a figure swirled out of the dust, white and scarlet robes billowing, mouth opening to cry out, and a gleaming curved sword twirling around and around over his head. Presumably, a lookout for the raiders, for the man was alone and under-armed for the knight he faced. With dreadful ease, Geoffrey parried the intended blow with his shield, long and kite-shaped, and ran the man through.

But there was strategy in the Turk's attack for Geoffrey heard a curse but a yard away and saw another Turk, who had come from nowhere, struggling with one of Guvi's long arrows in his back. The knight finished him with his sword.

They nodded at one another, Geoffrey lifting his visor.

"Stay behind me!" the Norman shouted.

"Always and ever!" Guvi returned, bowing in the saddle.

Geoffrey spurred Chestnut down the hillside in a flurry of sand-laden dust, Guvi still behind him. The clamor of battle did come from the arid valley below them where several purple tents had been set up beneath the golden standard of the Emperor Alexis himself. Ranging through the close circle of pavilions stormed perhaps twenty riders, Saracens by the glint of their embossed chest-plates and conical helmets wrapped with silk.

And standing in the exact middle of the confusion and conflagration were less than ten men afoot, hacking at the dancing riders with broadsword and axe. But the light, supple lances of the attackers were taking their toll, for the proud footmen could not hope to match their ten-foot reach. The bellows and screams were a never ceasing racket and Geoffrey blanched a little at the pain in them.

Brave men, he thought. To take on cavalry with only close combat weapons was the height of chivalric foolishness or utter desperation. They looked to be some of Alexis's Varangians that Geoffrey had heard much of, blood lusting berserkers from the frozen North, Vikings and Swedes from the emperor's own personal bodyguard. They were tough enough, he saw. There was no doubt that, equally mounted, the Vikings would scatter these infidels like water before a ship's prow. But who or what were they guarding this far from Byzantium?

Geoffrey turned in the saddle and gave the Finn a questioning toss of his head. He grinned. Guvi was obviously dejected that there had been no caravan to save or plunder.

Guvi shrugged.

Geoffrey laughed and lowered his visor. With a swift motion, he drew his longsword, noticing how easily it pulled free from the scabbard and gave Chestnut a nudge. Guvi followed closely, readying another shaft on his bowstring. At the bottom of the hill, they put the spurs to their horses and thundered in behind the Saracens.

"Deus vult!" shouted the Norman as he swept into the rear of the Seljuk hoard, catching the first unsuspecting, commanding with a down-ward stroke that clove the fellow, armor and all, from shoulder to cracking sternum, and cast him from the saddle in a wave of crimson.

"I-e-e-e," came from the Turk, in surprise and pain, much of it from the tear in his throat. The man's smaller steed itself was smashed, broken and dying, beneath the irresistible impact of Chestnut's superior weight and railing hooves.

Several riders turned to regard the knight's eyes, first wide with surprise, then narrow with fiery hatred.

An arrow winged past. Guvi cursed. Then another left his bow and an infidel pitched from the saddle.

Then Geoffrey was in the center of the combat, his razor-edged sword a ten-foot arc in the hot desert sunlight that spattered drops of red everywhere as if it rained. It was so damnably easy!

The Saracens were secure in their knowledge of the terrain and the two sentries they had posted. They would not have understood two foreigners plunging heedlessly into their band, outnumbered ten to one, slaughtering to save a group of strangers on foot. And because of this, they died.

A fearsome swing of his sword and Geoffrey sent another Saracen to hell, and with the return stroke, he laid open the back of another. Sweat gushed down his face and into his armor; his visor clogged with gritty sand so that he cast the helmet away from him and still he pressed farther into their group. Another arrow flew over his shoulder into an infidel's back. In less than three minutes, Geoffrey and Guvi had dropped six the desert riders.

At the onset, the infidels found it hard to determine what was happening for two additional riders were hard to discern in the choking dust of the attack, and the riders themselves were caught up in a frenzy of slaughter. They had watched the camp for nearly an hour before they attacked, so they were certain that these brutish Franks had no mounts of their own. They had herded these doomed foot soldiers together with their lances, and ringed them in for quick destruction. Yet, suddenly the followers of the prophet were being hurled from their saddles.

They were soon to learn that Sir Geoffrey of Westwall was among them. But it was the Finn who actually alerted the enemy to the danger from their rear when he sent a thirty-six-inch arrow, steel tipped and barbed, through the bearded throat of the infidel captain as he called out his orders. The man choked hideously an instant before he died and the Saracens realized that these Franks had archers.

They turned inward into the melee, seeking. And finding. There was the fiery flash of a lone blade, straight, unlike the Saracen steel, and the whistle of air in the press of combatants halted only by a sickening thud.

Another Moslem heaved over in his saddle, scimitar cast away, both swarthy hands clutched at a ruined face between blood-soaked fingers. Geoffrey struck him again, to be sure. The wounded were still deadly.

Then he hurled Chestnut into a cluster of the riders, jamming the tip of his narrow shield into one horse's rump so that it started and reared, throwing the rider beneath the hooves. His sword he buried in the guts of a second.

"For William and Westwall!" cried Geoffrey, delivering a death stroke.

"For the Sultan's gold!" cried Guvi, mockingly in imitation. And another Saracen's heart leapt at the end of his arrow.

Geoffrey twisted sideways as a lance point raked across his chainmail and sent the attacker's arm flying free from his body with a backhand slash. Sweat poured into his narrowed eyes and his brain fairly boiled beneath his chainmail hood as he paused to wipe the perspiration from his face with the leather underside of a gauntlet. A rider sent a glancing stroke of his wickedly curved scimitar across the steel cloth of his hood. But the Finn was at his back still and the rider did not take a second stroke; an arrow was shot point blank, propelling the man back into his comrades, screaming.

Geoffrey felt the heat of his own blood run down his neck and throat but it was not gushing as he had feared. He wiped his face again, unintentionally spreading the flow into a red mask across his Norman features, causing a horrific appearance.

"Sleep well, dog of Islam," sneered Guvi as he fitted another shaft to string. "Wink at the devil with that eye, you son of a bitch!"

Geoffrey strained to see if any of the foot soldiers were left. All he saw through the haze was the swarthy Sultan and his men. But there were fewer now.

Still, they were as ferocious as wolves after his life. For he had shamed them badly with his skill and they had watched too many of their comrades fall before his strokes. Most, if not all, of the Vikings had been slaughtered, Geoffrey decided; the infidels seemed to have abandoned that attack. Ten or twelve of them tried to close at once with the pair, but Geoffrey's death swing was a cobra, gliding and flickering in the air.

A scimitar pierced his right forearm eventually, so that he was unable to continue with a firm grip on his sword hilt. He withdrew apace while Guvi sent shaft after whizzing shaft into the group of lightly-armored infidels. Eagerly, they sought to finish off the two, thinking the knight defenseless, but Geoffrey gave them insight into the matter when he seized up his heavy mace, wrapping the leather thong that was laced through its handle about his throbbing wrist so that it not fly from his grasp, wound or not, then he set the spurs to Chestnut and sent that huge, magnificent beast barreling into his foes, mace weaving overhead.

The twenty-pound weapon was frightening to witness. Flesh could not stand before it. He crashed into the riders lustily, bringing the heavy ball down with all his might against the nearest foe. The enemy's shield bent and cracked, falling aside, and the blow continued onto their heads, mangling the Turkish helmet and breaking the head within like a melon. He heard Guvi cry as Guvi's horse was cut out from under him and turned Chestnut to intercept the man bent on riding his friend down. The mace bowled the infidel from the saddle and he fell dead without a mark on him, his spleen ruptured. Geoffrey parried a deluge of lightning sword strokes across the long length of his shield, and just barely missed a final one that lightly kissed the flesh of his cheek, opening it like some budding flower and bringing forth a considerable quantity of blood, though the wound was not a mortal one. However, the Saracens saw the blood flow and thought the knight had slain again. They pressed him for the kill, harrying both sides with their strokes. Guvi watched as best he could but he was caught up with a pair after his own.

Geoffrey was tiring; they were not falling as fast now.

"Allah-h-h-h! Akbar!" they screamed and cried. "God is great!" And they pressed him hotly.

"In God's name!" Geoffrey roared back, returning stroke for stroke. "And King William!" he bellowed with sick fury that caused even the stanchest of the desert dogs to pale beneath their swarthy skins. Then Chestnut rose mightily and lashed out on Geoffrey's command, like the superbly-trained destrier he was, to dash a Moslem's face to pulp with steel-shod hooves. Before the rest could rush in against him and over-whelm the knight by sheer numbers, he spurred Chestnut to the charge, counting on the massive weight of the horse over the desert ponies.

But it was not this that finally drove the remaining infidels away, for they were still eight against one weary knight, wounded and dizzy in the heat. It was something else that occurred very suddenly.

First, there was some sort of commotion behind the infidel riders and Geoffrey swore he heard heavy words often laced with curses. But then it was the grumbling growl of a hungry bear that turned just as quickly to the snarl of a panther. Then, there was a roar that froze the riders in their saddles and even sent a chill through the sweat coursing down the Norman's back. One of the Vikings they had clubbed into the sand and left for dead was pulling himself to his feet, berserk with fury.

"Odin damn me for a weak-bellied boy! You cowardly, dung-colored, fly-crawling, ass-stinking band of women to count me down. Thor's blood, you scavenging bunch of maggot-mouthed dogs…!"

A hellish apparition had arisen amid the swirling storm of riders, set its shoulder under a horse's belly and stood to pick up both battling pony and protesting rider, to hurl them both beneath their brothers' hooves.

He stood shouting at their center, defying them to cut him down with their razor-edged scimitars. Blood and sand caked his tangled hair, but it still glared bright red in the sun and his long beard was a trail of fire. Arms laced with a hundred lesser cuts still streaming blood, he took up his instrument of carnage and made breathing space in the combat with ten-foot strokes of double-bladed steel edge, glittering wickedly where it was not crusted a darkening red.

And even in the steaming, broiling heat of the desert and the rushing press of battle, the gallant young Norman knew this Viking by the gut-wrenching stink of him. Even after all this time.

Eadric Siwardsson rose howling into the battle again!

"By God!" shouted Geoffrey, aghast at his ally. "The Siwardsson! Here is surely then, my true collection of foes!" Only the five or six heathen horse soldiers before Geoffrey stopped him from riding down his old foe.

"Get out of my way, you bastards!" the knight cried and took on two of the riders at once. "It is the Siwardsson I want!"

Wild Eadric paused in mid stroke to turn at hearing his name and caught sight of the young knight. A smile of surprise and pleasure creased his leathery face but he had no time to reply.

Suddenly, it dawned on Geoffrey that the Siwardsson was alone and nausea churned within him as he saw the awful implications.

Where was she then?

The Norman gritted his taste of bile away, angry and affronted at being put in the position of being this Saxon's savior but he needed to talk with him. So, he again put his back to the heavy mace with renewed vigor and another screaming Saracen thudded to the dusty earth with his side smashed. But still they fought him!

A thousand questions nagged at the frayed edges of his consciousness as Geoffrey fought with redoubled fury and ferocity. Was this really the Saxon bear in the Holy Land? Was she somewhere else, waiting for him? Where was he bound for? Who did he serve, this bandit? What was he doing here in this camp? Had another claimed her?

"Oh my God!" he cried in impotent rage, setting loose his impatience upon the Saracens in a flurry of mace blows that were dealt as lightly now as if he but bore a sword. He stood in the saddle and swung the heavy weapon with both hands in a blow his foe could never hope to stop in its utter recklessness. The face and silk-wrapped helmet of the Turk merged in the power of the iron club before both disappeared in a deluge of steaming crimson.

"Die, you dog! Die!" Geoffrey screamed as he hit the falling body with another unnecessary blow.

Even more insane with the frenzy and smell of battle was the ugly Siwardsson. His bear's eye was wild with unbridled hatred and gleaming fire, his thick lips stretched taut, white and foam-flecked. A thick and dry, seemingly dead tongue hung slackly from his mouth like a piece of spoiled meat as he dog-panted in his terrible exertions.

He raised his axe again to shear off a horse's head this time. There was no use in calling to him in the press, for he had become an unrea-soning predator now, descended back into the dim haunts of antiquity in a savagery that could only be called prehistoric, for no remotely civilized creature could howl and fight this way. Earliest man must have bellowed like this when he slew the great cave bears. All he wished for was to kill whatever stepped so ignorantly before his axe.

"Uhh—h-hh-hhh!" he grunted loudly as he fought. Then, he cast back his lion's head back and howled like a rabid dog.

The Siwardsson's armor, once decked out in the silver and gold raiment of the Byzantine emperor's own bodyguard, was now battered and dented, and the ornate molding crushed flat beneath the impact of so many lance thrusts and sword strokes. Blood ran in rivulets down his back and over his grim face, soaking his beard an even redder red, but by the way he still moved, whirling and dancing, Geoffrey knew whose blood it must certainly be. Again, that fearsome axe swung, driven so mightily that it cut the leg from one horse and slashed deep into the side of another. Both riders fell.

And the Saxon madman threw back his head and laughed at the sight of the two men scrabbling for footing and weapons. With a demonic leer, he advanced upon them both at once.

"Come, little birds!" he gasped hoarsely, his bellows-like lungs straining for air. "Do not fly so from your gentle hunter! Would you have him hunger? Ah ha, ha, ha, ha!" His maniacal laughter rang, chilling and endless, in the open air.

"Mercy!" cried one in French.

Eadric's brow darkened. "Better for you had you chosen your plea in my language instead of mine enemy's."

Both cast away their swords and ran for the desert, though they undoubtedly knew that they could not last long without transportation, which Wild Eadric had so unkindly taken from them. But the matter was settled, for one of them anyway, for as fast as he was, Eadric's stroke was faster. It deftly creased his spine from neck to buttocks.

Then suddenly, there were but four Saracens surviving, and the disheveled raiders broke off their catastrophic attack and fled, though the battle had only lasted on the lesser side of an hour.

Geoffrey turned, tired and feeling sore and shook his arm to restore the circulation. It had become numb with the wound and the weight of the mace but the bleeding was much less now and he was relieved. He saw the Finn cast off a dead Saracen who had fallen atop him and stagger upright with a broad grin, plainly happy to be alive. Then, he looked warily at the grim figure of the Siwardsson, leaning and wheezing over his sturdy axe.

Geoffrey leaned over in the saddle and vomited mightily from the exertion of battle in the hundred-plus degree heat.

The Siwardsson seemed to ignore him for the moment.

Anger burned hotter in Geoffrey's heart then the sun upon his head, but he was so completely winded that he had not enough breath left within his heaving lungs to speak so much as a single word. Probably the huge Saxon suffered similarly, perhaps even more so than Geoffrey did for Wild Eadric's bulk was heavy indeed. And it was not Geoffrey's muscular thickness, it was a layer of obesity added by too much food and ale, and not enough fighting recently.

For what seemed years to the young knight, the two surveyed each other in silence, broken only by gulps of air or dry coughing. Guvi, too, was silent. He was busily plundering the purses of the fallen—Saxons and Saracens alike, until his leather wallet bulged fat with the tidy sum of collected coin. The rest he relegated to the saddlebags he had also claimed from the fallen.

Geoffrey could not help but smile at the gleam of purest avarice in his comrade's eyes. But money held no lure for the knight now. Fate had taunted him for the last time; now there would be an answering.

Finally, the blood-smeared Saxon drew breath and grinned at Geoffrey, looking for all the world like some smirking monster-demon, risen from hell itself.

The Norman glared at him with his eyes hard and narrow with the frustration of still being too winded to speak.

Eadric found his voice first. "So, young wolf, you have repaid me for your life!" he spouted, half laughing, half gasping. His eye twinkled merrily for all his pain and fatigue. "They laughed at me when I spared you. But now, the laughter is choked by desert sand within. I wonder what brings such a wolfling to this barren, godforsaken land."

"Your death, now, Saxon," said Geoffrey. Had he had the power within his eyes to slay, the Saxon would have been struck down dead that very instant, his final word was uttered.

"I came to serve our Lord, though it be not your concern, Saxon!" the knight said through gritted teeth, strangely it seemed for one man speaking to another whose life he had just saved. The evil wretch plays games with me, does he, thought Geoffrey in suppressed fury.

The Siwardsson's grim smile broadened and lightened until it enveloped his full ruddy face, revealing twin rows of dark brown teeth, rotting in the gums along with his fuzzy, drink-ruined tongue. For a minute, he gazed at the ruined and burning tents over the mounds of the dead and finally over the hills before he spoke. "Thirst kills me," he rasped.

Without a word, Geoffrey cast a water bag to his feet and watched with steely eyes as the bandit gulped until he gagged. Eadric nodded amiably as he tossed it back.

"Only your sword will kill me, that's it, isn't it?" he asked.

Geoffrey nodded, unspeaking,

The Siwardsson pursed his grizzled lips in thought. "Why do you hate me so? I gave you your life once."

"And I have given you yours once!" snarled Geoffrey. Plainly the Saxon was toying with him. "Where is she, you bastard?! Better had you killed me than taken her!"

The Siwardsson's smile faded and a hint of true regret colored his ugly visage. His voice was almost quiet.

"I have wronged you, young wolf cub. I have wronged you both, for I tried to deny something I was jealous of, something I felt between you even though no one spoke of it; I tried to believe it did not exist, but I can refute it no longer. I should have admitted it to myself for you both were born to each other. She is as much a champion as a woman can be in this man's world. And you are everything I first thought when I met you in that dark cell. I have never believed truly in gods or destiny but, damn me, if there is not a feeling in my bones that I meddled in something better left alone."

Geoffrey could not reply.

"Did I miss something, friend Geoffrey?" asked Guvi casually as he walked up to catch sight of Geoffrey's scowl. There was an odd expression in his good comrade's eyes that worried the Finn for the hurt and anger it displayed.

"Nay, friend, only the introduction. Know you who this ragtag villain is?"

Guvi shrugged. "Who?"

"What!?" stormed the Saxon. "You lie! Everyone knows the wild son of a wild father, the son of Siward the Saxon!"

Guvi gazed at him coolly. "Can this be true?"

Geoffrey nodded.

"Then let us kill the fat, red bear," suggested Guvi with a casualness that was chilling. He fitted a shaft to his bow and raised it a quarter.

Eadric looked up, startled. The look on his face showed that he was decidedly taken aback for he knew he was no match for these two warriors at once, especially with Guvi's skill with a longbow.

He leapt high as an arrow struck the sand between his big feet, "Odin damn you, boy! You are going to get a spanking for that!" he blustered.

"Indeed?" cooed Guvi as he offhandedly reached for an arrow a second time. "You make a plump target, you bellowing pig."

"Now, now, here, fellows! Let us not be hasty in this," he negotiated in a more respectful voice as Guvi raised the bow. "'Tis certainly quite true that the cub and I have a minor dispute, but it can surely be settled with soothing words or at most a pouch of gold. There is no need for a bloodletting," he stammered. "I saved your life, cub!" he cried.

Geoffrey thumbed the sharp nobs upon his mace as Eadric had once done to an axe before the Norman's eyes.

"Nay," Geoffrey grinned with little humor. "I think not. Rather you simply did not take it, and you would have had no right to. Here, today, I saved your worthless hide, you pillaging vulture. What small debt I owe you is paid. Your worthless life is mine to take now, but I do not desire it. There is only one thing I want from you, Eadric Siwardsson, and I will forgive you all you have cost me if you yield it to me. Well you know what it is. Where is she!?"

Eadric hung his shaggy head in mock sorrow, "Ah, cub! How sad I am to say I do not have her with me. But still, there are many women in this new land that will…"

He was interrupted by Geoffrey's grated command to Guvi. "Be sad for yourself, Saxon. Send him to hell, Guvi!" snarled Geoffrey.

"Hold!" cried the Saxon, shaken just a bit by this crooked turn of chance upon him. "I said that I have her not, but I can easily show you where she might be found!"

"Tell me instead!" ordered Geoffrey.

"Better to show you," suggested Eadric, "that way I'm sure to live at least a little longer and…"

"Where?!" roared Geoffrey. Another arrow struck at the Siwardsson's feet.

"Most like, by now, she is in the Saracen citadel of Tarsus."

"What?!" cried Geoffrey. "You lying son of a bitch!"

"Tis true enough!" protested Wild Eadric.

"In God's sweet name!" swore Geoffrey, turning scarlet with rage. "You do not beg for an easy death, do you, rogue?"

Eyeing the Saxon speculatively, the Norman wrapped his blue surcoat tightly about his injured arm and then wiped the drying crimson from his cheek where the wound had ceased its flow. Was this vile fellow really telling the truth or did he lie, in hopes of saving his life?

And if she was in the Saracen encampment, what then? This was a tougher nut to crack than a handful of wild outlaws.

Siwardsson then spat his disgust into the dirt at his feet.

"She was given to my son, my own precious kin. But he decided that in this tortured land that the emperor's gold was more valuable to him than the love and blessings of his father. For this very reason, he stole all of the gold we carried for the Frankish forces and ran for the infidels."

"That *you* carried?" exploded Guvi. "Holy Moses, since when does the emperor appoint a fox to escort chickens?"

"Ere, well, he did not really know about our history of independence…"

"You mean thievery, you robbing bastard!" shouted Geoffrey.

"It's been called worse," grinned Eadric. "But to continue, Wulfhere Eadricsson hoped to buy his way across the East. But you Franks move too quickly and methinks by now he is probably trapped like a rat with his new friends in the city of Tarsus. Your Frankish leaders have attempted to put a ring of steel about it."

Guvi guffawed, causing the stout Saxon to glare at him. "The son sounds like a prince to me, friend Geoffrey, to value gold above the affection of this churl!"

"Have care, swine!" snarled Eadric stepping forward apace.

Guvi was not intimidated. "You have a care, you fat pig!" As if by magic, an arrow suddenly appeared between Eadric's legs, and the bandit calmed.

"No need for that, friend!" He smiled hastily, "I'm not your enemy!"

"Then whose enemy are you, if not mine?" asked the Norman dryly, "I can think of no one, excluding your ill-spawned son, that I would rather kill slowly."

"We could be allies, I also owe Wulfhere Eadricsson a debt!"

Geoffrey smiled grimly. "Tis fitting perhaps. You who have robbed me have been robbed in turn. Yet, still I ache for what I value always above all else and it seems that this offspring of yours has fooled us both in his knavery." Wearily, Geoffrey wiped sweat from his eyes. He felt an almost overpowering fatigue, a bone-deep weariness that stemmed from more than the energy of battle.

"Aye!" scowled the Saxon, "But I think he started..."

Guvi interrupted him, tired of the philosophizing. "Well, shall I slay the fat old buzzard and send his soul to the flames?"

Puzzled, Eadric said, "There are no flames in Valhalla."

"Valhalla!" snorted the Finn. "If there is another life for you, then it has to be in this hell the Franks whine about continually. There you can break hot rocks all day while the fiends bugger you in your hairy arse!"

Eadric looked at the Norman for salvation a second time that day.

Geoffrey sighed a rib-bending breath and turned his horse for the trail.

"Boy! I saved you!" cried Eadric.

"Let him live, Guvi. Let the dirty old bear live. His story should prove amusing on our journey. Come red-beard! Find a horse to mount and ride with us."

"You forgive too quickly!" muttered Guvi through gritted teeth.

Eadric stared at Geoffrey. "Where do you ride for in this hostile land? The Frankish encampment?"

"Of course," smiled Geoffrey. "And Tarsus."

"Shit!" muttered Guvi.

10

CHAPTER THE TENTH

The day was early but the sun hot as the odd trio rode into the huge camp of the Christian kings. It was not as Geoffrey had expected for his mind was still crowded with thoughts of glorious battles and an army banded together at the will of God.

But God did not, perhaps could not, stop the stink and the dust of this noisy city of tents. Hastily dug latrines baked in the sun, offending all but the thick clouds of well-fed flies and the dust seemed to hang permanently in the air, so many were the riders in and out. The tent city was brilliant in color with the stripes and banners of heraldry, though the colors were somewhat subdued from the layer of blowing grit overall. Everywhere there was drinking, gambling and whoring going on for this was an army at rest. For such a large body of fighting men far from home, such rest was a venereal disease of the body for it blunted their toughness and determination; it made them lazy and complacent.

This place lacks dignity, Geoffrey thought sadly. But his companions were of a different opinion. Guvi eyed the gamblers speculatively while Eadric stopped often to pinch the whores. Geoffrey shrugged in good humor. The pair was incorrigible.

Geoffrey dismounted and handed the reins to a page as did Guvi, while Eadric plodded off on some nefarious business of his own. Geoffrey faintly acknowledged to himself that he was not anxious to be seen in the camp for the spies of the emperor were everywhere. The two comrades strode toward the tent that flew the colors of Westwall, unmistakable despite their coating of filth.

The two serjeants guarding the door, however, were not men of Westwall, but part of a detachment that wore the colors of Lincoln and Geoffrey realized that his father had truly been appointed representative to King William. Neither so much as cocked an eyebrow as the young knight announced his desire and position.

"Sir Geoffrey of Westwall to see his father," he said, very businesslike.

"Can't be done, young sir!" replied the fellow before him, lowering a pike to bar his way. He winked a bloodshot eye and showed a mouthful of missing teeth as he grinned. "The Lord St. Denis haven't got no desire to see no one just now and his lordship himself haint one to tolerate no excuses. Tis only your own word I got that you are who you say, and I haven't never seen you before today. Best you be coming back around supper when his lordship takes visitors and he might be bothered with you."

Geoffrey slowly turned scarlet at the man's attitude and he deliberately reached down and half-drew his longsword.

"You dirty son of a bitch!" he snarled, mouthing each word separately for emphasis. "Since you are so secure in your position, I shall put it to you this way. Supposing what I say is true, and it is, and I am Sir Brian's son. Then it stands to reason that I carry weight here; and you may be certain that I will see to it that your coarse hide is slowly and lovingly flayed from your back for this insult, if I do not cross swords with you first!"

The serjeant gulped twice, a sizeable lump now in his throat and his moronic face paled.

"Gor, blimey! You has for certain the mouth of his Lordship and I believe you just might be who you say. But still, his lordship…"

The reply was not finished for the entry flap to the pavilion was abruptly thrust open to show the mail-clad figure of Sir Brian St. Denis.

The eyes of father and son met suddenly and held each other, the experienced ones of age searching the impetuous ones of youth. Eternities of emotion passed through the seas of sight and long-unsaid thoughts brimmed bright with the need for expression.

Sir Brian gave a bitter, wry smile and shook his head. "So, it's you, is it?" he murmured. "The prodigal son returned to the fold? But where is your lady, if I might apply that term to her? I see only yon rascally knave standing with you, or mayhap you have lost your heart over a truly plain and unwholesome wench? Did you not find her, as I predicted you would not? A pity, I sympathize with you deeply, but that is life, is it not?"

"The arrogant shit!" muttered Guvi beneath his breath.

Sir Brian paused as if to say something to the Finn, but Guvi gave him a look of open hostility and the commander thought the better on his desire to reply. He continued, "Set what stores you have with the men of Westwall for they have saved a place for you; you have played false knight long enough. It is they who have kept your place, not I, for no longer do I name you a knight of either Westwall or England. You have put your own foolish desires above your code and a man who does so is a coward to himself. But still, you seem to have a strong sword arm and God knows that is what is needed these days in this land of heat and flies. Why God chose this hell to birthe Christ into I shall never understand, but I suppose it does give you sinners a taste of what might come. You will rule over the men of Westwall for it was William's request that I marshal the entire contingent of England. He gave me his ring to command with," smiled Sir Brian proudly, extending a bejeweled hand.

"And his unbridled conceit as well, I think!" murmured Guvi again.

Sir Brian eyed him with distaste. "You would do well to watch your speech, varlet. My patience is not without end."

Guvi's face went dark and he opened his mouth to reply, but Geoffrey interrupted. "If your contempt for me is so great, Father, why do I retain command at Westwall? Why not Alfred or one of the others born in the English force?" he asked without much feeling.

Sir Brian ran a leathery hand through his gray hair thoughtfully as he examined the situation in his mind. The old knight's eyes narrowed in concentration and Geoffrey thought to himself how aged the man looked. It was as if he stood before a stranger.

Sir Brian's reply brimmed with bitterness and unconcealed disappointment. "Firstly, because although you have sadly failed in your vows of knighthood, you are still my son, and I would not set another above you, if for no other reason than my own pride. Secondly, because the men will follow you into hell itself; you were always their leader, you know. Even when you were small, the other children listened to you. The more hot-headed ones of our group swear they will follow no other now that you have returned, and I think that they would have followed you on your foolish search if they had known of it, forsaking their code in turn. Fortunately, I did not have to when I said I knew not where you had run off to."

"If nothing else, that gladdens my heart," smiled the son.

Brian's eyes were stormy. "It does, does it? It pleases you that there are others to join you in your treachery to our codes, to abandon their honor so easily? Is this how you have found this rogue? Who is he? He has the look of a fugitive about him and a lowborn one at that." Sir Brian's disgust was unbearable.

Guvi stepped forward with a sneer so menacing that the two men-at-arms stepped forward also. Sir Brian waved them back.

"Rogue, am I? Who are you to so haughtily name an honest thief and scoundrel a knave and a rogue? I have seen many of your kind before, self-satisfied and self-righteous. You think the world is yours to command, but I tell you that I serve your son alone! Tell me, my lord, when you fall, will they mark your grave with a cross?"

Sir Brian stood, speechless and purple in the face at the Finn's mad audacity.

Guvi continued, "Do you read the book of Him who you revere so much?"

Sir Brian gave him a lofty look. "If you mean the Bible, of course I do. Every knight of Christ reads the *good book*!"

"Phah!" snorted Guvi. "Then you must not remember what it says about condemning others!"

The elder St. Denis smiled mockingly. "Ah, so you are a student of theology, as well as a knave and a rogue? But you cannot catch me, fool! The Bible tells where Christ says to the crowd that only the one amongst them without guilt or blame should cast the first stone. But I say, you cannot hold that up to me; I have never foresworn my loyalties. What judgment I pass on you is fair." His steel-blue eyes sparkled in the triumph he felt over this miserable young puppy that bearded him in his own den. Ha! Best the scurvy fellow cross wits with the commoners! But he stopped his revelry at the thin smile on the Finn's dark face.

"Nay, good Christian," Guvi said. "I speak of a simpler command-ment. Your Lord said, 'Judge ye not at all, my brethren, lest ye also be judged in turn and found wanting.'"

With a dark scowl, Sir Brian turned from the Finn in disgust. He continued with his back to them all, hands locked behind him. "Well," he grated woodenly, "after all, we are not here to discuss the scriptures, but to fight for them. Talk is useless anyway. All the infidel comprehends is the bite of the whip and the cut of the sword. You will find the men of Westwall beneath their banner at the front of the English section. Now, I bid you both good day!" He stood with his back to them until they left.

"Arsehole!" snickered the Finn.

Geoffrey shrugged, lost in thought. He was hot and tired in his heavy armor and wanted nothing more than a cool tent and a flagon of cool wine.

Guvi openly grinned at his friend. "So, we are here to fight for your religion, but damn me if we might discuss it, eh?" He slapped his thighs in mirth, eyebrows curled up and strong white teeth gleaming. "Tis a good thing I carry my religion in my purse, friend Norman! Gold is an easier weight to bear than your father's religion, I think. What think you?"

"I think you talk too much, villain. But he does not concern me over much. He is set in his ways and speaks with too much pride, but he is a good knight and an able commander and we will follow him. Remember that, you knavish rogue!"

"I'm afraid that I will," sighed the Finn.

Geoffrey shook his head again in disgust, but Guvi continued in a more serious vein. "Twill be the pompous fools like him who see to it that good men, such as myself, are sacrificed needlessly in the hot press of combat!"

"If my father had his way, I'm sure you would lead the advance, my sardonic friend. But I'm sure that when the trumpet sounds, you will be comfortably nestled deep, deep within the rear ranks."

Guvi beamed. "Protecting your naive behind as always, master!" He bowed with the elegance of a cavalier and Geoffrey kicked him roundly in the buttocks.

The pair found Wild Eadric Siwardsson already embroiled in a heated debate with three of the emperor's Viking mercenaries, who had also arrived to reinforce the Christians. As minions of Alexis, they openly spied on the Christian armies and insured there was no treachery toward the empire. But they also fought as well, and they were grudgingly given respect, not in the slightest diminished by the fact that they were the hereditary foes of most of the Frankish knights. But a problem had arisen; by some oblique line of reasoning, Eadric Siwardsson had come to the conclusion that, since he had lost his command in the desert, these men were rightfully obligated to follow him in the emperor's service.

"Mon Dieu!" laughed Geoffrey. "First, he is worried that Alexis will find out he is in camp, then he wants to openly command all of Alexis's detachment."

"Mad as a March hare," agreed Guvi.

But Wild Eadric was not to be deterred. Too long had he commanded men; if he had lost one command, then he would gain another. However, a gigantic flaxen-haired Northman, larger even than the Siwardsson, saw fit to be a trifle disturbed at this as he was the undisputed, until today, leader of the Northern mercenaries. In heavily accented Saxon, he asked Eadric to sit on his sword.

Eadric screwed up his bloodshot eye and ran a grubby tongue across fleshy lips in anticipation.

"Let us fight instead, you wet notch of womanhood!" he blandly suggested.

The chieftain, whose name was Gunnar Tibaltsson drew himself up to full height and gazed deeply into the remarkable face of this red bear baiting him. It never once occurred to Gunnar that he might fail in such an encounter. All he saw before him was a grime-encrusted, stinking, flabby brigand with a mouth the size of his doubled fists.

Gunnar's nostrils flared but he had commanded too long to lose his temper so easily. He informed Eadric that leadership was not so decided here in the east. The Saxon bear nodded in understanding and smiled at seeing Geoffrey and Guvi approach. Already, a crowd was starting to gather, attracted by Eadric's braying voice. The Siwardsson gave the pair what Geoffrey took to be a wink, turned, cleared his throat with an enormous inward snuffling sound followed by a deep-throated hawking and launched the collected prize into Gunnar's face.

"Do we fight now?" Eadric inquired blandly.

The big Viking went from scarlet to white and his massive, scarred hand clenched about his sword hilt.

"We fight!" he roared. The crowd gave a subdued cheer and stepped back. But this giant of the East had sorely underestimated the son of Siward. Before his longsword was half a length from his scabbard, Eadric's booted foot was deep in his groin. At this, Gunnar's two companions went for their blades but halted when they saw Guvi and Geoffrey do the same, only Geoffrey was smiling somewhat unnervingly as he drew his, corded muscles bunching beneath his chain mail and leather with his eyes cold and deadly.

Anyway, it was Gunnar's fight, was it not?

Eadric turned and grinned openly at his two friends as Gunnar fought for breath, one hand cupping his injured crotch. He could not even draw his sword.

The crowd hooted; they loved treachery so skillfully delivered.

"I'll wager he never expected that first blow!" Eadric cried to the group of watchers, holding his hands out appealingly and mugging. Geoffrey gaped as they applauded the bandit.

Eadric cocked his hands at his hips and danced a little jig for the entertainment of all. They roared louder than ever.

"Twould seem these Easterners are a bit slow in the fighting arts!" he bellowed, turning his back completely on the big Northman to smile at one of the female camp followers who had turned out to watch.

"And what is your name, little flower?" He leered at her, brushing back his matted red mane in a parody of grooming. "I'll wager you can keep a man warm all night!"

She smiled a smile of crooked yellow teeth beneath a semblance of a thin moustache and Eadric felt like lust was stirring somewhere deep within him. Coquettishly, she tossed her head.

"Watch him, you great oaf!" shouted Geoffrey, for Gunnar was up with a roar and going for Eadric's back with sword flailing. But instead of turning to parry the attack, Eadric threw himself to one side as the giant rushed and caught him with a mighty kick in the arse as he ran past, unable to stop his own momentum. The crowd laughed delightedly and the Viking turned, fair features a livid mask of fury. He stood with his broad chest heaving and sized up his slightly smaller foe before he advanced again. As he did so, Eadric drew his sword but held up a hand. The Viking Gunnar halted and the crowd hushed to a few stray giggles.

"Well!" roared Eadric. "I wish to know if you have had enough, yet? Why don't you retreat while only your dignity is lost?"

"I'll carve your fat guts, Saxon," snarled Gunnar.

Wild Eadric guffawed and spat into the dirt at his feet.

"You're a bit slow for that, you big pig!" he laughed. The crowd echoed his merriment and Eadric took the opportunity to pinch the cheek of the little flower he desired. He gave her a pat of affection on her ample rear.

"Fight!" bellowed Gunnar.

Eadric continued to hold up a hand, stopping the fight, as he talked with the sullied dove.

"Come to me after this and we will celebrate, my delicious sweet-meat!" he snorted and merriment in the crowd progressed to hilarity. Gunnar's cry split the heavens as he closed with his Saxon foe.

But suddenly, clumsy, cloddish Eadric was all business and thirty years of sword discipline manifested itself. His sword stroke was a flash of quicksilver that belied his trembling bulk of fat-covered muscle. He moved with the agility of one half his size and Gunnar found his strokes countered with strokes of strength equal, if not greater than his own.

Eadric pulled his jerkin open in the heat and through the layer of fat, Gunnar saw slabs of steel, moving with the terrible meticulousness of a siege engine.

The Saxon bear blew his nose into his fingers, flicked the snot off into the dirt, and gave his enemy a wink of pure malice.

"Cry quarter and I shall let you live!" he shouted.

"I need no quarter from you!" the Viking screamed.

"Then cry quarter and I shall teach you how to use that pig-sticker that you swing like a shovel!"

"Arghhhh!" roared Gunnar as he hacked madly at Eadric, but the Siwardsson's sword was everywhere, a shimmering net of defensive strokes.

"You can be second in command," suggested Eadric sarcastically, barely out of breath. He stood with feet planted firmly while his foe wove all about him. But still, Gunnar could not get near the Saxon.

The Viking withdrew, panting.

Eadric stuck his own blade in the sand, stretched and cracked his big knuckles. The implied insult was too great for the Viking. He hurled himself forward, but Eadric's blade was there instantly, catching the Viking's. The red-beard took the opportunity to seize hold of Gunnar's wrist with his free hand. The Northman paled as he felt Eadric's true strength. His sword fell.

Exerting the full of his raw power, Eadric broke his enemy's wrist with a bone-snapping wrench and ground the bone splinters together until Gunnar fell to his knees. The Viking was too proud to cry out but his lips trembled visibly and his complexion whitened quite dramatically. Contemptuously, Eadric Siwardsson cast the man backwards and away from him before he turned to face the fellow's companions.

Both of them stepped back from him, arrogance turning to caution.

"You are weaklings, you men of the North!" Eadric laughed good-humoredly. "Your bones are as brittle as the icicles on a ship's mast! Now, I would still relish a position of leadership with your dainty band. Say you yea or nay?" His single eye was piercing and both Vikings found it hard to take their eyes from Gunnar, unconscious with the pain of his injury.

At last, the Viking closest to him found speech and replied, "I am Rolf Hensson, second in command to the emperor's detachment in this army and I say I will not fight you. You are captain henceforth!"

"Aye, I suppose!" muttered the second Northman, somewhat sourly. Eadric took offense at the man's tone of speech and dealt him a ringing crack to the ear.

"You suppose? You suppose! Why you maggot-mouthed spawn of a troll and a dead cow, I am the greatest warrior you will ever live to see; my name is legendary in Britain and the lands of the North. I am Eadric the Wild, son of Siward the Saxon and you would do well to remember that you stand before Saxon royalty!"

Guvi looked sideways at Geoffrey and the Norman shook his head in disbelief.

Then the Saxon hitched up his breeks, spat twice on the prostrate Gunnar and nodded approvingly.

"Tis well!" he decided. "I feel right at home already. You, Rolf, will continue to be second in this band. Now take yon braggart, this Gunnar Tibaltsson, and send him back to Alexis with my compliments in a message that I shall dictate, when I think up a story about lost ships and gold. Hmmmm. At any rate, your old captain is worth little to me but there is no point in being bloodthirsty about this episode. I am by nature a patient and gentle creature, as you all shall see, but beware you all of crossing to my bad side. My good humor is as bountiful as Odin's cloud, but it is not infinite; I tolerate neither excuses nor cowardice from others and sport not such habits myself!" He finished by asking if either of his new band had any complaints to make.

Rolf's companion began to voice a reasonable protest of the way the situation was being handled, but Eadric dropped him to his knees in the dust of the street, stunned, with a great, open-handed blow.

"And least of all, you rabbit turd, do I tolerate the sniveling of the complainer. If you have something to cry about, cry it in your woman's arms, but best you make sure it is snuggled deep in your furs, so deep that I do not catch so much as a drift of it on the night breeze. For by Odin, if I hear a single complaint, so much as the tiniest protest, then I'll nail you to a ship's mast in a winter squall and give you something to really feel sorry about." Eadric nodded and turned to the crowd.

"Spread the words, dear children. Eadric the Wild, the son of Siward the Saxon has arrived! The Holy Land will soon be liberated! Let the women make themselves sweet and the men walk with pride and respect. We will send all the infidels to hell!"

The wild red-beard was still ranting as Geoffrey and Guvi tugged him free from the crowd and towed him toward a row of tents, looking for their quarters.

"They loved you, you old fart," Geoffrey laughed. "No one else has your audacity, even here in the East."

"Perhaps that is just as well," murmured Guvi, sardonically.

WULFHERE EADRICSSON, SON OF EADRIC THE WILD, STOOD SOMEWHAT forlornly upon a windy parapet just beside the entrance to the twin towers of the main gate of Tarsus. Before him, the edge of the plain milled endlessly with the Frankish hordes stretching far and wide in both directions and back until he saw tents pitched in the hills and gullies that bordered the rear of the coastal flatlands. The dogs resembled nothing so much as an ant swarm and each day Wulfhere paced nervously as their numbers grew larger and larger.

He knew he had miscalculated.

The Christian armies, who Eadric and he both figured to be rife with conflict that would slow the march, moved effortlessly to the attack over dusty roads and tossing seas until they had caught the Saracens a full two weeks earlier than had been expected. It seemed that none of the clang of Christendom loved each other, but they all shared an equal hatred of the Moslem infidels and an equal lust for land and wealth. Differences in politics could be postponed while the riches of the East were waiting. Particularly disconcerting was the drive of Lord Bohemond of Otranto, a leader in the vacuum of political indecision. His iron-willed magnetism judged the minor disputes for the rest and forged them by his own deci-sions, into a real force. Whether threatening, begging, or cajoling, he had had the good sense to urge the blitzing of the coastal cities so that their ships might move through the sea lanes unhampered.

Huh! There had been only the most minimal problems with the Turks, for they had a gentry all of their own, not totally ignorant of ethics and honor. They had demanded only half of his gold, all of his female slaves, and his undying declaration of faith in Islam. In return, they gave him shelter and the freedom to move unhampered in a written pledge of protection by the Caliph himself, for it was his coffers that the gold filled. But the freedom was academic now, for the game might well be up. Tarsus had been built centuries before to well withstand a siege, but the Franks were devils. While they lolled about outside the walls growing stronger, and Wulfhere whiled away his hours drinking thick eastern wines and fornicating with the dancing girls, Bohemond and his party were slowly closing off the coastal roads and unwittingly netting the renegade Saxons. That Frankish bastard had cut off their chances to take a ship from the coast and return North, for Christian galleys now prowled like hungry lions from Tomuk to Karatas, bringing more warriors and supplies daily and searching and seizing all ships leaving the Seljuk coast regardless.

And while Wulfhere Eadricsson might just about escape with his life, assuming it was a Frankish ship that stopped his and not one of the Empire's, he could never escape with the great mass of gold he retained. For when all was said and done, the Franks as well as the Emperor Alexis, were little more than glorified thieves bent on plundering the Moslem nations. A shipload of ready gold would just suit them, and some patrol ship captain would hastily leave the Christian contingent and sail home a wealthy man. Bah!

It had seemed so easy when he was planning it all out. Still, there was certain to be a way if he kept his wits enough to find it. The treacherous Saxon cursed roundly the fate that had treated him thus. Twas bad enough to lack wealth, but worse was to have it and lack the chance to use it.

But even worse, now he must fight. He had planned to retire away, snug in some manor house where he would spend out his life in drunkenness and lechery and no longer play the high risks of the sword game. But now, with battle about to be joined, these heathen Turks, his Moslem brothers, would expect the Saxons to fight shoulder to shoulder with them, and rightly so. But while these imbeciles were fighting for their faith, for their Allah, he would be fighting so that his hide did not end up as the leather in some Frank's saddle. And worse, it would surely be, if any of the emperor's men took control of Tarsus for they slew a man slowly. When he had visited Alexis, they had watched Moslem thieves be maimed and disfigured during post-dinner entertainment. Brrr! And Alexis had not even born a grudge against those he tortured, how much worse it would be for Wulfhere and his nasty band!

Fate laughed at him. Neither the Franks nor the emperor relished the ideals of traitors. Damn! All that gold and there was no one he could even bribe. In his more desperate moods, he had considered a side deal with some of the Franks to let him pass. But if he was discovered, or failed, the consequences would be disastrous. The Turks would brand him a traitor or, equally bad, the Franks might decide that they wanted his life as well as his gold. Afterall, the dead never discuss their sins. And then there was the possibility that somewhere, somehow, Alexis had found out what had happened and was offering a reward for Wulfhere's safe return. He would die fighting first.

Tarsus was strong, though, a truly tough nut to crack. There was a real chance that it could hold out until the Christian tide ebbed or floundered in its own blood, thanks to its reckless leaders hell-bent for glory and salvation. The walls of Tarsus in some places were fifteen feet thick and thirty-some feet high, topped with steel spikes and cauldrons for superheated pitch, racks for hurling stones, mangonels, and catapults. But the Eadricsson was no stranger to siege-craft as the Franks certainly were not, and he wondered if the Turks were cunning enough to resist the ploys and strategy of a long-barricaded war. Would the Turks lose control when food ran low, when even the last rat was devoured and women looked hungrily at their babies and sallied forth to break a deadlock and be decimated in the field?

It must be Wulfhere's task to see that the Seljuks were not fooled; he knew they regarded the Christian knights as barbarians and were sometimes contemptuous of their abilities. Wulfhere must not let that contempt become a weakness. If the Franks lured these infidels out onto that low plain between Tarsus and the hills, the slaughter would be endless.

Then he was struck with the germ of an idea. When the battle wore on and the Franks hurled all of their men against the walls, intent upon breaking a stalemate, sure of themselves in victory, what if they were suddenly attacked from the rear? He gazed at the hills and gullies winding behind and to the sides of the Christian camp. A force of men could hide there in full battle gear and never be seen until too late.

But for now, he had more immediate worries. Hopefully, the fortress might weather the storm of steel and leather successfully, forcing the Franks to break camp and move along the coast for other cities. Certainly, they could not remain before the gates of Tarsus indefinitely, even with their access to the sea for provisions. Wulfhere knew that to the east there were other Saracen armies answering the call of the Jehad, or Holy War, as it was called. For the Franks to allow these storms to build unchecked while they stewed over a single fortress would be folly. And although Wulfhere expected recklessness from his attackers, he did not believe that their overall plan would amount to folly.

Ironically enough though, while Wulfhere's mind was filled with concern for the future, he had no way of knowing that the two most powerful talismans of his fate now sat within sight of the walls. One he assumed long dead, and the other he did not even know existed.

The ways of fate are inscrutable in the extreme, those of God only slightly less so. Both men thought of him though, for the battle was soon to be joined.

However, both foes of Wulfhere Eadricsson had their own degrees of composure regarding their shared hatred. For Eadric the Wild, this thing he felt clawing at his innards like a buzzard about to hatch was put aside when the eventide came, traded for a foaming jack of ale and a nimble-thighed camp-follower to sit upon his lap. Indeed, that pace which he set for himself soon left all the Franks sadly behind and even stretched prostrate the stoutest of his Varangian crew of Saxons and Vikings. Eadric Siwardsson was past a master at the art of imbibing.

And it soon passed that he alone wandered the encampment in the still of the night, oblivious to all but his own dark thoughts, startling the night watch with an occasional belch or fart of thunderous proportions, and even going so far once as to wake up the mighty Lord Bohemond of

Otranto who many called the leader of the armies, when he stood outside the sleeping commander's tent and howled at the moon.

When the guards came, he was flapping his arms and cawing like a crow, a wineskin in one grubby paw and an article of woman's under-clothing in the other. Life was good, he felt. A little drink, a soft, plump woman to bed, and the promise of action on the morrow; what more could a man desire?

But in the darkened pavilion of the younger St. Denis, there was no celebration. Geoffrey lay abed, his mind sleep-laden and clouded by ale-inspired dreams of the morrow, wretched and soul-chilling, and filled with her. He stood knee-deep in a terrible sea of lampblack water, clad in his full armor with his longsword clenched within a mailed fist, as he watched the rocking prow of an equally black vessel, almost indistin-guishable from the inky waves. The ship bobbed with the force of some mystical tide, just beyond his reach. He walked toward it with hard strides, yet the ship always seemed to draw away from him. There was neither sea nor sky nor land to be seen, there was just a swirling of shadows and varied shades of darkness. But he saw the boat with uncanny clarity and felt the chilling caress of the ebony current as it swirled about his steel-encased legs. And on the prow of that fearful ship, that vessel of the damned, he saw her.

She held her arms out to him in pleading desperation. She stood alone, her fair, pale form a single whitish blur against the enveloping curtain of night. At this close distance, he could see how she trembled in dread at some unspoken fate, and he witnessed the silent acceptance in her lovely eyes. She understood how powerless he was to save her, yet still she begged him for salvation.

With a groan that arose from the depths of his heart, he held out his arms to her and saw her smile in recognition. Geoffrey tried to call to her but the words were dust within his throat. She, in turn, called to him in a hauntingly beautiful voice, some syllables he could not quite compre-hend. Then, she fell to her knees, hands over her beautiful face as she wept, and the sound of her sobbing shook the unnatural stillness and set the crawling darkness to moaning with the terrible echoes of her misery.

"Claire!" he cried to her as he moved forward again, but the word stuck and cracked within him. The boat did not move now and he took another pace forward. Suddenly, he was so close that he might reach out and touch her.

For an instant, their gazes met fully, and he saw such an abundance of love and quiet peace there that his heart suddenly felt a calmness it had never known. Here, in the midst of mystery and impending death, in this horrible prison of dark waves and darker ships, her soul shone forth like a beacon in a storm, and the warmth of the love she radiated drew him to her with a force that seemed nearly physical. It was as if she read the words written across his heart for her gentle smile expressed all he could ever feel for her revealing love and hope, possession and pity. His sword slipped from his grasp and fell beneath the water, but he scarcely noticed. Now there was no need for death.

But as he moved that last long step through the current, he suddenly felt his feet slide from the sea bottom and instantly he was lost, sinking down beneath the surface, plunging with the weight of his armor. The water forced its way into his mouth and nostrils but it was not the brackish taste of unclean water, it was the salty taste of blood. He struggled hard against the tossing blackness that swept in upon him, but there was nothing to take hold of. There was nothing but shifting, choking blackness, and the breath fled too quickly from his screaming lungs.

He fought for air against the surging sweep of the current, and it was as if he were suddenly holding his own. He found air; his desire to live for her possessed him. But something gingerly wrapped itself about his left ankle and drew him ever downward.

Abruptly the scene changed to a torchlit room in the old hall of jarl Eadric, the hall Geoffrey had found abandoned in his search. But the rooms were no longer vacant, he saw. By the crude sleeping couch of Eadric's son, he saw a quivering, nude form huddled protectively against the rough furs, her ankles connected to the foot of the couch by a length of heavy chain.

Her eyes were upon the low doorway where a shadowy figure stood gazing in at her, and they were bright with terror, the doe's first sight of the stalking wolf. She jerked her head about sensing the awfulness of her fate, but there was no avenue of escape to be seen, and she understood this only too well. Futilely, she tugged at the collar and chain, but her small hands were less than powerless against its strength.

Geoffrey watched with a horror approaching her own as the massive, shadowed figure of the warrior approached his captive and laughed a laugh of pure lust, reminiscent of Eadric Siwardsson. The warrior jerked her to her feet by the length of chain. She fought; she clawed madly, but she was relentlessly drawn nearer and nearer to the assailant until his bulky arms enveloped her petite form and his head forced hers back to taste the sweet flesh of her throat.

He cried out in pleasure; she in pain.

And the young Norman watched helpless in his dream as the figure of Wulfhere Eadricsson, the warrior he had yet to meet, ravished his Claire within the inner sanctum of his own mind. Inside, he wept as he watched her roughly taken, for the solitary place where she should be safe, here, within his own heart, even this last refuge had been grossly violated by the son of a Saxon outlaw.

He roared out his anger and his hate from the shadows of the room, but they could not hear him. He was as a ghost witnessing the outlaw's brutality.

But the final dream that came to him that night was the most relentlessly horrifying of all for the fear it discovered deep within his brave heart was more subtly all-possessing then that which he felt for his Claire. Indeed, the dream did not even seem to concern her directly, although even deep within its mystery he detected her presence where he had not before. It was only a slight variation of the same theme, that dream he had not been able to escape from in the cold damp tower of Castle Ayrin so long ago, and although he could not quite discern its true significance, still its aspects churned his insides raw with its implications.

There was that damned hill and the same heat burning white-hot from above though much was shadowed darkness and the feel of a stout horse between his armored thighs as he held his sword hilt tightly. But gradually, all of the desert before him dissolved into nothingness; hot black emptiness swirled about the foot of the hill. He sat poised in the saddle somewhere upon a precipice overlooking a vast cavern, yet within the void, he could see neither wall's bottoms. There was only the hill and the horse and him.

Without warning, the heat became coolness and then cold until the knight shivered with bone-shaking intensity. It was a coldness unlike any winter he had ever experienced; there was something wrong about its feel. It was not the frozen ferocity of the glacier that assailed him, it was the all-encompassing chill of the grave.

A freezing wind blew forth from that abject and total blackness, a wind with a stink to it that he had smelled only in combat the day after the butchering was done; it was the filthy scent of rotting corpses and from the intensity of the odor, there must be thousands left to decay in that grave he stood above. God! It was the stink of a grave so full that the breeze seemed the very breath of the molten floors of hell. And, incredibly, on that reeking wind there was the sighing murmur of many, many voices in many tongues, all linked together supernaturally until the breeze was weighted leadenly with the burden of countless expressions that lingered siren-like to caress the steel covered ears of the mounted knight.

Who were they, those voices? His mind screamed the question into the thick silence that exists only in man's deepest dreams, in that twilight world of distorted shadows and time-slowed motion. But even deeper in his whirling mind, a calm voice answered him, a voice apart from the others, that he knew was also his own. It answered the question in a way he did not wish to know.

These were the voices of the dead, he understood, inviting, coaxing, calling to him to join them in their everlasting carnival of stuporous peace. Ah, peace! There was so much peace to be had after the pain and loneliness of life was at an end; all he needed was to come with them.

No. No! His mind screamed it over and over. They laughed at him, not harshly, but rather as a father laughs when he sees his beloved son attempting something foolish.

Yes, they laughed, you will come with us; it is written that you cannot avoid us for we are eternal; we are the left hand of fate! We have the patience to wait for you as we have for so many others.

But the wait for Geoffrey St. Denis will not be long! You drive yourself into our arms; you hurl yourself headlong into death, into the scythe of the Grim Reaper. They chuckled comfortingly, after all, they were not his enemies. But they would have him. Yes, they would certainly have him.

The stench of them, of their words, gagged him. The taste of sour milk was in his throat but he choked it back. But in the uncanny perception that a man often finds only deep within his dreams, Geoffrey sensed they were being honest with him. His quest would be the death of him.

Anger flowed through his veins like scalding water, thawing the icy grip of the dead. Inside, he raged, raged like the lion he was! He was tired of mockery, of deceit! Did they imagine that he was afraid to die? But he was! And he knew it and it made him sick; he was more afraid of death than any other thing he had ever experienced, save one. He was more afraid of shame than death. And he would not be shamed before others by his own words. He drew himself erect, furious!

Then so be it! He thundered in reply. Damn you all to hell, my brothers! If death was the price he must pay to win her then it was still a bargain in his eyes, and the laughter of a few lousy corpses would not change that. And in this realization, the laughter of all the voices died, awed at the power he radiated. A lone voice remained speaking to him, feminine and soft. He had never spoken with Claire, yet he knew that the voice was hers. "My love," it whispered so softly it brought tears to his eyes. "My champion!" Then it faded until all that he heard was a strangely haunting echo of the words. But the words did not die off as natural echoes do but changed until they were a rasping of air, unwholesome, fearful, then a hideous croaking parody of the gentle words.

"Love! Champion! My, my," the voiced croaked like a trained raven and Geoffrey jerked back in the saddle as something dark and sleek separated itself from the blackness and winged toward his eyes. It was a raven, an enormous ebony bird with blood dripping from its pointed beak and tatters of flesh, ripped from the dead stuffed in its mouth. It barely cleared him and as it passed overhead, blood flew off and spattered his fear-struck face.

"Champion! Champion!" it croaked again before it vanished behind him, leaving only the windy whistle of its still-flapping wings to sound out its progress in the fetid air.

Geoffrey shivered awake and lay in the darkness of his pavilion as if he were truly dead. For long moments, it seemed as if even his heart had ceased to thump. Etched in the dim lines of the tent folds, imagination drew her face and the hunger that ripped his heart then and there was a burning brand set to the tender energy of his very soul.

Very slowly, he arose.

It was still dark outside as he drew back the flap that served as a door to the blue and red striped structure. A fresh, clean breeze, cool and smelling of the open desert behind them blew into his pinched face. Above him, the sky was a woven tapestry of pure black velvet and glittering diamonds scattered in random handfuls of patterns across the bowl of heaven. There was very nearly no sound in the night air, save for the occasional barking protest of a watch dog or a snore from a nearby pavilion, yet he felt himself tense and on edge, as if he were listening for something or expecting a vision.

But nothing came to him. The only sound was the blood pulsing at his temples, the only sights the stars and the shadowed pavilions of Christendom.

With a low curse that was for either love or fate, or both as well as himself, he struck flint and lit the small lamp beside his couch. Before him, his armor gleamed quite brilliant in the smoky lamplight. It was but hours before he would wear it in the fight for his life and those of others. He ran a strong, thick-calloused hand across his longsword, smiled at the thin line of blood that appeared attesting to its sharpness, and hefted the familiar weight of the weapon in his grasp. It was somehow comforting.

One could say much against the strength of the infidel armies, yet one still could feel calm holding this stout length of razor-edged steel up to the light. How wickedly the blade gleamed! Killing bright, he thought, from an odd verse that a passing minstrel had taught him as a boy.

Death comes once, and death comes twice,
Deathly polished killing bright;
As the falcon hunts the mice
Gleams the sword in awful might!

A song it sings; death comes thrice;
Blood runs red as souls take flight!
The devil stands to cast his dice,
With sword that gleams, oh killing bright.

Aye! he thought, the song was true. This day, the blood would surely run red and the soul take flight, but whether twas his or not was more a matter for the silvery blade to decide, the blade and the arm behind it when the two armies locked in the press of combat.

Almost reluctantly, he buckled on his armor and sword, tucked his folded gauntlets within the confines of his broad leather sword belt and grasped in his hands his freshly painted, kite-shaped shield. He stepped out into the night air. Geoffrey hesitated only an instant before he nudged his squire awake and bade him saddle the chestnut destrier for him.

"Milord!" stammered the young fellow as he saw Geoffrey's armor, and more foreboding, the gaunt, lined face it framed. "Is aught amiss? Do we ride to war at this hour?"

Geoffrey smiled at the boy's concern before he answered. The boy would make a good knight one day if he lived through the coming battles.

"Nay lad, not yet, anyway. The battle fight now is within my own boundaries, not those of God or Islam." He ruffled the gaping lad's hair with a common display of affection before he took the reins and led Chestnut out to the edge of the camp.

Before him loomed Tarsus, black and squat like a block of solid granite, and the hills about it were immobile and silent like dozing camels against the starlit sky.

11

CHAPTER THE ELEVENTH

The light of false dawn did little to make Tarsus seem more approachable. Silhouetted against the gray twilight sky of the unrisen sun, the high walls loomed gigantic in the near distance upon that low, flat hill. Here and there, spaced at precise intervals among the parapets, warming fires of the night watch twinkled brightly, exuding thoughts of warmth and companionship. Geoffrey found curious lapses in his thoughts when he stared at such sights; he forgot why there was war, for the fires seemed to him to be too much like those at Westwall or Cornwall or any other English manor. At these moments, he found himself wondering if men were not alike, regardless of what land they lived in. There was something cozy and comforting about flames in the night and Geoffrey pictured the Moslems laughing and storytelling about their own fires.

Save for such reminders of life, Tarsus sat hollow and deserted, blocky and forbidding as mountain peaks against a moon. It was squat and broad astride that hill, giving the impression of intense strength, a grim formidability that would be measured before long, this day of combat in Christian and Moslem lives. In little more than an hour, the battle would be joined and that peaceful, cool plain, slumbering now beneath the stars, would turn molten red with hot sun and hotter blood.

Geoffrey shivered at the thought. It was still too much like a dream, sitting here in the night air. He turned, a frown creasing his face, at the sound of hooves galloping up the hill behind him. He wanted no companions in his brooding. Let them find their own damned hills to ponder upon.

But the sounds swept up the dusty, rock-strewn path to the hilltop without pause to where Geoffrey sat astride Chestnut. In the growing light, Geoffrey discerned the worry that had etched itself across Guvi's face, masking even the lines of sardonic humor so characteristic of the Finn. As the young knight realized who the rider was, he turned back to his thoughts and contemplations of night's ending.

How oddly peaceful the morning was. Did not God and Allah realize what ferocity would soon shake this tranquility? But morning in the desert was always deceptively peaceful and Geoffrey smiled wryly that its uncommon beauty should do so much to bring out the philosopher in him.

He thought again of the universal question that has ever entered the warrior's mind before the battle when waiting is gut-tensing, a soul-chilling feeling of its own, a kind of clammy unreality when the man realizes with a start, whether it's his first battle or his last, that within the hour his entire existence may have vanished.

And if it does not, then it is only because that existence of someone else has? Why? Why must it be? What was so infernally wrong with him and his love for Claire, or so fantastically right perhaps, that he must seek her at the expense of others' lives? Why must they stand before him? He had no hatred for them.

Yet, they would try to stop him, unknowing his reasons for storming the gates with the rest of the Christian press. Was any love worth this cost in lives? Was it worth his life? Aye, he sighed. Alas, alas, he loved too strongly, he knew. She was worth everything to him…and more.

For the good or evil of it, he would kill for her, not so much to possess her, though possess her he would, as to see her free. It was so deliciously ironic that he nearly laughed aloud for the cause of love he would send as many Moslems to hell as stepped before his glittering sword, as stepped between her and him.

"Geoffrey, you shit!" Guvi gasped. "Where have you been? Tis not even the first trumpet to rise and you are up. I have never known you to be so afraid of battle that you could not sleep, and certainly with all the ale we quaffed last eventide."

The Finn halted his speech in mid-thought when he saw that his friend was dressed in full battle regalia. While Guvi had just arisen, early as he usually did, and was dressed only in tunic and curled-toe felt slippers such as the Saracens wore, his Norman comrade sat in the saddle of his full-dressed destrier, clad in his mail with his naked broadsword laid across his thighs and both gauntleted hands clenched about blade and hilt.

The hands were clenched so tightly that, had Guvi peered closer, he would have noted the areas where the razor-edged blade had bitten through the leather undersides of the ring-mail gloves, again and again.

The conical helmet, peculiar to the Norman knights throughout Christendom was set upon the high saddle horn and his chain-link coif was now thrown back so that the wind might sweep through his long hair, un-Norman like in its cut.

When Geoffrey turned to regard him, Guvi was jolted by the red-rimmed, swollen, sleepless eyes of his friend and the hard line of his mouth. Now, Guvi was not a superstitious fellow, believing in neither God nor devil, which was uncommon for that age, but an odd chill crept slowly up his spine as he stared at his comrade.

In those tired eyes, he saw the face of death but whose death he could not precisely say. The face was the grim face of a statue, unseeing, unfeeling, uncaring, and unreasoning. Oblivious to all but one purpose.

Guvi looked past his companion at Tarsus before them and his psyche received a jolt at the energy he could feel between the knight and the city. The citadel sat like a giant lodestone acting upon Geoffrey, drawing him ever closer, to swallow him. Never had he witnessed such an attraction of a man towards an instrument of his death and Guvi feared that Geoffrey had lost his reason.

"Eh, what say you, my friend?" Geoffrey asked him, having heard the clear tones of the Finn's voice in the still morning air, but not the meaning behind the sounds.

Guvi eyed him quizzically with trepidation of a sort. "I entered your tent in search of you this morning for I had trouble sleeping, and to my huge surprise noted that some rogue had stealthily entered after you had left but before I myself did enter, and hacked all of your fine furniture to pieces with a great sword such as you yourself possess."

The young knight's eyes lightened momentarily with a heavy humor.

"Indeed, you say, sir?" he questioned. "Tis easy to believe as all sorts of knaves and rogues abound in such a rude settlement as this camp. Has not my father intimated so? Mayhap it was some such person as he who will not tend to his own affairs but who plagues others with his unwanted and unwarranted consideration!"

Guvi sat bolt upright at the sardonic jest, scowling darkly, and muttered a wicked oath to himself concerning Christian morality. Anger struck him momentarily.

"Nay, friend!" he answered, rather heatedly. "Twas more like some fellow, still but a child inside, who takes out his rage upon objects, rather than those foes who…"

Geoffrey interrupted him with a snarl that caused Chestnut to shy, startled at the harsh, metallic sound of his master's voice. "When I mount that high wall yonder this morn, you will understand fully that I am both willing and able to deal out killing strokes to men as well as the trappings of my pavilion. I was but loosening my sword arm."

"I see…"

"Have care, Finn! I am in no mood for your mischief!" Geoffrey's voice was cold and deadly with danger in it; only his hatred kept him from dropping from the exhaustion he felt. He had slept only little since discovering she was here.

Guvi shrugged. "I noticed that you left your sleeping couch intact, my friend. Do you plan on returning with a prize to warm it?"

For a long instant, the knight sat silent. Then he turned to reply. In that second, when the young St. Denis turned his head to look Guvi in the face, the Finn realized that he had miscalculated, for there were hellish furnaces glowing within those pools of icy blue.

This was no longer the boyish champion Guvi had grown so fond of; this was another warrior, awful and menacing, with absolutely no regard for his own life and even less for the lives of others. Guvi blinked his eyes for suddenly he saw Geoffrey as the devil's champion, a knight of the darkness and with the appearance of his friend's hard-lined face, he needed but a crow or two upon his shoulder to convince Guvi that he was the Grim Reaper incarnate.

But his vision cleared and he felt only concern for this wayward friend of his. There was something terribly wrong here, he knew. The anger he saw was awesome, a killing force from some time primeval when all of man was savage beyond logic. It was as if an entirely separate entity possessed his companion, a demon cast from some black, hell-spawned pit to this world of light and air and imprisoned behind those fierce blue eyes. And yet, as quickly as it had been birthed, it died.

It was not Guvi who had earned such hatred, it was not the Finn who would die. And Guvi wondered in that instant when the storm in those eyes calmed back to rationality, if it was himself that Geoffrey kept the anger for. "Aye," was all the young warrior said.

Guvi laid an awkwardly gentle hand upon Geoffrey's armored sleeve. "My friend, my best comrade, you push yourself too hard. What will be will be and you cannot alter the will of the gods, or fates, whatever you choose to name the forces of destiny. By driving yourself as you do, you but decrease your chances of having her. You would have done well to have slept this night."

Geoffrey shook his head wearily. The day had not yet begun and he was tired beyond exhaustion from running in his dreams. But when the trumpet sounded, his head would clear; it always had.

"There was no rest for me, friend, only sleep filled with evil dreams of her. How could I close my eyes when with each darkening of sight, I saw her kneeling and weeping upon that cursed boat, or chained naked and trembling to that son of a bitch's couch. You call yourself too wise for this; so be it then, I am a fool. Yet I can change naught. She has instilled a fire in my veins and sent the quicksilver flash of lightning through the chambers of my heart. These are the thirsts I cannot quench, save by behaving as a hero."

Guvi shook his head and began to speak, but Geoffrey held up a gauntleted hand to hush him. "Give me leave to finish, friend. I will say this to you this one time and then will no longer burden you with it."

"Tis no burden, Geoffrey. You must know better than that!"

Geoffrey shrugged. "For over two years, this fire has glowed within the wretched hollowness of my sinner's soul. I have taken much upon myself in this quest, this fool's quest as you name it. I have sacrificed my honor, my obligation to my family's familial love, and duty to my king. And I have not cared; contrary to all I was ever taught and learned to respect, I have not given a damn about any of this when compared to some peasant's daughter.

"This fire I speak of has altered me terribly inside, though you could not know it; it has tempered the chambers of my heart into a temple for her and with each new day and each new thought of her, it has drummed thunder loud in my bursting temples and brought a frigid rush of some inexplicable fear to my mind. It is a river, a cataract of some awful burning substance that makes me hot and weak at the same time. And I have suffered all of this these years until my entire soul has been reworked into something of iron, of but a single purpose.

"And now I sit before those ugly, dirty walls. And, as I do, as I see that those thick layers of yellow stone are all that keep me from her, the pain of the burning river has swollen my veins until they are bursting and the witch-fire that has eddied to and fro these years inside my blood has been fanned from lamplight to bonfire.

"I am consumed by what I feel and I can think of naught but possessing her. It can go on no longer; I am spent with my own desires. It ends here. If I cannot have her then I will die for her. If I cannot take her from the wretched slavery she has suffered as concubine to that bastard of the Siwardsson's, then I will perish as much by my own hand as yon Moslems. I say to you truly, my friend, if Lord God ever created one true test of my worthiness for these gilded spurs I wear, this is it. I must have her, Guvi, These years have left my soul shriveled and wasted like a leper's body; if I cannot free her after seeing her so close to freedom, then most surely my soul will rot inside me, until it chokes the very life from my chest."

In the face of such a confession, even the salacious wit of the heathen

228

Finn was stilled. For long, clumsy minutes there was only the soft tapping of the steel links of Geoffrey's coif upon his shoulder steel as the quick wind tore at it.

Guvi ran a swarthy hand through his sleep-tangled hair. "Methinks I will ride with your father this morning, though I like not the man at all, for fear you are bent upon suicide. I can hear the recall trumpet being sounded and see you still alone, assaulting the gates of the Saracen citadel with a thousand infidel arrows leaping for your fool's throat!"

Geoffrey snorted at the black humor. "I am touched by your mother's concern, knave!"

"Better the sting of the words of a friend, then the deadly sting of the infidel weaponry."

"It will not be me that dies this day, Finn, woman of Finn-land. This fire that enrages the spirits of my blood also lends strength to my sword arm. And the rage that denies me sleep is a two-edged sword for it also raises the arm that wields my weapon. Nay, friend, I think that it will be many a foolish infidel that steps before me this morning."

Guvi was silent again a few moments before he replied, "You confound and amaze me, Geoffrey. We sit amidst the greatest of the Christian armies, where every man is dreaming of either wealth, power, or salvation and you sit mooning lovestruck over some female you have never bedded."

Geoffrey glared at his slender companion. "I have already confessed to being the fool among us all, have I not? Do you wish more?" he asked curtly.

"No, I only think..." Guvi stammered.

"Good. It is settled. Cease your old wive's prattling like a scolding wood squirrel!" Geoffrey thundered in a voice so stentorian as to cause the early risers in the encampment to pause in their chores and stare up at the hill where they sat in the saddle.

Guvi chuckled. Here was speech he could appreciate and deal with and he replied in kind, drawing a rather pointed comparison between Geoffrey and the leavings of several different types of farm animals. Then he was off for the camp kitchen for breakfast.

For some it is so easy, Geoffrey thought as he sat alone once again.

What was it inside him that drove him so? Was it love alone? He knew he needed her more than life itself; but was there not a limit somewhere and was there not a point where the walls could not be battered down no matter what the ram used? Was there not a point where a man might honorably acknowledge defeat? Not while he lived. There was only one alternative to having her...death.

There was a raucous booming voice behind him again and Geoffrey turned impatiently, this time to see the robust form of Wild Eadric Siwardsson staggering up on foot. He seemed to be very drunk.

"Odin's blue balls, boy!" he roared good-humoredly. "I see that there is at least one other in this stinking, chicken-hearted camp who is not such a dainty flower that he needs sleep before such a minor contest as this!"

While the Saxon was still yards away from Geoffrey, the knight could detect the pungent, heady scent of ale in the air, mixed in thickly with the burly Saxon's even stronger aroma. Quite obviously, the bandit had remained awake all night drinking as his ruddy face was one continuous flush and his single eye puffy and bloodshot. His eyepatch was gone and there was dirt stuffed into the empty socket where he had obviously tumbled down one of the camp hillsides. Geoffrey looked him over, sniffed in distaste, and resumed his silent vigil.

Eadric blinked comically so that the grit in his empty socket gently sifted down into his beard. He was hard to ignore, this one.

Geoffrey's thoughts were on Claire as the sun began its ascent, marking the end of night. She was within those stark walls; was she awake now? Was she thinking about the coming battle?

What would she think if she knew he was there, for he would hope she welcomed his love. Did she fear the army of her countrymen camped outside the gates? More than two years had passed. Would she be different now?

Geoffrey winced as he felt the sword bite through the leather again, and into his hand where he unthinkingly clenched it.

What if she had fallen in love with him, this Wulfhere, this Eadric's son? On the trail, Geoffrey had attempted to discreetly search out the Siwardsson about this but no sooner had he broached the suggestion to

Wild Eadric than the man, embarrassingly, collapsed into convulsions of laughter. The red-beard beat his fists against his thighs and his massive belly shook with the humor of the thought.

"Love Wulfhere?!" he cackled. Geoffrey had been too flustered to ask further. But he always wondered; women were strange in their loyalties. But if it was this way, she was wasting her love on a dead man for Wulfhere was going to die!

Eadric was not to be denied his audience. He belched twice, quite indelicately, and the second time hiccoughed and spat some regurgitated ale upon the ground. He blew his nose into his huge fist and wiped it casually across his fur breeches, causing Geoffrey to turn and stare at him hotly. It was then he saw the Siwardsson still held a half-full horn of ale in one ham-handed fist. The fellow was not to be believed! He had been drinking continuously for over fourteen hours.

The Siwardsson farted loudly and spoke, "Had I known you were up, cub, I would have gladly fetched you to drink with me! These other Normans are much too soft! After several hours of horn-hoisting, they roll over and puke their guts out. Then, they crawl over the floor like dogs and collapse. But come, I think you might be worthy to drink with the Son of Siward the Saxon, Eadric the Wild!"

He belched blissfully and smacked his full fleshy lips in pleasure. Geoffrey contemplated his strange comrade, standing beside him drinking with one hand shoved down the rear of his breeches, scratching away at his broad bum like there was salvation to be found there. The knight shook his head in amusement, as weary and impatient as he was.

"I shall forgo that dubious pleasure, thank you," muttered Geoffrey, stiffly, his shoulders slightly hunched against the pre-dawn chill.

But Eadric's face took on a strange cast abruptly, and he was uncommonly serious as he again raised his voice to his young companion. "But then, mayhap it was not through thine own choice that you went sleepless. Mayhap it was more due to softness, not steel, in your backbone!"

Geoffrey's voice was dry of emotion as he answered. He did not so much as turn his head about to look at the Saxon; his eyes remained focused upon the dark walls of the infidel city, still stonily silent as a burial vault. "One more word, one more sound, one more of your stupid insinuations, you ugly brute, and I shall slay you as you stand there, and not a man of this camp would gainsay me or defend you!"

Eadric howled with glee, the ale horn half-risen to his thick lips. "Ah, cub! The trumpet is not sounded, the contest not yet met and already bloodlust sings in your soul. You are edgy indeed this morning; perhaps you should sleep more next time, But you have the fire kindled up, it is well. Look to me when the hunting horn sounds and we are into the Seljuks like hounds after hares."

"I ride before the men of Westwall."

"Are you afraid?" laughed Eadric.

Geoffrey wheeled Chestnut back to face Eadric, intent upon either silencing the red bear or riding him down and slaying him. The knight was angry to the point of madness. "Eadric Siwardsson, I warn you but this final time!" Geoffrey rasped with dry throat and thick tongue. His hands tensed upon the broadsword, and Eadric, ever watchful of details, caught this.

The Saxon considered his words now, before he spoke. His sarcasm had been rough, but well intended. He did not wish to goad the young knight further. "Posh, boy! You'll not cleave this red pate atwain for a few ill-spent words. I know you better than that. Here! Drink instead! Twill settle your gut for the blood to come, and more so, dull the pain that cuts through your heart, my friend."

Geoffrey's look was unfathomable, yet he reached down and took the ale horn. There was a large amount left. Eadric raised one bushy eyebrow as his friend drained the vessel with a single tilt and cast it over his shoulder to clatter, startlingly loud in the quiet morning, upon the stones that littered the hill path. Geoffrey let out a belch and ruffled the tangles in his hair, his steely eyes beginning to heighten with the bite of the brew.

"My thanks, red-hair. Twas a far better breakfast than I have tasted in a while, and most certainly does more to sooth my weariness than your idle rambling!" he laughed tiredly.

Eadric beamed benevolently. "When the contest is ended, we shall drink again, cub! If you are not too busy with your prize."

"Enough of this! I do my duty for God and King William," Geoffrey said, not unkindly.

"And for them both you wander the hills sleepless and moonstruck, eh?" smiled Eadric. "Well, tis not such an awful thing, I suppose. Many a man has been motivated by much less than this foolishness!"

"So say you?" asked Geoffrey, sarcastically.

"Aye!" thundered Eadric, his boldness returning. "You Normans always were a bunch of pleasant daisies to be plucked by any maid's hand or trampled into the rich English soil by a stout Saxon boot."

His voice trumpeted over the awakening camp, a large portion of which was Norman, but he was oblivious to the hot looks he garnered from the milling Franks. His braying call was meant to evoke only good humor, but many a vassal of William II took offense.

"As at Hastings, do you mean?" inquired Geoffrey, owlishly.

"Ah!" chortled the red bear, though his face darkened a bit. "There is a difference. I was not at Hastings. Had I been there, you Normans would still be growing your grapes across the water!" He broke wind loudly for the third time before he finished speaking. "The sun rises! Make ready! Let us go to the cook for a bite to eat before we struggle and die!"

Geoffrey spit at his feet. "And how do you propose we do that? While we talk the entire camp lines up before us to breakfast."

Eadric grinned mightily. "There are ways," he said.

He turned and cupped his hands to carry a shout down the hill to the sleepy soldiers who sat eating their morning bread, dried meat, fruit, and ale.

"To arms! To arms! Help! They are upon us!" he roared.

The effect was instantaneous and shocking, if not outright laughable. Plates of food sailed through the air and half-dressed Frank and English knights and men-at-arms ran to their pavilions for arms and armor. In a split second, the kitchen compound was totally deserted with even the cooks racing for their crossbows.

Eadric casually looked around as he surveyed the effect. "That will chase the sleep from their eyes and make them better prepared for this day; they are a lazy lot anyway. Ha! Now we might eat uninterrupted and enjoy perhaps, a moment of meditation as well. Come!"

"You are most surely lower than the deepest dug latrine, red-hair!" muttered Geoffrey.

"I have been called worse!" smiled Eadric with his yellow teeth.

The Saxon started down the hill; Geoffrey followed.

Within the hour, the lines of assault were forming around Tarsus. The lines of the Franks stretched out for what seemed miles and were deep with the closely packed armies of the Christian countries. The first of the attacks would be against the main gate; Bohemond of Otranto was not one to waste time shilly-shallying about with devious plans when a head on collision might just as well do the job. And God knew his army was ready; they were tired of the inaction of building camps and awaiting reinforcements and even of ale-guzzling and whoring. Their money was long gone and now all they thought of was booty. Stories circulated of the charms of the Arabian women and even the most wretched of the common soldiers knew if he were in the right place at the right time, he might snare a rare prize.

Cries for Allah and his prophet Mohammed went up throughout the city as the white-burnoosed Saracens ran to the parapets with bundles of throwing spears and quivers of steel-headed arrows. Stones had been piled for days along the walls at intervals of twenty feet, masses of rock large enough to crush a siege-ladder full of men. About the gates were piles ten times the size of the others, for the Saracens well knew how vulnerable their gates were. Cauldrons of smoking pitch or olive oil sat at intervals between the stone piles, giant pots fixed to wheeled dollies so that they might readily be pulled along the wall's trouble points. The infidels were ready; they had awaited this day for two months.

CLAIRE HAD PROMISED HERSELF THAT SHE WOULD NOT WATCH THE combat this day, that watching would only worsen the torment of divided loyalties that raged inside her. But this morning, she rose early and dressed, bade the ancient Moslem nurse take her daughter Helgi, and stepped out onto the terrace less than an hour after first light. She quietly closed the gilded latticework doors of her balcony to peer over the army gathered before the lofty walls of Wulfhere Eadricsson's sanctuary.

In the center of the field before Tarsus flew the colors of Bohemond of Otranto, a crafty, experienced fighter who might match sword stroke for sword stroke with the lions of Islam as well as he matched wits with the poisoned mind of Emperor Alexis. To his left sat the knights of Raymond of Toulouse, distinguishable by the fleur-de-lis upon his flapping standard, and to his right were massed the chivalry of Godfrey of Bouillon. But there was also a small, hard wedge of knights sitting between the ranks of Otranto and Toulouse, beneath the pennant of William II of England. The rest of the English had either taken to the flanks or were lax in massing for the attack. There was also the possibilities that they were held in reserve or had been sent to other gates of the city to storm them as well. In this army of united Christendom, the English were but another contingent.

And although Claire could not see clearly enough in the rising dust of the horses to distinguish it, just behind the proud banner of England was one of purest sky blue with the green color of twin trees upon it—the honored standard of Westwall and the clan St. Denis.

The armor of the Franks was dazzling in the sunlight and the colors of their tunics looked like a rainbow had spilled from heaven to the plain below. At that instant, Claire felt some small comfort that she was more a captive in this city than a defender, though she knew that she also might suffer if the walls were breeched for all too often the attackers were drunk on blood and killing lust and made no distinction between the citizens of a defeated city.

Directly beside the banner of St. Denis sat a young, steel-muscled knight she might have recognized astride his massive chestnut-colored destrier. His fair skin had been burnt shades darker by the unforgiving desert sun, a tribute to its intensity, yet he wore not the customary white surcoat to ward off the heat. Instead, his loose outer garment was a copy of the banner of his family, blue with the twin trees, the heraldry of generations of pride and success. The heraldry he thought he would never wear, marked him as redeemed. Behind him sat the men of Westwall in their high saddles, silent as their master's son, watching and awaiting his command.

They were proud soldiers all, and although the fear of death shone deep within their eyes as it did with every soldier of the great armies, still they sat calm in the stale breeze. Few words were spoken but they jested lightly among themselves or made quiet wagers and eyed each other with many unasked questions. Westwall was not a large contingent and those behind the blue shields knew each other intimately for they had grown to knighthood together. It was a hard thing to accept for the inexperienced of them, that within the hour a trusted friend, or master, or even the ones who had taught them, might be lying face down before the walls, coughing out his life. But they masked their thoughts; morbidity would be counterproductive.

Most were experienced in combat, warriors conditioned to fears, veterans long-seasoned in other, lesser wars until their fear was no more of a hinderance than the weight of their armor or the heavy heft of their swords. They had been taught accordingly to use the fear within them-selves, to keep it contained, chained up, locked under control as the advance sounded.

And when they couched their terrible long lances to charge, they let forth in a veritable tidal wave of shattering emotion where the blood pounded hot, salty, and electric and the mind's logical reasoning flickered and went dark. The adrenalin within their veins changed them into machines made of steel as was the armored links they wore. And when they opened their dry mouths over the pounding of the hooves, the fear took to wing and the cry that rent the heavens asunder with its very ferocity, with its utter, total lack of human control became a weapon itself, to rise high over the dusty plain and plunge like a hunting gyrfalcon for the heart of the enemy force. As it always was since the dawn of man, and as it will always be, the roaring of a charging enemy has the power to shake even the strongest of the defenders.

They might die horribly, their reeling minds screamed. But with honor! With honor there was no turning back; the only recourse was to slay, slay wildly, slay madly. Let your sword-swing be a whistling, glit-tering arc around you that you might live. Each foe fallen was another minute added to your fleeting life and in the hot press of battle your life was measured indeed by minutes and by seconds.

One split-second was the down swing of an axe or the flight of a cloth-yard arrow shaft. He who laughed with you but ten heartbeats ago might lie dead ten heartbeats hence. Run wild to save your life! Howl! Fight like the savages you are beneath this thin veneer, this fine coating of civilization. Go berserk!

For this instant, they sat awaiting the trumpet call but all the power drifted just below the surface. The fire was lit; only the smoke had yet to be. And then it would be too late.

Geoffrey's deep blue eyes smoldered as he gazed over the terrain he would risk his life upon. A broad, dusty field changed into a cluster of low hills just outside the walls of Tarsus, fallow of grass or trees, sunbaked and cracked in this dry summer season so that even the dirty green scrub grass that dotted it at irregular intervals looked worn with the dryness of the weather.

Tarsus and Tartarus. How incredibly alike the two words were. Guvi had explained to him once that Tartarus was the field of the pagan dead, and Geoffrey wondered chillingly if Tarsus would be a field of Christian dead. The longer he stared at the high walls, the more lofty and foreboding seemed the gates and towers, the more packed with Moslem soldiers the parapets. Geoffrey's keen eyes caught groups of Saracen workmen moving about the walls and towers, heating the oil and pitch, filling the bow quivers, re-piling the rocks. How many stones and arrows would shower down upon him? How much oil? He felt bile rise in his throat with the tautness of his nerves. Would he die today? Would he die with nothing accomplished?

The young knight turned his sweating face to heaven and mouthed a small, silent prayer to God. No warrior's prayer was this, but one of love. Oh God of the Cross and Resurrection, if he must die this day don't let it happen before he saw her free! He wiped the sweat from his eyes and tilted the wineskin to parched lips.

The sun burned bright and clear, a curious orange-yellow. Flights of vultures were already circling, for across the lines of men they smelled death where man or beast had collapsed beneath the heat and died.

When they came close, the archers shot them, but there were always more.

Just like the Seljuks, Geoffrey thought. There was always another to fight. Par Deux! If it was this hot with the sun only just risen, how much hotter would it become thundering with Chestnut over that plain? He felt like a boiled shellfish in his armor already, but there was no discarding it. It was his edge over the defenders, for it turned aside their arrows and even their keen Damascus steel had to strike most powerfully to bite through it. Geoffrey pictured the battles as armored insects fighting each other, scrabbling madly over the hot floors of hell.

The blowing grit stuck to his face and tortured his eyes. He drank all of his wine, but still his thirst was not quenched. *One was always thirsty in this terrible land*, he thought ruefully and he wondered how much worse hell could truly be. Tangentially, his thoughts turned to the cold sweet brooks of England and he remembered winter mornings when icicles hung thick as leaves on the tree branches outside his window. Ah, what he would not give for a cup of pure snow!

But even with these thoughts about the wretchedness around him and his suppressed fear of death, Geoffrey knew for certain that he would be at the front when that trumpet sounded the assault call. His strong hand gripped together the long-handled Danish double-headed axe that Guvi had pressed upon him at the last moment with the words that it would serve him in better stead than his longsword when he was atop those walls and the Saracens were packed tight around him.

Geoffrey's armor hung heavy with weapons for he still retained his longsword as well as his poniard. A splay-headed mace was fastened at the saddle horn in case the Saracen horse soldiers chose to ride out and meet them. He saw others equipped only with sword and shield, complaining about the weight of extra weapons, but he knew in combat a man's weapon was his salvation, and, by the gods, he wanted as many chances as he could carry. Too many times had he seen death strike because of a broken sword. Would this Wulfhere Eadricsson be there to greet him? Would the renegade fight? Would the son of Eadric have any idea who Geoffrey was?

Where was his lovely Claire? Was she watching the ranks form, wind-swept like the swirling leaves of autumn until their mass was irre-pressible? He cursed the painful thought from his exhausted mind as he had often done before.

Instead of dwelling on the countless, morbid possibilities of the situa-tion, he turned to look for Guvi. The Finn tugged at his long moustache and winked encouragingly at him. He also wore the surcoat of the clan St. Denis, a privilege not allowed him under chivalric law for he was by rights not a member of the family or sworn vassal thereof. But the weight of Geoffrey's authority had paved the way for such liberties, and in truth the Norman was touched that his brigand comrade wished to wear his colors. And oddly, Guvi had foresworn immediate use of his bow and light sword; he now sported the Norman style of armor, carrying the massive axe of the North in addition to his round Viking-style shield of wood planking and center hub. Geoffrey had whistled in disbelief at seeing his slender friend so encumbered with the weight of weaponry, but Guvi explained in mock seriousness, that after all, they were not out hunting quail, and had tried to force one of the cumbersome round shields on his Norman friend. He claimed that you made less of a target secure behind one of the heavy things, and while Geoffrey was sure this must be so, yet he deferred, preferring to retain his lighter, kite-shaped shield.

It was pride in his heritage as much as anything else. The shield that he carried had been his grandfather's at Hastings, and there was some-thing stirring in just gripping its worn leather straps. His grandfather had been a powerful knight and a respected noble, and it seemed somehow that the shield was imbued with the tradition of such chivalry and Geof-frey gained strength from it.

The plan of assault was undeniably simple yet potentially effective. Or, one hoped it would be so. The Christian flanks would storm the walls of Tarsus with scaling ladders at the gate towers in the eastern and western walls, while a third party, the major attack force, hit the southern wall and gates. Logically, the infidels would believe that the one deliv-ered at the southern wall was the real force, considering its greater contingent of men and the fact that it would begin after the assaults on the other two walls. By Saracen thought, the first two would be ruses and the third one the final attack which they would expend all their men in trying to stop. Instead, while Saracen attention was drawn to the southern force, Geoffrey's group would storm the main frontal gates.

Theoretically, the very audacity of this would shelter them from the suspicion of the Seljuks, crafty as they were. Geoffrey's men would attempt to fire the gates with a strange liquid sent by Alexis the Emperor, called Fire of the Greeks. Geoffrey had never seen it work, but he was told it was an alchemist's compound that burned even in water. The idea was to burn the gates enough to batter them in. And Geoffrey would be there with his axe.

No one discussed the heat or the smoke that would assail Geoffrey's force in that narrow channel between the twin towers as the gates burned. His men made huge wooden shields as protection of a sort from the hail of rocks and arrows they would face, but each of them understood that these same shields might just as easily catch fire when the gates were torched and stop the attack. The entire plan needed immaculate timing, as well as bravery, and Guvi complained loud and long when informed that Westwall had been selected to carry the attack.

And suddenly, so incredibly abrupt in its coming, there was the trumpet. Now, there was no time for thought or trepidation; Geoffrey jerked his head in confusion at the coming of the moment he had needed and dreaded for so long. Something inside him screamed to run and flee. Nothing, no cause, no woman, no king was worth his life. But a calmer voice answered and Geoffrey drew a deep breath and gripped the reins more tightly. It was happening as it should.

The attacks hit the eastern and western walls with a flurry of rushing men-at-arms and scaling ladders. Bugles answered from the walls and the knight heard the cries of the first wounded as sheets of scalding pitch and oil cascaded from the parapets. Poor fools, thought Geoffrey, to die so horribly for a mere diversion. But they could not have known; they thought they were carrying out the main attack. No one discussed strategy with the common soldiers.

Then, there was the bugle blaring urgently from the north gate where the third and largest attack was forming and Geoffrey prayed to God that these Saracens were to be duped. If they suspected the mission of the men from Westwall, the consequences would be incalculably bad. The attacking army was hidden in its own dust until Geoffrey saw only the fortresses surrounded by a fog of sand, writhing with small figures, and terrible, terrible sounds.

Then there was the final trumpet. For him! Ha Rou! For God and William!

The rest was a blur of clashing hooves and dancing colors as the knights of Westwall charged. Dust and coarse yellow grit swirled up to choke Geoffrey as Chestnut pounded across the plain. From the corners of his eyes, he saw the forces of Boullion and Toulouse converge on the furthest corners of the city walls, intent upon drawing off the last defenders in one final ruse. Crooked scaling ladders were thrown up with the momentum of the headlong charge and already the first knights were being hurled from the walls to fall screaming into the mill of their comrades below. But all this was of little concern as he passed into arrow range of the gate towers and the gigantic gates grew up before him, looming larger and larger like some magic gravestones, side by side. As if in a dream, he saw little Hugh deLussac drop with a black feathered arrow in his chest, he whose own mother had wet nursed Geoffrey, he who had received his gilded spurs the same day Geoffrey had in the same ceremony. A lump formed in the young knight's throat.

Brian Fitzpatrick fell as they neared the high wall, a lance through his belly and God's name upon his lips. Guy deMontgomerie fell as his mount shied in the confusion and he plunged beneath the hooves of his comrades, to be trampled into a mangled pile of guts and bones.

"Au Secours!" came the cry for help from all around. But there was no aid for the injured in this rushing pell mell; there was no chivalry to save the fallen for this was no tournament stretched across an English green. This was war in its most brutal form and uncommonly lucky was the fallen knight whose comrades halted to pull him to safety. Too much depended upon the fall of the gates and Geoffrey knew this. If there was time, he would free them from the press, but experience told him that in this heat and dust that most of the fallen wounded would die quickly, literally choked to death by the dust of their comrade's destriers.

Geoffrey cursed the bards who sang of glory in conquest. Let them take arms in this madness, then let them write to thrill the ladies.

There were high, pointed staves of wood before him now, a barrier set just before the gates themselves. With a leap worthy of a champion, Chestnut cleared them, just barely. The horse of Peter deMais, caught unawares, plunged directly upon them and screamed, as it fell steaming onto the ground. Peter fell from the saddle, instantly transfixed by a volley of arrows. A plummeting stone ended his life mercifully.

A splash of scalding heat spattered Geoffrey's left arm and Chestnut cried as he also felt the sting of the oil. Those behind him took the full brunt of the discharge and went down, horribly. The young knight turned away from a knight who sat in the saddle dead, his destrier in shock from the pain. Only the markings of his shield identified the unfortunate warrior, but Geoffrey forced his gaze away. He had no wish to know who had suffered so; it might have been him. There was no time to mark in his mind the deaths of the fallen.

Then there was the arch with its tall gates, ironbound and seemingly impregnable. Geoffrey hurled himself from the saddle, flinging the reins to another rider who, miraculously, turned out to be Guvi, and waved to the others. The engineers brought up the firepots and the sticky substance was hurled against the gates. A torch was tossed and the strange pitch caught with such a wicked fervor that Geoffrey might have been standing before the gates of hell, begging admission.

But no supplicant was he! He howled like a banshee as the timbers took fire and waved his heavy axe about his head. His shield sloughed aside arrows and rocks and the deluge lessened as the Turks tried to pour water over the burning wood. But it continued to flame merrily.

"Burn, damn you! Turn to cinders!" roared Geoffrey, shaking a clenched fist at the flaming gates. He was so near the intense heat that his exposed face was blistered, yet he was so stubborn that he would not retreat so much as a solitary pace. He held his axe ready, waiting.

The gates popped and crackled loudly as they took the fire, for the wood was ancient and well-seasoned in the dry desert air. The iron bands that bound them grew red with the heat and Geoffrey saw that it was but a matter of time before they would fall, and...then, disaster!

It was neither the falling rocks nor the oil. It was the horse soldiers. Suddenly, the flaming gates drew inward, draw-chains groaning loud over the popping fire. They opened like a desert flower at morning and with such rapidity that Geoffrey saw they were superbly counterbalanced for use in just such emergencies. Smoke obscured the entry portal and the unsuspecting Franks behind Geoffrey pressed in, seeing that something was happening and assuming that the attack had succeeded. At once, they found themselves met by a solidly massed formation of Saracen cavalry. Dark eyes peered over shield rims and long, supple lances dipped for the bellies of the crusader knights. They had guessed! *Hell and damnation!* Geoffrey cried inside.

His group was in a catastrophic situation, and their only hope of survival lay in reaching their saddles in time to turn the charge, for he saw the infidel riders eagerly awaited their command. Geoffrey turned to look for Guvi and Chestnut, but his fellows had lost their wits and tried to bunch together with swords drawn, afoot.

"You stupid bastards!" Geoffrey bellowed. "Get to your horses! They will trample us!" But they were full of panic and unreasoning. With a cry of horror, the Franks attempted to retreat on foot, some looking over their shoulders for their horses. They were not quick enough.

A swarm of black-armored and white-robed bees rode down upon them, plunging couched lance and out-thrust scimitar into the bodies of the screaming Christians. The men on foot could not escape; they would be ridden down before they reached the safety of their other companies, slaughtered to the last man. Geoffrey cursed roundly as he saw there was no choice but to stand and fight, to look death in the face and snarl.

Whether outrageously brave or simply struck dumb by terror, Sir Geoffrey met the charge without flinching. What use to run? A Latin phrase pounded through his mind, or was it Hebraic, taught to him years before in his religion classes, the words of Christ upon the cross: *Eloi, Eloi, lama sabachthani!* My God, my God, why hast thou forsaken me? Then, there was no more time for self-pity.

With all the strength he could muster from his broad, muscular back, he swung his great battle axe sideways, having cast away his shield to swing the ferocious weapon with both hands.

"Come and die, you fools!" he cried. Bloodlust was setting in.

His spinal erectors bunched with the effort of swinging the heavy instrument and an intense play of muscle through his shoulders and arms drove the man-killing blade with the raw force of a storm-driven leaf. All of his weight was put into motion as he pivoted on his toes, twisting his body to add more momentum to the already whistling arc. He saw terror momentarily race across the swarthy face of the nearest Turk as the fellow witnessed the ten-foot swath of gleaming, glittering steel, razor-edged and utterly fearsome, burn a bright path through the desert air.

The broad blade of the weapon sheared completely through the muzzle of the first horse and smashed bloodily into the neck of the second, sending both white-burnoosed riders beneath the hooves of their own charge. Geoffrey saw that one wore the golden braid of an officer and thought it fitting that he be the first to fall. But there was no time for congratulations.

Suddenly, he stood completely enmeshed in a sweeping flood of Seljuk cavalry with flashing scimitars and probing lances, but he did not stand unaided. His men of Westwall saw what had happened, saw their young master turn his back on escape to fight. And they, too, took up the fight they had come for, now with more thoughts of saving their skins than of wealth or glory. They were rodents cornered before the feline hunter; they were ground squirrels beneath the talons of the falcon, but they could sting their predators. They, too, held hands filled with swift, silvery death and knew how to hurl it into the rushing enemy. To flee was to die and such knowledge can make heroes out of the weakest men; the Seljuks had made an error in their charge for they had not allowed their prey an avenue of escape. Most of the great battles were won by allowing the beaten enemy a chance to survive; to promise him nothing but death makes him bitter and savage and far more fearsome to face. There was to be no quarter given in the interlocked struggle; this was obvious to all of the Christian knights, so it was not even possible to sacrifice honor and to surrender. Perhaps it was only because of this unpalatable fact and the way the Saracen horse soldiers pushed them together like cattle, that they fought so wildly.

But fight they did. Awesomely. Powerfully.

And the infidel Turks were shocked to see that their light horses and light armor were not sufficient to overrun these well-armored men of England, these grim-faced warriors whose eyes held no hope.

The fiery-golden sun of morning shone down indifferently upon the clash of sweat-soaked, bloodied adversaries and the rest of the siege upon the city might just as well have been carried out in England or hell for all that mattered to Sir Geoffrey. His entire world—life and death, was centered in this short drama played out before the burning gates of Tarsus.

The heroes of Westwall were gruesomely decimated in that rush of Seljuk riders, sustaining better than sixty per cent casualties, most of them slain outright. Geoffrey nearly wept with rage as he saw the blue and green surcoats, sodden with gushing crimson, upon lifeless bodies that lay scattered around him. Men that had been his friends and comrades since birth lay cold beneath the furnace that was the sun, never again to clasp his hand by the fire in welcome or drink to his health at the feasts. Their blood washed in small pools about his chain sollerets.

But the Seljuk charge was ripped apart and flung into bits and pieces as a deer spitted upon boar tusks. They had been overconfident in their surprise; they had not counted upon the English anger nor the English pride.

"Westwall and William!" Geoffrey's cry split the heavens.

"Allah-el-akbarrrrrr!" he was answered.

On the hundredth stroke of his axe, the handle began to split. On the five hundredth stroke, it splintered with the force laid behind it as it was tested against men, armor, and horseflesh without prejudice. After he had ruined his seventeenth horse and smashed the helmet of his twelfth infidel, it was just a sharp-splintered jagged shaft clutched in his mailed fist and even this he drove into the eyes of a wounded Saracen who clutched at his legs, curved dagger in hand and seeking Geoffrey's groin.

His axe gone, Geoffrey drew his two-foot-long dagger and hurled himself at the throat of the nearest rider. His own throat was almost too dry to yell either curses or prayers.

Guvi was perhaps a bit more efficient. As a rider would rush at him, he would always step to one side or the other, duck under the stroke and strike the horse's legs with the handle of his axe, nearly always dropping the plunging beast rider-less. At once, his comrades, many of whom were too wounded to do anything else, would rush in to slay the man before he could rise. But nowhere was there to be seen the bright colors of St. Denis; all was a darkening crimson and the wretched dirt before the gates was literally red mud.

Geoffrey stood with his blood-encrusted, chainmail-armored back to the wall beside the gate, swinging a captured scimitar with one hand, his twin-edged longsword in the other. The dead Saracens were virtually thigh deep before him, motionless as pitched sacks of steel-dressed grain and still their heathen brothers hurled themselves over the bodies of the fallen in an attempt to bring down this Frankish lion who roared curses like a drunken demon and who slew at every side with the ferocity and utter recklessness of a maddened bull, whose actions left the battling Seljuks dazed and puzzled.

Why would he not fall?

But only those that had kept him imprisoned in Castle Ayrin could have answered the question for the Moslem riders, for only they had witnessed how the young knight had driven himself unmercifully in his training, had seen the weights he lifted and the instruments of death he became proficient with until none could stand before him. Here, now, he was tired and winded but the weapons in his hands were as familiar to him as his own boots and he had spent months on end making them a part of him.

His chest heaved mightily, sweat all but blinded him. But still the swords rose and fell, rose and fell, reaping carnage everywhere. The infidels were no more superstitious than any other group of soldiers but there was something distinctly unnerving about the way he fought.

Then, with a dropping of his stomach, Geoffrey heard the recall trumpet sound and realized the attack had been given up. But what of them here? Were they written off with the attack? But despite his anger and his outrage, he could not help but laugh as he heard Guvi's mocking voice over the din of battle. "Lord St. Denis!" he called. "I believe they are retiring for dinner. Could you tell me where the rear door is that I might follow the rest of your brave Franks?"

"God rot your balls, you cowardly shit piece!" bellowed Geoffrey lustily as he tore away a Saracen hand groping for his eyes.

"My balls for my life at this point!" Guvi retorted.

"What balls?!" growled Geoffrey. "Every Finn I ever knew had the sweet soul of a woman. God grant that I might someday meet a woman as dainty in manner as you, my friend!" Of course, Geoffrey knew no other Finns.

Guvi cursed him soundly in two languages before he shut his mouth. Now he must save his jests for breath, for the Moslems swarmed thick as bees at a hive.

In the bloody crush all he really needed to do was swing his blade and a Saracen fell, for there were at least ten infidels about him at any given time, each eagerly jostling the others to try to bring down the Christian champion. Geoffrey's skill was fading a little with his strength, but the Seljuks made it hard for him to miss, for it seemed as if even the lowliest Turkish foot soldier had run from the parapets to be in on the butchery, intent upon slaying these last of the courageous Franks now that their main force had abandoned them.

Geoffrey found himself ankle deep in blood with his arms growing heavy. He had the strength of three men, but three men would have fallen long before this in the hellish struggle.

Suddenly, the Turk before him gave a long keen of despair, turning to look panic stricken at the gates. Wasting no time, for he was sorely tired now, Geoffrey took full advantage of the distraction and raked his poniard deeply across the fellow's throat. With a kick, he freed himself from the dead man's embrace and blanched a little as a geyser of carmine splashed over him.

All of the Turks stood frozen an instant.

Turning to follow their gaze, Geoffrey saw the cause of such a curious reaction from hardened fighting men and smiled in relief. Neither God nor Bohemond had forsaken him!

The gates had slammed shut, closing out both Franks and perhaps two hundred of the dismounted Moslems. Somehow the Seljuks had managed to smother the fire before the flames had eaten too much of the wood away, and now the ponderous contraption of steel and timber clashed shut, smashing several of the combatants in the process. And with good cause. Geoffrey felt the ground itself tremble with the heavy thunder of hooves, and over the shoulder of the smelly, struggling Turk he grappled with, he saw the reason for the panic moving closer.

Nearly five hundred of the men of Otranto were charging the gates, alone from the rest of the Christian host, heading for the center of the wooden rampart of sharpened logs, and Geoffrey saw why. While Geoffrey and the rest had been fighting with their swords, Guvi had used his head and applied his heavy axe to the center spikes, felling them so that a charge of horse soldiers might pass through, hoping Bohemond was as shrewd as stories said.

And he was.

Someone in Bohemond's camp had seen the plight of Westwall and dispatched an armored avenging fury. All of the riders were armored knights astride armored destriers, and they rode with their massive lances couched for the kill. These were not the supple, thrusting lances of the Turks, these were the long, cumbersome, but deadly lengths of steel and wood used by the knights of Christendom. Pennants streamed in the wind as the trumpets blared out attack.

The weight behind the charge of such a body of knights is irresistible and unstoppable, save with like force. It would drown these lightly armored Turks like a tidal wave of steel, and the crafty Seljuks realized this. Had the gates been left ajar, the charge would have certainly swept deep inside Tarsus, and close behind it would be the Christian host.

Thus were a few sacrificed for the safety of the city. The rush of the Turk's death-bringers was horrifying for the pounding of the hooves alone deafened those on foot, shattering the air like storm-tossed clouds colliding in the distant hills. But what of the men of Westwall within the Seljuk confusion?

Geoffrey was no stranger to the military concept of sacrifice, but it was not so pleasant to dwell upon the prospects of becoming skewered upon a Christian lance like so much meat. Damn! Was the cure going to be worse than the illness? What sense was there in this? That he should survive the heat of combat with an overwhelming mass of infidels only to be cut down by his own fellows? How much of a chance was he being given? The gods of war are masters of irony indeed.

Suppose Bohemond really didn't give a damn about the trapped English, but only wished to slay the Saracens trapped outside their own gates? Or perhaps Bohemond cared, but the knights in the charge did not. Afterall, they were not of England and King William. Geoffrey hoped they all remembered the requirements of the chivalric code as they ripped into the struggling mass afoot.

Geoffrey, however, had no real time to dwell upon the predicament. For every Turk who sensibly tried to escape, there was another fanatically intent upon seeking Allah's rose garden and taking a last Christian with him when he left this vale of sorrow. The young knight plunged his dagger into the belly of another foe and ripped upwards with all of his remaining strength while his scimitar rang with sparks as he barely stopped the downswing of an infidel's short axe. Sweat burned his eyes, yet he could not pause to wipe them free of the salt, for his gauntlets were completely covered with Seljuk blood, and his own as well in a few places. Better honest sweat in his eyes, stinging as it might be, than blood turning thick and syrupy in the white-hot glare of the sun.

Then the Christian chivalry hit the infidels with a roar, five hundred lances lowered and five hundred heavy destriers pounding the infidel foot-men into pudding.

"Against the wall!" screamed Geoffrey, "Au Secours! Against the wall, my friends, if you value life at all!"

Those of his men who heard, wisely followed him in pressing flat against the yellowish stone for what little shelter it afforded. It was possible that they might keep the distraught Turks between them and the Christian reavers long enough for the charge to lose momentum and expend its crushing power amid the fleeing Moslems. If they could be that fortunate. If the saviours could comprehend what they were doing.

The ground shook beneath the weight of half a thousand Frankish champions as they hit the packed Seljuk mass as churning hooves kicked up double handfuls of thick red mud. In what seemed to Geoffrey's clouded eyes a line of gleaming silver stretching out into infinity on both sides, they ripped the Turkish mass, tearing it to shred with their horizontal lances. Heads positioned just above the rims of their broad triangular shields, they guided these instruments of needle-sharp death.

Geoffrey heard a bellow that all but drowned out the Islamic curses in his ears and he made out the figure of a knight all in silver mail, wearing a surcoat with the lions of England upon it, but his shield was the shield of Westwall.

"Ha! Rou!" the voice of Sir Brian St. Denis thundered. "For God and King William of England! God send the might!"

"Otranto! Otranto!" screamed other frenzied voices, unleashing their frustration for the first failed assault against the foot soldiers, eager to redeem their honor here in Islamite blood. The carnage was horrible.

They struck the soldiers of the prophet like a thunderbolt from God's right hand, Saracen after Saracen was pinned by Christian lance or hacked to pieces by stout longsword when lance lay broken. So tightly packed were the Turks, that they could barely strike in their own defenses; the Franks slaughtered them like cattle.

But twice and again Geoffrey saw a good Christian knight struck down from his saddle to fall into the ranting, clutching mob that was the enemy. Christian sometimes slew Christian with all of the blood and sweat and mud, it was nigh impossible to distinguish friend from foe.

And as Geoffrey saw one of the knights of Otranto racing in his direction, he grabbed the nearest Saracen by the throat and the seat of the silk breech he wore and jerked the unfortunate man up to intercept the head of that awful lance ."A-l-l-l-a-a-h!" cried the poor doomed fellow as his soul took wing upon the end of the Frankish shaft. The weapon's foot-long point passed completely through the man's gut area, splashing Geoffrey with a crimson bath of hot liquid and raked across the young knight's mail-clad army tearing off his bloody surcoat.

Enraged at this close escape at the hands of an ally, Geoffrey laid hold of the lance and, taking the knight by surprise, yanked him from the saddle of his destrier with his superior strength.

"Dolt! Pig's bastard!" Geoffrey was beside himself in his fury as he threw his ally face down in the mud and gave him a savage kick to the backside in passing. "Can you not see I am a Christian?" But the knight could be excused for not knowing, for Geoffrey was covered with blood from head to toe.

Cursing still, Sir Geoffrey seized the destrier and pulled himself into the saddle, sword swinging.

"Avant Avant! Westwall and William! Westwall and God!" he shouted like a madman, swinging his sword with both hands to behead a Turk who wandered too near his English fury. He raced in and bowled over a Moslem horseman with the superior weight of his mount and ran the man into the earth as another of his men of Westwall seized the empty saddle.

"Au Secours!" came Guvi's familiar voice from the wooden rampart, laced with his peculiar sarcasm even in this desperate moment and Geoffrey saw him upon his knees, crimson streaming from beneath his helmet, fighting for his life against three frantic infidels. Even in the face of impending death, the Finn could see life as nothing more than a jest delivered in poor taste.

Geoffrey cried out and battered the three into oblivion with the flailing hooves of his beast, a warhorse nearly as large as Chestnut and as well trained. Guvi found a horse in his respite and, being blessed with common sense as well as intelligence, turned it from battle and raced for the Christian camp.

"Withdraw! Withdraw," called Sir Brian and the company broke off the contest and wheeled their horses for the tents of Christendom.

With the Moslem dead lay piled three layers high at the gateway, the city defenders had once again begun their avalanche of rocks and fiery oil, but most of the Franks had already moved out of range. And of the few hundred Turks who had poured from the walls intent on Christian blood, not a man of them stirred. The men of Otranto were thorough.

All of the gleaming armor, the bright colored pennants, the rich trappings of silk and polished leather, all of the fiery ornaments of the horses and soldiers of both sides, all of this lay dull and discolored beneath a uniform coating of darkening blood.

It was a victory of sorts for the Franks, or so they proclaimed it, for they were in a hurry for victories in this campaign. But it was a hollow one for Geoffrey, for only twelve of his comrades from Westwall rode back with him. The rest lay fallen from both Turkish and Christian swords. Westwall was now barren of her manhood and Geoffrey wondered what his father would say to the widows and children.

When Geoffrey made his way to his own pavilion, he dismissed his squire and friends, Guvi included, so that he might be alone. Only then did he fall upon his knees, still wrapped in his filthy armor and wept despite his strength.

He had been wrong, he knew. Nothing was worth this.

~

CLAIRE HAD WATCHED THE ENTIRE BATTLE BELOW AT THE GATES, BOTH fascinated and repulsed by the bloodshed and screams. Several times, she had tried to turn away, to exit her high balcony, but something within her held her there as well as frightened her. Perhaps it was the raw vitality exuded by these bold adventurers below; she did not know. It was a spectacle she had never witnessed before and it took her breath away.

She was in a quandary now, for if the Franks took Tarsus, it was likely that she and Helgi would be slaughtered with Wulfhere and his men as traitors. Yet, these were her people outside, not these savages manning the walls, nor these traitorous Saxons who left their own brother for dead in the sands. She sighed quietly. The only characteristic more dominant in men than their stupidity was their greed.

She thought of Eadric Siwardsson, Eadric the Wild, who had fallen prey to his wilder offspring. By now, he was but a pile of bleached bones in the desert dunes and she should feel no pity for him, by rights. But there was something so tragic about the man that she could not but help feel a trifle endeared to him. He had treated her well and seen to it that Wulfhere did not abuse her as much as he might have. Perhaps she felt for him simply because he seemed so good when contrasted to his son. She had thought Wild Eadric to be so clever, such a crafty chieftain of his band of brigands, but he was not in retrospect; he was dull-witted for he had set a wolf to guard the sheep. For one who mistrusted everyone and everything, he had trusted overmuch, and paid dreadfully for it. God pity him, she thought.

But her mind turned to something else this day, something curious that she had seen and heard in the struggle below the parapets. The cries of terror, pain and vengeance had carried through the clear air to her ears high above the clash of the battle and one had struck a chord deep within her. She had watched the brave Christian knights attempt the firing of the gates, had watched them fail, and had seen them all but slaughtered by the unlimited number of Saracens that stormed from the walls.

But their leader with the broad shoulders and heavy axe had made a mockery of the infidel reputation of toughness. He was like demon out of hell in their midst, recklessly slaying on all sides. She had watched him cornered against the wall and bit her lips in fear for him until they bled. He must live! He must! For he had the courage of a lion and tossed aside the unbelievable odds against him, and she was so proud she was of his people. He was a champion and made her think of the knight she had left behind on that dark shore so long ago. He, too, had been a champion the folk had said, a lion caged, perhaps, but a lion, nevertheless. And suddenly this knight below, in the heat of the battle, had laid about him savagely with sword and dagger and cried, "Westwall, Westwall!" and she remembered…

Remembered what she had put aside years past, remembered what she had learned from guards bribed with honey cakes and mead in a fortress, that Westwall was the ancestral home of Sir Geoffrey St. Denis, the caged lion. Was it he who had cried out or had her ears deceived her? Or was it another from his home? But if the men of Westwall were here in the Holy Land, might not he also be here? And if he was here, might it not have been him she had seen below? All the guards at Castle Ayrin had spoken of his fearsome prowess with the instruments of battle; could there be more than one man at Westwall capable of this?

It was too confusing to dwell upon and it hurt far too much. She dared not think that the man she had wanted so much from a distance was now here before the gates, striking with his great axe to enter. What would he be doing in the Holy Land two years and more after he had sat upon that Cornish bank and watched her sail out of his life?

She was unaware how great a force this was, this First Crusade. Claire sucked in her breath as her mind ran away with her. Was this the knight whom she had dreamed would follow her? Was this he whose love she dreamed of?

Once she had asked Eadric about the man he had freed in the castle, for he had told the story of Geoffrey's grit many times over a cup of ale around the fire. Once in the silence of the winter night, when the others had retired, leaving only Eadric and Claire before the fire, she had asked Eadric to tell her the story again and he had stared at her a long time, his face sad. "You are my son's woman; it is not right that you ask to hear of other men, even if they are long past."

"I loved him, my master," she said quietly.

"I knew from the first that you did. But you will grow to care for my son in time."

They both knew it was a lie. The silence was awkward. Eadric became irritable. "If he loved you, he would have followed you and taken you for himself; he would have followed us all the way here."

"And then what?" she murmured.

"Die for you!" he grunted, guzzling ale out of his flagon. He stared into the cup, unable to meet her eyes.

"That is not love. That is foolishness."

Eadric banged the cup down. "You carry Wulfhere's child in your belly, little golden hair. Forget your dreams of the past; close your eyes to all the tomorrows for they are only the property of poets and children. Life is for living, but only today. Dwell upon the seed that grows in your womb, cherish it for it is much of you, and it is good. Accept Wulfhere for the man that he is and love him when you can."

"I can never love him. He is a villain," she cried.

"And you can never love this dream-knight of yours either, girl, for he is long dead to you. You left him with your life in Britain." Eadric's voice rose in anger.

"You know nothing of the heart, my master."

"I know it is the source of weakness and foolishness, and that a man without one is far better off for he can never wound himself!"

"But he can never know comfort or loving embrace, either," she argued in a low voice.

Eadric spat into the fire and was silent a long time before he answered. "There is no comfort in this life, girl. Security is only an illusion. There is only one embrace that amounts to anything at all, and that comes from death when we are finished living. Everything a man creates in his own mind, or with his own hands to prolong this illusion is a falsehood. Better an honest understanding, a more careful reckoning with the facts of life, golden hair. Then you might know what is real and what is not."

"I will keep my illusions, if illusions they be, master. There are those of us, not the warrior that you are, but there are those of us that need comfort and security."

Eadric shrugged. The fire burned low and he sipped the last of his biting brew. Then he looked up at her, and his eye was clear and young again, and he gave her a look of the most exquisite sadness. So said this hard leader, "Little Claire, though I have never said it and will never say it again, if I had known you then as I do now, and that you felt touched by some puppy who was mad enough to spit in my face, in the face of death itself, I would not have interfered. The fates play strange tricks on a man in his life, but what is past is past. You know of my affection for you, but all you can do now is live your life the way the gods have willed it."

"Nothing is forever," she said, and she knew not even why she said it. It was the expression of a nameless emotion that rose inside her at hearing his thoughts.

And she had been right, for the fates had turned them all on many twists in the path since she had spoken. The master was dead, the son an outlaw, and she could never say she had known more of this young knight than before. But her misery continued until Claire shut the lattice doors against the heat as her chamber was still relatively cool and she retired to silence, now. She went inside. To sit and think.

12

CHAPTER THE TWELFTH

F or two discouraging days, the Christians sat still within their camp, licking their wounds and planning for the next assault. The city itself was completely sealed off and besieged so that there was no real danger of supplies entering or citizens leaving. For a while, there was a peace of sorts, except in the council of leaders.

Bohemond, Sir Godfrey, Sir Raymund, Sir Brian, and two score of lesser leaders such as Robert of Flanders and Hugh of Vermandois met twice a day to review and discuss the proposed strategy. But, frustratingly, at each council another noble had a plan to put forward and each was vocal in his demands during the meeting. Unfortunately, each had a different solution to the problem, a characteristic which was to plague the leaders of every campaign from then on in the Holy Land. Bohemond, with his common sense as strong as his sword arm, was willing to opt for a standard siege while he negotiated for the city's surrender as their supplies grew low. He did not see where the Turks had the stamina of the Christians which was necessary to withstand a drawn-out Norman-style siege. Things were done differently here in the East.

But the others were vehement in their protests and Bohemond slowly went red in the face while they complained and mocked him. "What of our supplies?" cried Godfrey. "Can we afford to sit and wait as these followers of their wretched prophet mass in other parts of the land until they are strong enough to cut off our supplies and lay siege to us? I do not wish to subject myself to eating sand while fighting on two sides!"

"Hear! Hear!" called others. "Leave a force to contain the Turks here and ride for Antioch and the Holy City!"

"On with the conquest!" shouted another.

"Conquest, my ass," snarled Bohemond. "We have yet to take this city and you would have us march against others like children. You stupid, buggering gadflies! Is this how you have learned to wage war from your internal disputes? God preserve us if it is your brains that are to be used to free Christendom!"

"We are also barons, Otranto!" cried one of the lesser nobles. "We need not suffer such indignities from you!" The fellow, still young, proud, and completely inexperienced, stood up and brandished a dagger.

Bohemond paused an instant, gave him a look of withering distaste and suddenly broke a stool across his face so that he collapsed amid the splintered wood, bleeding from several small cuts.

"By God, you do so!" muttered Bohemond, giving the inert body a kick. "All of you have sworn allegiance to this Holy Crusade and duly elected me the leader thereof! Now, dammit, remove your thumbs from your arseholes and begin thinking. Sir Brian, we have not heard from Britain. Hopefully, you have something more intelligent to say than these hounds baying at my heels."

"I have said nothing because I cannot contradict what you have voiced, my friend. It is both foolish and dangerous to disperse our forces and attack several cities with none yet taken. Godfrey is so concerned about being encircled here; I ask how much easier would it be to entrap three or four smaller armies? How much greater would the logistical problems be; how much more watered down our strength? Let the infidels try to encircle us here; they will all die! If yon Saracens could match us in arms and soldiering, do you think they would be locked up tight in that ugly fortress? I believe that no Saracen armies will be sent to relieve Tarsus; they are too uncertain of our strength and will not commit all of their forces in what they feel might become a disaster for them all. These others talk of dangerous tactics, my friend. I say, let us crack this nut first!"

Bohemond smiled. "Here speaks sense!" he said.

But suddenly, their thoughts of siege were thrust aside as the tent flap was opened to admit a wide-eyed young knight with an incredible message.

"My lords! An emissary from the Caliph of Tarsus has arrived. He craves an audience with you and claims to offer ideas toward a peaceful settlement of our dispute!" The men of the council exchanged skeptical glances, but the man was admitted.

Geoffrey sat quietly beneath the olive trees that covered the hilltops overlooking Kazanli and the coast of the Mediterranean Sea. Here, he had rested the past two days, recovering from the shock of the first battle for Tarsus. His wounds had not been critical, but it was Bohemond's wish that any and all wounded be given a chance to recover fully during the lull. And that had gone especially for Sir Geoffrey St. Denis who had acquitted himself so well before the gates of Tarsus and almost died in the process. He had a narrow gash along his neck where he had barely halted a scimitar from relieving him of his head, and numerous shorter gashes along his hands and forearms where tempered Damascus steel had overpowered stout English chain-link.

Dusk was setting in. But as he watched the lights appear along the coast to signal the end of day, his thoughts were not upon his own wounds. Rather, he was plagued by a nagging philosophical insight; he pondered what guidance lay behind this first great crusade and his own role in the drama.

Why, for example, when the Prince of Peace preached love, did his Christian brothers so relish cutting down the Turks? That is, now that they had finished cutting down each other? He remembered with distaste the collection of Seljuk ears he had seen dangling from the belts of some knights and men-at-arms in the encampment.

That the infidels supposedly did the same thing was understandable in the very fact that they were heathen followers of the prophet. Yet, shouldn't the Christians forbear such unseemly action in the name of Christ? That they must fight to free the Holy Land was imminently understandable; the Turks and other Arabics were wrong to hold it so forcefully, and not at all willing to relinquish their power even for the nobility of Christ. Geoffrey did not wonder at their nature for he had been taught they were the devil's own minions. But still…

Were all the limits to be left behind in this type of warfare? He shrugged. It was not his concern for he made no decisions. He was here for neither the wealth nor the holy glory. The others were welcome to it and all that it entailed.

From below the hill, the breeze blew up salt-fresh, carrying with it the tangy aroma of the placid sea and of the fish the small boats were unloading. The entire scene before him was dreamlike in quality, a dream of peace away from the war and trumpets he was learning already to hate. Fireflies drifted lazily through the deepening twilight creating flickering patterns against a cloud-laced heaven like a myriad of moving stars.

A gusty nuzzle of wet air reminded him of Chestnut's presence and he smiled as he stroked his steed's glossy hide. It was odd, he thought, that only with animals did one truly know where one stood, for better or worse. Why was only man's nature so fickle?

A laugh broke him from his revelry and he turned to see the Finn grinning at him, grinning with some secret jest. "So!" his friend trumpeted. "They were right. The Lion of Tarsus has turned into a mystic and philosopher here atop some hill overlooking the sea of the poets and pondering the mystery of life."

"Arsehole," said Geoffrey thoughtfully.

Guvi still chuckled.

"Perhaps you should have been a man of learning instead of war with your odd penchant for hilltops and solitude."

Geoffrey lay back against a tree trunk and stretched. What was Guvi getting at with his odd humor? "And with your taste for women and wine, perhaps you should have been a whoremaster instead of a thief," he returned.

"Bah," mocked Guvi, "you think too much to be a Frank, my friend. Are you sure you are not a Jew? Tis greatly uncommon for any knight of any Christian host to have brains within his head, or heart, rather than inside his sword arm or cock." Casually, he picked up a rock to cast down the hillside into the sea, then sat down beside his Norman friend.

"How are your wounds healing?" Guvi asked.

"Well enough, except for the stiffness in my neck where that one bastard's sword near took off my head. Yours?" he murmured, his blue eyes upon the sea again.

Guvi snickered. "Mine are well enough. The only pain left is in my arse where I backed into some damned Frank's lance seizing that horse to escape." Both laughed and Geoffrey jokingly called him a coward.

"No coward would follow you into battle, my friend. Mental defectives, perhaps, but never cowards. Only a man with nerves of steel might stand side by side with the Lion of Tarsus before the burning gates!"

"Oh, stop this horse crap, you lunatic. Gods! Who started with this name for me, this 'Lion of Tarsus'?"

Guvi looked at him with feigned innocence. "Undoubtedly, someone who thinks a lot of you and wishes to see that you obtain your share of glory here."

Geoffrey pursed his lips in thought. "Or some scoundrel who seeks to capitalize upon the friendship of a hero, say with free drinks for his tales of blood and gore or extra portions of food to take to the champion so that he might keep his strength up?"

Guvi appeared quite shocked, but Geoffrey had known him long enough to see through the ruse. The Finn protested loudly. "Twas you who saved my life, your Christ! I thought it only fitting to see you with a title, and you know how glory hungry the entire Frankish camp is. They loved it! Now they wonder what the Lion of Tarsus will do next; will he tear down the towers with his bare hands; will he challenge the champion of the Saracens to a duel; will he..."

"Spare me your idle gossip, rogue. Shove your glory up your arse for I have no wish to see laurels won by blood."

"So speaks the philosopher. But do not spurn me and my friendship; I will make you great. And anyway, you worry me when you are so solemn, for I know you are quite strange, and neither of us are able to say what you will do next!"

"Neither of us?" Geoffrey inquired.

"Oh, yes, I speak of the Siwardsson, you remember him, of course, the gentleman's gentleman? He thinks you are quite mad, but then so do I."

"A pair of deserving rogues!" scoffed Geoffrey.

"So," Guvi continued," when you wish to commit suicide, please do so out of sight of my conscience for it might make things awkward on me. As you know, I have promised several women across the land that I would return to wed them when the bastards they carry are born!"

"Such salaciousness from a father-to-be! How unseemly!" Geoffrey guffawed.

"But tell me, you lump of quivering snot, why have you chosen to interrupt my well-earned solitude at this time? Are we to horse again against Tarsus?" he ended anxiously.

Guvi smiled slyly. "I am here with the hopes that you will soon find yourself in the saddle, so that we all might relax."

"Then we attack!" shouted Geoffrey, rising to seize Chestnut's reins.

"Not so fast, not so fast, my friend. If there is any attacking to be done, it will involve you alone." The Finn attempted to maintain a deadpan expression but Geoffrey's look of utter bewilderment was so comical that he could not help but hoot.

"Speak plainly, you pig!" swore Geoffrey, adding some hot adjectives concerning the Finn's dubious ancestry.

Guvi cocked a quizzical eyebrow. "If I could grant you but one wish, tell me what it would be!"

Geoffrey flushed and eyed him balefully. "Well you know what it would be, mocker. You have chided me for it long enough!"

Guvi snickered and rose also. "So, I thought," he smiled. He looked into Geoffrey's face with good-natured cynicism. "You will never learn, but I will show you the worth of our friendship. I cannot give her to you; that is beyond me. But would you settle for a chance to take her yourself?"

"You ask for a dagger in your gaping gullet!" snarled Geoffrey.

"My, my, I certainly hope she can modify that temper of yours, friend Norman. But we will see."

Geoffrey said nothing at this point but merely glared at his friend, for the most part enraged that Guvi would play with his emotions so lightly. But the Finn just laughed and slapped him on the shoulder with good comradery.

"Well, come then, you proud, lovestruck swine! Make yourself pretty, for you will quite possibly see her while you are there and you would not want her to behold you with all your dirt and bloodstained bandages."

"What?" cried Geoffrey. "You rotten bastard! What did you say?"

"Why simply that I have persuaded both the infidels and your Franks to allow you into the city of Tarsus on the morrow; indeed, even the Emir of the city claims he would welcome a chance to meet the one who they call 'Lion.'"

"What?!" stormed Geoffrey. "If this is a jest, you piece of Finnish shit, I'll carve your lying tongue from your ugly face."

Guvi doubled over with laughter. "Your gentle words have warmed me, my friend. You have a gift of saying the right thing at the right time in much the manner of the Siwardsson!"

"Well?" demanded Geoffrey, coldly.

"God grant that I should never fall so in love," Guvi chortled. Then he straightened to wipe tears of mirth from his dark eyes.

"Oh, Lord!" he gasped weakly "It was worth your anger to see the look come over your face! But rejoice, my friend! Lighten your heart and soul for tomorrow you will see your Claire. On the morrow, you are to enter the city as emissary of the Christian host as per the Emir's request."

"He requested me?" Geoffrey snorted skeptically. "And for what? To give me gold for slaying his men? To make me a priest of their Allah for having sent so many to eat lamb in paradise?" He fingered the hilt of his dagger meaningfully as he watched the Finn's face.

"Oh, nay! Be not so vain! He but wanted an emissary to discuss peace with. Twas me who said it would be you." The knight bowed deeply from the waist.

"Ah, forgive me, your grace! I had no idea that you wielded so much power in this poor camp. Tell me, though, sir, did you take Bohemond or even my father into your confidence in this? Do the lord commanders respect you so greatly that they immediately acceded to your wishes?"

"Again, nay. But after your disgusting bravery before the gates two days past, they would allow you anything. Your's was the only worth-while thing done that wretched day."

"Ours, you mean. The deed belonged to the men of Westwall; it was not committed by myself alone." Geoffrey eyed Guvi in some puzzlement.

Guvi sneered. "It was yours alone and you know it is so. Had it not been your own hide left on the line to dry, I would have left the party much sooner than I did. And if not for your thrice-damned example, so would most of your men, be they of Westwall, England, or the devil. Twas you who made them stay; none would shame himself before the master's son so they stayed and died with you for they were not the warrior you are, nor had they your luck. I heard even your men say that perhaps you are a fool in the mundane matters of life but you are awesome in battle. But the worst of this is that there are few who can match you, these lesser men that idolize your lion-like strength, your lion-like courage. They follow you and they fall around you for the battle you select for yourself is always the hardest one, one few others are capable of fighting. All of those men before the gates died because of you, because you were a leader who set too high an example for them. Not all of us are destined to be legends."

"I want none of their glory. Leave it with the dead!"

"But the others will not, Geoffrey. They need heroes in this crusade and it is a cancer that feeds upon itself. They die trying to emulate you, and the more who die trying, the more will try so they can be called lions. It is nonsense, I do not criticize you in what you do; you are my friend, but I tell you truthfully that you are too noble, too much a knight and that it is hard on those of us who must follow you."

"Mine was a hotter furnace," said the Norman, brooding.

"Yes," agreed Guvi. "I understand you. I understand you enough to remain unaffected by your courage and your recklessness, but that is why you must go to Tarsus and see her. You are past the point of wanting a woman, of loving a woman. You have made up your mind she is to have your life as some great gift, so you hurl yourself against all odds. Fate has allowed that you might see her, perhaps it will alter your view of her. Can she still love you so much?"

"She loves me," the young knight murmured and there was something in the tone that made Guvi unable to doubt the truth of that. Then he sighed and spoke again, "So they said they wanted an emissary and you said I wished to go."

"Not exactly. While I watched the old farts dithering on about who to send, I was struck with the idea and I suggested why not send the 'Lion of Tarsus' and really put the shits up the old Emir?"

Geoffrey laughed, despite himself.

"Are you not pleased?" Guvi beamed.

"Perhaps, but what if they hold a grudge, or merely seek someone to torture for information?"

"What if this is the only chance to see her and she rewards you beyond your wildest dreams?" countered the Finn with a revolting leer.

"Pig!" muttered Geoffrey, but without malice. He understood what Guvi was saying to him despite its coarseness.

He turned again to the sea. It was now slate gray with the coming of night and the last of the little fishing boats were docking, eager hands transferring the catch to shore, and deep male voices starting to sing their song of fishing the sea and drinking. It was nice to watch.

"Is this a chance for peace?" wondered Geoffrey aloud.

"Ha, ha, Odin's arse! On that account, you need have no fear, my friend!" spat Guvi, emphatically. "You know as well as I that both sides are merely buying time; that is all. They take us for fools and we take them for much the same. But here, all you need do is play the game and if you should see her, well, that's just so much in your favor. For all the good this conference is likely to do, you might just as well dally with your sweet Claire as discuss religion with the Turkish Emir."

Geoffrey stroked the scabbard of his sword unconsciously. "Tis well, then, for this is the only way I might have her. Eadric has told me of her master, and that she has born him a child. The Saxon thinks she would not leave the father of her child despite her hatred for him. I must kill this Wulfhere Eadricsson and for this kind of killing there needs to be war."

Guvi studied his comrade's face, brooding and dark in the twilight. It was better to be possessed by demons than by love, he decided.

"So, you will take a ready-made clan, eh? By the gods, Geoffrey, why you do not set your sights on another, I do not know, but as far as I care, I'd be the last one to deny you such simple pleasures as killing and wife-stealing. Just don't get carried away and slice off his turnip in the presence of the Emirs. They play the game also, but there are limits to this good humor of theirs, my friend," he cautioned. "And likewise, would I council you to discretion with your little dove. The Saracens have odd notions about love and fidelity in their wives and this Wulfhere is one of them now. But perhaps I am worried overmuch; Wulfhere is but a refugee of theirs and perhaps will not even be present during your visit, and with the gods' help, perhaps you can avoid seeing her at all and save yourself much trouble..."

"I will see her," ground out Geoffrey. "Come heaven or hell, I will see her."

"Hmmm," mouthed Guvi, sarcastically, "perhaps I am not worried enough..."

Geoffrey stared at him. "One day, your tongue will be your undoing, you villain. I have not yet spoken with her and already you make something bawdy out of my feelings!"

"Huh!" sniffed the Finn indignantly. "And after all this time of wanting, you tell me that if you do get her off into a quiet corner, you'll spend the time discussing her husband's health. Ha! How simple you are, or how blind to what you feel. Love begins with a warm heart but likely ends up with the heat moving to the loins. And anyway, in love, there is no importance in the words; speaking is carried out with the heart and the eyes and the lips. And who knows so much, or so little, is to say that the hunger of the flesh is not part of it all?"

"A poet with the soul of a thief or perhaps just the opposite!" muttered the knight, climbing with the stiffness of new wounds into Chestnut's saddle.

"Well, watch yourself at any rate, my friend," advised Guvi, attempting poorly to hide his concern.

Geoffrey paused and digested this. Then he threw back his head and laughed happily for a moment. "Fear not for me, my dear, dear friend. I trust your guidance will see me through and that you will protect my flanks as you have ever done!"

"What?" blinked Guvi, suspiciously. He did not like the implications of this speech.

"Oh, yes," Geoffrey snickered. "Be joyous, for you are going to see what other men will note. The Saracens await! Hurrah!" Then he calmed, but leaned down in the saddle to give Guvi his most charming smile. "I wouldn't dream of going without you, my friend!" he grinned.

"Shit and damnation!" cursed Guvi. Shaking his head, he also mounted but loud and long were his protests on the ride back to camp.

In camp, they pressed Geoffrey with well-intentioned advice that he did not hear, gave him orders and potions and amulets against poison and sorcery that he politely accepted, then cast into a heap upon the couch. His squire helped him into his armor while the Finn stood, identically clad, with a sour smile etched across his thin features. He was the only one who understood fully why the younger St. Denis wished to enter the city that had already almost cost him his life.

"These will be our burial suits!" grumbled the Finn, but Geoffrey chuckled. Although his heart palpitated wildly at the thought of the adventure, he was happy and showed calmness on the outside

"You are madly brave to enter their gates, my lord!" whispered his young squire as he laced up Geoffrey's leggings. "They have seen your prowess and would surely deem it wise to break the truce to rid us of such a champion!"

"Not madly brave, merely mad!" snorted Guvi in disgust. The boy gazed at him without comprehending and Guvi turned away, shaking his head.

"Mind him not, lad," soothed Geoffrey. "He is but edgy about entering the city with me for he has no spine for a small portion of danger!" And the young knight laughed so that the puzzled squire looked again to Guvi for an explanation but the Finn merely cursed and mumbled something about "moonstruck idiots and women" and strode from the pavilion.

"If you become anymore nervous," called Geoffrey after him, "perhaps you should wear your brown pants so you do not embarrass us both!"

Two ordinary riding horses, not the precious Frankish destriers that were bred for battle, awaited the companions. The Christians were careful about their men, but even more so about their horses for while there seemed an unending line of warriors ready to take up the cause, the heavy warhorses were harder to replace in this tricky climate.

"A bad sign!" swore Guvi, but Geoffrey cheekily whistled a crusader's tune as they rode towards the earthen ramparts that marked the outermost boundary of the Christian camp. Along the path through the tents and crude stables the other warriors eyed the two in silence, feeling somewhat that they were bidding farewell to two condemned men. No Christian trusted a Saracen.

At the main gate, several of the leaders bade them farewell and bonne chance, the elder St. Denis among them. But words were wasted, for both comrades were lost in contemplation, though of opposite natures. For while Geoffrey rode with an easy half-smile as if he laughed with the gods at the irony in his fate, the Finn's sly face was set in a hard scowl for he felt that he had finally, and fatally, out-smarted himself.

The plain was dry and dusty, the sun hot as it always was. The brilliant armor was soon dust-covered and by the time the Saracen honor guard was sent out to accompany the pair, the white flag of truce was limp and dirty.

A troop of the infidel horse soldiers surrounded them and caused Guvi's heart to pound within his throat. Geoffrey nodded at the hard-eyed, unspeaking riders and noticed that some of them were bandaged. He idly wondered if any of them had fought against them at the gate.

Then the gates loomed before them, fire-scarred but still impervious. Geoffrey openly grinned at the charred wood and rebuilt hinges, proud of the destruction he had wrought. His grin put the infidels in sullen humor and their unsmiling visages darkened even further, and Geoffrey almost laughed aloud as he turned and saw the look of dread on the Finn's face. Have a care, he thought to himself, these were proud men.

The gates creaked open and the aroma of the city rushed out to hit him as the group plunged into a mass of gaping onlookers. Here were smells far distant from the stink of his camp, pungent spices and exotic fruits mixed with the hot scent of horses.

Burnoosed traders and armored soldiers eyed him with curiosity;

veiled women spat in his path for the Moslems he had slain. Brown-skinned children cast pebbles at his mount's tough flanks, but most of Tarsus was an unfocused blur of moving colors until he stood before the gold-plated doors of the Emir of Tarsus. With scarce time for a gulp of breath, the doors were cast open by turbaned eunuchs and he entered the high-ceilinged hallway of the throne room.

Suddenly, he was serious, his good nature dissolved. Here was one of the men who held the shrines of Christ. Here was one responsible for the deaths of untold Christians, with more to come. They wished to see what steel the Franks were made of; he would show them it was stronger than their own.

Geoffrey strode down the long hall, the very picture of knighthood. Slaves had washed the dust from him as he entered the palace and, once again, he was brilliant and well-polished. He carried his conical helmet in the crook of his left arm and his stride contained both grace and power. His armored feet and gilded spurs clanked ominously upon the tiled flag-stones. Guvi marched two paces behind him, also freshly scrubbed; his pointed beard and moustache had been trimmed elegantly. Although his build was slender and without the power of Geoffrey's broad shoulders and narrow waist, he was still impressive for many Moslems still had not seen close-up the intricate chainmail of the Franks. Geoffrey seemed to radiate power as he moved, lithe as a cat, as powerful as a lion.

But it was his scarred, tanned face that gave the infidel guards the most to stare at for it was an impassive mask, aloof and unapproachable with the warm blue eyes turned to glittering ice and the jaw set hard so the mouth was pinched into a set, straight line. Here was a man of much pride and violent emotions, they thought. Here was a warrior.

One of the Seljuks guarding the hall muttered something in Turkish as the Franks passed and the tone was one of amusement, though the words were gibberish to Geoffrey. The Emir's man stopped and eyed the man coolly, his face tightening and eyes-of-ice speaking a promise to the dark-desert eyes that returned his gaze. Although Geoffrey was permitted neither sword nor dagger, the Turk paled a little beneath the scrutiny of the Norman's stare and turned away. Without a word, Geoffrey walked on, but Guvi paused to give the churl a thin smile of the purest contempt as he passed.

At the end of the corridor, were two more huge doors, also gold plated but more elaborate and studded with precious gems. Here was the sanctum sanctorum of the city leader. Two huge Saracens in the black armor of the palace guard stepped forward and opened the doors automatically and the two from the Christian camp entered into the chamber of the Emir of Tarsus. An interpreter announced the name of the Emir but Geoffrey remembered it no longer than it took to pronounce it. Woodenly, he handed his message to the man's emissary yet his eyes saw neither the small, wiry Turk before him nor the fat Emir upon the gold and red leather throne across the room. His eyes had searched the people within the chamber, intent upon only one subject and now he was peering past the smiling fellow at the company of people who stood obediently next to the throne.

The fates were kind this time.

In that massive chamber with its gilded walls and ornate ceiling with its huge windows open to the brightness of the sun, the walls shone with a near-blinding brilliance; no gold gleamed warmer or more beautiful than that of her fair hair. Geoffrey felt his pulse rate leap and he was momentarily as dizzy as a drunkard. Was that really *her* behind that gossamer veil? Logic told him it must be, but logic was unnecessary. His heart would have recognized her anywhere.

Geoffrey's blood raced as he took a step forward unbidden, violating all protocol and causing even Guvi to raise his eyebrows. Had he less sense, he would have made a dash for her at that moment, though he knew he would not have had the barest chance of reaching her with no weapons.

He smiled inwardly at the painful irony of fate as he regained his composure, knowing with relief that only the Finn would understand what was running through his scheming mind. Guvi explained to the translator that Geoffrey's actions were the result of a head wound still healing and the Emir accepted this with a benevolent smile for he admired the young lion before him. The Seljuk translator beside him did the introductions and presentations as the Emir himself knew not a whit of Norman-French.

"The Emir of Kazanli!" he announced. Geoffrey nodded condescendingly, trying to conceal a smirk, for Kazanli was garrisoned by Christian troops. The fellow was more a refugee than an emir, a leader without a city. But the eyes of the proud Turk burned hot in his dark face and Geoffrey realized with a start that the man understood what was going through Geoffrey's warrior mind and he felt both shame and rage. The Norman realized that he had underestimated the man; the Turk was also a warrior. He marked the emir's hawkish face and sturdy build, tall and muscular. He would be one to reckon with in the heat of battle when much hung in balance.

Geoffrey stepped forward and stared the man face to face, his smirk gone. Yes, he thought, a warrior indeed. He bowed as had the other, showing his respect and he noticed that the face of the Emir of Kazanli was cooler now. Without words, they had reached an understanding.

The other introductions passed without Geoffrey remarking upon anything noteworthy in the rest of the Turks. For the most part, they were overfed nobles who led their troops from the rear, or rich merchants who bartered in spices and slaves. He shrugged. If these were all that held the city together, he would be over the walls soon enough. They were all soft, these rich Moslems, all save for the Emir of Kazanli and the dog who stood before him now.

"Wulfhere Eadricsson, consultant to the Emir of Tarsus!" the emissary announced.

"Wulfhere Eadricsson!" Geoffrey muttered mildly. "Much have I heard of you. Unmatched in both sword lore and treachery." His lips twisted into a sneer as he sized up the Saxon renegade.

"Geoffrey St. Denis!" Wulfhere spat out, white teeth gleaming evilly, "An unknown knight in a land unknown to him. A lamb of his god come to be slaughtered. Met by our swords so that the carrion birds might feast!" The Saxon smiled a slow smile of contempt and Geoffrey felt red rage choking his throat. For this smile, more than anything else, Geoffrey decided that he would slay the man slowly.

"Eadric Siwardsson sends his greetings, traitor. He bade me say that he is well and that he hopes to embrace you soon!" Geoffrey said and laughed quietly.

Wulfhere's smile died and he stared dumbfounded at his antagonist.

"Who is this Siwardsson?" asked the emissary. The Emir watched the two fair-skinned enemies with interest, although he could not know what they were speaking of. But it was plain that they shared common ground and the Moslems found this interesting, if not astonishing, for it ran true with their theories of fate.

"Eadric Siwardsson is the father your consultant left to die upon the open desert," grinned Geoffrey. "I rescued the man so that he might live to chastise an ungrateful son."

The emissary translated and the entire room gasped at the implied outrage.

"He lies," shouted Wulfhere.

The emissary turned to the Emir who said something in a pleasant voice. Turning back, he addressed the pair.

"His highness instructs me to say that such a discussion might better be carried on in private. For now, we will finish with the introductions and then dine. He stepped between Geoffrey and Wulfhere who were ready to leap at each other and introduced, "Claire, Lady to Wulfhere Eadricsson!"

She stepped forward with a tight throat.

Brendon gazed into her eyes and saw her pale just a little, a parade of emotions leaping through those clear pools. She tried to smile but could not.

Slowly, his pulse pounding in his ears, he lifted her smooth, light hand and put his lips to it chivalrously. "My lady," he said, with a gracious smile. "I see that my adversary chooses his women well for both grace and beauty and is to be envied in his fine selection. For such a lady, I would willingly travel across the world, even to a land such as this."

He alone heard her gasp.

Geoffrey could feel Wulfhere's hot eyes upon him and he enjoyed goading the man as much as he enjoyed touching her. He knew well enough that he most probably would never again be this close to her unless the fates granted his wildest dreams. Yet, seeing the object of his yearning so close and yet so unobtainable, oppressed him with a grim fatalism concerning the future.

He knew quite perfectly what a cruel jester fate was, giving all one moment then taking all the next. He must be wary. Even faith was not to be laden with too much trust.

At length, she found her voice and spoke in words that were soft music. "Then it was you on the shore that day they took me?"

"I was too late. I am sorry," Geoffrey said quietly.

"Be not sorry, gentle knight. The thought of what was in my heart, of what I dared to dream is true," she smiled.

Wulfhere fumed while the emissary gave them both a quizzical look. These Franks were full of mystery and surprises.

"The thought of what you did gives wings to my heart. I shall carry the dream always in my heart and draw strength from it."

The emissary stepped in and whispered to Geoffrey.

"I can stall the Emir no further. If you do not proceed with the introductions, he will wish to know what is being said. And her man Wulfhere champs at the bit to know what is passing between the two of you."

Geoffrey looked at her a final time, his eyes smoldering. "The dream has not yet run its course, my love. It will not until I die."

Claire was speechless before the meaning of these words and the determination behind them. The emissary, a wise man with no ill will toward the Christians, led Geoffrey away and made a chatter of ingratiating nonsense as he introduced the remaining nobles and Geoffrey greeted them with honor. In a few minutes, the episode between Geoffrey and Claire was forgotten. The Emir chose to believe that all the Franks were incurable romantics and could not help but be entranced by a pretty face. Wulfhere had the same suspicions, but he could not think that Claire had ever met this Norman before so he believed her story of Geoffrey's flattering eye.

But he had noticed how her hands had trembled ever so slightly after Geoffrey left the chamber and it seemed to him that she had been as reluctant to end the meeting as the knight. And her eyes could not meet his.

When he had the chance to approach her alone, he should probably beat her again. It would be harder now, for she slept alone with the child, so that he might enjoy other women in his own chambers. But he would watch and wait. Eadric Siwardsson had taught him patience in stalking. Huh! Could it be that his father was truly alive and before the walls of Tarsus, seeking him? It was a terrible thought, for he understood only too well the anger of the man who had raised him. But how else could the Norman know of Eadric Siwardsson, named Eadric the Wild? There was something wrong here.

Minutes later, Geoffrey was ushered into a smaller chamber, but one furnished as elaborately as the throne room. It was here that the real diplomacy would take place, free from all the court guests with their wagging tongues.

The Emir sat before Geoffrey and Guvi, relaxed and smiling. Here the attitude was more informal, one in which plain speech was appreciated. Geoffrey declined a chair and stood before the Emir, the emissary-interpreter next to him. At length, the Emir spoke.

"He wishes to know what message you bring him," explained the little wise man in slow, dignified Norman French.

Geoffrey smiled disarmingly. "You may tell the Emir of Tarsus that the message I carry is a call to surrender within the space of a day. He has twenty-four hours to consider his plight before we will sweep you from the walls and smash this wretched city into the earth so that it will never rise again. We have both the determination and the warriors to do this, I might add."

The little Turkish sage shrugged and smoothed his long black moustache.

"What Allah wills, will be." he said, fatalistically. "Allah Akbar!" Then he addressed the Emir of Tarsus who sat plump and squat upon his throne with small shifty eyes. Geoffrey did not understand what was said, but thrice he saw the flash of white teeth in a leering grin; the guards at the door grinned also.

He heard Guvi behind him. "The shits plot even before our eyes. Let us both beware of poisoned wine if they entertain us."

Despite himself, Geoffrey was forced to chuckle at Guvi's salaciousness, startling the Seljuks.

"Laugh, you infidel pigs!" he muttered under his breath.

Geoffrey's smile approached a sneer and his murderous thoughts were only too transparent in his blue eyes. The Turk paled as it suddenly occurred to him that the Franks might have sent one who understood the speech of Islam to spy upon them.

But the emissary said nothing of the suspicion. Again, his face was a mask of hospitality and pleasantries. "His magnificence asks that you allow him to entertain you for this evening and that you take his reply to your leaders on the morrow," he said politely.

"Decline! Decline!" whispered Guvi frantically.

"We will attend," said Geoffrey laconically.

"Ah, the request is for you alone, Sir Norman," the interpreter apologized.

Geoffrey surveyed the dark expectant faces. What game was this?

"Decline, damn you," hissed Guvi sharply. "I smell treachery!"

But Geoffrey was thinking of Claire who had stood near Wulfhere and still had the courage to speak of her love for him.

"Very well," said Geoffrey blandly, "I wish but a second of privacy to discuss this with my squire, however, that he might carry my actions to our leaders, so they might not misdoubt the Emir's intentions."

The interpreter relayed this to the fat Emir who again smiled and nodded benevolently, and the two Franks, Christian and heathens walked casually to the rear of the chamber.

"Squire, am I?" whispered Guvi in irritation. "You Norman dolt! I am well tempted to leave you alone here that they might amuse themselves with your arse, but fortunately for you..." The Finn groped habitually for his sword and shook his hand nervously when he realized again that he was unarmed.

"Fortunately for me, you will not be here to haunt me!" smiled Geoffrey, who realized that all eyes were upon the two. They must play at good fellowship and lack of suspicion. Cordially, he took Guvi's hand and announced loudly and with a flourish, "Then tell my Lord Bohemond that I shall join him on the morrow, hopefully with a solution to this bloodshed!"

"My only hope for your longevity is that they will believe you are a great fool and let you live, you giant arsehole!" Guvi smiled back and nodded. Cursing under his breath, he allowed a guard to lead him out of the courtyard toward the city gate.

Geoffrey hoped that he had calculated correctly. It made more sense for the infidels to hold to their honor and treat him as a guest, and perhaps buy his goodwill, if nothing else. They were planning some attack, of that he was sure. And would not the wisest course of action to be to stall for time?

Time. That was what hung in the balance.

But Geoffrey was not worried yet. He knew the strength of the Christian force unless the Saracens were joined by a much larger body of their brothers; the Franks could hold their own or better against any threat from them.

So, for tonight, feasting and the games of power politics. War would come quickly enough on the morrow.

As he was led from the chamber, he was escorted back through the throne room where the others of the court awaited the Emir's return. Claire was still there with Wulfhere. She turned briefly to look at him, an unfathomable expression upon her beautiful, veiled face.

Then, both turned away from each other, frightened at what might happen.

The banquet had a sort of barbaric sumptuousness to it, thought Geoffrey. Or perhaps it was simply that he was unused to the Eastern culture of this Holy Land. Instead of sitting behind one single high table with the Emir overlooking the rest of the feasters as was done in Norman lands, Geoffrey and several of the Turkish nobles sat about a circular, low table of glossy ebony, ornately carved with designs and Arabic figures, reclining upon plush silken pillows of outrageous hues. Perhaps a hundred other guests sat about such similar tables scattered throughout the area of the room with a space cleared centrally for an entertainment troupe of jugglers, acrobats and near-nude dancing girls.

To Geoffrey's dismay, Claire was not present since Seljuk women did not formally dine with their masters.

At the Emir's table, Geoffrey joined the Emir of Kazanli, the emissary-intrepreter of the Emir of Tarsus, and two other Seljuk lords as well as the Emir of Tarsus himself. Geoffrey noticed with some humor that Wulfhere ranked only the third table, but he was well within the Norman's field of vision and the two exchanged periodic stares for the length of the feasting. The food was excellent and the wine strong.

As Geoffrey tore his way through beef roast, baked goose, delicious fruit pastry, melon, and a host of more exotic dishes such as humming-bird tongues smothered in honey and the pickled brains of a nondescript rodent, he did his best to exchange pleasantries with the two Emirs. The interpreter was named Isbah, he learned, and was a genuinely pleasant distraction as he had turned out to be both intelligent and humorous, both traits well-accented by the fact that he was already slightly drunk even though the banquet had just begun. Geoffrey wondered at this as the Moslem religion forbade liquor.

"We frown upon drunkenness, it is true," Isbah explained. "But the juice of the grape is as much a bounty of Allah as any other fruit juice. Or so the Emir rationalizes…"

"And you, Isbah?" smiled Geoffrey.

The little Turk winked. "I would be the last one to tell the Emir he is wrong either by word or action!"

The Emir turned to address Geoffrey and gestured at the knight's armor.

"The Emir wishes to know if you would care to remove your armor and be comfortable among friends," Isbah smiled crookedly at him, his great beak of a nose and dark eyes making him look for all the world like some sort of giant owl to Geoffrey.

Geoffrey smiled and took a sip of wine.

"Tell his excellence that I most certainly would, yet duty demands that I remain so."

"Ho, ho!" chortled Isbah, winking again. "You do not mind if I somewhat rephrase your reply, to aid in the translation, you might say?"

"And to aid in the longevity of us both, eh?" the Norman asked slyly.

Isbah shrugged his narrow shoulders. "To interpret faithfully one needs to keep a tongue within his head; I would not like your reply to cost me my position before the Emir."

"Or your tongue either, I suppose?" asked Geoffrey, reaching for a large dish of melon.

"Sir Norman," Isbah smiled thinly, "you are quick to grasp the politics of the East."

The Emir of Tarsus had watched benignly, albeit ignorantly, throughout the exchange and his smile broadened as the interpreter gave his version of the young knight's answer.

Then Isbah again turned to Geoffrey after the Emir's reply. "The Emir wishes you to know that he truly respects a warrior who is ever ready to champion his cause, but bids you understand that there is no danger here for you tonight."

Geoffrey's face did not betray the outrage he felt. He nodded courteously and answered in a cheerful voice. "Tell the Emir that I am decidedly unimpressed with both his sincere efforts and his threat. It has not escaped me that my life is in his hands, yet do not expect me to cower or fawn like a dog before him for favor. I would lie if I said I did not fear death, yet the fear is not so great as to overcome my honor."

Isbah hesitated.

"Well spoken, Frank!" thundered the Emir of Kazanli in near-perfect French, causing Geoffrey to choke upon the wine. So! These Turks were full of games indeed. Now, how did the Emir of Kazanli speak French?

The lesser Emir threw back his head and laughed a deep, strong laugh. Reading Geoffrey's mind, he replied that the Norman need not worry; only he and Isbah spoke the barbaric French tongue and luckily for Geoffrey, the Emir of Tarsus was not legendary for his toleration of insults.

And in that moment of heavy humor, Geoffrey decided that he respected the Emir of Kazanli, if he could convince himself that he did not actually like the man. Hopefully, they would not meet in battle.

The feast itself dragged on for hours as was the lavish custom of the East, until Geoffrey's appetite was surely forever driven from his stuffed body and the richly spiced wines and unbelievable delicacies no longer held any enchantment for the jaded Norman palate. Indeed, it was with no small feeling of relief that he greeted the announcement of the banquet's end and wearily allowed himself to be led to his chamber.

No guard was posted before his door; he had no need of escape for he was not a prisoner. In the morning, after breaking his fast with the Emir of Tarsus, he was free to return to the Christian camp with the Emir's reply. Additionally, he had pledged himself not to spy upon the infidel fortification and the Emir realized, as did Geoffrey, that he would not get far nosing around in the foreign city. Of course, the Frank would be watched, but only from a distance as befit the Emir's trust in him.

The young knight stripped off his armor to sleep only in his under garments but he pulled a heavy silver candlestick near his bed to serve as a weapon if need be. He was too much the warrior to sleep totally defenseless. Before he slept, as was his habit now, he knelt to pray to Him who he now served over and above the Christian host. "Oh, Father of us all, grant that I might serve you in freeing this land so holy. Use me as your sword to strike out against the chains of slavery and set right the wrongs done to the name of your blessed Son."

Inwardly, he hoped that the Lord understood that there were other Christian fetters to be struck free, ones that meant as much to him privately as those that he now named in prayer. Yet, he felt it selfish and sinful in his heart to ask for another man's woman, so he spoke her name only to himself, while dry lips finished the prayer for the Christian lords, leaders of the crusade.

But the creaking of the door put an end to his meditation, for it had shifted upon its hinges so slightly as if someone outside were testing the sturdiness of its bolt. Soundlessly, he separated the hot wax of the candle from the heavy stand and brandished the instrument in his strong fist as he crept nearer the slowly-opening door. Treachery!

But it surprised him little in this place. Well, he would send them all to their Allah that they argued so much about. Silent as a cat, he stepped next to the door and raised the candle stand and paused; dim light shone in from a far-off torch and Geoffrey saw a solitary shadow peering into the darkness of his unlit chamber. Then, the door opened half-way. Apparently decided, the phantom figure entered and Geoffrey raised his weapon high for a killing blow but waited.

He saw first a flash of dark skin as a slender leg stealthily slipped over the threshold, only to withdraw quickly, accompanied by a small, feminine squeak of surprise at the realization of an "empty" chamber. With a hoarse curse, Geoffrey wrenched the door free from the intruder's small hands, flung it open its full width and grabbed a struggling woman who had plainly been frightened near to death. Somewhat brutally, he eased her to his bed and hastily checked the hallway to see if any others lurked in the dim twilight of the castle corridors.

"Cry out and you will die!" he cautioned her. He would take no chance on her signaling a gang of cutthroats. He checked the hallway once again. But there was nothing there.

Satisfied that they were alone, he turned and regarded the trembling girl. She was of an age of about thirteen or fourteen years with dark doe eyes, jet skin and long ebony hair, silky-straight. She was pretty and exotic and very nearly naked. Her only ornaments were the golden rings she sported on slender ankles and wrists. Other than her tresses, her body shone like a statue, revealed in the dusky light from the hall. He shut the door tightly and lit a candle, watching her all the time as he did so.

The girl's eyes grew large as she regarded him; his face was inscrutable. The stories she had heard of him returned to her; this was the one her masters called the champion of the Franks. He was a dealer of many deaths among the faithful. Some said he drank the blood of the dead.

But his tight mouth relaxed and his eyes softened as he looked at her. Suddenly, he was quite different and she was drawn to his easy smile. He had wondered at first if she were sent to seduce him and entrap him; but if so, she was a poor little actress for she inspired pity in him instead of lust with her childlike fear. Geoffrey realized there was a mystery here, but it was not a hostile one.

"Well," he cocked a quizzical eyebrow at her, "I await your story."

"Mercy, Sir Knight, I meant no harm," she whimpered in French.

"Then you will receive naught in that direction from me, lass. But you have a rude way of imposing upon a man's well-deserved slumber. Aye, but the sting of that wine makes my belly grumble and my head ache. But tell me, how is it there is one such as you in this city of infidels that speaks the French tongue?"

She spoke in a low whisper as if fearing spies, "My mistress taught me her speech when she first came here, so that she might have a companion. She is a kind and gentle mistress. This night she bade me find the chamber of the Frank within these walls, the St. Denis."

Geoffrey started as adrenalin roared through his veins. Without thinking, he reached for his tunic and armor. "I am the St. Denis, little flower of the night. The fates are kind, as is your mistress, to grant me an audience. But this is dangerous and I have not the will to ask what she desires. By leaving with you, I might condemn us all to death for betrayal of the truce."

"I had not thought to find you afraid, my lord. Not from what I have heard about you in battle," she whispered.

"Only the dead do not know fear, small one. But it is not myself I fear for. I am not sure what she plans…"

"She wishes to repay you for what you have rendered her, Sir Knight," she said with her dark eyes shining.

"What mockery is this that you make of me? I have rendered her no service for I have accomplished nothing for her. She is generous in saying that a debt exists."

The little slave smiled and answered with a maturity belying her tender space of years. "What fools you men are, to measure your devotion with sword strokes and combat as if that meant anything. Tis plain to me that you have done more for my lady by merely following her than you could ever achieve by heaping bodies at her feet, Now, she wishes an audience with you, this instant. Am I to tell her that you shall wait until you feel you have earned it? Or is it that you are afraid of her?"

"Nay," scowled Geoffrey. "You mock me, girl, but I fear not she who I have loved so long. Tis only that…"

For a second the slave's face lost its impishness and warmed with a glow of understanding and compassion as she answered his own thoughts.

"Nay, sir. Tis that you are afraid of yourself. I know, I can see it in your eyes. And my lady is also afraid in that same sad way. The wine of love is bittersweet the poets say, but if you pass the night alone, will you not experience only the harshness of the draught? Would it not be better to accept a word of comfort from my lady?"

Geoffrey smiled to himself. Was this not what he had prayed for, such a chance? Was this not the reason of his visit to Tarsus? And here he stood trying to talk otherwise. "And if things go beyond our control, then I will die for her, but even that death would be palatable."

"Pooh! Men!" said the girl with disgust. "You all fancy yourselves such lovers that the woman will lose her head over you, yet, how often is it just the opposite? Mayhap she only wishes to talk with you!"

Geoffrey opened the door. "So say you?" he asked casually.

"She is a lady!" snorted the girl.

Geoffrey frowned. "Aye, that she is. Perhaps I think her wrongly in this for she still belongs to another man; perhaps, I do act the fool," he said solemnly with a sudden inertia of spirit that slowed him.

"Indeed, you might!" answered the girl haughtily, taking him by the hand and pulling him behind her down the deserted corridor.

But she smiled secretly to herself for well she knew the Lady Claire and how it was that her man treated her. And though the wife of the brutal Eadricsson was by all means a lady, she was still a lady in love. And perhaps the girl understood this fact better at that moment than did either of the two uncertain lovers, for she had a forbidding feeling at the back of her consciousness, a sort of sensing of what was to come. But the knight beside her walked on without giving so much as an inkling of what he felt; his brain now seemed numb with his good fortune. Or by the singular image he saw before him at every step.

For near a half hour, the odd-matched pair made their way through ill-lit hallways, always avoiding the pacing of the watch with a near-sixth sense. The girl had been born into the Emir's slave pens and had grown up wholly within the bounds of Tarsus, such growing as she had done. Her ripening body was still more that of a child, but her mind was as full of common wisdom as any aged midwife's. For all of her ease in Claire's service, she was still a slave and slavery makes life a quick teacher, for either one learns swiftly or one does not survive.

"How far yet?" hissed Geoffrey.

"Shhh!" she whispered, clenching his hand in good camaraderie. "Still your pulse but a few minutes more, my good lord. We are almost there. But I like not the looks of these hallways for now we are within the limits of the chambers of Wulfhere Eadricsson, and since the day he arrived with his gold and his band of cutthroats, these halls have been footed by none but his own men. Yet, now I see no one."

"Perhaps they sleep off the banquet?" he asked hopefully.

She pursed her lips in thought. "Nay, his men did not attend, only he and his few captains. Tis muchly unlike him to leave his lair unguarded!"

"A trick!" muttered Geoffrey. "I have fallen for it without so much as a dagger in my grasp."

The girl looked at him anxiously as she pulled him within the shadows of the torches. The hall was dark and silent, unnaturally so.

"There is still time to flee, if you wish, my lord. What has entered the mind of this devilish Saxon I cannot tell you. But if you desire, I will help you escape before we are set upon. The choice is yours, my lord. I would not judge you for it. Under these strange circumstances, my lady would understand, I am sure."

So close and give it all up? God! Why could he not be left in peace with her? Why must there always be the fear, the suspicion? And what now? Return to his chamber and pretend she had not wanted him, sacrifice the only chance he might ever have to be with her?

No, no, it could not be. He was intoxicated with the need to see her, if for nothing more than to look into her bright eyes a final time. What he intended was folly, the risk too damnably great. But had he not already sacrificed everything for her?

Geoffrey shook with his need for her, his lover's heart taut and quivering, stroked by the memory of her soft smile. And his breath came in a sigh with his decision of utter fatality. "What will be, will be. Lead on, girl," he murmured, squeezing her small hand within his. And she saw then why her lady loved this man so greatly.

13

CHAPTER THE THIRTEENTH

S aheera, the slave girl, bowed low as she tugged at the brass ring to
open the ornately carved door of gilt and lacquer. Then, golden
rings about her ankles bobbing with her quick walk, she was gone down
the dark hallway.

Geoffrey brushed aside the filmy purple and red curtains and strode
quietly into the chamber, obviously the richly furnished bedchamber of
some high Moslem lord or lady in this heathen city. With mild disgust, he
surveyed the splendor the infidels lived in. Colored carpets of complex
patterns covered every inch of the floor and thick-padded couches sat
behind low, glossy-wood tables. Rare draperies and tapestries decorated
the walls and at the far side of the chamber, there opened intricately-
carved lattice doors onto a spacious balcony, open to the night and stars.

The moon was high and brilliant in this infidel fairyland; its silvery
color bathed the open porch and illuminated the inside of the doors. A
cool breeze drifted in off the desert hills and Geoffrey smelled the exotic
spices of the East. In corners of the room, scented candles burned with
the fragrance of jasmine and, despite its foreign flavor, the scene was
warm and inviting.

Upon the balcony, silhouetted against the pale light of the moon and stars, Geoffrey made out a slender form wrapped in the sheer robes of the land. In his heart, he knew it was her.

She turned as he entered, though he made not a sound upon the cushion of the carpeting. For long moments, she stood unmoving, regarding silently the man who was her champion across oceans and years, the man she had loved and been loved by for so long and so tragically. Now the pain was numbness. The hour of night made for deep dreams, but none more beautiful than this.

He was the supplicant come to beg his lady's favor, knowing it could not be denied. He stood as though turned to stone by her presence, hypnotized as he watched her ever so slowly enter into the soft light of the chamber.

Gracefully, she slipped the transparent hood of her robe back upon her shoulders and he smiled as she revealed herself. He was stunned by her beauty here in the flickering amber of the candle lamps, stunned as if he was seeing her again for the first time. Time fled from her face, and he saw again the girl he had loved from so high in that wretched tower of the Castle Ayrin, the little one who loved him despite his wrongs.

Claire watched him intently as she entered, mouth set in a polite smile of greeting, though fearful and trembling inside lest either of them give up the game and collapse weeping into the other's arms.

She had almost thought it innocent when she planned it out. She wanted but to thank him and talk with him, to hear his voice again as she had heard so quietly for the first time that day. And it had been just as she had imagined it would be. But now...

There was a fire behind his cool blue eyes and an aching within his heart as he gazed at her, even lovelier for the time that had separated the two of them. For what seemed an eternity, neither of them could speak, as if each were afraid of breaking the enchantment that lay over the warm chamber. There was only the soft rustle of her silks as she approached him, until she stood, eyes lowered, before him.

At last, Geoffrey reached out to take her small, trembling hand, lifting it lightly so that her eyes followed it until they met his. She smiled timidly and Geoffrey saw that her eyes were bluer than the lakes of their homeland, and just as deep. Gently, he kissed her hand.

They were both playing a game, but then all lovers do whether they realize it or not. Having fantasy turn to reality before one's eyes can sometimes be a frightening experience, so dreams are often left to simply run their course without encouragement. But here the need was too strong, the desire too long pent up. Geoffrey played the game of gentle wooing, and Claire played the lady, but each was fire to the other's heart, and the flames of what they felt slowly consumed all between them that was not real.

"At last, I am at liberty to thank you for what you gave me so long ago, my lady, indeed what you have always given me from that day I first saw you in the wood with the morning sun in your hair as you walked," he said gently. But his blue eyes smoldered.

What did she see there? Was all this too sudden?

What he felt for her was still adoration, yet now, unexpectedly, he loved her in every one of the infinity of ways in which one person might love another. She was so indescribably lovely standing before him, half-hidden in her diaphanous gown, as gentle-eyed as a young doe. The musk she wore filled his nostrils and pounded a rhythm of need through his body.

Again, she smiled, lowering her head a little to look at the rough hand that held hers so gently. "And what is that, Sir Geoffrey?" she asked, very, very quietly. She looked up after she had spoken to peer searchingly into the sparkling wells that were his eyes.

"Hope, my lady," he replied. "For two years, you were my sun in the morning and for nigh two more you have been the star that guided me. Never has there been a need stronger, a promise greater than that which you made me put into my own hard heart. When I would have rested, it drove me. When I would have lost, it succored me. When I was alone, it walked with me…"

"I had not thought my sympathy for a prisoner could ever be so much to him, especially a noble born one. What was I, but the daughter of a craftsman and what am I, but the wife-slave of a Saxon traitor? You are kind to hold me in such esteem, good knight, but I fear you overestimate me," she tried to explain, her eyes misty with tears. She felt she had no right to lay claim to him, for they had always existed worlds apart. But the look upon his face stopped her.

"You have never been aught else to me but my most dear lady, the one I cherish above all else. For love of you, I sacrificed friends and family at the beginning of my quest. I left my honor on the doorstep of my father's manor house at Westwall. And in my search for you have slain many men who have tried to stop me for their own reasons. Because of you, I led the attack upon the gates of Tarsus, for you alone. When I thought the attack had failed and I would die, I regretted only that I would not see you free, and the shame of such knowledge lent strength to my arm and sent many of the heathens to hell. To me, there is nothing else, but you. You do me an injustice when you belittle my love for you; it is all have."

"Oh, Geoffrey," she cried, "I did not mean that you..."

But he seized her face very gently in his calloused hand and lifted her lovely eyes to meet his. He watched, smiling, as a whirl of emotions flashed through the windows of her soul. First, he saw abrupt surprise at his boldness, then shyness, then realization. Then want.

So softly that she scarcely knew herself touched, he kissed her pretty lips. And although she did not return the kiss, neither did she push him away. Geoffrey heard a sigh but whether it was his or hers, he could not say. She had tasted sweeter than he had imagined and her lips were soft and moist.

Again, he kissed her, harder this time so that the enveloping softness of her ripe mouth was all he could think of. As he lifted his lips from hers, he stroked her smooth cheek very, very softly.

Still, she did not return his kiss, but Geoffrey felt a quick shiver course through her.

"Sweet, my Claire, oh how I have loved you! I thought never to see this night that I might hold you so."

"Oh, Geoffrey," she wept, tears running down her cheeks. "I cannot be yours for I belong to another. I have born his child and what might have been, can never be...for us." She bowed her head in misery so sure of the absoluteness of the situation.

"No!" he said as he pulled her close. "You talk now of my life, for to lose you now is for me to die. I am stronger than those who would destroy us!"

"Geoffrey!" she pleaded as he bent her head back, placing his lips upon hers in both want and need.

She gasped at his touch this time, for the determination of his mind was easy enough to read through his touch and his kiss. He pressed his lips to hers this third time, not intending to remove them until she either yielded or found the strength to walk away from him.

But she had not the strength. Nor the desire.

Claire threw both her slender arms about him, forcing her mouth up to meet his with the sudden fury of a summer storm. Her deliciously supple young body meshed against his hotly, sending a sharp thrilling through them both, and they realized they had gone past stopping. For what seemed forever, they caressed in this way until both were gasping and shaking. Claire broke away and threw herself upon the sleeping couch, sobbing.

Tenderly, Geoffrey lay her upon her back and cradled her head with one strong arm while he kissed the tears from her eyes. She alternately clung to him and then tried to push him away with the intense emotions of a woman in love, until at last resistance ceased and she clung to him only, lips melted fiercely against his and her arms entwined about his strong neck.

Geoffrey smoothed her blonde hair away from her wet face where curls lay soddenly pressed against her soft cheek. He smiled at her with his love evident across his hard-lined features.

"Geoffrey," she sighed.

"Hush," he murmured. "Now is the time for those words found in the language of love."

She closed her eyes and smiled a smile of utter contentment. For the first time in her life, she was truly happy. And so was he.

Geoffrey let his lips trail lightly down her exquisite throat's full length and she gave a little moan, lifting her chin that he might kiss her more readily. She stroked his hair as he nuzzled her, eyes closed in a fantasy that they were both home in Britain, in a summer field of trees and brooks. It had been long since she had known such tenderness.

But a love years in the making, and just now realizing fruition, becomes deeper abruptly and without the participants realizing it. At last, Geoffrey was no longer content to kiss her face and throat, nor was she content to allow him that only. Both wanted the stronger possession; it was not to be denied. Geoffrey looked only an instant into her hot flushed face, reading the answer in her blue eyes and in the sensuous twist to her lips.

Claire shivered again as Geoffrey's hand moved beneath her light gown to find her flat belly and then her petite breasts, although his touch was clumsy at first for all the times he had practiced this act with others. Was it perhaps that now he was touching something sacred?

Yet, the awkwardness was soon gone, vanished wholly into the depths of the emotion he felt, the pent-up longing of four years. It was a sea that shed clean reality's clumsiness; it was an endless roaring ocean that maddened the pulse and quickened the blood that made the breath come hot and wet and fast and drowned the endless pettiness of a mundane world in a deluge of deep, deep dreams.

He stood and pulled his armor from his strong body, and then his tunic, hose and boots. Claire watched in fascination as he slowly revealed his hard musculature, full and powerful, so different from Wulfhere's leaner form. She winced as she saw tracks and ridges of scars from his years as a warrior and ground her teeth against the pain they must have caused him. As he moved, with every movement, his body rippled with steel hard sinews and Claire saw why the Turks had surrounded him before the gates and why the Turks had died horribly. She saw the new scars from that contest still painfully puckered and angry red, and she felt tears overwhelm her as she understood more fully what this man had suffered out of his love for her. She had never wanted to look at Wulfhere as he drunkenly paraded his nakedness before he ravaged her; but she found Geoffrey's body beautiful in her eyes and inviting.

He knelt next to her and smiled at the seriousness of her gaze.

Her lips were tender-sweet and the ineffable beauty of her body was as nothing compared to the beauty of her soul as Geoffrey cradled her ever-lovingly within his arms. She protested not as he slowly removed her robe until she was totally, and unashamedly, exposed to him. She was as innocently lovely as spring's first flower.

And as Geoffrey looked at her lying there unmoving, his pulse stilled just the slightest bit and the carnal desire he felt was transformed into something he could not name just then. Call it want or desire, although these pale weak words cannot fully name it; but it was not lust. They did not fornicate; they made love.

Events of magnitude were happening within and without the fortress, but the couple was oblivious in the cocoon of her bed. The fates had set the hourglass for the city and thousands of lives to its final turn, though no one yet understood this. An era was ending, another beginning. But the boundary between the two would be an ocean of blood from which not even two lovers would be exempt. Even now, hulking warriors with blond hair and longswords were padding silently down the hallways of the fortress, intent upon a dark revenge.

But the young knight and his lady, another man's so-called wife were not interested in any of this. They were too much in love.

That night, the dreams of each were realized in each other and, though neither had been prepared for it, a flame that had flickered steadily for four years was now fanned into a raging fire, and both lovers tasted the flesh of both bitter and sweet fruit at the same time. There was nothing new in this awakening; it is always the same when the meeting of souls includes the meeting of flesh. Neither was there shame in this.

Geoffrey reveled in her warmth, but a voice inside him whispered unnerving predictions of the future, for he understood her well. In the rearmost corner of Geoffrey's mind, he knew that although she would always be his in her heart, she belonged to another. And between them stood the infidel world. *Do you make sport of me, God?* Yet, if there was mockery, it was lost in emotion.

There was nothing but the sweetness of Claire's lips, for he was well and truly intoxicated, drunk on the taste and touch and smell of her. Her breath in his face was honey-sweet as she whispered to him, dreamy now and half asleep. "I love you, my Geoffrey!" she murmured, "I love you so!"

Geoffrey trailed kisses down her slender neck, her soft shoulders and delicately curved back. The words poured forth from his soul so rapidly and so effortlessly that he scarcely knew he spoke them. "And ever have I loved you, my Claire...even before I saw you framed in my window, I saw your veiled form in my sweetest dreams. You are all that I have ever wished for and worth more than life itself!"

Guvi would have laughed at the warrior turned poet, but Geoffrey did not even think such thoughts.

Claire smiled sleepily and rolled over to face him, resting her head upon his broad muscular chest and stroking his steel arms. It was hard to understand how this warrior's body could be so gentle with her or so caring. She felt the strength in him and marveled at what it must do when encased in its protective armor, when wielding the awesome weapons of war. How strange it was that this man's body that had so often functioned as nothing more than a killing machine had been the source of her greatest pleasure.

The memories of this night would bring solace to her forever, no matter what hurt the future might bring. Does the gift of prophecy go with that of love? Shadowy figures gathered in an archway and plotted. Time fled; the sands were running too fast.

Claire touched Geoffrey's cheek as if discovering it all again. How was it that he loved her so intensely, yet so tenderly? He might have wondered the same.

"I love you!" she breathed, and she smiled to herself as she felt his heart jump at the words beneath her palm. Raising upon her elbows, she looked awhile upon his serious features, now full of calm and thoughts of peace rather than warfare, her face bright with the emotion she felt. Then she took his face between her small hands and took a turn at tasting his mouth with a form of exploration that began playful but soon roused again the passion they shared.

It was as if she had known him forever; never had she thought to be so bold with a man. But with Geoffrey she was comfortable, an unusual sensation in her hostile environment. She surprised herself at the strength of her need now, at her desire to initiate. She wanted him more now than she had when he had first had her; she needed him more and more and she felt a surge of joy come over her that she could share and care so much with another. What had been pain with Wulfhere was indescribable pleasure; what had been shame was now joy. For the first time in her life she felt complete, complete as even her child had failed to make her feel.

Geoffrey groaned and pulled her so that she was atop him and, one strong hand holding the back of her head, positively ravaged her seeking lips as his other hand stroked her sleek back. But she pulled away with a grin of total mischievousness and kissed him but lightly.

"Nay, sir knight," she laughed quietly. "This time, it is I who shall be the conqueror!" And before he could react to the challenge of her words, she had pressed herself back upon him and kissed him savagely.

It ended too soon. When it was over and both spent lovers lay peacefully still, her head again upon his chest and as he stroked her golden hair, there followed a heavy silence for both understood that cockcrow was not to be long in coming. There, night was but minutes long in their closeness; the day would prove to be an eternity.

At last, it was Geoffrey who broke the quietude. "Will you come with me?" he whispered, his throat dry with apprehension at what he sensed her answer must be.

For a long while, she said nothing as she stroked his calloused hand.

A chill breeze blew in from the desert. He felt her shiver but found it impossible to move closer to her. She was withdrawing from him, steadily. Then she sighed wearily, but it was not from their lovemaking.

"I cannot," she said. "I cannot risk it for Helgi's sake as well as my own. I am sorry, my love, now is not the time."

"There is no more time," said Geoffrey with the saddest of smiles, and he was yet to understand how right he was.

"We would not make it," Claire murmured. "They would know."

"Let them know. Let them come and die! None will stand before me!" the young knight said.

"For what?" she asked. "That I might watch you die for me? Is that how you would prove your love for me? It is a foolish way. I would see you live, my dearest love."

Geoffrey wrapped his arms about her and kissed her lightly. But the determination in his voice when he spoke had a steel edge to it.

"When it is for you that I stand, my Claire, none will stop me. The strength of my blade will do for us what my cunning fails at. And if I die, then I die to free you and there is no shame in that as long as I have worn my gilded spurs accompanied with death by my side as all soldiers do; death no longer frightens me. You say you would see me alive, my dove; now, I wonder how it is that you expect me to live in honor while the woman I love is chained to a barbarian's couch. You deny me this night; it is your choice and I cannot gainsay you in it. But know that when the trumpet calls, I shall again be at the walls and I will each day until I see you free."

"Or until you die," she whispered, horror etching the words across the silence of the chamber.

He nodded solemnly.

"No, no!" she breathed, touching his hard jaw. "It must never be as you say it. I can have no lives upon my conscience, not even for the love I have for you, my Geoffrey. You must not take me over other men's lives."

"That is not your choice to make," he said, frustrated, turning from her.

"It is, more than you realize, my Geoffrey. It is," she said evenly.

The meaning of her words sank in and he was stung. "Does my love not mean more than that, more than everything?"

"It does mean everything to me, my dear Geoffrey. But everything in the world is not enough to change wrong to right. And I cannot live to lie."

He rose to dress, features set hard. "Better to live a veritable slave, then?" he asked.

She put her head down. "It is bearable. I will learn patience and if God wills it, you and I will find our way together again. You must have faith."

"My faith is in my sword arm, sweet Claire. It will cut me a path to you. If you wish to be a slave, then you might as well be mine," he said, with a small attempt at humor.

She gave him a slow smile of infinite wisdom. "I understand what you are thinking, but it will not work. I am who I am and could not live like that. You would condemn me to worse slavery than I have now, for you would have robbed me of my dreams and proved all my hopes false."

"That is a riddle!" snapped Geoffrey, pulling his tunic closed. Frustrated as he was, he could not take his eyes from her nude beauty.

"Not so, my love. You would not understand how much your affection has meant to me, how I have dreamed of the handsome knight in that forlorn tower, that knight that followed me to sea's edge that day to fight a clan of raiders for my freedom. And now…to know that you have cared so much, so very, very much that you have followed me across the world and risked your life for mine. Everything you have done is more than mortal; you are the Prince of Dreams to show me such honor and such courage. But I have seen war, my dearest Geoffrey and I have seen bloodshed wherever we have traveled and it sickens me unto death. Not even the animals fight as man fights, for lust and booty. Wulfhere has done me much wrong, but in his own way he has taught me much about how life spins in this empty universe, and I tell you that I wish to be no man's prize of blood or see bodies piled high on the battlefield in my name. Most men are ignorant savages, too quick to show their anger or their greed. I have loved you because from the first, you were different, and I know after tonight just how different from all the others you really are. So, I beg you, my dearest, be not like your brothers; do not think to take me by the sword for that game sword will slay my love for you."

Geoffrey felt the bitter pill of tears film his eyes and his voice shook. "So, you will remain this Saxon's slave and subject your daughter and yourself to his will?"

"If God wills it," she said quietly.

"And where will you be when Tarsus falls and Alexis sees to it that all the renegade Saxons are put to death, mayhap tortured. The emperor is not revered for his charity!" Geoffrey retorted.

Claire closed her eyes and shook her head. There was nothing more to say.

Geoffrey finished dressing in silence and bent down to kiss her. She said nothing but clung to him for a long time, helplessly. The young knight felt his anger overwhelmed by his love for her, but not his determination. Then he walked to the door and put his hand upon the latch, but before he left, he turned to gaze at her a final time. "I understand you perhaps better than you might think, but it does not matter. You call freedom a prize of blood; it is. But it is a worthy prize. The blame for what happens next will be upon my head. And I swear to you by the love I bear you, that I will see to it that this wretched citadel falls, if no one else does. If I have to pull it down rock by rock, timber by timber, it will fall. And then I will come for you; let no one stand between us for they will die. For you, I will spare the Saxon, if I can, but I will have you, my sweet. Make no mistake about that! Or I will perish in the effort."

"Geoffrey!" she wept. Still unclothed, she ran to him and threw herself in his steel-clad arms.

But his eyes were hard and proud. He was the warrior again. "You would be his slave before being my wife. But you will be mine, my Claire."

Her tears ran down the front of his chainmail as he held her close. "But I *am* yours, my love! Can you not see that?" Her tears were a cascade of amber in the warm lamplight.

He appraised her a moment before he spoke. Then, his voice was tired. "You do not say it so," he said, nearly choking upon the emotion. "But I will have you. Even death cannot still my love for you!" He kissed her a final time and flung open the chamber door.

And drew back in horror.

"Pretty words, Sir Knight, noble emissary of the Christians, adulterer and woman-stealer!" laughed Wulfhere the Reaver. Geoffrey saw the gleam of steel in his fist and over his shoulders, the bearded faces of two of his Saxons. "We will see them put upon your gravestone. But first, I will permit you to watch while I punish your partner in crime!" he finished.

Instinctively, Geoffrey shoved Claire roughly behind him and he spoke to gain what moments he could. "I beg you, hear me out before you slay me, Saxon," he entreated. He lowered his eyes in humility and counted upon the enormous ego of Wulfhere to aid him. The ruse worked; a gloating smile spread over the renegade's thin lips and his companions laughed outright.

"The hero of the gates begging for his life? Is it the life of his dearest love, he begs for? Ha! Proceed, fool. Convince me to slay you!" Wulfhere the Reaver was enjoying himself immensely and Geoffrey tensed to strike.

"I can reward you beyond your wildest dreams, Saxon," assured Geoffrey.

Wulfhere snorted. "Wealth I already have, knave. Rather tell me how to get it safely away from here!"

"I can do that also," Geoffrey promised, confidently. Wulfhere' s eyes widened in greedy speculation.

"This should prove interesting, indeed!" he agreed. "Speak, dead man, while you still have breath in you to move your tongue."

Geoffrey nodded amiably, apparently relieved. He took a deep breath to begin. "Good, I wish to first say," Geoffrey began, but he finished by launching his armor-encased foot into the Saxon's groin. Wulfhere's scream was a shrill cry that echoed eerily through the corridor.

As Wulfhere doubled over, the Norman smashed a hard knee into the man's face, breaking his nose and wrecking upper and lower jaws, and sending a gush of hot crimson over the floor. The renegade was rocketed backward by the force of the blow, into his fellow traitors. Without a pause in his movements, Geoffrey wrenched loose Wulfhere's dagger and plunged the steel-glittering weapon into the throat of one of the other Saxons, to the hilt. The fellow collapsed, choking briefly on blade and blood, dying. At once, the young knight was grappling with the third Saxon in grunting silence, as Wulfhere flopped along on the stone floor like a fish out of water, trying desperately to regain both breath and wits.

Claire stood naked in the doorway, paralyzed by the intensity of the struggle. Her mouth was open for a scream, but no sound issued from it.

The guard was terribly strong, as were all the hard-fighting Saxons of the renegade Wulfhere. Geoffrey was stronger. He broke the man's left wrist with a bone-snapping twist. The Saxon howled madly and slashed at Geoffrey's face, but the Norman stooped and picked the fellow up with one leg, throwing him off balance, so that the long poniard missed his face and furrowed a path along the flesh of his left hand, stopping only when it met the steel links of his armored cuff. Blood streamed down his torso and legs as they grappled, although the cut was not as serious as it appeared.

Geoffrey hurled his opponent to the floor and the man lay still as his head struck the flagstones. Geoffrey crushed his larynx with one booted foot, to be sure.

He had thought the contest ended as he stood sweat-soaked and panting, but as he turned to Claire he saw a look of horror flash across her face and her lips twitched as she tried to speak. The fear in her eyes warned him and he stepped aside as Wulfhere's weapon thrust for his back. Wulfhere was upon him with a vengeance and Geoffrey felt the dagger tip pierce his mailed left shoulder, halted by the chain link after no more than a half inch had stuck him. He turned like a striking cobra and pulled the Saxon's hands loose from the hilt and his grip on Geoffrey's coif. Wulfhere tried to back away but Geoffrey brought the weight and power of an armored elbow up against the renegade's temple and Wulfhere collapsed.

Geoffrey stepped forward to finish the man off but paused as he remembered his promise to Claire. Phagh! Let the fellow lie here in his agony; Geoffrey had beaten him twice in less than half an hour. Even Wulfhere must know who the better man was.

But now they must fly! He looked at Claire's terror-stricken eyes. She was still naked, standing there with shock at what had happened. In this one moment of desire, she had precariously altered her future irredeemably. There was only death for her here, but the odds were against their escaping. She had still to fetch Helgi and...

"Dress!" Geoffrey snapped, his blue eyes gleaming in the lamplight as he panted for breath. "We must be long away from here by the time this bastard finds what wits he has."

"I cannot!" she cried, "He is..."

Geoffrey's look was ugly. "He is a renegade and a killer. He will slay you slowly for what you have done with me. For your daughter's life as well as your own, you must forget what has passed and come with me now." In a lower voice he added, "God or the fates have chosen this night to make you mine. I know not which, nor care. All I care about is that I have you now. God witness that I did not force this upon you but say to you that this night you have become mine completely. Now, come, my sweet, you must trust me in this!"

"I can't," she said, confused.

Geoffrey looked back at Wulfhere and placed his foot upon the Saxon's throat in a threatening gesture. His meaning was clear. "Then I will slay your husband before I leave that he might not live to do you harm!" Geoffrey snarled. He bent and picked up a bloody dagger.

Claire sighed, realizing that she was fighting fate. "Spare him, my love. I will come with you; here, let us hurry!" Shuddering, she dressed hurriedly and followed him into the hall.

"Where is your girl?" Geoffrey asked. He had to repeat the question before he received a reply, so mutely stricken with fear was Claire. She pointed a way down the corridor and Geoffrey paused to spit upon Wulfhere's prostrate form.

"Thank the gods you worship for this woman's goodness, you son of a dog!" he muttered through gritted teeth. Then they were off down the hall. A guard challenged them in a corner that they had turned blindly; they could not evade the man so Geoffrey turned upon him with a desperate fury that left the man bloodily slaughtered in a trice. But he had to drag Claire for she stood transfixed, gazing down at the man's corpse.

"It cannot be this way!" she cried. "It is not right..."

"Then close your eyes, little one, that you might not see. And cover your ears that you hear nothing for these Turks do not speak our language to be reasoned with, and I doubt if we can smile our way past them all."

"No, please!" she sobbed.

"It is their deaths or ours. I am no lamb to be slaughtered nor will I see you returned to Wulfhere. If your heart is heavy, then pray no more of them confront us for they will also die!" Geoffrey said coldly.

"Please..." she implored. But he was right.

He stared at her helplessly. "There is no other way, my angel. I ask to kill no man here, but neither will abandon you to them. If what we do is sin, then it is my sin alone for the deaths are mine."

"That is all the worse, for you are no killer!" she said.

"Neither am I a coward, my Claire. For you, I would defy the Creator himself! Now hush! We must find your babe and be free of this place!"

Claire saw what lay within his dark eyes and silently followed. The nurse of her child was little enough problem; she told the old woman that she wished to see the child for loneliness. Nodding assent, the aged crone wrapped the small girl in a warm blanket against the night air and handed her to her mother. As Claire stepped into the torch-lit corridor, Geoffrey took the babe in his arms for speed, pausing only long enough to brush away the blanket and gaze closely at the face of the sleeping girl.

His smile for her was very special, full of gentleness and care. "Her name is Helgi, you say, my love?" he asked.

Despite herself, she returned the smile. "Aye, she is a sprite of the North breeze, so Wulfhere named her thusly."

Claire watched the smile that lit her lover's grim face grow broader with the warm outflow of emotion for the helpless girl and mother, as well, and she understood all over again why it was that she loved him.

"She is the perfect image of you, my sweet! God has blessed her with your beauty, may he grant her your soul as well."

All of the killing fever had fled from his eyes at touching Helgi. She stared at his handsome face and felt an all-encompassing helplessness. But her fear was dying before this strong knight that loved her.

As he spoke in that firm voice, her terror calmed and once again hope sprang into her heart. Without further words, he took her hand in his, cradling the sleeping daughter against his mail-clad shoulder with the other, and led her down the hallways in the general direction of the walls. He pondered many plans as they walked hurriedly, but there was no time for either disguise or plotting. They must depend on the fact that he was the only enemy Frank within the walls of Tarsus and presumed to be under guard at that. The only ones who would know that he had escaped were dead or drunk or still unconscious, he hoped.

With the sharp instincts of a seasoned warrior, he led them down dark hallways and through ponderous unguarded doors, and finally and thankfully, down deserted moonlit streets. Twice they stepped secretively inside black archways to avoid the tramp of the night watch; twice were they successful. Geoffrey felt his spirits buoyed by their momentary good fortune, and even began to think that they might emerge unscathed from the infidel city.

He imagined that Tarsus, for all its exotic mystery and strange denizens, was much like any other city in a civilized land; the small streets and back alleys led to large ones and gates, and the large ones led to squares or to the gates in the walls. The tallest and most splendid buildings lined the main avenues at the city center where more activity and soldiers were to be encountered, while here, where they were now, was a maze of small shops and semi-secluded merchant houses leading to the less desirable tenements close to the outer walls. As long as they proceeded in the direction of the poorer sections, they were certain to encounter the walls eventually. He hoped.

For a long while, they had skulked along a minor artery that he had detected behind the palaces, remaining for the most part parallel to it in a series of side streets.

And, incredibly, their luck held, or so it seemed at the first. What was to happen next was to have a far more profound effect on Geoffrey's relationship with Claire than anything that had passed.

Abruptly, they came upon a gate, ideally suited for their purpose. It came almost too soon for Geoffrey had yet to think out his next moves. It was a minor gate in size as well as importance, little more than a mere opening in the yellow brick of the wall a man's height and breadth. It served as a portal for scouts and spies sent out. For Frankish purpose, it was nearly useless for it was so low that a large man might enter only by stooping low, and naturally, it could be easily defended by very few warriors.

But on this dark night, it seemed to the young Norman to be a gift from God, for it was guarded only by three sleepy footmen. The rest of the watch would be walking posts high up on the wall but they could not see what occurred in the black shadows at the foot of the parapets.

If the deed could be done in silence, they would be safe. Geoffrey stood behind an abandoned hut and surveyed the scene in grim silence. What would happen next would be life or death for them all and it was far easier to make the wrong move here than the right one. He cursed himself silently as he realized that his knees shook. He was unafraid to face these warriors alone, but he had no illusions as to what would happen to Claire should he make a mistake. God help him.

He turned to Claire and handed her back her small daughter, noticing in what pale light there was that she was also shaking.

His throat was dry. "What I must do, I do for us."

Closing her eyes, she nodded. Her face bore a pained expression.

There was no way to approach the guards without being seen for the buildings ended fifty feet from the wall, but this disadvantage was offset by the fact that the guards were by no means prepared for any type of assault. Two squatted together smoking a pipe filled with hashish and laughing contentedly to themselves; the third leaned upon his spear, dizzy already with the effects of the drug and dozing. They could not have presented a better target if they had tried.

To engage them, he must approach them and be sure that none cried out for the watch. One shout and he was done for. There was really only a single way. He would be mad to attempt it. But desperation breeds mad measures in the sanest of men, and how often had the Wild Siwardsson's madness worked superbly? He would do it; he must do it.

Geoffrey closed his eyes a moment in silent prayer before he stepped from the shadows to begin his approach for the gate. Casually, he strode across open, silver-lit, hard-packed earth toward the three men. Claire watched him and wondered at his self-control; one watching might actually believe him one of the heathen warriors out catching some night air to clear a stuffy head or some scoundrel out seeking easy prey in alley ways. Her own heart was in her throat, pounding thunder-loud.

Geoffrey pulled his cloak tighter about himself to hide his Christian armor and weapons. He doubted if they were discernible in the darkness, but he was taking no chances. His attempt was madness, but sometimes caution was the watchword of such adventures, he reasoned. He had watched the red Siwardsson and had learned that there was much underlying his madness, much of it logical reasoning and careful planning. Eadric had laughed once and told him that the truly mad perish quickly in battle for a mind lost to logic is a mind without a defense. Geoffrey had no choice this time but to trust the great red-bearded bear.

He got to within thirty feet before the standing guard said anything to him, and even this was spoken in a casual, affable manner that excluded suspicion. But there was surely some sort of challenge delivered, some demand for intent or purpose. This was the moment of truth.

Trying to halt his churning stomach, he equally casually replied with a salty Arabic curse. Although he could not speak the heathen language of these Turks, he had picked up in his travels a few of their more disgusting comparisons.

He pointed to their pipe and muttered the Arabic equivalent. The smokers immediately relaxed, but Geoffrey watched the third who had not smoked like the other two.

"You drink your mother's urine, straight from the breast!" he called. The effect was instantaneous, yet not altogether alarming. Perhaps it was the effect of the narcotic smoke upon them, but none of the three took actual offense at the insult, each turning to look at his companions and chuckle. One of the men hunched over the pipe rose somewhat warily, but his attitude was more like he felt he was being approached by a guard captain than anything else. Plainly, they were violating their duty and were perhaps anxious that they had been discovered. The man standing, who had challenged Geoffrey, stood chagrinned a moment before he replied with what Geoffrey took to be a cursing reply from its tone. Clearly, he did not think the Norman an officer of the guard.

But their minds must be whirling with suspicions about the stranger. Geoffrey prayed that their hashish was strong. Had he judged correctly? Geoffrey made a great show of snorting in derision before he again cursed.

Incredibly, the man shrugged and yawned. He waved Geoffrey over.

How foolish they were. But then, what would a single Frank be doing walking the dark streets of the city at this hour? And what reason would he have to approach three armed warriors of the sultan in such a casual manner, and curse them as freely and as bountifully as any Seljuk sailor along the Bosporus?

They were just soldiers, uninterested in their dreary night duty as they were uninterested in the conflict their nation was now embroiled in. Like many of their brothers on both sides of the walls, they wished only for enough money to fill their purses and amusement to while away the boredom. The ideology of war and religion was beyond them. Glory was a tasty morsel, but hashish was safer.

It was not within the scope of their limited imaginations to picture this stranger as he really was; that smacked of madness. Nay, it made sense to them more that one who came to them so, must be a brother.

Geoffrey smiled as one of them held up the pipe for him. Perhaps he could find some way to pass without slaying them. But fate overruled him, as it always would.

The guard stepped toward Geoffrey with the pipe, a lazy smile spread across his dark features. Then he stopped, suddenly. For no understandable reason, the fellow halted barely ten feet from the knight, and surveyed him with the suspicion Geoffrey had first suspected,

Damn! He swore softly. Somehow, the fellow sensed something amiss. He kept one eye warily on the Frank as he turned his head slightly to address his companions. His pipe was shifted to his left hand and his right slowly drifted toward his sheathed scimitar. Geoffrey flipped his cloak from him in a blur; now all the speed he had taught his body before must come to his aid.

There was a gleam of quicksilver in the night air as Geoffrey's long tapered dagger took wing like a hunting falcon and thudded home, not in the throat of the man nearest him, but in the throat of one of the others still at a distance. Geoffrey knew that he could eliminate the Turk before him if he acted quickly enough; it was the other pair that could do him in either by circling behind him or by running for assistance. The odds were better now as the first Turk died in the dirt before the gate, a clean kill. He hoped that the other two would become so enraged at this that they would try to finish Geoffrey off themselves as a matter of pride, without sending for the watch.

The young knight saw that he was right in his estimate. These two would be no match for him.

With a grunt of surprise, both soldiers pulled curved swords free and moved for the Christian. Geoffrey had no time to contemplate upon his first success for they moved in swiftly, belying the effects of their narcotic smoke. Geoffrey hurled himself forward at the nearest opponent, intending to overwhelm the man with strength alone. But the young Frank received a shock, and a blow to his ego when the wiry little Turk deftly slipped the blow and was suddenly behind him. Soiled robe and dirty armor that marked the man as a lesser of the sultan's pride notwithstanding, the slender infidel turned out to be an experienced, supple fighter much to Geoffrey's dismay.

The knight silently cursed his own arrogance but settled down to the task at hand. There was still no alternative to what he had to do and the thought of Claire waiting lent strength to his arm and swiftness to his thrusts. The little man danced aside from the knight's whistling strokes, but Geoffrey also parried each of his opponent's strokes. He knew without looking that the other infidel was skulking behind him, awaiting an opening.

"Well," Geoffrey muttered to himself, they would see who would tire first, the dancing Turk or Geoffrey's methodical offense. Let the Turk twist and turn, out-distancing Geoffrey's blade; Geoffrey could deal a thousand strokes and not tire. The fellow should pray to his Allah that his feet not tire, for one misstep would be death. Steadily, Geoffrey maneuvered his enemy in a wide circle so as to always keep him between himself and the other Turk.

The Norman was profoundly insulted by the look of confidence that came over the foe's narrow features before he realized that it was not because of his fighting skill but because the second Turk had finally gotten behind him and was poised for the kill. Dammit! Could he not get closer to the stringy little man? Something had to give soon before he received a scimitar tip between his shoulder blades.

And it did. Barely in time to save his life, Claire, who had watched the entire pantomime in horror-stricken silence from the blackened mouth of the little streetway, suddenly found her wits and realized that it was up to her to save Geoffrey's life. She saw him hard pressed and bewildered by the tactics of his opponents and although she knew he would win in a normal contest, she understood that he was taking grave risks here because they no longer had time to pass. He was risking every-thing by letting the second fighter behind him and she thought he might well have been in error.

"Here! Help me, please!" Claire cried in Arabic.

Amazed, the Turk turned his face a split-second to the shadows and never saw death rushing to meet him.

Geoffrey's longsword shot forth like a beam of God-driven lightning and pierced the Seljuk soldier's throat so that Claire saw a foot of steel stick out through the nape of his neck. But instantly, it was gone as her knight's blade flickered back like a cobra's tongue and he wrenched himself about to check the rush of the final warrior.

Geoffrey hurled himself forward to crush the momentum of the fellow's attack and felt the scimitar clash against his mail, staggering him and numbing his arm with the shock. But the knight was desperate and although his sword arm was leaden, he deflected the Turk's second blow long enough to take hold of the fellow's wrist. Dropping his own sword, he retained his lock on the wrist and took hold of the man's elbow on the game arm with his other hand. With a wrench of the elbow up and the forearm downs, he shattered the joint and shook the scimitar from nerve-less fingers. The Seljuk gave a short, sharp cry before Geoffrey's gauntleted hand thudded into his throat, crushing voice box and windpipe at once. The man fell to his knees gasping, though Geoffrey was no longer touching him.

All three were dead. He had succeeded. But the fates knew otherwise. Something was wrong here. He grabbed the guards' weapons.

Claire should have run to him now that it was over; there was no time left to dither about, they must away. But she did not come. He turned dizzily and saw her standing just outside the shadow of the nearest build-ing, still and silent. Was it possible that she was so shocked by what she had seen? Geoffrey wiped the blood from his blade and slowly walked to her, trying to see into her eyes. They were glazed with fear and Geoffrey slowed.

"Claire?" he whispered.

Still she did not come to him. Terror flitted quietly across her pretty features. Suddenly, she cried a warning to him and he knew she risked her life to do so when he at last understood. "Run, my love! Fly! He has followed us and we are undone. You cannot save me now!"

There was a low snarl from behind her and a hulking form shoved her roughly aside, no doubt sparing her further abuse for now, since she held his child.

Wulfhere Eadricsson laughed and stepped into the moonlight.

"Well met!" he cried happily. "Let us see how skilled you are with your sword rather than your cowardly foot. Were I not so convinced that I can kill you myself, I would call the Turks and let them boil you in lamp oil. But come now and meet your death!" And he threw back his head and laughed again. His long blond hair shook free in the air and Geoffrey was reminded of a wolf scenting his kill.

"Make ready the pit, oh Satanus!" Geoffrey muttered to himself. "This night will I send to you a great villain!"

"Come, dog!" goaded Wulfhere. "Or must I hurt our delicious Claire to bring you to me?"

"I should have killed you without honor in the hallway. I was too weak in my love," said Geoffrey coldly, his eyes flickering from the Saxon's gloating visage to Claire's pain-wracked features. "But come then, you monster. You are so eager for death; this time you shall have it. If naught else this damned night, I will see to it that your wretched, cowardly ghost never haunts her more! Fall on, you bastard! Come to the kiss of the steel; this sunrise will see you sleeping with the devil!"

"Geoffrey!" wept Claire. "Please! Please, my love. Not this way! You cannot have me this way!"

Geoffrey's voice held a terrifying chilled quality to it as he spoke, and even Wulfhere Eadricsson paused an instant at the tone. It was full of self-mockery and bitterness, rife with disgust at the whims of fate. The Norman shook his head almost sadly. "There is no other way, little one. There has never been any other way, not even from the beginning. Our love will always be mingled with death."

"No!" she cried. "Not if you do not will it so!"

"In truth, I know not another way to will it, little one; too much and too many stand in our way. Too few are those who can help us. I am no man of wisdom to argue them from our path."

"Little one," mocked Wulfhere. "Bah! Just because you have rutted the bitch you fancy yourself in love with her! Ask her! She knows not what love is, do you my little whore!" he snarled over his shoulder to her.

But Geoffrey did not react as he expected. In that instant, he saw Wulfhere for the petty villain he was and he knew that it would be no matter to slay him. Here was a man conquered by his own dark vices until he could no longer read his enemy as every soldier must do in combat if he is to survive. Wulfhere had attributed his views and perceptions to Geoffrey; he could not begin to comprehend Geoffrey's feelings for this petite blonde woman.

The Saxon had counted on stinging the Norman into unthinking combat, but the knight merely stood there weighing his weapon in one strong hand, the corners of his hard-set mouth turned up in a sneer of contempt, showing his strong white teeth. Again, he slowly shook his head and he strode toward Wulfhere with no apprehension at all.

Wulfhere found Geoffrey's confidence unnerving and insulting. Angered at having failed in his ruse, the renegade Saxon sprang forward with his steel flashing in the moonlight as a blur of silvery death. But Geoffrey was not there when it flashed, nor was he at the second lunge nor the third. Grimly, Wulfhere realized that the knight was no novice to sword lore. And when Geoffrey's scimitar blade finally met his fully, it jarred him to the bone and drove him backwards so that he nearly fell. The Norman's power was formidable. Wulfhere snarled defiantly and circled his foe with caution.

Then, astoundingly, Geoffrey threw back his head and laughed a deep, magnificent laugh full of ferocity and madness. "Best call the watch, dog! I will kill you soon!" he derided.

"Words! Only words, braggart!" Wulfhere retorted, and Geoffrey's scimitar point shot out marking Wulfhere's face both on one side and then the other. Wulfhere had not even seen the thrust and now he was silent, backing up slowly, unsure.

Claire shivered at the tone of her lover's voice and huddled her daughter closer to herself, for there was something contained within the man that lay dark and foreboding, something to be dreaded, seething just below the surface, something unseen but not un-sensed. There was enjoyment in that chill laugh, reverie at the thought of taking this man's life. And why? Because of the love he bore her? Aye, solely because of that. She understood the intent for the Saxon was strong and treacherous.

But would not the blood be on her hands as well, for the murder of the father of her child? How could Geoffrey relish the taking of life? Could he not see he was mimicking the wild dog? There was much darkness here.

But Claire did not see that this is the heinousness of mankind in general, not that of a single tired young knight, trying to set her free. It was all the same in that awful moment in her heart; all men were alike. They all were killers.

"Spare him!" she entreated.

Yet Geoffrey had spared him once already and to what avail? He was forced to risk his life again for her! But how many lives would be ended before he brought her to safety? When would bloodletting and butchery end and happiness begin? Could happiness ever exist upon such a foundation of fight and slaughter? How could it?

She closed her eyes in misery as the swordplay resumed in grunting silence and held the child closer in the darkness for the sounds of steel upon steel caused the child to stir uneasily in her dreams. Please God, she prayed, let them both live this night. Let no more die because of her, no matter what her fate. But God's love was one thing and the love of a man quite another.

She heard them grappling in the shadows, cursing and condemning each other to fantastic fates. She heard sword edge against armor and a soft tearing sound as blade found cloth and flesh beneath and one of the combatants moaned in pain.

Geoffrey swung his razor-edged scimitar with both leather-and-steel gauntleted hands and Claire saw it flash like lightning in the pale light of the open courtyard, to smash against Wulfhere's scimitar, ramming the Saxon's weapon back against his own breastplate and staggering the fellow again. Without mercy, Geoffrey swung again and this time drove the enemy to his knees in the dirt, blood pouring from a scalp wound. He had barely missed the kill, but Wulfhere's time was nigh. It was no longer even a contest, for even Wulfhere's unbridled arrogance was ended by Geoffrey's steel-smashing strength and long-winded endurance. Geoffrey was more than a warrior in combat, he was the best. He was a killing machine that could not be wound down. Shattered, perhaps. But not wound down.

And here, this night, it was Wulfhere who was ruined. On his knees, bloody from a myriad of wounds, he tried to raise his weapon once more to fend off the final stroke, but a backhand slash from the Norman sent his curved blade spinning away into the darkness and opened another line across his fair-skinned cheek.

There was no sound save for the panting of both men as they glared into each other's eyes.

Claire summoned up her courage and stepped nearer the two, wanting to intercede, yet hesitating lest she cause the brutality to proceed further. Timidity was hidden within the weariness in her voice; fatigue was all that remained of the awe she felt at what she had seen revealed within Geoffrey's soul.

"Aye, love, we are safe!" she whispered. "He will not cry out or follow; he is beaten. Please, there is no longer a need..."

Geoffrey gazed from Wulfhere's face to hers, pale and lovely behind the tears. He measured her coolly with his stern blue eyes, peering into her thoughts and desires.

"If you love me, then..." she murmured, using those timeless words of leverage. And she saw the fiery pits behind his eyes calm as she spoke, for such was her effect upon him.

"He must die," Geoffrey spit out.

Claire turned to Wulfhere, pleading with him to save himself. "Tell him, son of Eadric. Tell him you have had enough! Live!"

Wulfhere glared at her, savagery etched across his features. "You are mine, Claire, as much as the child you bore with me. You will always be mine and I will not have my woman stolen! Better death than the jibes of others!"

"Then die, fool!" Geoffrey shrugged.

Claire turned on him, imploringly. "I have seen you victorious many times this night and I ask you for this final life, for the magnanimity of a champion. If you slay this beaten man, wound him further, then by my love for you, Geoffrey St. Denis, I swear to forsake our bond! I will never live with, nor love further, the murderer of my child's father!"

Geoffrey cursed, but made to put his sword up. But, stung by their condescension, Wulfhere raised his voice in defiance and challenge. He looked mockingly at Geoffrey.

"By Odin, if nothing else, I'll see that you never have the wench! Guard, guards! Here by the…!" he cried, but the shout ended in a frothy gurgle as Geoffrey's already crimson blade bit deep into his skull and stopped its downward rush only when it nicked the steel neck rim of his breastplate. The hideous gurgle came only a fraction of a second before Claire's shrill scream of despair. Wulfhere fell into the bloody dirt, sprawling, and gushing crimson. She turned and blanched at the callous way her savior wiped his steel free of Wulfhere's blood.

"No-o-o," Claire whispered in despair, running forward as her master fell. "He was my daughter's father!" she cried in some vague sort of accusation. "There was no need. You might have rendered him unconscious or…"

"There was every need, my Claire, and I do not understand that which makes you say otherwise! I have severed the head of a viper this night, this and nothing more. God grant his soul a quick trip to the pit so that we might hurry from here in peace," Geoffrey growled.

"Peace?" she asked in a tired voice. "What peace is this? Shall I ever find peace in my dreams? Will I ever spend a night where I do not witness this sight over and over? You could have forgiven him his weakness."

"Forgiven?" queried Geoffrey. He sighed and gazed in confusion at her, looking deep into her flashing eyes. "How innocent you are, little one. You would forgive Satan himself. But come now, for I hear footsteps upon the parapets. The Saxon's shout has aroused the rest of the watch from their slumber and we must leave while we can!" He held out his hand to her, but she merely hugged her child Helgi and turned toward the gate, moving mechanically. The child whimpered with fright at the strange sounds and voices and Claire cooed her back to sleep.

The young knight shrugged and kicked open the small portal with a booted foot, revealing the desert night and freedom. Claire walked before him, but together they entered the sanctity of nature's sheltering darkness to make their way by the stars for the Christian camp. Geoffrey sighed in relief, unable to believe that he had finally succeeded, that his daring gamble and headstrong courage had paid off. He threw back his coif and shook his hair free in the cool air, smiling up at the moon that would light their way. He felt like a man who has beaten his own destiny But no man can long escape the clutching hands of fate.

For the longest time, it seemed that they walked across the desert in silence matching that of the lengthening night; but time was an illusion, night was nearly ended. It was a frozen, dark night that had descended upon Geoffrey's heart that he felt not perceptions of a real nature. Sometimes, there was the breath of the cold wind in his ears, another time the hum of an insect. But his senses did not register these puny interruptions to the grief that had sprung up between the two of them. In the wan light, Geoffrey saw the face of his beloved set hard against the pain that coursed through her heart. She felt betrayed.

As clouds passed beyond the moon, he saw always the light reflected within the tears that ran the length of her beautiful face. He longed so to comfort her, so much so that he stumbled on, oblivious to all around him.

There could not be much left of the night. Would they make camp in time? Were they followed? That was his darkest fear. But the desert was silent behind them, as it was in front.

Surely mother and babe must be in need of rest for Helgi stirred impatiently in her mother's arms. Geoffrey yearned to carry the child himself, but what could he say in the asking, after he had slain the father? Best let time ease the cutting edge of the emotions she felt. Best give her time before he rightfully claimed her as his own, if any claiming need be done. But as he thought this, he pondered the selfishness the thought contained, selfishness alien to this knight. He had sinned before, perhaps less than most men, but he had never felt the sin of desire so strongly as he felt it now. Now that he had found her, he could never let her go. Nay, it would kill him to do so.

And as he realized all of this, a prophetic chill coursed through his sturdy body, but he shrugged it off as the night wind. He had her now; they were safe. And soon, they would be within reach of shelter. Afraid with a fear that had no name, he quickened the pace so that she walked behind him. With every pace toward safety and comfort, his fear that he would lose her grew and grew for he had never known the fates to be so charitable as this.

Dizzily, they mounted a small cluster of hills midway between Tarsus and the Christian camp. The highest was known as the Hill of Stones for reasons ancient and shrouded. It seemed to be little more than any other hilltop, barren and rock-strewn, a knob of earth that arbitrarily jutted forth from the desert floor. The plateau was covered with small rock formations of no consequence, yet they were as thick about as bristles upon a boar's hide. As they paused, Claire wearily scanned the horizon for no other good reason than that she was ashamed to look her savior full in the face. She was too confused, too angry, too hurt by his perceived brutality.

"My love?" he whispered, standing next to her and checking her child.

"I was looking at those lights in that little valley below, there, where the hills converge, isolated and hidden," she said tiredly. "I know of no outposts either Saracen or Christian here; it is too far removed from the world."

"A convent," grunted Geoffrey. "It is named that of the Sacred Heart. Those lights twinkling like fireflies in our lost Britain are candles for the Christian dead. The sisters have condemned themselves to solitude here away from everyone, yet aid infidel and brother alike, with no regard for belief. As such, not even the heathen Saracens have the courage to molest them for the simple souls for miles around would be up in arms. These nuns nurse the sick and feed the hungry; most consider them saints, although their Mother Superior is said to be an even match for the devil himself!" Geoffrey chuckled a bit as he chewed upon a dry twig. He thought aloud, his eyes fastened to the glimmering candles.

"Odd, they are, I think. They make no distinction among sinners but offer shelter and salvation, to king and pauper alike. But none can doubt that they are good women all, though they are unlike any Christians I have ever encountered."

"Each candle, a dead Christian," Claire murmured sadly.

Geoffrey shrugged. "The wages of war," he answered fatalistically. "Guvi said that if they did the same for the heathens, they would be building bonfires instead of lighting candles. But don't pity the dead, my love. They understood what the gamble was and if you listen to the bishops, then they are now in a better world."

An awkward silence followed. The two felt like strangers now and Geoffrey felt her slipping away from him.

She brushed wet curls from her forehead and shivered against the wind. Geoffrey saw this and moved as if to shelter her with his cloak, but she drew away from him and huddled by herself with the child.

"How blessed it must be to live such a life," she whispered, "to be free of strife and bloodshed, to exist to help and shelter others. To know for certain, you would never have to take a life and do injury to others."

"Do you reproach me, my love?" he asked quietly.

"I reproach all of man who can settle his differences by no other means than by death and destruction. Wulfhere died to keep me a slave, you slaughtered scores to set me free; I marvel that I am that desirable," she replied.

"You omit morality, Claire," he commented firmly. It wasn't in his mindset to understand her point of view.

"Then I marvel that a greater immorality was committed to save me from a lesser one," she said sadly.

"You do disservice to yourself in saying this. You alone consider the morality. The others would have killed us both for lust *or* revenge; I slew only to stay alive. The very fact that you feel guilt shows that you are worth the saving. If not for me, I assure you the dead ones would have felt no remorse at our own demise."

"It is all too much, Geoffrey."

He tossed his long hair. In the light that presaged the false dawn, he saw her noble profile and shoulders hunched against the cold and found her infinitely appealing in her pathos.

"If all were as you, my sweet, it would be a fine world indeed, but you dream, as do the sisters. The world is a harsh place where there is no real justice other than what is found in a man's own strength. I am a good knight; I have kept my oaths, though they have lost me the respect of others. Yet, an oath is no proof against a churl who deals in villainy. Where there is law, it is the law of the strong enforced upon the weak. There is nothing noble about it; life is hard and many men are worse than animals. But you cannot run and hide from them; they will follow you and persecute you at their leisure. Tis better to make yourself strong enough that they will let you be."

She stared at him. "You talk only as a man might. It is different to be a woman," she answered with bitterness.

"Aye, love, that is a cruel thing to say to me for you have seen me stand for you many times this night alone. I freed you when no one else could. The strength of our love is all the strength needed," Geoffrey replied to her, hurt and stung.

"Aye," she whispered in a broken voice, "you have stood for me often, my love. The good earth has drunk deep of men's blood that I might walk free. Tell me, love, how many more will there be?" she said in anguish.

"How many more will seek to harm you?" the knight asked evenly.

"It is that easy, is it?" she asked. "All you need to know is that I am threatened with insult or injury and you kill for me!" She said as tears coursed down her cheeks. "Am I to be an omen of death?"

"What would you have me say?" he groaned.

"I would have you say no!" she wept.

"Then you would make a liar out of me!" he said bleakly.

"Please, no! Tell me no, Geoffrey!"

"You have put it to me unmercifully, but I shall answer you anyway. Yes, it is that easy. For you, and you alone, I would damn my soul if need be. Yes, curse you, all I need to know is that you are threatened. Yes, I will slay without hesitation. And this you find it so hard to understand!"

He tried to look into her eyes but she would no longer face him. She was more than crushed by his stubbornness and immorality.

"No," she said quietly, "this I will never understand."

"Those who would hurt you are not fit to live, my sweet. The world is full of evil and wretchedness, but any who would hurt you is past redemption."

"No, Geoffrey. It is not so. You but love too much."

"And do you love too little, my love?" he asked.

At this, she looked up at him, but her look was unfathomable; too many emotions welled up within those eyes. She was frustrated in a way he could not cope with, for her moods and ideals were in a different plane from his. Had he not silenced only the brutes without feelings? Where did so heavy a burden of sin lay, that she should so receive his deeds? Did not one good person merit more than a thousand evil ones? But this was all the worse, for how could he deal with one who was so faultless, to not even see the truth of the fact.

"The fertility of our love has produced an evil flower, I fear," she sighed, turning again to the horizon.

"You must not speak so!" Geoffrey burst out, horrified. "I but did what any knight would have done for you!"

"No, for you are indeed more noble than the rest, I have seen. But still, it is a hard code you live by, too hard for the tenderness that has existed between us." She turned to him and touched his cheek with much gentleness.

"No!" he cried.

"But yes, my Geoffrey, my wonderful brave Geoffrey with the body of steel. Yes, speak true. Our love was not meant to be for there has been too much pain, too little comfort!"

He grasped her shaking, outstretched hand and kissed it, his tears mingling with her own upon it.

"My Claire, it is all past now! We have won; we are together now, forever, my dove!"

She gave him a look full of infinite pity, new tears sparkling in her eyes. "No, my love, it is Wulfhere who has won, for all his evilness. He tempted you that final time and you succumbed. We are more apart now than we were when only oceans separated us. A greater gulf lies between us after this night than all the countries or years or seas. Your life is too far different from how I must live, from how my little Helgi must be raised up."

"How say you?" he pondered out loud.

"You are a warrior and a true champion. But it is always your destiny to kill or be killed, to wage war and to destroy. Better I had loved a minstrel," she said slowly.

Geoffrey rose to his feet, flushed with anger and anguish at her attitude.

"A minstrel! A soft-handed, soft-bellied heart-plucker. May the gods damn me should I ever revert to such a skill. But, in time, wars end, my love. And they are followed by peace. In Britain, we can live as you desire!"

Again, there was that smile full of pity for him. "I think not. There would always be wars for you to fight, men for you to slay."

"No!" he spoke, emphatically. "You are all that I desire, my love!"

She looked up at him curiously. "Then leave this war now, this night. Let us fly for our real home and forsake all of the treachery and bloodshed."

Geoffrey peered up at the heavens, lightening now with a faint forecast of dawn, as if trying to see the face of God. "I have taken an oath, Claire. I cannot leave, not at this time."

Her smile was sore. "'Tis as I said, my love. There will be other oaths to other lords. It cannot ever be. I cannot go with you; I must leave you here."

"What?!" Geoffrey was incredulous.

"I shall go to the convent below and ask the sisters for shelter so that you need not worry about me, until I decide what I must do, but for now, I must leave you."

He grabbed her as she rose, restraining her. "I will not let you go. By force, if I must," he halted, appalled at his own words.

She gave him an icy glare. "Yes, Wulfhere?"

He released her at once, at a total loss for words or action. And she said not one more word to him, but slowly, wearily, turned from him and began to make her way down the hill towards the convent. Geoffrey watched her pale form, illuminated very faintly by the growing light, make its way down the hillside and finally, safely, enter the gate of the convent.

Then he fell upon his knees and wept for all of the heaviness within his living heart, and the sinfulness and wretchedness of the world, weeping as only the damned can weep.

14

CHAPTER THE FOURTEENTH

A t the heels of morning, came a great band of Moslem dignitaries all grim-faced and dark with rage. Without explanation, they rode to the tent of Bohemond of Otranto and quickly spoke their business. The other leaders of the Christian camp were rapidly called and a council formed to listen to the grievance. The complaint was with the young St. Denis and his conduct of the night before. The Saracens, completely embarrassed that one lone knight could make such a shambles of their defenses, enjoined the council to silence concerning the matter of honor, but the guards outside the pavilion heard also the story, and great grins spread over their grizzled features at the pluck of one lad alone and they eagerly rushed off to spread the story. The end result was that when the mob of heathen diplomats withdrew with the assurances that the young knight would be punished, riding through the camp festooned in all their bright trappings, great crowds of knights and men-at-arms ringed them crying out Geoffrey's name amid much merriment.

"The lion has struck again!" one cried. "The Lion of Tarsus!"

"He is but a young knight!" another called. "Beware of us that are the veterans."

Scarlet beneath their swarthy skins, the Saracens set spurs to their horses to outdistance the jibes. When at last his antagonists had left,

Bohemond of Otranto sat down, laughing so hard he wept and sent word to Sir Geoffrey that when he was finished with his lady that he should present himself to the leader for congratulations.

But Sir Brian was not amused. He viewed the codes of knighthood far more sternly and he was aghast at Geoffrey's temerity in violating the Saracen hospitality. He had summoned his son privately to his own pavilion.

Sir Geoffrey entered with something less than good manners and Sir Brian was beside himself with rage. Twice, he came very close to slapping his leather riding gauntlets into his son's face, but twice the silent fury and despair he saw in those features stopped him. There was more wrong than he could know about, but he did not desire explanations. His anger was self-righteous and consuming and he thought only of punishment. For now, he contented himself with pacing about the rue-covered floor and ranting out his anger.

"Fool!" he cried, running a leathery hand through his silver hair. "You have cast Christian honor into the dirt! The council selected you as a diplomat and how do you display your abilities? As an adulterer! As a murderer! As a woman stealer! It makes not a whit of difference that these were crimes committed against heathens, perpetrated upon infidels who have no right at all to complain. You have dishonored the entire English host with your actions. And for what? Twice now, you have forsaken your chivalric vows and run off after some chit to rut; I should have you gelded like a stallion so that you do not bolt at every scent of female heat. How many more will there be?"

"There has never been but one," said Geoffrey sullenly.

"You mean one at a time, still nothing to brag about!" roared his father.

"Shame not her honor, my father, lest I must take up sword against my own sire and doom us both to hell's fire."

"What?" blinked Sir Brian. "You dare…why you must be mad! Is this woman a witch to turn you against all England? I do not understand you and I do not choose to, any more than I care about you breaking our peace with them, for we were but purchasing time. But our honor! Do you not even regret breaking your word as a guest to the emir?"

"I regret naught but losing her. She has my heart, so she might as well have my honor. Without her, I am finished." Geoffrey shrugged woodenly.

Sir Brian stroked his beard, grown long since his arrival in the Holy Land. "And still, you refuse to tell me what passed this last night, or where."

"Tis naught to you, sir!" muttered Geoffrey.

"We will see," murmured his father.

"She is safe enough from you and your treacherous thoughts, my father. You meddle in matters you know nothing about and I cannot see why you hound me for freeing a Norman-English girl from heathen captors who had made a slave of her."

His father's face was a mask of frozen contempt. "There is little more to be said. Do you understand the effect you have wrought upon this camp? Every man of honor despises you, although the churls that mill about now sing their wretched ballads about Sir Geoffrey of Tarsus, woman-stealer and champion, who pulled the emir's beard and lived to boast of it. My God! They have idolized you. A singular honor indeed, to be loved by the masses!"

"Are you finished?" asked Geoffrey, tiredly.

"Yes!" said his father curtly.

Geoffrey rose to take his leave. "If you have had your say, Father, then I shall attend to my horse and weapons. It would seem that they are needed soon!"

"Needed? Phagh!" came the answer. "What need do we have of a false knight? By my judgment, you would not be allowed to ride with us, but Lord Bohemund, the meddler, has invited you to ride with him personally. He has called over the colors of Westwall, for you are no longer a son to me!"

Geoffrey laughed mirthlessly.

"I have worn them thus far, I will not relinquish them now, not even for you!" He drew on his gauntlets and pulled up his coif to make ready for battle.

Sir Brian spat upon his blue surcoat with the twin trees of Westwall emblazoned upon it. "Then may they be your burial colors, false knight!"

roared the father at his disloyal son. Geoffrey casually wiped the spittle from his cloth and strode from the tent. Sir Brian sat upon his couch and put his head in his trembling hands. "My son! Oh, my son!" he cried.

~

THE DARKNESS WAS JUST BEGINNING TO LIFT AS CLAIRE APPROACHED THE convent by its narrow front door of steel-reinforced timber, out of place in the peaceful atmosphere of the setting. But she knew that not all respected the workers of God and there were times when defenses must be taken against a determined enemy. She saw dents and gouges in the old door, but it was still sound and protective, and somehow reassuring.

No one answered her knock. Perhaps the sisters were not yet awake. She hugged Helgi close and, somewhat hesitantly, rapped a long, halting beat with her small fist upon the portal.

After a few moments of silence, she heard a soft scuffling and through cracks in the planking, saw a flickering candle lazily approach the entry from down a long hallway. A sister approached sleepily and the metal visor of the door drew back with a harsh click to reveal a wrinkled female face, shrouded by a disarrayed, and hurriedly donned habit, obviously thrown on in haste by sleep-drugged hands. The elder face, though not openly hostile, nevertheless, eyed her quite warily.

"Is this more mischief of the emir?" a querulous voice demanded.

"What?" stammered Claire, taken aback.

"Does he never tire of provoking us, child? What is it he wishes this time? To nurse a child not stricken ill? To try to make his youngest wife miscarry so that he might have her sooner? Well, speak! But well you know we cannot help him in his unclean ways, and I tire of his constant tests of our virtue and sincerity," the old nun rattled on.

Claire's mouth opened and closed, but no sound issued forth.

Then, for the first time the nun noticed, with some degree of embarrassment, that her supplicant was a Frank, although the girl's blonde hair was soddened with perspiration against her pale face, looking dark in the weak candlelight. Then, too, did the aged sister see the miserable child held protectively against the desert cold in the poor comfort of her mother's arms.

"Ohhhh! Dear Lord!" she breathed, unbolting the door to admit the two strangers. "Come in out of the cold, child. Forgive a foolish old woman her silly distrust, but the infidels take us lightly and constantly make short of our duties here. I thought only that..."

"Sister, I would not intrude my problems upon yours..." Claire began.

"Hush! Hush! Here, let me hold the child. Come in, my dear. Let us sit by the fireside while I rekindle a blaze. For a burning land, the nights are often fierce with cold. Here! Here, take this quilt and wrap it about you for you shiver and ahhh, what a beautiful little girl you have." The nun crooned soothingly and Claire felt drowsiness already beginning to overtake her.

She slumped into a warm, stuffed chair by the fire's red embers while the kind sister stooped down, Helgi cradled securely in the crook of one arm and placed more wood upon the fire.

The compassionate nun rambled on. "Anyway, it is our code to aid those in need, and it certainly seems obvious that you are in need of help of some sort. Here, look at you! You are soaked with sweat like a race-horse run raw and covered with the dirt and scratches of the desert. You have journeyed far in a short time and in this country that can only herald danger. Here, take back your babe for a moment while I find you both refreshment and warm, dry garments."

"Did you say that the men of the emir come here often, Sister?" Claire asked nervously.

The sister gave her a long appraising look. "You are Christian?" she asked mildly.

Claire nodded.

"They will not enter then. In truth, they do not do us any great mischief for we are occasionally of use to them. Also, the Lord understands that the good we do is not for Christian alone. They tolerate our presence, these so-called infidels with sometimes more manners than their Christian brothers. But they play their pranks upon us, to teach us that we are...less than they, and they seem to ever love this wretched hour for such pranks. But here, I talk on and on, and you are tired."

Claire was lost for speech as the sister padded out of the chamber to find food and clothing; she had not rightly considered how to plead her case to the sisters. She had assumed that she would be accepted, but how much of a crime had she and Geoffrey committed this night? Would the Saracens see this as a debt against their honor, to be paid in blood? Would they disregard the sanctity of the convent to pursue her? Did they know she was here? Would they find out?

The sister's idle, though well-meant prattle had thus far saved her from any awkward explanations. But they would want to know why she had fled.

Oh, she understood well enough why she had, yet two tones played from the same pipe whirled through her pretty head. If she had been less good, that is to say more human, she would have accepted them both and reconciled her bitter emotions of destruction with the sweet ones of love. But at this time, she was blinded by her own naive, yet intensely felt, concept of what was right and what was wrong. But then, who is it that can truly define right and wrong?

The wise men say truth is a sense of knowledge that springs unbidden from the furthest recesses of the grasping mind, a feeling of deep harmony with the surrounding environment, a tranquil feeling of being. And yet, in the infinitely subtle twists of a man's mind, how many times does need stand mistaken as a desire for harmony? How many times does the intense pleasure of desire gratified surpass the more gentle, truer feeling of comfort achieved?

And, equally terrible and infinitely more dangerous, in those who strive all their lives for comfort, too much so, how many times does a false sense of self-righteousness surpass a true sense of need, as it had with Claire? As unwise as it is to allow desire to rule over what is right, far more foolish is it for one to seek all too actively for the harmony one desires, for one is then capable of losing perspective, one's most precious element of humanity and finally ceasing to be what God made him. It is passion controlled that makes the person, not passion denied.

But there are those, in addition to the ones who ignore this truth, who

never even perceive this great axiom of humanity, for they are too inse-
cure in their own emotions, or too concerned with artificial concepts of
good and evil. Pity them. Pity Claire. Ever-lovely, infinitely gentle, she
was one of these.

A soothingly warm fire was roused from the coals and in its cheery
light, Claire saw for the first time the age of the sister aiding her. She was
nearly fifty winters, though still full of quick smiles and in possession of
a pair of laughing brown eyes that nearly always sparkled with her enthusiasm for living. She was a grand lady and plied Claire with hot tea
seasoned with herbs, and warm wine, and goat's milk for her child. Soon
the small child was sleeping comfortably again, wrapped naked in a thick
blanket. Claire, too, sat cozy in a good dry smock after casting before the
fire her own damp garments.

For a brief awkward interval, there was the silence that often exists
between youth and age. The two were content to watch the dance of the
flames that flickered in warm, golden tones across Helgi 's sleeping face.
Such peace there was to be found in a child's face. It was good here in
this close chamber, so full of His love for men, and equally as holy, love
of man for each other in the dedication of the Sisters of the Sacred
Heart.

Then, with the sure knowledge that only years of experience can
bring, the aged sister prodded the heart of ashes amid the still burning
logs and queried in a low voice, "Fugitive?"

"Aye, Sister, but not such a one as you might think me," Claire said in
a hoarse whisper.

The nun smiled wryly. But it was not malicious sarcasm. "How say
you truly what I think, my daughter?" She laughed a friendly comforting
laugh and passed a hand across the tired wrinkles in her face. "Are you
sent by Him that you can so read my thoughts?" she added.

Claire shook her head, unlaughing. "Nay, good Sister, I think there is
little holiness within me."

"Then you should not think, my child, but feel. If your faith is the
size of a grain of mustard seed, it can grow," the nun interrupted in a curt
but gentle manner. "You err, child. There is holiness within every person
for we are all created the same, in His name. In His eyes, we are each of

us precious and though we sin wrongfully, there is still good in everyone if one but searches for it," the sister finished.

Claire set her jaw against the shame she would bare to her good listener and began her story in her abject misery, portraying herself more harshly than the facts warranted. "I have betrayed the father of this child, my child, for another man. I have slept with this other man and given myself to him. But now, I cannot bring myself to go with him for he is a warrior and has slain, in my poor name, those who stood before us. I cannot forget the arms of one and the memories of another; one died hating me and the other perverted our love with shed blood. Now, I have neither of them."

Claire stared at the stone flags of the floor as she finished, unable and unwilling to raise her eyes to her listener. Slowly, she brushed her blonde hair away from her eyes as it dried in the fire's heat.

"So, you are a fugitive from yourself," the nun said.

"Perhaps. I do not know, Sister."

The sister's eyes were grave, as gray in the flickering light as her hair that showed in wisps from beneath her habit. She pursed elder lips in thought as she examined minutely the young woman's face, searching for the key to the secrets that lay locked within her aching heart. The nun sought the young woman's memories that she used to condemn herself with, falsely so, thought the nun, for she was apt at judging the soul through the eyes. And when did sin so blot out such innocence as she saw in these sad eyes? When was shame so merited against such gentleness?

The sister smiled. She had seen into the soul, and she knew. "Your words are convincing, child, yet there is much I see in the softness of your eyes that belies just such treachery as you confess. Will you tell me this entire tail, that I myself might judge whether such sin belongs to you?"

"Must I, Sister? In my own heart, I know my guilt. Is this not enough?"

The old nun frowned in thought as pondering the basis of all theology. "Perhaps it would be, if the guilt is deserved, but look at it this way;

if I am to grant you shelter here, then should I not at least be entitled to know what sort of criminal it is that I have rescued?"

Claire nodded her head slowly, sleepily, as if reaching some serious decision, some turning point in her life. Which, perhaps, she had. "Oh, aye, Sister. In truth, I have not enough shame left to hide the tale of my foolish love," sighed the lowly fugitive with a slight yawn and a sad, sad smile.

And from the depth of her smile, and the immense sorrow in the young girl's eyes, the wise sister knew all along where the truth had to lie. "Then tell me, daughter, and open up your heart again to love."

"'Tis not love I need now, good Sister. It is only that which has brought to me so much pain. I seek instead but comfort and shelter from the future."

The Holy One smiled endearingly. "You are young to forsake the rest of your life. Perhaps you should ponder what it is that the future means."

Claire grimaced. "I have, Sister. I have."

Her host stirred the fire, thinking. When she again spoke, it was as if she but pondered philosophy aloud. "When you have seen more of life, you will understand what comfort and shelter springs from the mind, rather than from superficial walls and boundaries, what grace the heart can give to its owner in place of civilized establishment. And there is truly no richer source of comfort and shelter then open love, real unselfish love."

She offered her sleepy guest another goblet of wine. "Now," said the sister softly, "tell me of this love…"

And Claire opened her heart completely to her good listener. When the tale was finished, ended with the history of her love and lust which had caused so much death, the sister sat silent and visibly moved. Her lips pursed and unpursed behind a steeple made of praying hands and it took her some time to find speech for what she had heard. Finally, she expressed profound sympathy, that which is only felt by the truly generous.

"Child," she sighed, "you are too young for such grief and you punish yourself too strongly. This man, Wulfhere, was not your wedded husband but a barbarian who took you for his slave. That you and he conceived a child matters not a whit for it was not even out of love. Yet, you treat him respectfully, perhaps wrongfully. For in a moment of his slavering want he gave you little Helgi."

Claire looked up, lips trembling and fear flashing across her features. "But I did not protest enough!" said Claire, alarmed that her sense of guilt should be questioned. "Not the first time and not every time, but, oh Sister, there were times when my body cried out to be touched!"

"Lust is not the same as love!" said the nun curtly. "Not any more than having sight is the same as seeing."

She held up an aged hand to still Claire from further protests. "Hear me out first, my girl. You would try to impose your rightful love of your daughter upon the memory of a harsh master, and in so doing, reconcile his brutality with your guilt. You forgive him his crimes against you and that is wrong."

Claire started. "Wrong?" she asked. "How can forgiving someone be wrong, Sister?"

"Despite what we preach and our Lord himself taught, there are times when it is wrong and foolish to forgive. It is wrong if the person revels in his wicked ways and desires no forgiveness, and it is wrong if by forgiving a guilty man you injure an innocent one. You see the difference?"

Claire shook her head.

"There was no treachery in your loving this young knight, this man who cared enough for you that he would follow you to war and ruin. You have done your best to see it as something shame-laced, but I know from your eyes, and speech, that you sincerely love this Geoffrey. What you say of killing is true; it cannot be a foundation for love and it never will be. How could little Helgi call him father, he who slew the giver of her seed.

"Could you reconcile this paradox of love and death in your own mind? I would tell you to return to this man of yours for it certainly appears that his love is faithful. But for now, you cannot do so, and I understand why. So, I offer you shelter and sanctity within these poor walls for as long as you need it. Perhaps with time, the hurt will dim enough that love will again win out. I hope it does so and I feel with enough time, you will see these terrible memories as less and less and feel again in your heart what you once felt for him."

"And what of him, Sister?" Claire asked timidly, confused now of her own feelings.

"He will wait for you, Claire. I know him from your heart and he will wait whether it is twenty days or twenty years from what you have told me. I can see the everlasting brightness of his love for you; there are few who can love with such strength or devotion. I pray that you reach the right decision."

The young woman raised her eyes to the sister in her request, "Then may I stay here in the tranquility of Christ, and do His work and be free of all the killing and strife?"

"What of your love for this man, child?"

Claire stared into the fires filled with regret for what might have been. "Can I love him every morning when I know that he rides to the press of combat seeking for those enemies only death? Aye, he says he will do anything for me, yet when I see how his blue eyes smolder as he holds that terrible sword of his, and feel the reckless, fearsome strength behind the arm that raises it, I am chilled to the bone. And when he has seen me threatened but a little, his eyes smolder darkly with that same terrifying coldness and he becomes but a machine of steel. Perhaps it is that he is too great a warrior, or is it that he feels too great a love for me?"

"How do you mean, child?" the host asked quietly.

"I could not wish for one to love another so much that he would do harm in my name. I am free of Wulfhere now, but does Geoffrey not impose another horrible limit upon me?"

"Perhaps your Geoffrey seeks only to protect you. That is not wrong."

"But why must he kill so easily and so thoroughly to do so?" protested gentle Claire, her eyes hot with emotion.

"Why must any man?" shrugged the nun. "It is, for all His love, a hard, hard world. There are those who will not listen to reason any more than they can hear cries for mercy. What can a man do against such as these, but defend himself and those he loves?"

Claire was thinking hard now. "Could we not leave this wretched land that stinks of death and carrion? Could we not return to England or Normandy and peace?"

The sister shook her head sorrowfully. "Nay, girl, I think not. A fellow who follows your face, pretty as it is, must have more honor than sense. Oh, frown not so! I only jest, but even in a jest the words might ring true. From what I know of this knight through your eyes and lips, it seems to me that he is true to his beliefs, and loyal to his lords. He cannot leave this Holy War just begun and not nearly ended. To do so would shame him as a coward before his peers and in his own eyes as well. He would finally grow bitter towards you at being the center of such heartache."

"So, he will stay without me until this war will kill him? He would select killing over me? That is love, Sister?" Claire wept.

The sister studied the flickering flames as the young woman cried silently. When the nun again found her voice, it was with a hard sort of realism that held no comfort other than what naturally occurs in truth. And such comfort is only of the logical variety, rarely does it give surcease to the heart.

"Claire, he will kill with you or without you, for he is destined to be a warrior; it is unkind, but it is apparently God's will. It is not right, yet it is not entirely worthy only of condemnation for his skill has saved you, and no doubt others. There is a vast difference between the act of simply killing, and the act of killing for survival as there is between a man killing and a man being forced to kill. If nothing else, you have doubly damned him for now he has not even the comfort of your love, the love he has slain for."

"He has damned himself!" Claire cried, causing the child to stir fretfully.

"Ah, yes!" the host whispered. "But you have helped him! What God wills, be done!" the sister patiently murmured. "You are welcome here with the child. These memories are still raw; there is nothing you can do to ease them for you believe that your love of Geoffrey gave Wulfhere his death. But what if it was his own stupid brutality that ended his life? If not Geoffrey, then another. Child, do not weep so. God sees and forgives all. Though it might be sinful of me to say it, I think it was God's will that Wulfhere meet such a fitting end. I am only sorry that it was by your lover's hand, a good Christian knight who can at least care for another of God's creatures. Now, hush, child! There is naught more to be said tonight. You are safe. You have the word of the Mother Superior on this."

"But I should talk to her," murmured Claire.

"You have, my child, you have," the old nun's smile was caring and beautiful.

"Mother," whispered Claire, finally drifting off into an exhausted sleep by the embers of the dying fire.

Silence again wrapped the convent, and with it...peace.

GUVI AND EADRIC FOUND THE YOUNGER ST. DENIS BRUSHING HIS chestnut war-horse in preparation for saddling the animal for battle. Geoffrey studied their raucous approach at the mount's back as the odd-matched pair, one young, slender, and dark and the other aged, stout, and fair approached him, but he said nothing in way of greeting.

Guvi gave the Saxon a puzzled glance before he addressed his friend. "Well?" he asked.

"Leave be, Guvi," muttered Geoffrey quietly as he continued the brushing.

Eadric growled something to himself at the young knight's tone. But the Finn laughed aloud.

"Leave be?" he cried in good humour. "You force me from your side to depart upon an adventure so extraordinary that the entire Frankish camp holds you more than a little in awe, but you won't tell me what passed? How cruel and vain you are! Have you added false modesty to your list of vanity, you who used to brag about your exploits when we sat about the watchfires? Is she free or not, tell me that!"

"She is free enough, in truth," Geoffrey murmured with tight lips.

Eadric beamed benevolently and nudged the Finn with a heavy elbow. "Small wonder the lad is so still and thoughtful; methinks he is loathe to go into battle for the bedrest he is missing. Be content with having her there when you return, boy. Odin, give your horn some rest. At least you know she is yours now."

"She is not here, Saxon," replied Geoffrey. "She left me."

"What?!" roared both comrades at the same instant.

Geoffrey smiled ruefully. "Love is not bought with blood, she said. She cannot be mine for I slew her master and the father of her child."

"Wulfhere?" asked Eadric with dry throat.

"Aye," said Geoffrey as kindly as he could. "I gave him every chance to live, old man. But he wished only death. I'm sorry."

Eadric smiled with a gentleness it was hard to believe he possessed; he understood what Geoffrey was saying.

"Do not be sorry, my lad. Wulfhere was meant only to die; it was his destiny from the beginning. Better it was by your sword than mine. But you do not mean that..."

"Aye, red-hair. She at least is free and sheltered at the convent."

Eadric blew his nose noisily into one cupped hand. "And you stood for that?" he asked incredulously.

Geoffrey smiled at the man's attitude. "She is free. I succeeded in my dream, but not exactly as I had planned," he said ironically.

"By the red hair on Odin's arse!" swore Eadric hotly. "If you Franks call that success in your sniveling Christian way, then, by Thor, let me give blood offerings. I am a heathen! It is beyond my belief that she could do this to you. Golden-haired women! Bah! They're useless except for two things! Well, when are we going to take her back?" Eadric spat into the dirt, hitting a scuttling lizard who blinked expectantly.

Despite himself, Geoffrey laughed with Guvi at the giant's comical actions.

The young knight shook his head. "She must come to me on her own, else it will never be well," he said.

"What!" bellowed Eadric. "You'll sleep alone at night because the girl cannot make up her mind? Take her by force, I say! Put your sword in her sheath a few times and when she's twisting hotly on your horn, she will soon enough grow used to sleeping with you and greet you eagerly in the evening. My advice is to put your sensitivity aside and just take her. She will grow used to you in time. Many relationships were built on a less solid foundation than this," Eadric finished sagely. He drew himself up proudly, secure in his theory.

"Nay, twould not work, red-hair," Geoffrey smiled.

Eadric frowned darkly, but then his face again brightened. "I could fetch her for you, lad. Then she could not blame you at all! Why, I could just kick in the door to the convent with a few of my fellows so that it looked like some…"

"Red-hair! A convent is a sacred place!" protested Geoffrey. "Control your desire to help, my friends!"

"Humph!" muttered Eadric. "You are the one who speaks of this God that you eat and drink in your services, not me. What would such a god of man-eaters care if we tore down some old barn full of aged cows?"

Geoffrey shook his head in disgust, but Guvi crowed.

"See here! See here!" the Finn cried. "Our outlaw friend imagines he is back on the high seas with a deck beneath his heels and a coast to sack each night! Ha! You'll find the waves of the desert a harder rowing, old walrus, for they are made of sand and rock, not water!"

"And you have the backbone of a worm, Finn. And soon you'll have an arsehole shaped like my boot if you do not shut your filthy mouth!" cursed Eadric with much gesturing.

"Nothing will work," interjected Geoffrey, trying to make peace.

Eadric wiped his greasy hands on the seat of his breeks and hitched up his sword belt before he lumbered off in the direction of his own tent and stable.

"We shall certainly see," he murmured, planning his dark mischief as he went.

Guvi listened patiently to the entire story and sighed as Geoffrey finished. "Never scold me again for my pranks, friend Norman. I know not quite what to say in the face of such audacity. God, Odin and Thor! You are not content to bed the woman of an enemy in his own castle, but you must also send him and a bunch of his fellows to the fire below. Stay before me in today's combat; surely the fact that you still live is cause to believe you are blessed from what gods may be."

"And?" asked Geoffrey irritably. He did not need chiding now; he felt himself a miserable failure even in the face of the reputation he had earned.

Guvi sighed again. "Methinks you should have bedded the little slave instead, friend. Your heart would be much better off. Truthfully, I would help you if I could but I know not what to do. My own advice might well be to take her for yourself as old fire-and-stink said, but then you are cursed with love, thrice as hard to be rid of as lust."

"I will wait for her. If she loves me truly, she will decide."

Guvi shrugged. "Perhaps. Perhaps not. Women are stupid in that way. But I worry about you going through battle with so heavy a burden upon your shoulders, strong though they are. I fear you will lose your head and exceed yourself today, for you are a mad bastard when someone crosses you. I must be certain to stick close to you and watch your flanks. But have mercy upon me and remember that your life and mine share the same destiny, and I will not perish in this ill-planned siege. Mothers of my little bastards all across the Northlands would mourn me without end."

Geoffrey laughed good-humoredly. "Fear not, old woman! As long as I live, there is hope within my heart that she will come to me. I will not shirk my duty this day but neither will I seek to tempt fate."

Guvi's dark face brightened noticeably and he wiped the perspiration from his forehead. "Wise words, friend. Be sure they are foremost in your mind when the trumpet sounds for you have a slight tendency to lose your head. Today, you fight for her, but just not how you planned. She will come to you, Geoffrey. Never doubt it; in the end she will come to you."

Geoffrey felt an odd chill at the prophecy but shrugged it off stoically. He stopped and stared at Guvi, suddenly realizing something the Finn had said in passing. "Why is this siege ill-planned, my friend?" Geoffrey asked, curious at the devious turnings of his comrade's mind. When it came to treachery, thievery, plotting and skullduggery, the Finn was ahead of practically anyone else and the Norman guessed that the Finn had picked up on something the crusades leaders had missed.

Guvi squatted down in the dirt and drew a diagram with a stick that appeared to be the assembled Christian host as they sat before the walls of Tarsus. Making a wide sweep with the stick, he indicated the unguarded flanks of the army. Geoffrey's eyebrows raised. He saw it now.

Guvi nodded solemnly. "Your Lord Bohemond has ordered all but a handful of us into the field for a little wall-storming party, leaving the rear completely unguarded. I suppose this is safe enough for there are no other Saracen armies within a hundred miles, but I wonder. See here this gulley that winds up through the hills behind the Christian camp? Why, an army could march through that without being observed and fall upon us from behind. My point is this, friend Norman, should the Seljuks sneak their men out of the city in some way or should another troop of their brothers arrive, they might attack us from the rear, pinning our army between the walls of Tarsus and the high ground of our camp and slaughter us. If they do not have the troops to effect this, as lord Bohemond believes, we are secure. If yon Saracens can approach us with a strong body of horse soldiers unopposed, we are lost along with this entire crusade. Today could be more fateful than one realizes."

Geoffrey did not reply, but shivered, despite the heat of the risen sun as he gazed across the camp at the wide swale between the hills.

A dream came back to him but he shook it off. There was nothing to do. "We will know before long," he murmured. Then he brushed Chestnut more.

EADRIC POUNDED FEROCIOUSLY UPON THE DOOR OF THE CONVENT UNTIL the very cross-bracing creaked and cracked. Then he growled low in his throat, spat twice for good measure and gave the timbers a weighty kick. The small hatch door swung open abruptly to reveal a youthful, plain face in a habit. The small nun eyed the redheaded monster in silent trepidation.

"The girl!" snarled the Saxon. "Where is she?"

"Which girl?" enquired the young sister, bewildered. "We have many such here at the convent."

"And damn them all for their pious do-goodery, too!" thundered

Eadric. "But it will do you no good to stall me; I know you have her here and by the hair on Odin's arse, I intend to leave with her!"

Furious at the Saxon's lack of respect, the sister stared at him in silent indignation. Eadric was never one to flinch from a stare so he returned her look as he stood scratching at his underarms.

"I repeat, good sir..." began the nun, sarcastically accenting *good sir*, "which girl do you wish to see?"

The red-hair slowly inhaled a deep, full breath in preparation. "Which girl?!" roared Eadric so loud that the very dead in the convent cemetery must have started upright. Drawing himself up to full height he added, "Why the one I followed here after she ungratefully left the lad who saved her pretty arse, that's who, you tight-thighed little virgin! Now run and fetch her so that we might leave without further..."

"No," his adversary said simply.

Eadric halted in his speech, amazed at her response. Perhaps she had not heard him properly. Perhaps she did not know who it was she stood before.

"No...?" he asked mildly, unsure, his bluster put aside.

"No," she repeated. "Good day, sir!"

Anger flooded through him. His hands shook and he turned his head from side to side to see if anyone else had observed this singular and humiliating experience. A rumble began deep within his chest and struggled up his windpipe. Finally, it emerged in a thunderclap of exclamation. "No?" he boomed. "No?! Is it? Why, you listen to me you cold-blooded, little bitch! I came to see..."

He was silenced abruptly and painfully by the hatch door slamming with some force in his face, nearly squashing his sensitive nose. For an instant, he gingerly felt the large red protrusion, wincing a bit before the enormity of what had happened struck him.

"Odin's prick!" he thundered. "Where's my axe? I'll batter your little damned door to kindling and use it to set your black skirts afire. By Thor's moody hammer, I'll bash your wicked little building into..."

"What is this silly commotion!" raged a shrill voice from behind the portal.

The hatch door was flung open suddenly to reveal the livid face of the Mother Superior who sized up the situation in a glance and surveyed the rude Saxon with a caustic stare. Her burning eyes traveled up his thick legs from his horse-dung-stained boots, over his miserably-patched breeches, to his tarnished silver belt, turned contemptuous as they roamed across his fur jacket splattered here and there with unnamable and disgusting substances and went completely icy with revulsion as she examined his face.

The corners of her mouth twitched as she studied the countenance of the great bandit before her. Almost hypnotized, she watched as a large louse ambled over the surface of his long, hopelessly tangled red beard. His eye was bloodshot from days of careful drinking and his breath foul to match. His thick lips emphasized the wild red hairs reaching down from his nostrils below the large nose to mix with those of the moustache and as she watched, he further endeared himself to her by nervously picking his nose only scant inches from her astounded face.

Here was a man she might possibly really and truly hate were it not for her sworn ministrations of God's love. Hastily, she stepped back and crossed herself causing Eadric to jump at the movement.

"No witchcraft!" he muttered, holding up his axe defensively. For several minutes, they studied each other. No words were spoken but it was obvious that their perceptions of each other were not kind.

"Well?" she asked finally.

Eadric was put off by the iron in her voice.

"I come for the girl," he said lamely, the monstrous axe still clenched in his ham-sized hands, at the ready while his face bore a faintly imbecilic expression.

"So, you did," stated Mother Superior.

That was all. Nothing. She refused to add even so much as a 'get out.' Eadric's mouth opened but no words issued forth. He was plainly taken aback by her attitude. Then she relieved his doubts for him.

"Sister Farie has just explained to you that the girl you seek is to remain here. Now if that is all you came to inquire after, you are dismissed!"

Again, the door was shut rudely in his face. Eadric stood a moment, pondering this disastrous turn of events. Then his rage caught up with his wits and he brayed like a wounded dog.

"You old hag! I'll give you not over the count of three to produce that ungrateful little wench kept here or I'll rip your miserable hovel apart stick by stick and shove each post up your arsehole."

His stout Danish axe gave the door a quick kiss, ever so fleeting, that ripped a furrow an inch deep across the surface.

Then, he drew back from the threshold, spat into both hands, wiped them in his red beard and really pulled back to swing.

The heavy main door opened to reveal the Mother Superior. "You would not strike with me in the way of your axe!" she said, drawing the door closed behind her.

Eadric heard the latch click shut from inside. Had she lost her wits? "Ha! Ha!" he laughed, throwing his head back.

"You would not dare strike me!" she addressed him.

"What?" shouted Eadric the Wild. "Why, I'll splatter your old buzzard bones across that stinking door so that the sisters will have to paint it red from this day forth just to hide the blood! I give you but one chance, you old whore!"

"And I give you the same!" she snapped back. "Unless you leave this instant, I shall bring down the wrath of God upon you, down upon your head as you have never had done before. I will take your armor and weapons from you so that you might no longer be a threat and steal your gift of speech. I will further…" she warned him.

"Har, har, har!" Eadric roared his mirth at the threat. "Your God cannot even protect the city of his Son from the Saracens. Should I fear him? Don't bandy words with me! Fear only Odin!" he boasted.

She stepped forward enigmatically and pointed at his broad warrior's chest. "I warn you, pig," she hissed.

Eadric drew back his axe so that she paled a little.

"And I warn you, bitch! Prepare to meet your God."

Slowly, dramatically, she reached a hand up to the heavens and cried in a voice so strong that it momentarily halted the Saxon. "Then look up, look up and see the vengeance, see the justice, see the fury of the God you scorn, he of both strength and wisdom whose words will surely stop you when you feel the weight of them!"

"Heavy words, huh!" snorted the red-hair in disgust. But he looked up just the same, just to be sure.

Too late, he saw the two sisters on the convent roof above him, with a water jug loaded with rocks. For the briefest instant, this fate hung over him. Like the very sword of Damocles, but abruptly the anticipation was ended as the jug dropped. Eadric the Wild had time but for a single curse before the vessel struck him full atop the head; daylight turned into an inky, pain-filled night.

Mother Superior stepped forward and toed his prostrate form, then nodded to a host of nuns swarming out of the door behind her. She had not lied to him; her God was the one who preached self-help matched with faith. That is what she had used.

Grunting and groaning, the little group of sisters dragged their heavy burden off behind the convent, to a suitable resting place for the big red bear. Far away, it seemed they heard the first of the assembly calls from the plain before Tarsus.

So, this was the day, the elder Mother thought. She had prayed that it would not come and that the uneasy peace could be prolonged, but God moved in his own ways, she knew. It was not for her to know them.

Another trumpet joined the in the cry of first assembly for battle. Then she saw dust in the distance as the first cavalry formations formed. Tears came into her old eyes as they had so many times before. She knelt there in the dust and prayed, those nuns about her doing the same. She knew this was destined to be a dreadful day.

THE FIRST ASSEMBLY CALL ECHOED AND ECHOED ACROSS THAT HILL-strewn plateau before the high walls of Tarsus, somewhat mournfully, Geoffrey thought. But perhaps such feelings were due more to his melancholy thoughts than the army's morale, for certainly all of those knights and men-at-arms swarming about him were eager enough to come to grips with the infidels. Many paused to greet him and there were cries of,

"Lion! Lion" as he walked his horse to the assembly area. Clearly, great things were expected from the knight who carved his way out of a Saracen city. Great things indeed, he thought. But his heart was not in it.

Guvi sat in the saddle next to him, a watchful brother, secure and protective of his friend's back. They watched many colored pennants drift lightly on the hot breeze as the knights mounted and sought out their companies. Here, there was no glaring armor seen, for white scarves and surcoats were the order of the day against the desert's great heat, draped over hauberk and helm to ward off sunstroke. Upon each surcoat was the big red Crusader's Cross, to protect the body from blows and give strength to the arm in this holy cause. Only the men of Westwall kept their azure coats in a show of pride, perhaps excessive pride, among the Christian host. But on the long sleeve of the undershirt, they also had sewn on the cross. Line after line of the fearsome knights formed, sporting flags from nearly every Christian country. Row after row of the massive destriers, rearing and plunging, scenting the electricity in the air, filled the rear of the plain. This time, they waited at the rear of the massing forces to advance slowly behind the footmen so as not to outdistance their support. They would protect the rear with their long lances and wait to exploit any break the front lines might open up. Each prayed that the Seljuks might sally forth in battle madness to engage them in close combat like men.

Before them formed the ranks of the poor mercenaries and disinherited knights armed with poleaxes, pikes and bills. These were tough, vulgar churls in general, those without gentle birth or raised among the peasants, yet not of a mind to live the life of a serf. They could ill afford the armor of the knights, but they were well enough equipped with their jerkins of thick leather and thick broad-brimmed helmets. Although more than one sported armor taken from a fallen knight, most of those who had added to their battlefield accoutrements had breastplates and daggers taken from the Saracens. Hard men all, they knew the long and short of stopping a charge by mounted knights with their long-stemmed weapons, amid the tricks of close in-fighting with their two-handed swords and long battle axes.

Behind them assembled the ranks of the archers, divided into squads of longbowmen and crossbowmen. Neither of these groups were well armored, but with the rate of fire they could sustain, they needed little protection other than the ranks of the tough infantry before them. The pike-men before them were their shield, and by the same token, their imposing presence behind the infantry served to discourage penetration of the front ranks. If the Saracens charged the front ranks of infantry, they would lose nearly half their men from arrows and crossbow quarrels before they closed with the ranks of the Christians. It was an excellent, time-tested layout that had won many a battle on the green fields of England and France, and here the Saracens were learning to their despair, that the Franks were not entirely ignorant of tactics.

Their greatest fear was of other archers, for they could be decimated at a distance when opposed by equal strength in archery, and from this they might lose the battle, all at a distance. This was the way of warfare, for every weapon there was a counter, for every tactic, another plan.

But there was no fear this day before Tarsus for the Turks that manned the walls who had only the short, curved bows of the horse soldiers…deadly, but not to be confused with the great English longbow or the heavy crossbow. And even at close range, the Seljuks on the walls were not massed tight enough to give rise to the great gray goose flock of arrows that the Franks used with devastating effectiveness—the vest cloud of feathered shafts, fired simultaneously, that filled the sky and landed upon the enemy like all-devouring locusts. Several arrows might a man shield himself against or dodge, but the goose flock fell as thick as hail from the heavens, carrying needle-sharp death with it. The flock was as close a thing to a true lightning bolt the Christians had to hurl in the name of their God.

Each warrior checked and rechecked his own particular weapon. The pike-men were in place, still filing their blades. The archers were sticking dozens of arrows into the ground at their feet that they might more readily be available when needed for rapid firing. The knights rested their lances comfortably. Most of these chores had been done but instants before, yet they would be done again and again before battle was joined, for the hands often trembled before combat and it helped much to have something mundane to do. It stilled throbbing nerves, taut with waiting. It was said that the waiting was the worst part. In this waiting, a man experienced every fate he might find for himself in the press of combat, where the fates had only given him one.

At first, you were calm; you deceived yourself that you were ready, that you were mentally prepared for what was to come. But you weren't.

Calmness faded as the seconds ticked away; involuntary tremors shot through muscles as they released and relaxed out of coordination with others. You watched the trumpeter, who watched the commander, and you jerked every time he moved, for you knew that he was about to sound the attack. Yet, even as you watched him in those final moments, that gleaming brass instrument with its song and richly embroidered pennant rising to his lips, you still started and your blood momentarily ran cold as the harsh sound filled the air, echoing end echoing over the hills.

For just an instant, there seemed to be no breath left in your lungs and it passed through your mind that perhaps you were ill. But no, that was obviously not the case. You stared hard at the pale face of the fellow next to you and you saw fear shoot across it and especially through his eyes. His eyes were the worst and they gave you a sort of strength when you realized that he was more frightened than you were. Obliquely, you hoped that your own eyes were not revealing as much, for you knew how desperately you wanted to keep up the pretext of invulnerability.

Fear traveled down the line of soldiers like a lightning bolt passing from one to another, until the whole line shook.

The tension had to be relieved or you felt your head and heart would burst, so you opened your mouth and screamed like a bone-chilling banshee. Other voices caught and held the cry, which somehow became a war cry to the enemy in his equal confusion. Across the field of battle, your foemen heard that cry and shivered at the anguish it contained, and the terrible unnatural strangeness. They thought your cry beyond description, but in truth you were only screaming for the icy hands that gripped your legs to let you go.

To follow, you run forward with the others, making yourself believe that you really did want to kill. All across the plateau, they heard that call and rallied to it. One, however, was a bit slower to answer it than the rest.

Eadric Siwardsson, Eadric the Wild, rolled over and stared up at the fiery sun above him, opening and closing his eye with great effort. Somewhat sheepishly, he felt his tender scalp where a cluster of raised bumps made it seem as if he had set his paw upon a hen's nest. Cursing himself, he remembered.

He sat bolt upright and sank a bit in the soft earth he had been thrown upon, but halt! Twas not earth, after all; twas the dung pile out behind the convent stables. Well, it could have been worse. After all, it was not like they had thrown him into bathwater or something equally detestable.

But his weapons and clothing, including his rusty armor, were taken from him. They had left him only his filthy loincloth. For Odin! This exceeded his patience! But what was he to do with no weapons nor even clothing? Twas kind of the sisters to at least leave him his mount, though he realized that it had not been an act of charity. They merely wished to be easily rid of him! Ha! They were wrong!

Then he heard the trumpet for assembly. His rage was without measure. He held his hands up appealingly to Odin, but still his back remained naked and his sword hand without a weapon. He shook his fist to the blue heavens. Muttering hair-raising oaths to himself, he then shook his fist at the convent walls and climbed upon his horse to rejoin his men, for there was no question of priorities here. But he paused before the convent gate to shout his defiance at the nuns watching from inside. He thought he heard a few shrill giggles at his language and demeanor, but he was all too busy inventing new and colorful swearwords to express himself.

"Get down upon your knobby knees and thank the Saracens, you scabby whores, for I must join in the battle! But you may bet your saintly relics that I shall return. There will be a short interval here while I go and obtain a city for these dainty Franks, but my anger will not be assuaged by it. The very instant the combat is over, I shall be here with fire and sword, and then we will see what your god in a water jug can do!" And with a final jet of spit launched at the door, he galloped off for the milling Frankish host.

Geoffrey found it hard to believe his eyes as he stared across the plain at the high walls of Tarsus. The infidels had opened their high gates and swarms of horsemen were slowly spilling out onto the field. What madness was this? There was no reason for them to engage Frankish knighthood for they stood to be overwhelmed. He turned to Guvi and gave him a questioning glance. The Finn sneered and nodded his head; both smelled a trick.

Geoffrey peered off into the distance at the flanks of the Christian host. They were still clearly defined and in good order; there seemed to be no threat of another force striking from the sides. But why the ruse? He only hoped that those in command would not be overeager to engage. The Franks had the battle won with superior tactics and weaponry, if they would but be patient. Unfortunately, the rest of the Christian host was not as suspicious. The first catcalls went up.

"God has smitten them with madness! Attack!" cried someone from behind and Geoffrey felt his heart sink at the cry. The fools!

"Stand your damned ground," came also from behind Geoffrey and he heard the heavy thud of leather striking home on shoulder mail.

"God works no miracles thus!" He recognized his father's voice and was proud. Whatever were his faults, he was a seasoned warrior and he would not spend his men's lives recklessly. But his voice was not enough for many who had not yet tasted first blood; they broke ranks and swarmed like bees for the Seljuk riders.

"In God's good name, hold your ground!" roared Sir Brian, causing his horse to rear in the face of rushing troops. But the result was minimal. He succeeded in retaining only about half the horse soldiers. They watched as the infidels met the rushing Franks in the middle of the plain, did battle for a few moments, and then ran for the gates of Tarsus as though their very souls depended upon it. Naturally, with their swifter, smaller horses they made it safely to their walls and the Franks halted well out of bowshot, so they too were safe.

Geoffrey sighed in relief. Whoever had led that foolish rush at least had brains enough to fear the Saracen archers. Perhaps they had not lost anything. It had certainly been a ruse, but what had been gained? He looked at Guvi; the Finn shrugged. He, also, was puzzled.

Possibly, they had been testing the reaction of the Christian army, but for what intent? Geoffrey smiled to himself. Aye, let them think all

Franks were reckless and undisciplined. After Bohemond was through kicking the butts of those who led that pell mell rush, the Saracens would encounter a wholly different army in their second attack. And that could be decisive in the long run for it is often fatal to misjudge the tactics of a clever army.

The knights who had bolted, returned unrepentant and brandishing their lance, eager for another go until Sir Brian began pushing them from the saddle with his sword pommel and spitting upon them, calling them undisciplined traitors and fools.

No, it made no sense at all. If the Saracens were attempting to tire the Franks, they would need to do better than this poor display. And after Sir Brian's gentle persuasion being carried out all along the Frankish line by the leaders upon the lesser, there would be no repeat of the blind rush.

The younger St. Denis turned to Guvi again. "Do you see what happens?" he asked.

Guvi nodded but did not reply. Something was amiss, but it was too early to see it with any clarity. Geoffrey only hoped that he might understand the Seljuk trick, and counter it, before it did any damage. Again, the Franks formed for the attack, but before the trumpet sounded a bloody squire raced along the front ranks and stopped before Sir Brian who he recognized as commander of the English host.

"My lord!" he gasped, falling from the saddle. "A large number of the Saracen lancers broke through our ring outside the western gate and headed southwest, a large number, my lord!"

Sir Brian dismounted as several knights, including Geoffrey, helped the wretched fellow up and gave him water.

"How many, fellow? How many?!"

The squire struggled for breath while two pages wrapped his wounds.

"At least a thousand, my lord! Perhaps twice that. I could not see clearly for they overwhelmed us and mowed us down as ripe wheat!" The man was near fainting and when he spoke, it was a barely an audible whisper. "They outnumbered us heavily and the knights to our flank had left their positions to engage the Saracens at the front gate. We were alone and on foot; we could not stop them. I'm sorry, my lord. We tried..."

In a rare show of compassion, Sir Brian ruffled the boy's hair and smiled. "Nay, lad. You stood your post like a brave man and that was all we can ask of any. Come to my tent and relax, but I say this to you, that each of you who are a squire who fought at your post when you could have honorably retreated against such odds, each of you this day has earned his knighthood by my hand, in the authority of William, King of England. Now go and rest, my son. You have done your part; now we must do ours."

When the squire-made-knight left, Sir Brian turned to his captains. He said, "If they capture our north, then we will starve. But they cannot move as fast as a single rider. Geoffrey, return to camp and relay this to Sir Charles. Have him send a rider to warn Kazanli at once! Then return to me. These Saracens can scarce afford to lose such a band of soldiers in such a gamble; forces will stop them on the road to Kanzanli while we smash the walls of Tarsus here!"

Geoffrey hesitated as he turned his tanned face toward the camp in deep thought. Sir Brian eyed him with distaste. "Well? What ails you lad?" he asked curtly. "We do not have much time!"

"Father," thought Geoffrey aloud, "what if instead of trying for Kazanli, when now they find the port forewarned, they try to outflank us, to come from the rear and put a sword to our back?"

"Don't be an idiot, boy!" shouted Sir Brian. "Their attack was meant to slaughter us; they would have wiped out the soldiers so that not a single man could come through as that squire did!"

"But what if it was all a ruse to try our rear?" persisted Geoffrey.

"Hell's damnation!" cursed Sir Brian, brandishing his longsword in fury. "Our rear is safe enough! Now ride, damn you!"

And the old knight slapped Chestnut with a gauntlet so that the brave destrier raced off in the direction of the Christian camp.

It was logical enough, Geoffrey thought as he rode, for the Turks to cut them off this way by taking the port, but the Emir was not stupid; surely, he knew that by the time such a large gathering of horse soldiers arrived, the port would be up in arms and awaiting them.

But if the sly Emir chose to attack the Frankish ends, why had he not begun with the men of the side gate? Would no other choice precisely fit in with his plans, the way he would have thought it out? Mayhap? Or was it but a fatal oversight on the emir's part not to realize that a messenger could reach KazanIi before them. Or perhaps they had cohorts waiting along the road for just such a messenger. Or did they think all Christian horses as big and ponderous as Chestnut? But it was odd that they did not understand that Bohemond had also brought many swift ponies for just such events.

He thought again of the possible plan and its faults but shook the thought from his head. It was too complicated. Surely, someone would notice a large column of horse soldiers in the hills, if they came. This time Guvi's instinct was wrong. It must be that those loyal to the Emir were awaiting a messenger along the road; he would have Sir Charles send several to insure delivery of the message. That detail satisfied his mind for now. He knew logically that the troop of Saracen horse soldiers was heading for the port.

But the fates are often unkind. In this thinking he was wrong, as was Sir Brian before him. It was a fatal error.

15

CHAPTER THE FIFTEENTH

S ir Geoffrey raced into the Christian camp with hooves pounding
madly and drew Chestnut to an abrupt halt before the maroon and
white pavilion of Sir Charles of Brent, second to Sir Brian in repre-
senting William of England. Two squires ran to hold his reins should he
wish to dismount but he impatiently waved them away.

"Sir Brian St. Denis bade me deliver a message to Sir Charles!" the
younger St. Denis called from the saddle. There was little time for polite
niceties with the battle to be joined.

"Word must be sent to the garrison at Kazanli; they are to move
along the coastal rode for Tarsus and engage a force of every horse
that they will encounter, driving them back against our flank. It is
believed that such a body of Turkish horses has escaped the city and is
moving southwards for them. They must be countered before they are
close enough to strike our supply line and held at least long enough
that we might strike them in their rear flanks after this battle for the
city!"

Geoffrey acknowledged a salute from one and turned Chestnut for
the battle again, but as he rode to the top of one hill on the fringe of the
Christian encampment to survey the battle now levied, something made
him turn his head to the side and examine the hills behind the Christian

pavilions, the hills that held the defile. Call it fate if you will, for divine destiny is a cruel, cruel phrase to justify what he saw.

And what he saw was the vision of a slaughter of war, for as Geoffrey turned Chestnut upon that flat hilltop, he caught the glitter of spear-points in the late morning sun. A long column of horse soldiers where there should be none. In the scalding sunshine, beneath the hot weight of his armor, Geoffrey shivered.

These were neither Normans nor even mercenaries sent by the Emperor Alexis, for Geoffrey could discern their conical steel helmets topped with the tell-tale crests of green-dyed horsehair and a neck covering of iron links. Even in the harsh glare of the sun that they rode out of, Geoffrey saw that there was at least twelve hundred of the infidel soldiers around the hills and down a narrow valley that ran between the sides of the Christian encampment like a backbone. They were well-armored for battle, although Moslem armor was light, aiming more for speed rather than strength.

Geoffrey saw then that they would drive a wedge of crimson steel up the rear guard of the Christian host. Unless there was built a gate, a mighty dam, to stop this flood of pending death.

He reacted instinctively; he had no time to ponder whether it was an act of destiny or not that he should return to camp at this time of need. If he could have stopped to consider what was happening, he would have been frightened more than at any time in his life, but, mercifully, he had no such time. All that lay in his whirling mind was the question of whether he had seen them in time to build a dam of horseflesh and armor.

"To arms! To arms! For God and William of England!" he roared, drawing the attention of the pitifully few knights and men-at-arms left in the camp either as wounded or in sore reserve. None of the leaders had even dreamed of the Seljuk hoard positioned within the city, thirsting for a chance to strike at the back of their enemy.

There was no extra garrison to fall back on. Even those on medical duty had been ordered into the final attack upon the city. There was no army left here.

But those remaining here knew the crest of Westwall and St. Denis;

they knew the one called the Lion. And they understood the urgency of the knight's cry, for he could not keep the hint of disaster from it.

The men of Otranto and St. Denis swarmed to him, if a swarm of such a pitiful offering of men could be rightfully called. There were wounded and stragglers from the pavilions of Toulouse, Bouillon, deChamps, and the rest of the levies, squires just into their teens tending their masters reserve armor and destriers; all grabbed for sword and armor, many not entirely unhappy, for it gave them the chance to become knights, and in the armor of their sponsors to boot. They would fight well.

The camp came alive with the cry. Geoffrey saw a page of no more than eleven years pull on a too-large helmet, take his special smaller sword and scramble into the war saddle of a destrier the size of Chestnut. Even in the midst of the confusion, Geoffrey had time to pound up next to the boy and pull him, struggling fiercely, from the saddle.

"Give a man that horse, boy!" he commanded.

The lad kicked out and cursed him. Someday he would be a fine knight, but not this day. His death would serve nothing.

Geoffrey had wished for Guvi to guard his back as always and to carry the standard, but a young knight who had obviously just been knighted in the field during the previous battle took the streaming pennant from Geoffrey's gauntleted hand, calling the young St. Denis "Sir Lion" as he did, though Geoffrey had never seen the fellow's face before.

They drew up before him. More than one hailed the Lion of Tarsus. All totaled, there were less than three hundred men.

Geoffrey sighed to himself as they formed their ragtag ranks and he tried to arrange them so that the most heavily armored knights would lead the mad charge, followed by the more lightly armored men-at-arms, and finally the less experienced squires and footmen who found mounts. Squeezed together as they would be, all the Turks would see would be a row of tightly packed knights and destriers and the swords behind them; hopefully, they surmised that three hundred of Christendom's best knights had been sent to greet them, and then so much the better for the surprise that the Franks would already have. And if, in the surging dust, the infidels saw ten times the three hundred and panicked, then perhaps there was a chance of saving the day. A small chance, true enough.

Then, Geoffrey turned his eyes to the clear, hot heavens. The fresh sun beamed golden and beautiful for all its aching heat, unhampered by clouds, the beginning of a warm, sunny day. The shadows were driven from a night's end and the cold ridges of the distant hills were again warm with a promise of life. All of nature was tinted amber-gold with the bright sunbeams and even the faded Crusader surcoats of white fustian with their dull red crosses, even the rusting armor and weapons of the Christians, never looked brighter nor prouder.

He saw not the rows of haggard, sleepless faces before him worn through from pondering whether a Turkish lance would rip their guts open today or on the morrow. Nor did he smell the stench of clothes and armor worn in the heat of battle for days without change, nor did he see those pinched faces, cramped with the pains of sicknesses or abject, nerve-chilling fear that had answered his call anyway.

The morning was magic. The sunshine banished all human frailties. Before the Lion of Tarsus, sitting proud and straight in their saddles, there were only three hundred champions.

Geoffrey looked up to God. Across the hills, the Hill of Stones was lit by this beautiful light, the hill where she was sheltered in the Convent of the Sacred Heart. For an instant, his eyes filled with tears for all that he knew, he would never have her. Then, suddenly, self-pity vanished and he was overwhelmed with a deep, burning anger. He had lost.

He had lost all that he had ever cherished and hoped for. Why had his love for her been so wrong? Why? His head pounded. Why could he not have held her to him and gone back to the cool, green hills of England to live like everyone else? Why had he been constantly confronted with villains who would stand up to be cut down, and in their dying, beat him? Lion of Tarsus? Hah! Geoffrey spit on that title of respect; it had come between him and Claire. Why was he the one to suffer; he was no Christ to take on the salvation of his brothers! Let them fend for themselves; he would leave them now and take her up on her word. He would flee with her to England or Scotland or Ireland. He would live his life an outlaw as long as he had her beside him. It would be easily and quickly done; all he needed to do was be rid of these searching eyes, these brave, hard, terror-filled eyes that looked to him to lead...and die.

The bubble of fantasy burst. He threw back his head and laughed madly, a full, magnificent laugh that the men misunderstood for courage, and they laughed with him, wildly, savagely. They could do no less. They followed the example of the Lion.

But he laughed so he would not weep, for he had lost everything. Everything. Except honor. And without the sighs and tears of self-pity, he realized that he would not survive this day, that he and his fellow dead men were too brave and too foolish to realize it. It was not that he was so very brave, he thought, for his stomach was turning inside out with fear at this point. Rather, it was that he saw no logical choice.

If he should flee now, the entire crusade might be ended this day, and how many of his friends would die because he had saved his own life. No, the alternative was not acceptable; he knew his conscience only too well. That same entity that had driven him on his search for Claire would condemn him and damn him for failure just as readily. If the price of his comrade's lives must include his own, then so be it. God is wise. It is not for man to question his will.

How many times had the priests said this to him? And he had never believed it until now. Perhaps he was part of Divine Destiny. He spat. Divine Destiny and the wars of man both be damned. If he could have Claire by a warm fire in winter, and hope, that was all he asked.

He looked a last time at the sun climbing over the Hill of Stones, and silently mouthed her beautiful name a final time, his lips and tongue lingering on the lovely syllables and remembering the overwhelming sweetness of her kiss. For a selfish second, he allowed his mind to picture her face and golden hair, and he thanked God that he had lived to set her free.

Perhaps God did hear his prayers. After all, was that not what he had prayed for every night for two years? He laughed to himself. Now he was but being greedy, wishing for a life with her as well as her freedom. Perhaps in these troubled times, God had rationed his answers. Ah, well. He shook his head sadly for what might have been.

She would have come to him, eventually, he knew she would. His love for her, and hers for him, would have triumphed over the nightmares she had. Strangely, this knowledge was comforting in a perverse way. He desperately wanted to believe that she loved him as he did her, despite all that had come between them and her harsh reactions. God is wise. It is not for man to question.

Then his voice came to him, but it was different, a barely human, nerve-shattering roar that made those nearest him start from their saddle. He had locked her dear memory within his heart, so deep that even the sharpest infidel shaft might not seek it out. And in doing this, he was again the warrior.

"Avant! Avant! For God and William. For our Sweet Saviour who died for us on the Cross! Today we die for him!" Geoffrey cried.

And so it was.

Even in the field before Tarsus, where the fighting was heaviest and the din of bitter struggle loudest, they heard the meager offering of souls. Swords clashed upon shields and lances with foot-long heads bobbed in the cool air. In their fervor, they were no longer merely three hundred, they were three hundred of God's chosen knights.

"For God and Honor!" they cried.

"William and England forever!"

"Otranto! Otranto!"

They glorified disaster. They reveled in their fight. The spirit of the crusade, the true spirit that did exist, had possessed and filled them. They raged and cried in all their glory for today they would repay mankind's debt to God; they were to be lions set loose among wolves, ultimate destroyers of the blasphemers of their Lord's name. Today, they were invincible.

Then, as straight and as murderously swift the flight of an arrow, they receded into that narrow defile and set spurs for the Saracen host.

Such was the narrowness of the gulley, thick with yellow dust, that no more than perhaps ten riders abreast might approach, a like number of the enemy when the opposing forces engaged. The infidels rode confidently beneath their green banner, knowing well enough that they would strike a tired host from the rear in a devastating surprise blow that would rip and scatter the Franks across the field, hopefully beyond repair. The others from within the city would join them in finishing the rout and the first Crusade would be ignominiously ended.

And it almost had happened. Almost.

So surprised were the Saracens when they rounded that final bend in the gulley, that last curve in the twisting, snake-like path, that their pace slowed nearly to a halt and the rear ranks followed the foremost in confusion.

By Allah, it could not be! Their plan was too well thought out! But it was. They met death in that defile and it stunned them.

"Ha! Rou!" cried a voice in the war cry of William the Conqueror, father to William of England. "William and England forever!"

"For God and honor!" cried three hundred voices and a thunderbolt was sent hurtling against the Saracen riders. There was no time nor room for fancy tactics, no desire to outwit a cunning enemy. Raw anger seized hold of the Christian troop and they roared defiance against all odds as they closed with the enemy. Let their longswords do for tactics; let their iron-shod destriers do for cunning, and let their mad courage do what they had no numbers for.

Geoffrey had chosen his spot well, for in the slithering of the defile's course, the Moslems could not clearly see how many attacked their blood-thirsty horde. All they were able to discern in the choking dust was a frightful, swift-winged charge of Frankish horse soldiers, lances couched and gleaming in the sunlight, pennants streaming proudly, and a screaming mad din as they hurled their heavy steeds into the fray as though they were impervious to the infidel's weaponry.

In this crucial time of indecision, the Christian knights hit the Saracen column, staggering horses and riders back to the twentieth line of lancers. The front lines of the Saracen host were more than decimated; they were crushed into nothingness by the heavily-armored knights on the sturdy horses. Twenty-foot-long lances driven with strength and steel-thewed arms pinned two and three lightly armored riders together, writhing and screaming. Their lighter horses were literally trampled by the more massive ones of the Christians.

Then lances became entirely useless and were cast aside if still unshattered, in favor of wicked double-edged longswords, short axe, mace and the more exotic morning star. With these instruments of dark and terrible death whirling over their heads, the heavily-armored knights smashed deeper into the Moslem ranks and lay infidel after infidel out into the bloody dust. The carnage was horrible but both sides understood that more was at stake than mere lives.

"Onward!" roared Geoffrey, lashing out. "Before God, onward!" And the enemy fell before him, screaming and panic-stricken.

For an instant, one majestic beautiful moment fleeting across the face of time, Geoffrey succeeded; the infidels tried to fall back in disarray for so lusty were the Christians in their pursuit of slaughter and scorn of death that the infidels truly believed themselves outnumbered.

But it was not to be, for some men there is no salvation.

If they had fought in an open field, Geoffrey would have driven the enemy horse soldiers into the horizon. But here, their ranks were packed too tightly and they could not turn to run and give quarter to that of the Christian ferocity; they were forced to stay and fight. The unyielding courage of those few pitiful knight's squires had also doomed them, iron- ically. They were also unyielding. But then, perhaps they would have had it no other way.

The Seljuks, in turn, cast away their supple lances and ripped back against the Franks with scimitar and battle axe. But they were outclassed and died.

Seven had fallen before Geoffrey's singing sword and another was losing the contest. They all knew though, those Christian champions, they all knew that time was against them, time and the weight of the infidel troop. Soon, the press of sheer numbers would begin to tell for the mightiest arm can only lift a sword so many times. Geoffrey feared most for the untested squires.

The whirling combat was the height of confusion as infidels, frus- trated at being kept in the rear while battle raged, jostled their comrades aside in an effort to reach the struggle, only to regret their decision as they beheld the larger, steel-armored knights that held their line with remarkable precision and with meticulous accuracy hacked the front line of Turks to pieces. When a knight fell, he was at once replaced by another or a tough men-at-arms so that the Christian line remained strong.

"Kill! Kill!" chanted the Seljuks in Arabic. But the intent was clear.

"God rot your souls, you cowardly does, spawned from the devil!" returned Geoffrey with a bellow and a whistling blow to the nearest Turk who tumbled, screaming, from his saddle.

"In God's name!" shouted a voice behind the knight.

"In God's name!" chorused several others, and although Geoffrey had thought the attack pressed to the fullest it might be, nevertheless the Christian line edged forward inch by inch, incredibly.

Already, Geoffrey was bleeding from superficial cuts upon his arms and the glancing stroke of an axe knocked the helmet from his head, leaving him only the mail hood as protection. But he was far more fortunate that the fellow holding the axe, for his head left his shoulders, not merely his helmet.

A hulking Saracen commander in a gold-burnished breastplate of authority loomed before the young Norman and for an instant; Geoffrey thought he recognized one of the swarthy faces he had seen as emissary to Tarsus. The man's hooked scimitar rattled off Geoffrey's shield with a ringing that sent sparks dancing like witch fire before his eyes. The Turk was immensely strong. Almost as strong as the young St. Denis.

It had not been for weakness that Geoffrey had sweated and toiled with leaded sword and mace for longer than two years. His longsword rose in a high shining arc, seemingly brushing the cloudless heavens and caused the air to whisper in dread as it rushed down upon the man. Only to be caught squarely on the infidel's low, small, circular shield.

"Dog!" hissed the battle-wise Turk in Norman-French.

Geoffrey forced moisture into his dry mouth and spat the precious liquid into the infidel's face. The Turk's eyes blazed as the spittle struck him and he stood in the saddle to deliver another powerful blow. But Geoffrey bravely held position and kneed Chestnut so that the destrier rammed against the Seljuk's lighter horse, throwing the warrior off balance. For an instant, Geoffrey read fear in the man's eyes as he realized his disadvantage in both strength and weight. Then fear left his dark eyes as the Norman sent his soul home to Allah.

"Deus vult!" the Christian cried savagely. "God wills it!"

The man fell backwards from the saddle with his shield, cloven through so that his shoulder flapped free, attached to the corpse by only shreds of flesh. It was terrible to see.

"God wills it!" they roared, and wept, and howled. "God wills it!"

And while they battled, the sun rose higher and more fearsome.

As soon as one dying infidel was swept under the tide of hooves and sword strokes, there was another in his place, another fresher and stronger. Geoffrey's men were holding well so far because most of the Christian front rank still consisted of the seasoned knights, veterans of other campaigns and all-knowing of the techniques and tactics of cavalry confrontation. The real test of the Frankish mettle would come when these men had fallen and the grizzled men-at-arms and young squires were called to fill the opening ranks. But for this instant, hope was not yet dead.

The infidels were being slaughtered by the dozens trying to breech the steel wall of the Christians. Although the knights could no longer advance against the steady press of the Seljuks, neither were they giving so much as an inch, and the Moslems were anxious, too anxious. They had forgotten the lessons they had paid dearly for in other battles against these armored beetles from Europe; they had forgotten that they could not match them weight for weight or stroke for stroke. To attempt so was to invite slaughter. But they did so anyway for the killing lust was not confined to only one camp.

Sweat soaked Geoffrey's surcoat so that it clung to him darkly sodden and perspiration ran the length of his chainmail armor as does summer rain over a leaf. His eyes stung. His breath came leadenly from lungs that felt heavy and his vision was tinged with a deep red haze, both from the sun that broiled him and from the angered bloodlust he felt.

Two more fell beneath him, already dead before they reached Chestnut's thrashing hooves. More rushed in, swords and axes flailing. Geoffrey felt sharp pains in his sides as his body craved oxygen. It was stifling in his armor but he was glad for it being upon him.

The Saracen armor, although of high quality steel, could not stand up to a solid blow from his good longsword, but something was happening inside Geoffrey now that made even the most bloodthirsty infidels weak men in comparison; the intense young knight was possessed by a strength of emotion so singular, so peculiar, as to come upon men only once in their lives, if ever at all.

It was a fatal emotion; it was the means to an ending. It was a grim abiding of outrage at the world, a sudden and illusion-shattering realization of all of life's vile rotten-ness. It was something that shunned care and caution, and momentarily submerged the will to live within a man's own soul. It was a poison of snake venom and boiling pitch, caustic past belief. There was only that explosion of righteous anger; nothing else mattered, nor ever would again. There was no love, no comfort, no goodness in the wretched world for poor Geoffrey; there was only the reality that he was truly alone. Friendship was dead and faith dying; there was only the stinking wind out of man's own oozing insides to cool him. Creation was a monstrous joke for the Creator had thought up a world of muck-lapping dogs. And the dogs swarmed about him now, baying and tugging at him, attempting to pull him down to their level, and death. Fate had betrayed him; God had betrayed him.

And all of this outrage and sense of betrayal was transmitted into a drunken fever of physical action and the purest of naked emotion. Geoffrey hated as he had never hated before, perhaps as no man had ever hated. Two more Saracens fell before his sword sweeps, crying out to Allah.

More, far more than the Saracens, did he hate life itself. In this fateful moment, he felt himself awakening as if from a deep, dark slumber and he perceived life as everything it really was. By the most lenient standards, it was but a grim game of the gods, a horrible jest created by some uncaring power that played out the lives of men as mere pawns upon a gameboard that stretched from far horizon to far horizon. The gods, those damn-ers of dreams, had given man something as beautiful as love, let a man taste it and revel in it, only to deny him its final possession. That same deity had made them take the coming of the marvelous Christ and demean it with death, made it something to kill another man over. Good was but illusion, joyous and tear-swept.

Evil was reality, grim and all-pervading. The gods cast their wretched dice and laughed while good knights, on both sides, fell and bled. Reality, where was reality?

Here, in his chain-mailed fist, here was reality, as real as the death that stopped the intake of breath in a Saracen gullet as Geoffrey plunged down his wicked sword for the justice the gods decreed. Aye! He laughed ruefully, here is the secret of life itself! Man wields his own soul with his own two hands. And it is a thing of cold, cold steel, with no heart or gentleness. It, too, more than anything else, is an instrument of death and mortal destruction. Burning brightly, it is an engine of hell.

Somewhere beyond the fray, Geoffrey heard the devil laugh. And he tossed his handsome head and thundered his own black mirth. God and his angels be pitied, for he had learned the secret of all life. Laugh, Satan laugh! Laugh as our swords sing you a song!

All Geoffrey desired now was to slay madly and finally be slain in his turn. He saw the markings of fate in the enemy before him; he knew it was not ordained that he possess all he had ever wanted, so let him die; let a sword stroke ease his suffering; let the bloody stroke of an axe give him comfort. It was as pointless to continue as it was to stop. Ego rules supreme in these fierce moments. The feeling of "I am!" is a raw, nerve-clawing, gut-churning feeling that makes killing a thing worthy of exultation and sends the mind of even the most civilized man spinning back into times that were long forgotten when he was little more than an animal.

"Westwalll, Westwall!" Geoffrey screamed, and he laid about himself with his dripping blade. Crimson droplets flew everywhere in the fiercely hot air, and with every stroke, left a red rainbow of spilled blood.

"Ha! Rou!" came answering cries. He saw the pennant of St. Denis dip as the proud young knight who had called him sire fell, streaming blood, and Geoffrey knew he was dying. But he held the brave flag up long enough for a fresh arm to seize hold of it and raise it again proudly, to the cheers of the Christian host. Blood-spattered and slit, it was the very essence of pride and defiance.

And, God, they must be proud now, for it was slowly coming to an end. What was left of them but their pride? Even the lowest of the Christian host understood that when the battle had reached its inevitable conclusion, that there would be no Franks left standing. There was but one hope, and that was to render the Saracen unit ineffective as a fighting force before they all expired.

Then why not die well, if it was too late to fly?

Geoffrey cheered hoarsely as he saw a young man-at-arms, weapon lost and wounded terribly about the face, leap from the saddle upon a Turkish lancer and bury his strong teeth in the infidel's throat. Both fell beneath the pounding press of Frankish and Seljuk horseflesh.

The gulley was so tightly packed with thrashing horses and squirming men in armor, that, save for the brilliant colors of the Saracen scarves, one could not easily discern friend from foe. Twice, Geoffrey turned to grin encouragement at a good comrade, only to find the man's position replaced by a narrow-lipped, eye-rolling Turk. His longsword was scored and nicked its entire length from its meeting with Moslem blades and armor of good Damascus steel. And still there was no end to the foemen.

Geoffrey cast chivalry to the winds and raked a sharp-spurred heel across the eye of a Seljuk mount, causing it to throw its rider. An arrow thudded home into the leather of his saddle from a short Turkish bow and another whistled so near his mail-covered cheek that he heard the whisper of its short feathers upon his armor. He cursed Guvi savagely for not being there to match the Turkish archers.

A huge, dark rider loomed up before him waving two scimitars and gurgling hideously from a mouth with no tongue, a servant of some Seljuk lord no doubt, promised his freedom if he acquitted himself well this day. Better had they taught the poor fellow how to fight. The Norman lifted his narrow, pointed shield and struck home with it between the man's gleaming white eyes, opened wide in the surprised face. The dead man rolled off his horse after a brief grunt of despair and was lost in the sweaty, dusty melee. "Sleep well, friend!" Geoffrey muttered sadly. "Keep a place open for me!"

He surveyed his men and saw that scarcely fifty remained, although their winding gulley was piled so high with infidel dead that in many places the horses literally had to leap over the mounds of the fallen to attack the Christian host. Geoffrey lost sight of the dry foreign earth for all the blood and gore that ceaselessly splattered the ground, drenching the thirsty defile with the salty perversion of gushing crimson instead of the sweet, clean taste of the rain it needed.

And still they came for him. Growling, cursing, panting, praying, the infidels of the Emir's horse cavalry clamored forward to clash swords with the Lion of Tarsus.

"Westwall! Avant! Avant!" he roared wildly. But now there was no advance. They were tired and dying, pushed further than any of them had thought possible. Muscles screamed in protest as creaking arms brought the swords down woodenly, strength evaporating with each new stroke. They longed for the grave now; they longed to end this agony of endurance. They had done their best; they were content with their lot. All except Geoffrey.

His hatred was stronger than theirs. He refused to die until he had played his game to the limit. Let the angels carry off the others; he would stand side by side with Lucifer and spit in Death's eye. And he was a wolf with his unyielding savagery, for he would not let the others retire gracefully either. His strokes were also turning wooden as his muscles cramped, but still they killed. Still they killed and killed and killed.

The battle had turned upon Geoffrey as he knew it must. It was only the merest matter of instants before the tide of Saracen lancers swept them all at last into the grave. His men were too tired to continue; they were fading, but their fatigue only served to fan the fever that smoldered within him. They all but needed a breeze for their embers.

"Cowards!" Geoffrey cried, hot tears in his blue eyes. "Would you betray our Sweet Jesus and our brothers both? Would you see our task fail and our cities fall before the anti-Christ? Fools! Dogs! Cowards! You shame me as you shame both your king and your god! Fly from the field if you will not fight! Fly and tell the world of the brave men who died here!"

Geoffrey screamed at the weary men he was already more than proud of. And stung, they renewed their press against the infidels, like madmen, like demons out of hell. Fatigue was banished to misty recesses of the mind, driven off by both love and honor, by both shame and fear.

"Avant! For Christos!" bellowed Geoffrey.

Their roar split the heavens, and they hurled the milling Saracens back and back. And the sweating, slashing Seljuks who had counted their battle won, fell like ripe wheat before a finely-honed harvest blade.

"For Christos! For God and Christos!" the Franks cried.

No longer did the Moslem cavalry need to come to the Franks for death. Geoffrey witnessed the remaining Christians leaping the piles of dead like wounded lions, laughing aloud in chilling ferocity. They hurled themselves up high and then down upon the Saracens who drew back in total fear.

These men were not human. The Turks were as courageous as any man living, but this...this was beyond comprehension. They were mad, these Franks. When they should be crying for quarter, they thundered like victors. Geoffrey watched helplessly as one of the few remaining knights sent his destrier rocketing over a mound of corpses to crash down upon the screaming infidels, crushing with his weight at least three to the bloody earth.

"No quarter!" he cried. "For William!" The knight swung his sword. They surrounded him like a pack. It cost them six more men to do it. And still more. He was granted no quarter, the wolves were tearing him to pieces. A cut to the Norman sucked the lifeblood from his throat. Geoffrey's surcoat became wetter. But his arm grew weaker, more and more of the infidel blows reached past his shield to his arms and legs. Despite their armor, they bled freely, bleeding away his energy and his life. And it hurt so.

He might have even cried out from the pain, but he had no breath left. It was but a matter of time. Then it happened.

A long-shafted Moslem lance, clutched in the hand of a dying lancer whose brains already dripped from a cloven skull, rammed upwards and ripped into Chestnut's soft underbelly. The horse screamed like a child and coughed up blood, then fell and Geoffrey leapt free from him, finding the strength to weep for the noble animal. "Good-bye, my truest friend!" he cried.

Then he stood splay-legged next to the animal, afoot and desperate, clashing on left and right with the horsemen of death. His shield was battered and bent, the crest worn completely off so that only bare metal and leather showed, though it was hard to see for all the blood. Two more horsemen went down before his singing sword, never to rise, but by now others were behind him and probing for his back.

A sharp pain penetrated just below his ribs, but he was oblivious to it. Turning rapidly, he staggered the Turk with a blow to the helmet, but he found it impossible to deliver a killing stroke for his arm was numb and heavy.

"Au Secours!" he cried. "Au Secours." But now there were none left to aid him.

Three hundred Moslems, all that remained of the great troop, swarmed at him, eager to be the one to end the Lion of Tarsus. Like dogs, they savaged him only because he was too weak to fight. The rest of his men had found their glory, and peace as well, he prayed. Perhaps it was that the instinct to survive in him was so much stronger, or perhaps it was because of his fighting skills, skills long ago encouraged by his worst enemy, and he would not relinquish his life.

Whatever the reason, he was one of the mightiest champions the world had ever known, one who might fall before fatigue and incalculable odds, and still not be beaten. And while all of his brothers lay silent in the rich, red mud, he stood alone. And he fought!

He saw the flash of gilded spurs and prayed it was another knight. But he realized abruptly that the spurs had been stripped from some dead Frank by a Seljuk captain. Furious, he drove his sword with both hands through the officer's small leather shield and into his belly. The horse bucked the dying rider but Geoffrey lurched forward and tore an ornate Saracen mace from the saddle as the horse raced past.

A grinning infidel loomed before Geoffrey, eyes bright above a thick black moustache and beard, intent upon the kill. Geoffrey's mace ruptured both helmet and head beneath with a sickening thud. But another jagged pain tore through the red fog of his senses and he was dimly aware of the weight of something protruding from his back that hindered him curiously when he moved.

He smashed a horse's knee and beat down the rider as he fell. How many had he slain this day. Twenty? Thirty? More? More! Many, many more, but the sands were running out. The drama was entering its final act.

If Allah's followers sat at his right hand, feasting upon lamb when they died in battle as the infidels believed, then there would be many at the eternal banquet this evening with the name of St. Denis upon their lips and the cold kiss of Geoffrey's steel upon their torn flesh.

He cried out aloud as a Seljuk raced in and, turning suddenly, struck out with his spurs and caught Geoffrey across the eyes. Nerve-crushing pain shook his entire body and he was blinded by his own blood. Wildly, he struck out about himself with his mace, striking yielding flesh of foolish men, men who thought a dying lion already dead. But where once his strength would have slain, now it only broke bones or dented steel. He was finished and the Turks knew it. Suddenly, none of them wished to be the one who ended this magnificent lion. They drew back apace, silent, to allow him to fall, and die in peace.

But he would not.

Blinded and bloody from a hundred wounds, he stood screaming madly, terribly proud with a defiance none of them could match. He brandished his captured mace over his head and roared, "Avant!" as though he led an attack against them. They could only shake their heads in wonderment.

He looked up at a sky he could not see and raised clenched fists to his God in final defiance of His Will. Then he cried her name out and although his enemy did not understand the word, its intensity frightened them.

"Claire!" he wept furiously. "Claire!"

And finally, blood streaming across his features, he fell first to his knees and then face down into the crimson mud.

The captain of the Saracen troop gazed over his decimated band sighting the few less than three hundred remaining, so few left out of so many. He looked down at Geoffrey and smiled at the irony; this Lion of Tarsus had been finished here, and still he had won. There were no longer enough men to alter the battle; the troop was ripped to pieces and by a handful of their foe. Now, all they might do is join the battle and perish with the rest.

"Rest easy, oh Lion of Tarsus," he whispered in Arabic. "You did not fail them. We will talk about you in Paradise."

Then there was only the sound of pounding, slurping, muddy hooves as they raced past his still form. But not a one dared to tread upon his motionless body; no one was that brave.

16

CHAPTER THE SIXTEENTH

O n that same fearful morning, late after the sun had risen, many of the nuns of the Sacred Heart walked the hills around the convent, gathering the deep purple Turkish grapes for the heady wine they made. The steep hillsides were terraced with engineering precision and laced with vines whose fruit was ripe for harvest.

Claire walked with them. She wore the white linen robe that marked her as a novice and carried a light wicker basket to fill with her share. She moved gracefully through the tangled vines, fingers plucking busily. It was pleasant to be out this day despite the always oppressive heat; the sky was clear and the beauty of the Lord's nature in rich abundance. She loved the reassuring smell of the earth that held the fruit vines for it reminded her of the ease with which everything grew when left to God's care. The human spirit included. There was beauty in everything if one but opened one's eyes, she had learned. Nothing is so base as to be worthless or meaningless.

She looked up at the horizon, sadly. Carrion birds in great flocks wheeled in the distant sky over Tarsus and Claire knew this was what the Turks called "the day of the great struggle." Distant sounds of armies clashing occasionally came with the breeze and she knew that the city's fate would be decided this day. Geoffrey would be there, slaying.

She shook her head sadly and blocked all thoughts of the struggle from her mind. There was nothing that she might do about it. God's will be done.

She walked on, slightly flushed with the heat but smiling at the others. She was content, more so than she had ever been. It was good not to worry about life and the many trials she had endured; sometimes it was hard to believe they were over with, all the rape and robbery and slaughter. It was good to have little Helgi protected by the sisters.

Sometimes, it seemed though, that there was a void in her life, a space unable to be filled by prayer and meditation and service to others, and her thoughts returned to Geoffrey while her body throbbed with almost painful desire. But Mother Superior had told her that these feelings would leave with time, if she wished them to, as her spirit outgrew the needs of the flesh. Claire wanted very much to believe her; indeed, her conscience gave her no other alternative but to believe. So, she was content.

But as she made her way among the rows of twining stems, she was abruptly distracted from her tranquility by a raucous squawking and the frantic sound of hard-flapping wings. Several shadows raced across her face in the forms of large black ravens, fat and well-fed from Tarsus's siege. They seemed intent upon something tangled in the vines a hundred feet from where she stood.

Oddly enough, she thought of Geoffrey an instant before she reacted. Swiftly then, she scrambled over the steep-terraced banks of the hill to see what struggled so furiously in its deadly confinement. When she was but twenty feet from the spot where the scavengers swooped low with triumphant cries, pecking furiously at their prey, she saw a dark thrashing form amid the grapes. It appeared to be another bird of some sort. A thorny bush tangled her hem and slowed her rescue of the creature. She grappled in exasperation with the branches as she watched the drama, a helpless trapped bird acquitted itself nobly for as the ravens taunted it, it slashed back with hooked beak and talons, blindly, ferociously.

Claire cried out in fury as she tore her hem free and cast aside her basket with its harvest, for she knew that without immediate help, the small champion would fall beneath the weight of so many. The ravens rose as one with a dark cry of protest as she lashed out at them with a stick. "Away! Away, you savage feasters! Today this little brave one will not fill your greedy gullets!" she cursed them.

Only temporarily discouraged, they alighted but scant yards away, determined to outwait her and have their prey. She saw that it was a young falcon entangled within the vines. "Oh, my sweet little one," she cooed, tears forming. "Here, here, let me take you from this place." She reached in and touched its sleek feathers, and, curiously, it seemed to welcome her touch. But it could not free itself from the twisting vines.

A slim, powerful reddish-brown bird it was, with steel-clad talons to mark it as a hunting falcon, probably flown wild from some Turkish lord in the area. Its proud black eyes glittered in the sunlight as it regarded her and she saw its fiercely curved beak was bright with blood.

Claire could not help but smile at the pride in the creature's bearing. It seemed the noblest of all birds.

Another shadow raced past and just missed her face as it tried to drive her off.

"Fly! Fly!" she cried, infuriated at the circling birds, "take your death elsewhere, corpse seekers!" She began to remove the vines from the little prisoner with infinite tenderness. Poor, poor tiny babe, she thought. One broken wing hung limply and through gashes in its side feathers, she saw the dull white of bone. And still it struggled to be free from her grasp, to fly and fight against all the odds.

"Hush you, brave one," she murmured. "Your flight is over this day. No longer will you need your slashing hooked talons or your scimitar-like beak to rend and tear your enemies; I will teach you gentleness and peace." Overhead, beaks clacked in protest and the cries hounded her; they were hungry for blood. But Claire concentrated her energies on the warrior she had saved; she withdrew it from the prison in cupped hands. The falcon was quieter now, Claire knew he was tired beyond life.

Its one black-tipped wing beat sporadically while the broken one was now twisted beneath it in a way that caused more bones to protrude through the sleek, tattered flesh. Here and there, its glossy feathers were streaked with blood.

Saddened unto sickness, she realized that she could not save the beaten champion, but she held it well, free from the vines so that it might die in the free air it had lived in. Feebly, it tried a final time to take wing.

"Fly away! Fly away, my love!" she sobbed. "Rise to the heavens and never come down."

It fought for the air with a spirit far stronger than its flesh. "Be free, my love. Rise, rise…" she whispered hoarsely. But it failed. It rose from her hands in an attempt at flight, at life, and finally fell back, exhausted. She caught and held it while its painfully quick breathing slowed and became shallower. And suddenly…terribly…stopped. With the barest of sighs, it accepted its fate nestled securely in her delicate hands. It was free now…just as free as if it had flown.

There arose a horrendous cry from the gathering of ravens as if sensing the death that they had initiated, and they flew lower and closer, each one more eager than his brothers to feast upon the fallen. But Claire came a third time between prey and predator as she clutched the falcon against her breast and walked away from them. She resolved to bury the fragile creature in the convent courtyard, that it might at least escape the ignominy of providing food for the desert scavengers.

But as she pressed the bloody bundle of feathers to her white robe and felt the hot blood soak into the linen and against her soft skin, she experienced a sensation so striking that it was tantamount to a vision from God or a glimpse into the fires of hell. Her soft heart was filled with pity for the poor little thing that sagged limply in her arms, its flesh still warm as if it only slept, and the beat of its warrior's heart but seconds gone. Her despair for the fallen was monumental.

And in this ineffable sadness she felt, so vast was it, that she took fright for it did uncanny things to her eyesight and mind; it opened dim corridors behind her eyes. Corridors never before sensed that led to the heart.

Other thoughts and scenes suddenly manifested themselves and Claire felt as if she had physically been torn from her plane of existence and subjected to a netherworld of frightening sights and sounds, and events that she had no right to witness. Events that only God should have witnessed or the devil initiated.

Claire sensed a brooding darkness swirling about in the cold caverns of her heart, a lurking, stalking substance that chilled her to the bone and was neither wholly creature nor entirely force. But it was a dark, damned, dangerous shape that ripped shreds from her warm soul and clawed, howling, at her insides. It compressed her lungs with fear so powerful that she was faint of breath and she was too horrified at what she saw behind her eyes to cry out.

She saw man's final visitor.

Slowly, she felt the spinning world slowing down until there was no longer the hot sun above her nor the gravelly sand beneath. She saw a hundred skulking forms approach her out of nothingness and inwardly screamed as she saw they were men in warrior's garb, each with hideous wounds, raw and gaping.

A form more vile than the rest approached her, gurgling hideously, and leered at her in stark mockery. Claire, although frightened past despair, returned his stare with defiance. And looked deep into the pale face of death.

She understood a fear stronger than the rest, but curiously, one not for herself. She did not fear death. But in a fierce instant of black knowledge, knowledge never intended for humankind, she knew the purpose of the grim dark figure and shuddered. The face of her adversary contorted in a grin of purest malice. Laughing in the caverns of its empty eye sockets, it turned from her and the creature she still held futilely and drifted off through her raging mind like smoke on the wind, blowing for a battlefield miles away. The weight now gone from her chest, she drew breath and waited...for what sound she could not know.

But she suddenly knew it when it came; it was Geoffrey's voice. "Claire!" she heard him cry in mortal anguish. "Oh, my Claire!"

She shivered and let forth a scream, a loud, long soul-chilling shriek of totally helpless terror. "No-o-o-o!" she wept.

And it was matched on that bloody battlefield, in that savage gulley, amid another flock of ravens, by a hoarse cry of pain and rage. And of inevitable coming death.

As the black irony of fate allowed it, it was Wild Eadric Siwardsson who first saw the pavilions burning and the enemy riders sweeping up the narrow gulley, headed for the rear of the massed Frankish armies.

Ever the rogue, he was high upon the hill nearest to Tarsus where he had built a mangonel. There, he and several of his cohorts were busily engaged in their own version of total war; they hurled barrels of animal and human excrement over the city walls in the hope of hitting the water supply or the food storage bins. A barrel of the stinking, nasty slop weighed five hundred pounds and could do considerable damage when it landed. Massively thewed beneath the layers of fat and filth, Wild Eadric lifted the barrels himself to the mangonel.

It readily appealed to the Siwardsson's sense of humor to imagine the Emir's cavalry on parade before the battle, all dressed and prancing proudly upon their magnificent Arabian horses just as a load of the slushy dung cleared the walls to fall into their laps.

Pigfeet called the barrels, "Eadric's farts," and howled insanely as another arced from their huge weapon, leaving a dark-colored comet's trail behind it to mark its passing.

"Heigh-ho!" cried Eadric as the ponderous shot dropped into the city. "Let them taste the kiss of the wind that blows brown from the camp!"

"Eadric's Wind!" one of the Saxons called.

Eadric beamed proudly. It had been all his idea, and although the English captains stared at him aghast when he started his bombardment, many of the rank and file foot soldiers laughed and cheered him. War was, after all, war.

"May it poison their water and make their streets slick and disease filled; may it give the Emir himself a face full of our best wishes!" Eadric blessed the barrel with almost religious fervor.

Arrows fell a ways away from the hill, signs of the Saracen irritation at their shooting. But Eadric had picked his hill well; they were out of range.

"I'm coming for you, you puckered arseholes!" the Siwardsson bragged, brandishing his sword at small figures watching him from the city's parapets. Laughing, he hoisted another barrel up to the launching arm.

Pigfeet was a bit put out that Eadric refused to hurl his dead and putrefying horse over the walls right now, and several of the other Saxons had thrown themselves into the game with enthusiasm, each dragging equally disgusting objects up the hill to be launched. But Eadric, ever practical, opted for the dung above all, for it generated more splash when it landed and, of course, inferred more of an insult. When Eadric decided the barrel was not sloppy enough, his motley crew gathered about and diluted the mix with their own urine.

The English and particularly the French gave them a wide berth.

That each takeoff splattered Eadric and his men a little with the foul sludge did not matter a whit, such was the grand sport of it. Eadric had initiated the game and he was pleased with it. Only once did they incur a complaint when a barrel of the goop went awry, and for some mysterious reason shattered in midair to rain down in a thick stinking storm upon the High Lord of Stanbury's tent. The pavilion was occupied at the time solely by the shrewish Lady Stanbury who at once sent a young squire to protest and demand apology. The lad further dismayed the huge Saxon by crinkling up his nose at Eadric's aroma.

Eadric the Wild opened and shut his mouth without saying anything. For an instant, he was completely taken aback at the boy's insolence and haughty demeanor. Not even the leaders of the armies had the effrontery to make demands from Eadric Siwardsson. Eadric hunched his vast bulk over to peer closely into the face of the teenage boy.

"Are you ill? Do you have a fever?" he asked kindly.

"I say, you stinking peasant," the squire snapped, "I don't have all day, you know. Give me what I've asked for and I'll be on my way!"

Eadric glanced over at Pigfeet who was openly grinning.

"Should I?" Eadric asked quietly, his face suffused with mock humility.

"I say, you stinking peasant..." replied Eadric's big brawny second in command. "Give him what he's asking for!" The band of adventurers howled. Slowly, Eadric shook his head, almost mournfully. Then, there was a ringing slap across the ear followed by a quick upending of the lad into the next barrel ready to fly.

"Launch it now!" cried one of the Saxons.

Eadric reached out and pulled the gagging, puking boy free from the muck. "Take that to your lady and with my compliments!" he roared, flinging a handful of the stuff at the boy as he raced off screaming. For an instant, the war was forgotten in the general hilarity.

Then he saw them.

Was it instinct that made the Siwardsson turn towards the Frankish encampment? Or was it fate? Mayhap it was because Eadric Siwardsson was nearest to being an animal in the camp, and his senses would be the first to detect the tinge of smoke in the air, smoke fueled by burning tents and supplies. He sighed deeply. Ah, well, war was, after all war, he thought.

Eadric turned again to his men, looking over their heads to the city beyond. This then, was how the game was played, was it? Ah, these heathen fellows were crafty indeed. However, they had reckoned without one vitally important factor in mind. They had not considered that Eadric the Wild was in camp!

Slowly, terribly, a thin smile spread its way across his face and his meaty hand stroked his scabbard. He began to tremble from coming bloodlust and his temples pounded. Small animal noises squeaked and grunted inside his hairy gullet as civilization slipped from him. His mouth turned into a moist cavern as he roared to his force a form of request heavily laced with his own peculiar brand of enthusiastic encouragement.

"Odin's balls, you slime-eating bastards. The infidels are upon us from the rear and those delicate Norman ladies most certainly will not see them. Get off your lazy arses, you half-bred Vikings spawned from toothless whores! We shall all be heroes and I myself will be acclaimed the greatest of them all!"

He dealt the nearest a kick in the arse that sent him and the others racing for horses and Wild Eadric himself blew the trumpet call of distress to warn the armies on the plain below. But it was a short one for he suddenly thought the better of it; he did not need the help of a bunch of damned Normans to deal with a few hundred infidels. Thor's Hammer! If he and a hundred Saxons could not butcher at least five times their number in these infidels, then he was not fit to be the son of Siwardsson.

He thundered down the hillside and leapt into the saddle of a Norman knight's destrier, pausing only long enough to kick the outraged noble out of the way and blow his nose in the old-fashioned way upon the man's coat of arms.

"Out of the way, you slackard! Go find a bed to hide under or something. This is the day of Eadric the Wild, Eadric, son of Siward the Saxon who raided your thrice-damned shores and butchered your father and grandfather! Today, I am a hero! Today, I will save all of the armies even though I wish you all dead! Tell your children you gave your horse to Eadric the Wild, the man who saved the armies of your god!"

Eadric Siwardsson was nearly incoherent in his glory.

"Go fuck a horse!" grumbled the knight, dusting himself off and stepping out of the way of his own destrier as Eadric raced past.

"Today, I am your savior!" bellowed Eadric as he rode by.

More of the Saxons found mounts, many in a similar manner. What they lacked in riding ability, being sailors for the most part, they made up in their brutish enthusiasm. The madness he had started was epidemic.

Swords were scorned now as being effeminate. These burly, ragged wild men carried only axe and shield, dagger and war hammer. The Siwardsson himself rode with the reins of his captured mount held tightly between his two lines of rotten teeth, brandishing an axe held high above his head with either bull-muscled arm.

He was a figure to strike terror into the infidels indeed with his sleeveless vest of wolf fur and breeks of tanned red leather. A dagger was tucked within one wolf-hide boot for the most dire emergency, sheathed in the lacings running up his thick legs and his silver oval-shaped belt caught and held the sunlight so that it glittered as though it held the brightness of the universe captive. No helmet did he wear but his wild red mane raced free with the wind and he had cast away his eyepatch, stuffing the hole instead with a blood-red ruby that glittered wickedly in the sunlight. No demon out of hell could have looked more ferocious.

"Onward, you puny sons of aged whores! Now Is the time to show these vomit-licking Normans how a battle is fought! O-d-d-d-i-i-i-n-n-n!" He spat the reins back into one fist still retaining his axe and trumpeted encouragement to his men. "Here now. All the heathens you can kill! Odin is good to our thirsty blades!"

"O-o-o-d-d-d-i-i-i-n-n-n!" they answered.

372

He raced ahead of them, aiming straight as an arrowshot for the Saracen multitude that was emerging from the enflamed Christian camp, awash with smoke and the smell of burning canvas and human flesh. He paused not in his run to even see if he was followed.

But he was. By a hundred rabid Saxons and Vikings. "Eah-h-h-h!" they groaned as they rode. Their bones ached for combat and their tongues lolled outside their mouths as hounds on the chase. Their massed voice was a fearsome cacophony of animal calls, curses and the most blood-curdling screams as though they led the advance of Satan's infernal legions. And the voice of Eadric Siwardsson was loudest of them all.

Lord Bohemond of Otranto stood directing the assault upon that same frontal gate the men of Westwall had stormed that first day when a breathless messenger brought word that a force of Turks had attacked and set fire to the Christian camp. Outraged, Bohemond demanded to know if they were being met and contained. Must he dispatch part of his army to meet them?

"Oh, nay, sire. I suppose not!" remarked the men-at-arms in a manner so casual as to cause the Lord of Otranto to go deep purple and question the fellow's sanity, and desire to live.

"How say you, fellow?" grated the First Crusade's greatest leader.

"Why, the Saxons of Emperor Alexis are to horse against them this moment!" the messenger proudly imparted. Bohemond eyed his dirty armor and several bandaged wounds a long moment before he spoke.

"How say you with so much certainty?" he asked.

The young soldier stared back mischievously, trading glance for glance. "Why, my Lord Bohemond, they thundered past me quite close, uncaring whether they trampled me or not, and I near swooned from the stink of them. I left my breakfast upon the ground there and they laughed as…"

Bohemond frowned darkly. "None of us are bathing these days, lad. All you saw was a detachment of Varangians or Vikings. I will have to…"

"But my lord," interrupted the man-at-arms, "they were led by Eadric the Wild himself. They stank of dung!"

The leader from Otranto gave a short, "Oh!" as he digested this amusing turn of events. Indeed, these Saxons in question must be the men of the wild and reckless Siwardsson. Stinking of dung. Who else could they be? Then, Lord Bohemond nodded and turned back to the gate. No longer was he concerned with the outcome of the contest, for it was no longer in doubt.

Even their Allah could not help those Saracens now. He dismissed the messenger and for the first time since the siege began, laughed heartily.

As the Seljuk lancers raced out of the gulley to where there should have only been the rear echelon of the Christian army, they came face to face, and axe to sword, with a host of wild-bearded boars who either grunted like rutting hogs or roared out the most disgustingly obscene and ridiculously bountiful oaths and insults about the Moslem god.

One of them even cawed like a crow and hurled a war hammer so that it knocked a neatly-bearded infidel from the saddle where another of the Saxons seized the hapless man and bit both his ears, then allowed him to flee in disgrace.

These were opponents who rocked precariously on the fine line between normalcy and insanity, even in their calmest moments. Now, of course, they were all quite mad with the war fever.

Eadric the Wild stood high in the uncomfortable saddle and caught infidels passing on both sides with his twin axes. A spearpoint pierced his thick-muscled left arm yet it slowed him not a bit; he was oblivious to pain. With a deft swing of his right axe, he cut the head from the lance that the foeman could shove deeper or withdraw and pulled the lance head free from his arm with his teeth. This he spat with a mouthful of blood from the wound into the face of his attacker. He looked into the eyes of the astonished Seljuk and laughed. It was as natural as spring after winter that Eadric the Wild was drunk, very drunk.

Then the foe's eyes bulged with fear and he tried to duck the swing of the avenging axe, for the ale had slowed neither the Saxon's instincts nor his reflexes. The first swing came high, or rather the man was lucky to stoop low and dive beneath it. Eadric merely slashed free the green horsehair crest that adorned the fellow's burnished helmet. But the wily

Turk made his last mistake when he stood again to launch an attack of his own.

The backswing of the Siwardsson's weapon carved a second mouth for the fellow directly above the first one with a horizontal slash that removed half of the man's nose and all of his upper teeth. For an instant, Eadric got a curious insight into the mechanics of the human gullet before it disappeared in a bubbling froth of blood that choked the Turk's dying scream.

And he fell as others would fall before the Saxon jarl. They were insane, these wild, bushy-bearded men! And they smelled of dung! What type of warrior rode his steed into the press of pitched battle stinking of offal? And again, that day the Seljuk cavalry had cause to feel some sort of stark awe in the presence of their foes. Outrageous bravery was a thing they could grasp for the Saracen attack had called for the bravest of the brave. But these pigs? And more frightful, for pigs, their axes drank deep and their war hammers cleft skulls right and left.

"Thor's cock, you infidel leavings of unclean arseholes, but I'll show you how to put your backs in it! You puny little men had better take lessons in sword lore ere you face me again," roared the Siwardsson. He dashed another Saracen to the ground and howled like a dog, delighted.

Corpses fell all around him, but still he laughed in his dementia. And even the worse for Turkish morale, the dying Saxons laughed just as heartily as the victorious ones. The wild men of an even wilder leader stopped the impact of the attack.

Stopped it dead.

The Seljuks had no avenue of retreat left them except the winding gulley they had littered with corpses earlier. Before they had traversed its twisting length, they would all be overtaken. So, with the fanaticism typical of the infidels, they bunched together and held as best they could on the defensive against less than a third of their number. But the hunter was now the hunted; the victor soon to be vanquished.

The hawk that had mercilessly slaughtered its prey there in that same wretched gulley earlier now fell quarry to an even fiercer beast. Eadric's ruddy face was contorted with an animalistic snarl of sheer bloodlust, his large nostrils dilated with the rich smell of hot crimson and his thick tongue protruding slightly from one corner of his big mouth. The prey was treed; the chase was over. It was dying.

And then, suddenly, it was over. The last rider fell struggling, buried beneath the weight of his own horse, to roast in death beneath the hot desert sun. There was only the sound of Saxons panting and the whipping of wings as the carrion birds descended to feast.

Eadric pulled a flask from his belt and emptied it down his parched throat. Others did the same. Then they dismounted, daggers in hand, to dispatch the wounded and search the corpses for gold.

All except Eadric.

He wanted to know the beginning of what had happened, for the men he had slain were already bloody and winded. The only battle he had known of still raged before the gates of Tarsus, so how did these men come upon the Frankish camp from the rear, already battered. There had to have been a larger force for a few hundred infidels attacking from the rear could not have altered the battle. He paused briefly to survey the damage to the camp.

Had it been simply some sort of diversion?

He did not think so. He rode down further into the gulley and saw that here and there were droppings of blood, leading back away from the camp. A battle had been fought this day, a savage battle just beyond the camp in this gulley. But who had blocked the Saracen attack? Who had weakened them so that Eadric and his men could finish them off so easily? He rounded a high sharp bend in the defile where he knew he must find...

"Jesu!" he breathed softly as he came upon the silent mounds of the dead. He had known it would be thus; he had known from years of experience. He had expected the remains of a brutal battle, but this...this defied description.

Only the wind made any sound at all. A brisk breeze whispered through the defile, whistling over bent and dented steel weapons, and rustling the sodden cloth to make it flap excitedly against the sides of the corpses of men and animals.

"See! See!" it seemed to be saying, "Look what I guard here!" Nowhere was there a sign of life. Nowhere.

Eadric sat motionless in the saddle as his eyes trailed over the piles of Moslem dead before the slaughtered heaps that had formed, and held, the Christian line. Nearly three hundred knights and men-at-arms, even in death, formed a wall across the width of that bloody gulley, a sort of useless dam against all of the churned up red mud. And if the sight of the Christian effort was awesome, the sight of the tall pile of infidel corpses, already crawling with insects and birds, was a vision out of a nightmare.

Horses and riders lay twisted and tangled grotesquely, here and there laced with dead Franks, all of the brilliant silken scarves and coats a uniform dull red-turning-brown with the vast river of blood that had washed over them and dried. Their armor was filthy with blood and sweat and dust. Man was sometimes noble in dying, but never in death.

The stench was overpowering as well; over a thousand corpses lay packed together beneath the sweltering Arabic sun, brave men all. There had been no quarter given and none asked, Eadric supposed. This was what might have been the final great struggle of the battle for Tarsus, the do-or-die of the best of the infidel army. And they had been pulverized by three hundred, more or less, of the men they held in contempt. Many looked to be only pages and squires, not yet seasoned warriors. Eadric dismounted to squelch through the mud, searching...

He needed to see the brave, mad bastard that had ordered this defense, the man of iron who had thrown his life into the winds of death with the rest of them, all uncaring.

He must have been a Saxon, Eadric reasoned with his own peculiar brand of logic.

The jarl cleared his throat and hawked casually upon the helmet of a dead infidel. He hefted one of the scimitars he found in so many hands. Huh! Lightweight stuff with no impetus behind it other than the strength of the arm holding it. Too bad he had not been there with a few of his reavers and their axes; all of the Saracens would have been stopped in their tracks. Still, these Franks had done well, he thought.

Bending over, he seized a fat pouch off one body, opened it to count the gold and silver coins, and then stuffed it into his belt. One man's loss, another's gain, he reasoned philosophically.

But the wild man's attitude changed abruptly when he turned to follow the sounds of approaching horses. He stared in the direction his men approached from and suddenly, amidst the corpses weltering in their own blood, he caught a familiar burst of sky blue, a slight patch of azure among all of the darkening crimson on the ground.

By the beard of Odin! Let it not be...

Snarling, fear welling up in his throat and half-choking him, Eadric the Wild clawed away the English and Islamite corpses. He slipped and fell forward in the sickening mud and finally crawled forward on his knees to roll over the remaining bodies and saw the familiar form lying broken beneath them. Great was his howl of rage; the heavens rang with his anger and the air became charged with murderous tension. His men, now dismounted, stayed back from him when they caught sight of his face and heard the growling within his chest.

His hands shook as with palsy. With an uncharacteristic gentleness, he rolled the fallen knight over and cradled his bloody head with one strong arm. With some small satisfaction, he noticed that the knight still had a little breath left in his lungs, though it was plain that he was badly wounded. Lightly, Eadric wiped away the blood obscuring the features, and grimaced as he saw the gash that would not stop bleeding. He felt the broken bones through the once-strong body and turned his gaze a moment from the skull bone that showed over his eyes. The auburn of his hair was matted with blood and dirt and his bright blue eyes, now unfocused and unseeing, were sunken darkly with the shadow of approaching death.

Geoffrey was conscious in Eadric's arms but it was evident he could see nothing about him, though his eyes burned bright with pain. Eadric pulled open his mail collar so that the knight might breathe easier, and although the young knight knew him not in his delirium of agony, Eadric saw the faintest trace of a smile cross those pain-pinched lips and the broken mouth tried to form words of thanks.

Those same warriors that had followed Wild Eadric now blanched white at the molten gleam throbbing within his good eye.

"You stopped them, young knight!" he rasped into Geoffrey's ear. "The only infidels in the gulley are dead men, food for the ravens."

Geoffrey nodded weakly and tried to speak. "I am dying, my friend," the young knight whispered and Eadric's face darkened while veins stood out at his throat and temples.

But his voice was calm and reassuring. "You will live a long while yet, my boy, There is still much to be done. Why, if you give up now, you will not have your little golden hair..."

Geoffrey coughed up a little blood. Then his voice was but little more than the sighing of the wind as he tried to make his peace before Eadric.

"At least, I saw her free, Eadric. Give her..." he murmured as his broken hands fumbled with his family ring, the one remaining from the three he had been given so long ago. Then he fainted again from the pain.

Eadric looked up at the men of his who stood in stunned silence before him, hands still clutching bloody axes and the reins of their horses. Their faces were calmly impassive; they had seen too much death and carnage lately to be muchly affected by a Norman knight's dying croak. But none of them understood the intensity in the Siwardsson's gaze, and none could face Eadric's fierce dark eye as it glistened wet with suppressed tears and they noticed how his strong warrior's hands continued to shake. For a space of time he said nothing, yet the fire in his face grew hotter and hotter with each passing instant until the men expected something dire to occur. Eadric looked in their direction and they shrank back further, but he was not studying them. His gaze was past them and past the barren hilltops, centered on a city that lay squat and imposing beyond, that unconquered city that claimed his young friend.

Within his gaze, universes collided and burned; entire solar systems perished and the very most elemental forces that propelled the realm of life were twisted horribly and turned awry. It was not hatred nor rage that tore at his innards and sent his soul a quivering; these were but the mildest manifestations of what he felt. It was something without a name, something much darker, much deeper, some primeval emotion unseen for thousands upon thousands of years within mankind. It was a return to the most basic impulses of life, involuntary actions that emerge machine-like from an unconsciously functioning brain operating alertly in only one category and all reactions pushed into, and centered around, this whirling vortex of demonic desire.

There was a curious sensation of thought seeming to embody the will of the gods and seeming to contain the sanction of everything spinning by the lawful forces of nature. It was an incredible sense of right and wrong, a contrast so astounding and so perfectly illuminated in this flash of fanatical emotion as to dim the very boundaries and limits of reality. More than a gross injustice had been committed. Some cog within the eternal machine of the universe had slipped free.

But it was done.

And in its happening, it had fanned a fire hotter than the most brilliant star and more consuming than the flood of Noah. It was an inferno in every sense of the word that could be extinguished by only one liquid. It could neither be smothered out by might nor beaten out by exhaustion. Only blood could end this flame.

Eadric gazed up at the fiery heavens and his speech came in a shaking rasp, long-drawn and choked with the terrible weight of the emotion he felt. Still, his gaze was in the distance, but his fists clenched until the pale knuckles shone even whiter in the sunburned flesh of his hands as he lay Geoffrey gently back for the others to attend to. He stood, still staring. His trembling hand floundered for the axe handle of his weapon set in the red mud, and it pulled free from the earth with a sucking sound that the silence magnified.

All eyes were on that fearsome axe as it slowly came up from the ground and rose in the Siwardsson's hand. It was a massive, heavy weapon that most men needed two hands to heft, but now it might have been a housemaid's broom that the jarl hoisted. Muscles ridged and writhed in his arms but he was like a moving statue now, devoid of pain or fatigue. The city that had taken his friend from him drew him inexorably.

"Tarsus," he said quietly, his voice but a whisper and more terrible for that reason. Then he led his way through the gaping men for his horse.

17

CHAPTER THE SEVENTEENTH

Geoffrey lay still within the confines of his darkened pavilion, his wounds bandaged tightly to limit the loss of blood. His eyes were closed in light slumber but his face was not peaceful; he had seen too much and suffered too much to ever sleep innocently again. At any rate, sleep rarely lasted, for the pain of his wounds was all too great, even for him. Flies swarmed greedily in the air, smelling the slow putrification of his flesh, rotting on his very body in the merciless heat.

Across the dirt floor from his bed sat the Finn with a mighty axe resting across his knees and his hawkish, sly features never altering. His eyes were flint in a drawn face, his lips but one tight line with worry and fear stamped upon them. His eyes never left his Norman friend and the darkness of them lightened only a little when Geoffrey opened his swollen eyes. The young knight smiled slightly as he saw Guvi hovering above him with an intense expression upon his face.

"Can you see, brother?" he asked quietly

"Aye, and what a fearful sight to awake to!" Geoffrey whispered, "Now I know that I am dead and gone to hell for all my sins! Why I see the face of Satan's greatest helper before me!"

"You see well enough, then," smiled Guvi dryly. "But be still, you great fool; save your breath for rest."

The Norman nodded weakly but both men understood how near death he was. Both played the game for the sake of the other.

"We could have used you and your longbow," whispered Geoffrey. Then he was pensive. "How many others lived?"

Guvi shook his head sadly. "None," he muttered, "the Turks were thorough."

Geoffrey turned his face away that his friend might not see the tears splashing over his eyes.

The Finn continued with grim determination in his voice. "But there are four or five times your number in Saracen corpses before your men in that gulley. I care not for your way of waging war, or dying, my friend, but it is obvious to all that it is the Lion of Tarsus who won this siege. You ripped the lancers to shreds and knocked the guts out of the city. Those Seljuks we let live are in mortal fear of the Lion for he is no ordinary warrior. They say you stood with but five men and shattered the lancers; I tell them in reply that you stood alone. Heathen mothers scare their children with your name for they say you are a true lion disguised as a man."

"Then Tarsus?" murmured the Norman.

"Yes! Tarsus has fallen, my friend. The enemy is no more."

"What of the Siwardsson?"

Guvi smiled broadly and his eyes were far away.

"It was he that was first inside the city. I know not what passed between you and he when he found you in that gulley, but when he again took the field none could speak to him. Nor could they stop him from beating the French and English knights from the very gate Lord Bohemond had personally taken only seconds before. He was a demon, Geoffrey. He slew all about him with his axe and when they swarmed around him twenty at once, he threw back his head and laughed and sang and cried. He raged if any knight attempted to succor him and he hacked those twenty adversaries to bits. The rest ran from him for they thought Satan helped the Franks, and Eadric roared after them, "Be thankful it is only a Saxon pirate and not the Lion of Tarsus, you miserable weaklings! When he comes, he will tear your city apart stone by stone!"

And even after the city was taken, they found the red bear in the streets weeping uncontrollably and cutting the infidel corpses to pieces. He ate sand and drank their blood in his grief for you, but he has recovered. He is quite mad, you know!"

Geoffrey wished he could laugh. "And my father?"

Guvi snorted. "He is safe enough. At present, he is dividing the city among the other leaders with Lord Bohemond. All of his captains bade me greet you for them and tell you that you are in their prayers. Huh! Most of those old bastards have never dropped to their knees in their lives; I suppose it is a nice thought all the same, though; it makes them feel good to say it. They will be here shortly to see you."

The Norman forced a laugh despite his pain. Guvi was never one to hide his feelings from a friend or an enemy. For a few minutes, both warriors were silent, knowing the next question he would ask would have no good answer.

"Claire?" asked Geoffrey in a cracking voice.

Guvi poured some wine down his parched throat and nodded. "She was sent for."

"Will she come to me now, friend Guvi? Now that I am dying, will she come to me when she would not before? Will she come when she knows I have sent more of the infidels to the dark lands?"

Guvi shrugged. How could he answer that?

"Eadric himself went to give her your ring and ask her to come back. He is a hard man to turn down."

"He is indeed," agreed Geoffrey. Suddenly, he was tired again.

He closed his eyes against the pain that tore at his arms, legs and face. It was another dimension of its own, plunging him into a grotesque world where few men ever travel, and even fewer return from. But there was no peace, no solace in the darkness behind his shut eyelids; at the backs of his sockets the images of battle whirled in confusion and he could not drive them away. He witnessed again the deaths of all his wonderfully brave men and saw those awful, unmoving mounds that were once free to laugh and love and live until he had commanded them to give up their breath.

Would they have forgiven him if they could?

Tears wet his eyes and he felt a huge weight upon his chest. He prayed it was death come to relieve his suffering, to take him to join those he had slaughtered.

Nothing else mattered, for he could not forgive himself. He could justify the actions and even smile a grim smile when those living praised his defense, yet those lives lay upon his soul and such weight is a terrible poundage indeed. They were the ones who should be honored, not him. They had been the ones to pay the price of his brave foolishness, not he. Perhaps now, only in death, could he truly make peace with himself.

But he could not let himself die yet.

Guvi's gaze had not left him. They stared at each other, both mourning the common bond between them that was ending. "I have to ask you, friend Geoffrey..."

"Why?" smiled Geoffrey. "Why did I do it?"

Guvi nodded.

"I do not know how to explain it, my friend. Perhaps because it was expected of me. Tell me, has there never been something in your life that you would have died for without hesitation, some dream, some idea? Have you never found something so precious as to be worth more than life?"

The Finn nodded quietly.

Geoffrey went on, "I thought about it, high on that hilltop, watching those damned lancers stretching off into the distance. For an instant, thought much of running or riding back to the main forces and some sort of safety. But I knew then that many more men would die if I did, men who I loved and admired, men who followed me into battle. And I thought of the shame upon my head if I ran from the fight. I thought of what she would say if she knew..."

"Claire?"

"Aye."

"No one would have expected such a sacrifice of you, to man the gulley with sick men and page boys. No one could have shamed you for not doing that," said Guvi quietly.

"I expected that of myself, Guvi."

Guvi spat in mock disgust. "You probably did at that."

Guvi toyed with his weapon uneasily. "I would have fled, you know.

I would not have thrown away my life on this damned bunch of hypocrites."

"You cannot say that until you have your chance. I think you talk too much sometimes," Geoffrey whispered.

"Perhaps. Perhaps not enough! Perhaps you should have listened more to what I tried to tell you!"

Geoffrey gave him a slow smile of infinite understanding. "It is possible you are right, my friend. Yet I am content with my lot now. The struggle is over and I have been allowed to see those I love a final time. What more can a man ask for, really?"

"We have become good comrades, have we not?" asked Guvi quietly.

"The best. The very best, my brother," Geoffrey whispered.

"All across this land now, they speak of the Lion of Tarsus. Two more small cities have surrendered, rather than face the Frankish Lion."

Geoffrey smiled gently. "Ah, immortality within my lifetime; I have lived to see it all."

"My friend, you say you love her more than life. Why did you not consider her first before choosing that gulley. She does love you, I believe. She is stubborn, but in time she would have come to you," Guvi said.

"Time ran out," sighed the Norman. "Time and the fates were against me."

"Only because you allowed them to be. Why did you not take her and sail for Britain as she wanted, return to your home, both of you, and begin anew?"

"The price was too high, Guvi."

"You lie here at death's door and say that?" replied the Finn hotly. His grief was surfacing now in anger at the thief which was robbing him of his dearest friend.

"Losing only my life is the best of bargains. To abandon my comrades and the crusade, would be perfidy."

Guvi snorted. "You said you loved her more than life itself. And you already told me how you betrayed your knightly oath once to run after her."

"True, my friend, but more than her, I love you and those who followed me. For her, I would sacrifice my honor, but not the lives of my comrades. It is ironic, really. Many men in life go from fate to fate without choice; I was given many choices and each one tipped with poison. It was inevitable that I fall."

"Nothing is inevitable!" thundered Guvi.

"Except death," whispered Geoffrey. "We have come full circle in our discussion, my friend."

Guvi lowered his head and wept silently.

Suddenly, there were cries from outside the tent and Guvi turned to the opening drapery of the pavilion.

Eadric Siwardsson was outside, roaring at the top of his lungs for his Saxons, and fire. He had retrieved his wits from the blot of battle madness. Now he remembered a chore undone and a debt to be paid.

"By Odin and Thor!" he bellowed as his men swarmed round brandishing their longswords and battleaxes. I'll burn the home of those devilish bitches to the earth and quench the flames with their blood. Say they nay to me, will they! Defy the son of Siward the Saxon, will they! By Loki, then let them beware, for their lives will be forfeit. I am going again and this time will butcher any hag that dares to stop me. Here now, you puny bastards! Bring torches!"

The Saxon bear raged on as his men gathered and Guvi turned to his comrade with a sly smile reminiscent of old times. "He does ramble on, does he not? It would seem, however, that he has met his match, this ruffian. He has encountered someone who can say no to him and live. This time will..."

"No, Guvi, let it be until I talk with him. None shall go. Send him to me that I might make him understand."

Guvi smiled wryly.

"What is there to understand, Geoffrey? She is a woman, that is all. She will never understand you or herself; certainly, she will never understand you any more than you understand her."

"You are wise!" mocked Geoffrey.

Guvi shrugged eloquently. "Wisdom is useless in dealing with a woman. They know no sense of logic. They think with their hearts and those who do have the rudiments of a brain are as cunning as a fox, but still without logic. If you try to understand them you will only give yourself a headache."

"Headache, phah!" answered Geoffrey. "You give me an ache in the arse! But bring in the red bear and let me talk with the monster."

Guvi stuck his swarthy face outside the tent flap and said something to one of the guards.

Blustering and cursing, though somewhat more quietly, if possible, the hulking red-haired giant entered the pavilion and lumbered over to Geoffrey's bedside. He stank as usual.

"Ah, Cub!" he rasped, "tis good to see you awake again. Would that I had better news to bring you but just before the battle horn, I went to the convent and could not get in. The old bitch who runs the place stood before the door and you know me, cub, you know my gentle nature. I could not bring myself to harm her or even force her from the door," he lied blithely. "They say Claire golden-hair will not see anyone, that she wishes it to be so. But fear not! I have reconsidered and am willing, for you, to return to that hellhole and burn it to the ground and slay all of the sisters if they stand before me. I am here but to reorganize the attack. I know this surprises you as you have come to know me as a lover of patience and virtue, but I think that under the circumstances a cool head should prevail and we should not let misplaced charity sway us from what is rightfully yours."

Even in his pain, the young knight was forced to grin at the overbearing benevolence of the brigand. Eadric the Wild wiped his large nose on the back of his hand and bent low that he might catch Geoffrey's hoarse voice. "Eadric, it cannot be thus, my friend. She has chosen her path, rightly or wrongly as you may think, but she has chosen. For the love I bear her, and the love you bear me, I ask you to let it be. Do not put a greater burden upon my shoulders than is already there."

The huge Saxon stood up, digesting this strange request. By his reasoning, Geoffrey was mad or foolish, or both. But still the rage swept through him. "Bah! She is a stupid female who will admit to no one, not even herself, how great her love is for you. She but needs a kick in the arse to show her the direction of her path," he said blackly.

"And that she will never receive from either you or my friend, " murmured Geoffrey determinedly.

"But there is not much time left to change her chicken's mind," he began tactlessly. Geoffrey noticed how Guvi went white with rage and Eadric, after a moment, realized his error. His ruddy face turned a deep shade of purple.

"Know there is not," whispered Geoffrey. "It is all right, red bear. I wish only to see her a last time."

"As I say!" roared Eadric in anger. "The wench will be here ere you can say William the Bastard."

Geoffrey seized him feebly by a thick wrist and held the Saxon for an instant by brute strength alone. But the strength left as quickly as it had come, several bandages split open with the effort. "Aye," said Geoffrey hotly. "There is little I can do for anyone now, or anyone for me, but I will see her suffer no more on my account. I ask you but for a horse to journey to the Hill of Stones and gaze upon the convent at sunrise. Mayhap, I will catch a glimpse of her and set my heart to rest. It is as good a way to die as any," he laughed weakly.

"It is a poor way to die!" stormed Eadric. Then he softened. There were tears in his good eye now as he spoke. "Fool!" he admonished.

The young Norman grinned slightly at the show of concern. "Aye, red-hair! But you sound more like the Finn now. But let me keep my delusions until the end, old one. I have made peace with myself; do not shake it, I pray you," he said half-joking, half-serious.

The Saxon shook his head. "You are merciless, cub. You have given me cause to love you as a son, though you slew my only son, and now you torment me with your wretched nobility after binding my hands with promises. Tis you that are the cruel one, not I!"

Geoffrey gave a hollow cough. "Do you know how beautiful she is, Eadric?" Geoffrey asked weakly, drifting off into semi-delirium. "Do you know how sweet it is to kiss her, to hold her?"

Eadric shrugged, but his speech was hauntingly eloquent. "I know that she is a bright star you have gotten too close to. She has burned the sight from your eyes and the sense from your head and saddled you with a yearning that even having her would not quench. She has made too much of a man out of you.

"But I am no judge of heroes or fools, either one. Each man must make his own way through life, and his own peace of mind when that life too abruptly comes to an end. If it is your love for her, your desire to grant her freedom that has given you such courage in battle, and shaped you into the man that you are, and if it is this love that causes you to lie so still here in bed with festering wounds amid pain and fear of coming death, then who am I to call such love foolish?

"I think mayhap it is she who is the more foolish of the pair of you, for while one loves where there is none wanted, the other spurns what is offered in abundance with no restrictions. In the end, all that matters is the happiness you have grabbed for yourself in this shabby life. With some, it is done through gold, with others, it is power. Rarely, is happiness found so greatly where you have found it or for such a foolishly noble reason. Perhaps, if you grew older your ideas on happiness would change as mine have. They would alter if you saw more of the stupidity and cowardice of men. But then you would have lost forever the dream that you have followed these past years, that vision which has reinforced your young man's soul with the iron of warriors twice your age and made you the champion that none who have fought with you will ever forget. Perhaps it is better to die with your dreams still intact for I do not believe that the gods care about man at all; they play us against each other for their own jesting sport. Yet, I do not think that they wish us to live forever with all our pettiness.

"So, there is nothing left to hold onto when life is plunging towards an ending. The only dreams then for most men are what might have been; fortunate is he who can take such treasures with him and say on his deathbed what well and truly was, and not what might have been."

But in this unusual lecture, the Saxon was forced to halt, for Geoffrey had drifted off into light slumber, a pale smile casting light upon his lined and haggard face as he dreamed.

Eadric looked upon him and beamed, all of the darkness lifted for a moment. "Aye, Cub!" he growled. "I do know how beautiful she is and I know how sweet it is to kiss her and hold her hand; it is etched in the smile upon your sleeping face." And as silently as he could, he turned to exit that the young knight might sleep undisturbed. Guvi watched him silently. "I would have died for him," Eadric said hoarsely.

"I know," replied Guvi quietly.

And they left their young friend to sleep a very long time, waiting for the sunrise.

~

SISTER BEATRICE HASTENED INTO THE HALLWAY AND BEAT UPON THE chamber door of Mother Superior. Although it was still not quite daybreak yet, she had risen early as her duty involved setting out the bread, milk and cheese for the breakfast of the others. But now, what she had seen so affected her that she no longer worried about such trivial things.

"Mother, Mother, arise, for a Holy thing has occurred. I have seen a vision sent from God!"

With deeply-lined, sleep-swollen eyes, Mother Superior opened her cell door and peered into the dark hallway.

"Sister! What is this unseemly commotion? Tis not but first light and you are flying about the halls like a demented baby bird first free of its nest!"

The little nun gasped for breath.

"Open your shutters, Mother!" she implored. "There is a storm gathering, yet the light of our Lord's storm flashes has shown me a vision upon the Hill of Stones!"

The two women, one convinced beyond doubt and the other skeptical beyond belief, went to the shuttered window and thrust it open to the early morning. A gust of drizzling rain blew in upon them, a gift from the fleeing night wind, and the lagging sunrise was dimmed by row upon row of churning gray thunderheads. Both turned eyes to the dark, semi-shapeless mass that was the hill. Both gazed openmouthed as a brilliant flash of lightning showed that there was truly something there.

Against the writhing sky, they had seen the dark form of a warrior on horseback, sitting stiffly in the saddle and gazing down at the convent from the hilltop. They had but a glimpse of the man in the rush of quicksilver that served to light the landscape, burning its way to earth through the lampblack air, yet both sensed an uncanny air of grim determination about him, and with it, some sort of devotion. He was there for a purpose, obviously, but what purpose? To what purpose indeed?

Perhaps with age and love of God comes revelation, for suddenly and very clearly Mother Superior understood who this was and why he was there.

She shivered, and deep within her, her heart cried out.

"Awaken Sister Claire, Sister," she said in a low voice.

"I must awaken all the others!" cried Sister Beatrice, her small eyes glittering fanatically. "Surely, this is the angel Michael come from our Lord to help deliver this Holy Land from the infidels! Surely, he has been sent to conquer in the sign of the Cross."

Mother Superior cut her short by seizing hold of her robe and peering deep into her unintelligent eyes. "Hush, now! Let the others sleep for now!" she whispered.

"But, Mother!"

"No! Awaken Sister Claire, the novice helper, and bid her come to me here. I feel that this is a vision meant for her alone, if I have understood all she has told me about this man."

"Man?" echoed Sister Beatrice.

"Please! Just do as I say, Sister!" ordered Mother Superior, and she turned back to the open window and the hill, watching and waiting for Claire. She sighed to herself. It could not be the angel Michael; God had long ago given up on this land that men called holy, yet ruined with each brother's rushing blood. If saving were to be done, man would have to save himself.

Then, abruptly, her thoughts turned in a different direction and she found herself wondering what it must be like to be loved so fiercely by such a man.

THE RUSH OF WATER-LADEN AIR WAS CHILL UPON GEOFFREY'S ACHING body, even though his stiff form was covered with his proud armor and heavy cloak. It was good, after the scalding delirium of his dreams. But the throbbing heat of his wounds negated much of the delicious coolness, warming him where his cloak could not. The light mist of rain was actually reassuring, as if it were God's cool touch upon his fevered face and hands.

He could almost smile despite his pain at the marvelous feeling of dreamy solitude up on this barren, windswept hill, the hill where Christ Himself was supposed to have slept amid the stones. Geoffrey turned a pale face to the stormy heavens and drank in the lightly falling moisture, expanding his chest to taste the fresh air. If it were not for the stiffness of his extremities, he might almost believe he would live.

Morning upon that bleak hill was scarcely lighter than the night had been for the dark thunderheads completely obscured the sun and the constant rainy drizzle made for fuzzy and distorted vision. But it was all good; he had no complaints. As long as there was breath in his body, life was good. As long as he might see her, life was good.

Eventually, several of the nuns in their distinctive robes exited the convent proper and scurried through the puddles for the barn and stable area and their morning chores. But there was one who scurried with them who did not wear their uniform dress, clothing herself instead in a long robe of white, similar in design to theirs. Even in the dim light, there was no mistaking that blonde hair.

"Sister golden-hair," Geoffrey smiled sadly, but his heart sang at seeing her once more. All pain had vanished, conquered for the moment by the intensity of his emotion.

A Sister, never to be fully claimed by any man, never to be bent beyond her beliefs no matter what the cost or prize. Perhaps, he reasoned to himself, it was exactly because of this that he wanted her so badly. But now, what could he give to her? All that remained was his love. He wondered if she realized he was there upon the hill, watching.

Perhaps…perhaps not.

Even had she noticed him, she would have forced herself to repress any show of emotion, for that would have been admitting that she did care. And she was too proud for that. Mayhap she had never truly cared and he had wasted years of his life in pursuit of nothing more than a smoke-filled dream.

Geoffrey found himself smiling at the grim gallows humor. What if he had risked his life for her, slain her "husband" and given so much of his time and life for her, for naught? Well, he had never denied that he was a fool, and now he would die as one.

But as he watched her exit the barn, suddenly she turned in the rain, turned and halted, and gazed up at the hill where he sat in the saddle. The water wetted her blond hair, turning it dark, and ran in rivulets down her face, and still she stared. A basket of eggs slipped from her nerveless hands and dropped into the mud, but she did not notice.

And he knew then that his only foolishness had been in doubting her. Now, if she would only come to him, to hold him and…

A terrible, terrible need burned through him, causing him to gasp and what he had felt before was rekindled past bearing. But a gruff whisper broke the spell and he turned to the figure that had approached him so silently. It was the Siwardsson. When he turned back to the convent, she had gone.

Eadric shivered and pulled his stinking furs tighter about him. "Well?" he growled. "Have you seen the wench yet? God knows you have sat here in this foul weather long enough."

"To what? Catch my death of cold?" murmured Geoffrey, still staring down at the convent, unwilling to accept the fact that she had gone.

The Siwardsson cursed in a low voice and roughly he seized the reins of Geoffrey's destrier. "Come, fool. You will not see her this morning, with the sky as it is. I will take you back," he muttered.

"But I have seen her, Eadric. I have seen her and my heart is lightened."

"Bah!" snarled the Saxon. And he turned the horse and led it back to the Christian camp.

For four days, even as his sickness grew progressively worse and he grew steadily weaker, Geoffrey repeated this ritual, trusting Eadric to bandage his rotting wounds so that they may sit him in the saddle those few hours again to watch her.

A lesser man would have been finished, flesh wasted and growing puffy, but his spirit remained staunch and determined. The longing for Claire was brighter than ever. The pain in his body relieved him of all the earthly wants for Claire but the passion of his soul carried undying embers for her. He slept no longer, instead he lay abed staring into space, seeing her before his eyes and returned again and again to his short time with her. He should have died each night but even while his body's energy continued its ebbing to the other side, his love for her burned greatly and his soul hungered for her. His hope sustained him.

And every morning, an hour before the rising of the sun, the Saxon would wrap his Norman friend in his own great fur cloak against the night air and carry him to that destrier Bohemond of Otranto had awarded him in place of Chestnut. Twas said that the destrier was Lord Bohemond's own mount, given in gratitude for what Geoffrey had done for the Christian host.

Eadric never left his side, day or night. Guvi was delegated by Geoffrey to attend to the command of the responsibilities of Westwall and gloomily accepted the promotion, but Eadric would not be so easily sent away. His face set into a glare of impassive hardness, he sat beside Geoffrey as he slept, guarding him, and he changed Geoffrey's dressings when the wounds burst and changed the bed linen when the young knight soiled them in his sleep. Twice, he had sent away women who wished to attend to Geoffrey for he would see no one touch the young knight but himself, and no one dared defy him.

In every way, he was the perfect servant. A far cry from the authority he still commanded in the camp. No one had the courage to remark upon this, however. Eadric had become a brooding sentinel at his friend's bed, and some said Geoffrey still lived because of this. Everyone else was afraid to enter that pavilion and face the red bear nor did anyone want to see Eadric's face as he sat or served his strange master. One might believe that this was so for behind the stony calmness of the features was a fury not of this earth.

Each morning of those days as the false light of creeping dawn tinged the hills with reddish gold, the huge Saxon could be seen leading the horse with its master sitting as best he could in the high saddle, and as the true light of the sunrise illuminated the hills around with its warm brilliance, the young knight could be found sitting silent and ever watchful on the Hill of Stones above the convent with Eadric slightly behind him, standing mute. Waiting for a sign.

But each morning, she would follow the sisters about their chores without acknowledging his presence by so much as a glance. Novice Sister Claire would make a determined effort to keep her bright eyes from the Holy hill where her champion sat. And although there were many sidelong glances from the sisters, and hushed speculation, none dared to ask what had passed between the two lovers, or what now lay within her heart.

Yet, she did see him there, that was certain, if not to Geoffrey than to the Sisters of the Sacred Heart. For each morning as she went back into the doorway of the convent proper, she would rush hastily past the others and more than one of the good sisters saw the film of tears that glistened over her soft eyes.

And often in the evening, she sat silent before the fire, her child in her arms, staring without a word at the crackling flames and oblivious to the good-humored speech that passed around her. But no one asked what she saw in those fires. And this, too, lasted for only four days.

On the fifth day, Eadric entered the pavilion to see Geoffrey futilely attempting to dress himself in his armor, but his right leg and both arms were so badly swollen with the infection that they were as wooden weights, and the knight cursed weakly as clasps and buckles eluded his fumbling fingers.

Blood oozed thickly through his bandages and his complexion was white. No longer did his blue eyes gleam with the iron will that had marked him throughout his life for now he was tired, tired past bearing. The drama had entered the final act and the look upon the Siwardsson's face showed that he understood this as well.

"Here, cub!" said Eadric gruffly, turning to look at his young friend's back. The Saxon lifted up the undershirt and grimaced at the way pus and blood had soaked through the bandage, leaving a greenish crust.

"Let me first dress…" he began to say, but Geoffrey's whisper hushed him. Its tone was chilling.

"Nay, red ox. There is no time, and no need any longer. I dreamed of death last night and I know that very soon it will become reality. Spare your goodhearted effort and help me clothe myself instead. It is nearly time to go; I am so weary, Eadric, but still hope for her."

Eadric took his friend's pallid face in his two large hands and peered deeply into Geoffrey's hollow, haunted eyes.

"Must you do this, cub? Must you suffer for her until the very end? Can you not await with some degree of peace?" the Saxon stammered, but he broke off into confusion. The point was well made, however.

Geoffrey smiled wanly, that smile that was once so full of life and encouragement, and oftentimes, determination as well as patience. He shook his head. "I am sorry for you, Eadric, for I see how you suffer for me. But I cannot ever have peace, perhaps save when I am in the grave. Having her to hold until the end would be as close to peace as I could find here and touching her again. But without her, there is only pain, no matter if I sit the saddle moaning or lie in my deathbed. But come. At least, this way I can see her free, even from me, and untamed beneath God's blue heaven. And there is always some degree of peace in this sight for me."

It was Eadric's turn to shake his head, "I do not understand you, Geoffrey. You want her and need her, as she needs you. Yet you will not take her!"

The young knight stared at his friend with a patience learned only through a life-altering experience. "Although love may be given many times in a man's life, red-beard, it may never rightfully be taken. Not ever. If she loves me, she will come to me or give me some sign. And if she loves me not, then what matters any of this suffering for it is as nothing next to the hurting of my soul."

The Siwardsson grasped Geoffrey's biceps, swollen and soft from the wound there, and gripped it so hard that the knight winced. "She loves you, you hard-headed bastard! By Odin! By Thor! You tear out my very heart with your stupid nobility!"

"I truly am sorry, my friend. I am how I am, that you know. I fear that I ill conceal my emotions, yet I would not burden you."

The Siwardsson grimaced at the show of affection. "Let be, cub! Tis well known what a fool you are. Here, now! Drink this!" And he shoved a flagon of ale into Geoffrey's fist.

The Norman sipped the brew but immediately vomited it back up. He looked at Eadric with some embarrassment but the Saxon's face radiated only immense sadness.

"Come," said Geoffrey softly, "it is time."

And a fifth morning did sunrise find Geoffrey St. Denis, now called the Lion, atop that barren, rocky hill. But the Lion's roar was stilled.

This time, Eadric left his charge alone upon the hill to return to the pavilion and Guvi, who was talking with Sir Brian. The Siwardsson gave the elder St. Denis a malicious squint and spat.

"How long has he left, red-beard?" asked Sir Brian who had just returned from changing the garrison at Kazanli. "Perhaps I should have remained with him instead."

"Why bother about things you cannot change, Sir Norman?" growled Eadric. "Only one person can end his pain, only one! And I leave now to discuss this matter with her in depth! As for your question, Norman, I cannot say how long, but there is little time."

Guvi stepped before him as Eadric turned to leave. "Geoffrey said to let her be, Eadric. I know how you must feel."

The Siwardsson stepped forward and seized the Finn's collar. Effort-lessly, he lifted Guvi into the air with a single hand. Eadric's lips curled back over yellowed teeth as he spoke so that he looked like a wolf scenting the kill. "You dare to preach to the son of Siward the Saxon?" he whispered. "Are your brains loose? Shove your goodwill up your dirty pink arsehole, you fatherless son of a bitch! Long have I listened to that dying fool spread his nobility over a spoiled little bitch and have held in my vomit while the rest of you encouraged it. Bah! You weaklings disgust me. I don't care a fart about what any of you little flowers say; if my boy was to see her before death, well, by Thor and Odin he shall, and I give warning to you and those thrice-damned nuns and this entire army, if you set any value upon your miserable sniveling lives at all, then stand clear of me."

Eadric launched Guvi into space and the Finn crashed headfirst into several boxes of supplies and armor. Eadric hitched up his sword belt, eyed them with satisfaction, and lumbered out of the tent.

Through the pavilion opening, Sir Brian saw Eadric shove a horse and rider aside and deal a kick in the arse to hurry along a squire who ran before him. "Out of my way, you arse-kissing cowards!"

Geoffrey's father eyed the red bear with open-mouthed amazement. "Upon my word, he is a ruffian!" Sir Brian said indignantly.

Guvi crawled from the piles gingerly, feeling the bruises that laced his throat. He felt sure his windpipe was cracked and it was hard for him to focus his vision. But he was happy.

"Good old Eadric!" Guvi whispered.

Sir Brian turned to stare at the Finn. Dust-stained and sweat-soaked from a hard ride, he had some trouble in understanding what was happening, but one thing was evident. "That outlaw loves my son as much as I!" he muttered.

"At least!" answered Guvi sarcastically, but Sir Brian was lost in thought as he stared out into the compound.

That morning, Geoffrey awaited her as he had each day before, but this morning it was a trifle harder to focus his vision and the breeze seemed unusually strong, so strong in fact that he was in constant danger of toppling from his saddle. The dry, yellow ground swirled beneath him, but he held on. Yet, it was still good. As long as there was breath, life was good. As long as he had sight left to see her…

She seemed to float from the open door in his dizzy gaze, discernible more in the gray haze of his vision by her golden hair than anything else. But it warmed him to know that she was there. And free.

He watched her slender form drift among the others into the barn and stable, up the slopes to the vineyards, and finally back into the convent, all without so much as a glance for him.

"Oh, my Claire!" he whispered with dry lips, but the words were lost to the wind.

Geoffrey looked up, quite drunk upon his pain and delirious at the yellow-gold orb of the sun; he found himself smiling at some joke he could not quite name. Then he slumped half-stuporous in the saddle, his wrecked body refusing to even remain upright. Only his mind worked now. Only one thought filled it.

Eadric and Guvi found him this way when they arrived, the Saxon to ride for the convent and Guvi to return their master to camp. Eadric kept up a low stream of bloodcurdling threats of what he was going to do and, by this time, the Finn was too apprehensive of the giant to open his mouth. Eadric softened an instant when they found the Norman numb from his festering sores and dizzy from the heat. Guvi pulled him from the saddle into his own while the Siwardsson cursed both man and God.

"Take the fool to his bed!" Eadric hissed. "And bid him not to die until I return, no matter how bent upon his own destruction he seems to be!" Then the red bear set his horse down the hill to the convent.

Eadric had no more patience left for etiquette; the door of two-inch-thick planks, bound with iron strapping, could not hold him up. A massive booted foot shattered the contraption as might a thunderbolt sent from God and without warning, Eadric the Wild stood roaring in the doorway brandishing his battle axe. Brave in the face of the devil, the sisters who saw the hulking madman fled for their lives.

"Take flight, you buzzards of the soul! Eadric the Wild is here with a purpose not to be denied!"

Loud were the screams of distress that echoed along the narrow hallway, for the convent had only one hall before the door. Several of the terrified nuns were pressed like huddled field mice and their eyes grew bigger as the Saxon came slowly toward them, growling and spitting as the door splintered. Eadric stood up against the wall bigger than life.

"Which among you dropped the jug upon my noggin before, eh? Come my pretties, I would have a word with you!"

One nun ran for her life into a side room and bolted the door, two others fainted dead away and the forth was Sister Beatrice who stood, eyes closed and quivering, nostrils dilated like a cornered rabbit, saying her rosary over and over. Eadric wrenched the implement out of her hands and cast it to the floor. He spat a great glistening glob at her feet and bared his teeth at her. She ignored him and continued praying.

"Shut-up, girl!" Eadric thundered so that she jumped a foot off the ground. She opened her eyes to see his sweaty face and began to slump in a dead faint. Eadric supported her, none too gently, while a vast paw encircled her delicate throat. "All right, you whining bitch!" he snarled "I've come again, you see, and this time I will see her, oh yes, I certainly will."

Sister Beatrice made sounds like a chicken slowly being strangled. Eadric smiled menacingly.

"If I do not hear your trembling lips speak where she is in two seconds, hell will greet another nun!" And he tightened his grip with that huge hairy hand so that she might understand. And she did. A limp arm pointed down the hallway.

Eadric nodded approvingly and cast her aside like a sack of beans. He was functioning at full tilt and he strode down the hallway swinging his large arms ominously.

The door to Claire's chamber flew off its hinges, smashed in with only one fist and Eadric stood in the doorway to the darkened chamber scowling and trying to see. He feared treachery. A child cried out in the darkness and a candle was lit.

Eadric was taken aback by her appearance in the flickering light. She had not been sleeping, though the babe was in bed. By the appearance of her face, she had not slept for days, and although still beautiful, her beauty was haggard and uncared for. And Eadric's rage stilled just a little, for he saw now that this forbidden love had left her a casualty also. Dark circles surrounded her red eyes and her hair was poorly combed; her pretty mouth was set in a line of harsh, self-conscious determination. Eadric was struck by her grim, haunted look as if her heart were punishing her for what she had done to a noble man. This was of some small satisfaction to the hulking Siwardsson; Geoffrey was not yet dead and already his spirit was hounding her.

She regarded him warily, eyes flashing their old fire. Eadric blocked the open doorway so that she might not pass.

"You have no right," she said in a low voice.

Eadric's face clouded over. "Do not speak to me of right, girl! I loved you once as a daughter but now you have slain a knight who is like my son! If he loved you less, I would slay you here and think nothing of it so do not press me with a lecture. You have run enough. Now you will listen to me!"

Claire tossed her blonde head angrily and stood appraising the giant, defiant and burning with a rage of her own. Why could they all not let her be. "I have told you already, Eadric Siwardsson, that I am bound to this place by vows. No longer am I a part of your killing world; here I have finally found peace in serving my God. My vows command me..."

The Siwardsson cursed hotly and struck her open-handed across the mouth. "You bitch," he roared.

She sank to her knees sobbing softly. A thin trickle of blood dripped down her chin, but she did not wipe it away. She looked up and saw Eadric pull the axe from his belt and raise it over her head. He was shaking and he panted for breath like a wild animal. Sweat glistened over his face and hairy forearms and she saw death in his gaze.

"Your vows be damned! Your god be damned! You are a stupid, blind, selfish girl!" he said, choking on the words. "He has dedicated better than four years of his life to you, woman! He has followed you across the seas for what he feels for you, and you spurn him now! You reject him in his hour of deed! You should die slowly for that," he hissed.

Her tears made a small puddle on the flagstone floor in the pale candlelight and she quivered with emotion as she answered him. "Slay me, then. I have no wish to live anymore. But do not think that I do not understand! Aye. He loves me true. And for me, he slew the father of my child! Am I some rare prize to be won bloody-handed by the strongest sword? Am I some object to be claimed as victor's spoils and fated to warm his bed for the rest of my life because..."

"All women are," Eadric sneered. "Wulfhere taught you that, well enough. But this boy has loved you past all that; he has never made such claims on you! He loves you!" Eadric's eyes were icy with contempt for her. "Even though Wulfhere was my own son, he was evil; perhaps he was too much like his sire. But he who you condemn only slew when threatened, twas not his fault that he was a better warrior than that scheming braggart I spawned. And even then, he would not have slain except to save you!"

"Better my life than another," she said wildly.

Eadric lowered his axe at the echo of Geoffrey's words.

"You fool!" he said. But he was speaking to Geoffrey, not her. She looked up at him when she heard the tremor in his voice.

"You believe that even as he does. You are both fools," he said quietly. He stared deep into her blue eyes and suddenly felt all of his rage draining away. He could not hate her when she reminded him so much of the knight he loved.

By her one expression of goodness, she had bested Eadric the Wild.

"This, then, is how you repay his love? You cannot spare so much as a farthing's worth of goodwill for the lad? Do you understand that he is truly dying?"

"Yes," she sobbed. "I felt it in my heart before they told me."

"And still you cannot love him for the few days he has left? Surely your loving God would not begrudge you this?" Eadric suggested contemptuously.

"I have always loved him, as I have never loved another. Even to this very moment, I love him with all my heart," she said in a voice so low as to be little more than the wind moaning.

The Siwardsson was struck dumb by this confession.

"Then why?" he whispered.

"Not even the greatest love can turn wrong to right," Claire replied evenly. She looked up to say more but stopped at Eadric's face.

Great tears rolled down his cheek and his vast bulk shook with sobs. "And do you understand that each morning I wrap the lad in my fur cloak against the cold, and sit him in the saddle of his destrier that he may watch you at your chores from the Hill of Stones? And all the while he dies a little more?"

"Yes," she wept. "Yes!" She pushed aside her hair and wiped the tears from her eyes with delicate fingertips.

"And yet you can never succor him from his anguish, never give him so much as a sign or token of your love that he might die a bit happier?"

"It is kinder this way..." she began.

"For who? He grows weaker this and every day, and still you say it is kinder to allow him to die unloved?" Eadric's voice was chilled as coming rain.

"Yes," she answered, and she lowered her head again, unable to withstand the pressure of his gaze.

Eadric said no more but walked slowly for the broken chamber door. Abruptly, he turned and spoke to her in a voice oddly still. "May your God who receives him be more merciful than you, my lady," he whispered. And then he was gone.

A terrible numbness set in, a numbness that was to last all day. She thought of nothing else but Geoffrey that day, her mind churning as if there was some indefinable decision to be reached in the backroads of her mind. But what sort of decision could there be?

She had already chosen, and rightly, she felt. There was no need to fuel a romance that could never be, nor was there virtue in condoning the fierce slaughter that had begun such a romance. Her ways were no longer the ways of men.

Here in the Convent of the Sacred Heart, she had finally achieved some sort of solace, a refuge from her guilt at what their love had wrought. Here, Sister Claire could run from all of the cruelty and inhumanity and warfare and the twisted love and lust of mankind. She had found her ivory tower; none must be allowed to drag her from it. Further descent into the world of man would only prolong the pain and suffering.

She had said it was kinder not to see Geoffrey; she had meant it was kinder to herself. Claire had now surrounded herself with the only love she might cope with–her love of God, her love of the good, kind sisters, and her love of her growing babe, a daughter who would be brought up in a world of great gentleness and understanding. Her love for Geoffrey would only be a burden for her, for if she allowed it to exist within herself, she would also be remorseful for all the evil it carried with it.

It could never be so. Others, stronger than her, might bear it out. But her spirit was too fragile for such a test. Her salvation would be in self-denial and the aching of her woman's body would be comforted by her clear conscience.

She rationalized her decision over and again that entire day until all time escaped her. Evening overtook day and night overtook evening. Softly, she kissed her sleeping child and snuffed out the candle by her bedside as she slipped beneath her covers. She was tired, more tired than she could ever remember being and it crossed her mind what a dreamy and delicious sleep death must be.

There seemed to be some inexplicable tension in the night air. Open shutters let in a breeze already cool with the sun's flight, but still sleep did not come. Her thoughts played tricks upon her mind and she sat up suddenly, sure she had heard the clatter of horse hooves upon the rocky road up the Hill of Stones. Was he there?

She stood at the open window, waiting, her pulse pounding and her throat dry. But the moonlight bathed only an empty hill and there was the feeling of complete emptiness as she looked, a feeling as though she were the last person upon this plane of existence.

There was only the sighing of the wind to talk with or to comfort her, to caress her fevered cheek and soothe her. Night dragged on, barren and lonely, watching the hill for a sight she did not want to see, until at last, even her anxiety was overcome by a leaden lethargy and she sank to her knees at that window, asleep.

But the sleep that arrived was not a peaceful rest for her soul was in the throes of a tumultuous catharsis. She had fought the love for so long, denying herself the most basic needs of all human existence. She had not allowed herself to believe in what she knew in her heart to be true.

Now her soul cried out and her poor, tired form trembled in slumber. They were awful, these dreams, tormenting and unyielding, and all the more unbearable because they contained not sorrow but a form of haunting joy. They were beautiful and free from the dirt of reality.

And each was of him.

She dreamed no longer how he had killed the guards in their escape but rather how he had first kissed her in her bedchamber in a way reserved for a queen. She tasted again that wonderful meeting of lips and flesh, in a touching full of loving innocence and complete adoration. Again, she felt the reassuring caress of his strong hands, gentle for her, upon her cool cheeks and the feather-light touch of his warrior's mouth upon her. Again, her body trembled as her soul sang in a way no other man had ever allowed it to. She shivered at the depth of his love for her; she reveled in his hunger for her body. She was proud that he had risked all to claim her.

In her sleep, she reached out and moaned. She saw once more the haunted look upon his face when he was but a prisoner in Castle Ayrin and she but a low-born freewoman, casting her holy pity into his out-grasping hands. Again, she was touched at seeing him weep for her tenderness, his strong chest crushed against the window bars and his shaggy-haired head lowered in grief. She had wanted so much to stroke the pain from those blue eyes, to smooth his hair, to hold his knight's face. She had never believed him bad, this young soldier with the haunted eyes.

And being human and loving and needing to be loved in turn, she again felt the intenseness of the physical side of their love, the great gentleness of his hard-muscled body against hers in the way that had given so much pleasure, the way his steel-thewed arm had cradled her as he had kissed away her foolish tears and then the immense security she had found lying by his side with her hand in his and her blonde head upon his thick chest. All over, she ached lovingly for him as she had never done for any man before.

And never would again.

But more terrible than all the rest, was that final dream she experienced when cockcrow was less than an hour away. It began with their attempted escape from the infidel city, and now a second time did she stand with him in that dark hallway outside the room of her Helgi. A second time, she saw the look of honest love that crossed his grim face as he gazed upon the child, because although she was not his, yet Helgi was flesh of Claire's flesh and he cared that she was so small and helpless. Once more did she witness how his hard-lined features lightened with the warmest of smiles as he stared at her and then the babe. His words, spoken reverently in that hallway, echoed inside her heart. "God has blessed her with your beauty; may he bless her with your soul as well." Her soul...now it was cracking with shame and hunger both.

Then the words were gone and the city, and all the other myriad scenes that crowded her sleeping mind as well, until only the image of his hard-lined features remained, flickering unsteadily as a candle flame running out of air. She gazed a final time into those cool blue eyes and upon that intense mouth, that nevertheless lost all of its grimness when he smiled at her. She traced every line of his face, noble without attempting to be, and in her mind again stroked that tangle of dark brown hair.

Claire saw his lips move as they shaped her name, yet no words issued forth. And suddenly, she stared straight into those eyes she had desperately tried to avoid and finally caught sight of all the unworthy pain she had given him.

"Oh Geoffrey! Oh, my love!" she cried out, weeping. She awoke with bones aching from the damp floor and all the misery of her dream a yoke about her shoulders.

How wrong she had been!

Nay! He was no killing machine any more than he was the saint she had demanded that he be. He was but a man with the failings of all men, yet capable of caring with the gods! Oh, God! How utterly merciless she had been. Had not Christ himself preached forgiveness? And what was there even so much to forgive, that he had done the greatest wrong in her eyes in attempting to save her? Then, if his soul was truly damned, then it was damned for her.

"Oh, God! Oh, God," she wept.

"Oh please, my Lord!" she cried out upon her knees. "Spare him for what he has done! You are the maker of miracles! Oh, my Lord! Grant me this one for he who deserves it, I beg you!"

The first rays of daybreak shone in the window. It was time. Claire paused only to check her sleeping Helgi before she ran down the hallway and out the door into the sunrise. She knew now that it was right, this acknowledgement she had feared so long. She knew now what she must do.

If he must die, then he would pass from this earth knowing the true strength of her love for him. Tears filled her eyes again to overflowing as she thought of him, and she decided that she would give him the sign she had used so many times so many years ago, that of the cross. She would make the sign of the cross that he might know.

Still in her nightdress, she ran barefoot into the brilliant sunlight of the convent yard, her pretty hair still sleep tangled and her lovely eyes blinking against the unusual power of the new-risen sun. There was a half-smile upon her lips and her eyes sparkled with the resolution her heart had made and made gladly now.

God! How she loved him, this warrior. Why could she not have understood this earlier?

But as she stood there with the whisper of the morning wind gently ruffling her garment amidst the utter silence of the morning, a terror came upon her that was not to be denied. Something grabbed her with iron claws and fear made her breath heavy in her chest. She turned her face into the golden disc rising over the Hill of Stones, and the chill talons clutched harder at her tender heart.

"Oh, my Geoffrey!" she cried.

But he was not there as he had been. And he would be there never again.

EPILOGUE

The rain, uncommonly bountiful for such an arid land, was finally letting up. Deep puddles lined the rocky road up the hill and between the patches of coarse gravel there was only yellowish mud. At times such as this, the entire road would merge back into the desert floor and vanish until new pilgrims and travelers would reshape it with their carts and horses, and more commonly, their feet. Everything passes.

Water passes into the sandy soil, nourishes the plant and passes into the air; air passes into the lungs to nourish the body and issues forth as a different gas to nourish the plant. In nature and life, nothing is ever static; even the greatest mountains crumble beneath the onslaught of wind and rain until they are but piles of earth sinking into the dim horizon. So, too, must all flesh pass. The good and the evil, the strong and the weak, the meek and the arrogant; all must pass.

It was in the first bright days of spring in the year of Our Lord 1119 that they lay Claire to rest for eternity, outside the city of Tarsus near the Convent of the Sacred Heart.

As a sporadic drizzle did little to cool the sticky warmth of the Turkish morning, grown progressively hotter since sunrise an hour past, an overcast and dripping sky brought some respite, but the sun's fire still smoldered in the rocky soil. This land that men called holy, yet still killed for, was temporarily at peace now and temporarily Christian. Here on this hill, on this forbidding morning, there had been the rites of a Christian funeral. A great goodness had passed from this life.

Many had come to see her a final time; her gentleness was legendary and her friends legion. All across that part of the Holy Land, Sister Claire was loved for her sweet, sad smile and the kindness she held for everyone. Hundreds of men, women and children had topped the Hill of Stones as her shrouded form was lowered into the grave. Now, but three remained, a warrior, his lady and their child.

Periodic gusts of rain pounded them, but they could not leave. A great emptiness was upon them.

For nigh twenty years, Claire had cared unselfishly for the surrounding countryside from her station in the convent. She had never taken the vows of the sisters there, yet she did as much, if not more than they for the poor and forsaken. Indeed, there were few who had not heard of the compassion of the little novice everyone called Sister Claire, for she had dedicated her life to God and mankind. When she died, it was in serving several children dying of the plague. No one else had offered to help them, other than by an occasional drink of water, for it was obvious they were too sick to live. And they were indeed too ill to be approached by the healthy, but Claire smiled that sweet-sad smile of hers and entered into their sick chamber and wiped the fever sweat from their little heads and changed their bedding and held them one by one as they died, crying softly for each.

When it was over, the sisters came to the chamber door and offered her food, but her face was much too white, and they all knew she had contracted the disease. In the weak light of a high, narrow window, Claire looked very much like the Holy Virgin must have looked as she held the still form of the last child close to her. She looked up at the concerned faces, her own face transfigured by the love she felt for the children and whispered, "Our Father is good beyond measure. He has seen fit to use me to ease the suffering of the little ones and now he grants me ease from my own."

"Go in peace, my child. You have earned it," Mother Superior answered.

"Pax vobiscum," murmured the others.

And Claire Beaumont lay back and was gone.

Only the ancient Mother Superior understood why she had wished to be buried alone atop the Hill of Stones at sunrise, but she offered no explanation. And thus, the burial was carried out that May morning in spite of the rain. Now, she was at peace.

Helgi stood as lovely as her mother had been, holding the powerful hand of her husband William, Duke of Venice and nephew to the Christian Lord of Tarsus in one slender hand and the tiny hand of their infant daughter, Claire, in the other. Her gown of maroon silk was soaked by the steady drizzle so that it clung plastered to her slim form and her light blonde hair was wet and dark from the water. Husband and child were also thusly drenched, but no one wanted to leave the gravesite, so deeply did all three love her that they took no notice of the punishment the weather was delivering.

She was there upon that hill; they could sense it.

William saw her as the loving mother to his Helgi and the doting grandmother to his child, and perhaps a saint in her own right for her love for all men, no matter how wretched or undeserving. Little Claire loved her namesake with the purity and intense feeling as only a child can. Helgi loved her for love given and an example upheld. She had never known her mother to do a selfish or thoughtless thing. The trio stood silently weeping in the rain at the rectangular pile of stones set against the scavengers and the simple cross that surmounted it.

At last, it was William with his common sense that broke the terrible stillness, a stillness so intensely unhappy as to perhaps be the mourning of nature itself for the end of something fine and noble.

"My dove," he murmured, "'tis best we leave now. The babe is soaked to the skin and see how you are, also. Come, we can do no more here save to wrap her memory in our aching hearts and keep always the love she had for us."

Helgi stared at the grave as if she were studying something far away. "She is here, my William. I can feel it."

The Duke smiled patiently and gazed at his wife. "She will always be with us, Helgi."

Helgi slowly shook her head. "I do not mean that. I mean that she is here this minute and I feel her waiting for some great happening."

William shrugged. He understood how upset his wife was; he was also. Gently he pulled her away. "There is nothing left for those of this world to do. Come."

Helgi sighed. "You say true, my love. We must think of the future now." And she allowed him to lead her down the muddy, rocky path toward the convent below. Mud spattered their clothes and Helgi transferred little Claire to her shoulder.

William put his arm about her. "You are still troubled by something, Helgi. What is it?" he coaxed gently as they walked to shelter.

She sighed and shook her head sadly as she answered him. "It is only that I know that for all the happiness she brought to others, my mother's own heart was ever laden with the heavy weight of some sorrow, even unto the day she died," she whispered.

William smiled a soft smile of affection for her. "I cannot say with certainty other than what I feel within my own heart," he replied, "yet it does seem to me that one who lived and loved as she did, must surely be entitled to a final happiness before the judgment of God."

"Perhaps, perhaps," Helgi conceded. "But I feel the only chance for her true happiness was lost twenty years past, and she truly never found it again."

William shrugged his broad shoulders. What was there to be said? As a warrior, he well knew the injustice in the world.

But as the three passed through the open gate set in the low stone wall around the convent, little Claire shivered and whispered very quietly into her mother's ear, "Mother, who is he?"

"Who is who, my little monkey?" puzzled Helgi, half-turning to examine the area of the convent.

The child gazed off into the distance, over her mother's shoulder. She shot out one small hand in childish impatience at the Hill of Stones. "Him, Mother!" she whispered, insistently.

And the mother and father turned to follow their child's gaze, through the rain and up to the crest of the hill.

Seen dimly through the blowing water was the vague shadow of a powerfully built warrior astride a magnificent chestnut colored destrier. A fresh wind billowed out his cloak of purest sky blue to reveal gleaming armor of a type not seen for a score of years, covered with a surcoat of the same clear, bright blue but decorated with twin green splotches that might have been trees. He was attired as if for either combat or ceremonial circumstance, but his attitude belied both guesses for he sat mute and unmoving upon his massive horse, next to that low sad grave and cross with his helmeted head hung low. Watching, only watching.

William cursed in mild exasperation at having to plod up the muddy hill again to challenge the stranger.

"I best see who yon stranger is," he muttered and started forward up the hill. "He dresses curiously and see how he slumps in the saddle as if overcome with fatigue from a great journey."

But Helgi stood frozen with eyes wide and clutched at his arm to restrain him as she replied firmly, "Leave be, my love! This is something you do not understand!" And although Sir William thought his pretty wife must be just the smallest bit confused at this point, he complied and left the odd knight alone.

For long moments, the warrior upon the hill sat unmoving in his saddle. Finally, he dismounted and slowly approached the grave, removing his helmet as he walked to reveal a tangle of reddish-brown hair. Weighed down with sorrow, he knelt beside the grave and bowed his head in prayer.

As he did so, it seemed that the rain lessened just a bit. Then he arose, taking his reins in hand and casting a final backward glance at the stones and cross. Suddenly, he seemed in the throes of a despair beyond all endurance and he threw himself to his knees again, both arms stretching out to the gray heavens, imploring.

His voice was the sound of a thunderclap as he cried out in his agony and Helgi remembered the voice, although the wind carried off the words. Or perhaps, it was a cry meant for the Creator alone.

William stood shaken at what was happening, but Helgi wept with a happiness she had thought she would never feel. "He has come for her!" Helgi cried. "Even death could not vanquish him, or his love!"

Then there was an eerie silence, a complete cessation of sound that blanketed the morning and the rain abruptly stopped. The wretched knight arose, steel-clad arms still held out to his God in supplication.

And as he did so, there occurred something so utterly marvelous that the three silent humans below could only rub their eyes in astonishment. For as the strange knight turned his anguished eyes from the grave to the cloudy sky, his grief-stricken figure shimmered and faded in the wan daylight until it was as smoke, then mist, then air, until he was gone as if he had never existed and his mount with him.

But as that final proud outline of the warrior faded into nothingness, the thick gray clouds drifted suddenly apart to reveal a dazzling sun for the first time that morning. And in those final few drops of moisture still riding the air, there was born the most beautiful of all rainbows across the breadth of that hill, sparkling brilliantly with bands of amber and gold, red and blue and green in a fantastic bridge from heaven to earth.

And in the sweet, warm kiss of the spring wind blowing softly out of that majestic-hued morning, a wind filled with freshness and the promise of new life and the future, Helgi was sure she heard the faintest of laughter, that of two lovers in the sunrise.

THE END

www.ingramcontent.com/pod-product-compliance
Lightning Source LLC
Chambersburg PA
CBHW070742120726
47910CB00001B/150